THE TANNENBAUM TAILORS AND THE SECRET SNOWBALL

To Christine,
Always believe in
yourself and your
dreams! Believe!
J B Michaels

THE TANNENBAUM TAILORS AND THE SECRET SNOWBALL

JB MICHAELS

The Tannenbaum Tailors and the Secret Snowball

Published by:
James B. Michaels. Authorship: Text.

Cover illustration by Emily Michaels

Harrison and James

ISBN-13: 9780692540558
ISBN-10: 0692540555

To the man who told me I can do anything, thanks Grampa.

To my Grandma who always cheered me on.

To Charles Edison, love you buddy.

LOG # 1222

"I made the right decision. The lack of options led me to one conclusion: I had to breach the Code. The kid deserved Christmas, especially after such a traumatic event in his life. I talked to him (it was a little difficult, given I am a tiny tree elf) because I needed his help. I rarely ask for help. I pride myself on always trying to blaze my own path and solve my own problems.

I was a new Captain assigned to tend to and tailor Christmas trees to the needs of human families around the world. I am the person who needs to make the "tough" decisions and navigate "difficult" situations. Although the "difficult" situations I was trained to face have to do with water levels, faulty light bulbs, and dusty ornaments.... haha! Nothing like what happened that Christmas season and the following two seasons. Whoa.

I thought I fully understood the consequences of my actions. Boy! I was wrong!"

- Captain Brendan

Chapter 1

CHRISTMAS RUSH

The Icicle transport swirled out of control. The blistering cold winds brought sleet and icy rain.

"Lily, how close are we to the chimney?!" Commander Brendan asked while gripping his swivel chair on the bridge of the Icicle.

"We are only a few feet away, but on our current vector, we will smack right into the roof next to the chimney. Engaging SLEIGH thrusters now to stabilize," Lily, the Pilot and Communications Tailor, responded.

Four thrusters spouted from the top and bottom of the Icicle transport. They burned icy blue as they attempted to thrust the Icicle back to a stable flight pattern.

Another gust of wind spun the Icicle towards crashing into the roof. The SLEIGH thruster's icy blue flames sputtered and gave out.

"Lily, take manual control now. Get us out of this spin!" Commander Brendan ordered.

"Roger that. Switching to manual control." Lily put gloves on as the Icicle's candy cane flight stick popped up from the center console.

The Icicle descended faster towards the roof. Lily pulled the flight stick towards her, attempting to position the Icicle upside down with its top facing the roof and the point of the Icicle to the sky. The Icicle buckled, then jerked into the position Lily so desired.

Commander Brendan still strapped into his swivel chair, held his hand over the booster bow and wrapped it around the left arm of his chair.

"Lily, you let me know when to unwrap the booster bow." Commander Brendan turned his head towards the four other members of his team. "Tailors, hang on tight!"

The Icicle shook and almost went in to another spin. Lily gritted her teeth and held the stick tight. The collision alarm blared the first three notes of "Jingle Bells" repeatedly and more frequently the closer the Icicle approached the roof. Two inches from the icy roof, Lily yelled, "Unwrap the bow!"

Commander Brendan pulled on the starter ribbon of the booster bow. CHOOM! The booster bow ignited the secondary rocket thrusters on the domed end of the Icicle. The Icicle launched just an inch from suffering an icy crash on the roof. A bright blue and gold spark burned from the booster rockets as the Icicle, pointed end up, climbed to the top of the chimney away from the icy roof. The boost took them over the chimney opening.

"Stopping the burn in four, three, two…one," Commander Brendan announced.

The boom from the thrusters ceased.

"We have control sir. Starting free fall into controlled descent now," Lily said.

The Icicle now free fell and swung back to its vertical position, pointed end down. The Tailors were used to switching positions. Each Tailor sat on a swivel seat designed to shift with the vertical-hanging and horizontal-flying positions of the Icicle. Lily guided the Icicle into the chimney, down to the fireplace of their assigned home.

"Great job, pilot," Commander Brendan said.

"Thank you, sir," Lily replied.

"Everybody okay back there?"

A collective "ugh" resounded from his Tailor Team.

Commander Brendan laughed. "Okay! Lily. We have a Christmas tree to take care of! Set a course for this family's tree!"

Chapter 2

TAILORING

The Icicle was finally ready to hook up to the Christmas tree. Commander Brendan ordered the rest of his tiny Tailors to prepare the ramp. Lily initiated the vertical swing procedure in the proper place. The Tailor's Icicle approached a branch of the beautiful Frasier fir near the back as to remain hidden. Lily elevated the hook-scope from the top of the Icicle. Commander Brendan surveyed a good strong spot on the branch to hook onto and an adjacent branch to lower the ramp and unload.

"Down hook-scope," Commander Brendan said.

"Yes, sir," Lily said confidently.

"All right, initiate hooking procedure."

A hole opened at the top of the Icicle, the North-Pole, Elf-enforced steel hook rose up and latched on the branch. Lily, very methodical and dependable, always did a great job of making sure the Icicle hung safely.

"Team, lower the ramp. Unload! Let's do this."

"You got it, Commander," Steve, the fire tailor, replied with his usual unenthusiastic voice.

"Tonto! What are you doing down there?" Commander Brendan yelled.

"Slow as usual sir," Irene said.

"I am coming already. I couldn't find my instruments."

"You can never find them," Irene pressed.

"Don't get me started, little sister. How many bulbs did you go through last Christmas?"

"Oh shut it. I am older than you and am not your *little* sister!" Irene stormed out over the ramp and onto the tree.

Commander Brendan knew those two would never stop bickering, since they were brother and sister. The arguing may lessen with time, but never go away completely. Irene always takes care of Tonto, and he always looks out for her in his own way. They work together a lot since she services the lights, which lower the water levels of the tree Tonto tends to. They seem dysfunctional, but they always get the job done.

"C-Commander, we are all set here. Should I seal up the Icicle sir?" Billy asked.

“Yes Billy please do!” Brendan said. The ramp door shut but didn’t lock. BONK! He looked through the viewport of the slightly open ramp door and saw Billy sitting on the branch next to the Icicle, rubbing his head.

“I will seal it, Billy. You okay?” Commander Brendan yelled to Billy through the ramp door.

“I hit my head on the ramp as it was folding up! Ouch! I am good,” Billy said.

“Haha, as long as you are okay, your ornaments await!” Commander Brendan said. Billy is a perfectionist and very good at what he does. The ornaments always look perfect but his focus on his job, often, causes him to not pay attention to what is happening around him, hence his clumsiness.

“Carry on,” Commander Brendan replied.

“Lily, let’s get this command center up and running, right behind the star at the top of tree,” Commander Brendan said.

“Full equipment set up, sir?”

“Yes, make sure to double check the spirit levels in the house. That is always most important and yes, of course, the vitality, decoration, and lighting monitors as well. This is a big tree this year.”

“Roger that, sir.”

“I am heading to my crew observations and help where needed,” Commander Brendan said.

Commander Brendan helped Steve set up various hydrants and hoses at key areas in the trunk of the tree at the bottom, middle, and top of the tree. Next on the checklist, Commander Brendan met with Irene and Tonto, who roam from tree branch to tree branch making sure all the lights and needles remain vibrant and strong. Tonto headed down to measure water levels in the tree stand, while Commander Brendan assisted Irene check the wiring and temperature of a bubble light.

"How's he been lately?" Commander Brendan asked.

"He's been pretty quiet but I just know he is really hurting inside. Tonto bottles things up," Irene answered.

"Time heals all. How are you?"

"I am okay. It is just tough. They were the best, you know."

"I understand if you guys want to take leave. Just so you know, you two are the best Tailors for the job as were your parents," Commander Brendan said.

"Thanks, Commander, but Tonto and I will be okay. Work is good for us."

"Whatever you think is best. I love you guys. Okay off to see how Billy's doing."

"Thanks again. See you later," Irene ended.

Commander Brendan saw Billy on the end of a tree branch with his sparkle gun and polish making sure an old red ornament shined and wouldn't crack.

A smile crossed Commander Brendan's face as he 'lifted back to his post. On the way, he felt the air push against him as he steadily zipped up the tree. Commander Brendan's heart beat faster as he weaved in and out of the narrow spaces between the branches. The smell of pine refreshes with each ride, made possible by the grappling hook device that each Tailor wears on their belts.

With effortless momentum, Commander Brendan learned to master the Glimmerlift, the ultimate grappling hook, in the Tailor Academy and was number one in the class. Of course, Glimmerlift Training traditionally wins the most popular class in every Academy yearbook. The device looks like a tailoring needle attached to a high tension wire, but its locking mechanism provides the smoothest ride from branch to branch.

Commander Brendan's joy ride ended abruptly.

"High marks again, Tailor team!" Captain Emery Mas congratulated them on their successful virtual training session, mandatory before each Icicle Launch every year.

The Tailors removed the virtual reality helmets, shaped like Santa hats, and stretched after being in their training capsule for over two hours.

"Excellent, Tailors. High marks again. We truly are the best team! For reals!" Commander Brendan yelled.

"If you ever say "for reals" again I am gonna punch you commander," Steve grunted.

"Is that any way to talk to your boss, Steven?" Commander Brendan laughed.

"Enough already... Brendan we have to go. There is a graduation today, remember?" Captain Emery Mas said.

"Right. Okay everybody. Great job. See you tomorrow for another run maybe there will be another Icicle maneuvering challenge. Wouldn't we all love that again?!" Commander Brendan said, smiling.

Once again, the Commander heard a collective "ugh" from his Tailor Team.

Chapter 3

CHRISTMAS OF '87

Being a Tailor officer means Commander Brendan is required to attend all Academy events. He stood in attendance as Captain Emery Mas congratulated the new recruits on their graduation day. The ceremony carried on in the usual joyous fashion in the North Pole's Home Tree. All the new recruits' families fawned with pride over their newly-named Tannenbaum Tailors.

Suddenly, every light in the vast Home Tree turned an eerie blue. The Blue Alarm sounded. It fills one's ears like a screeching banshee hocked up on too many gingerbread men. Not only is the sound deafening; it chills everyone to the bone -a difficult thing to do to those who live in the North Pole.

The Blue Alarm was followed by a voice. "Fire reported, Lower Branches, Branch 18, Requesting Home Fire Battalion and Emergency Water and Needle Response Team." The Captain calmed everyone on the assembly branch and assured them he would personally check the source of the emergency. Commander Brendan raced to catch up to him as he took off down to the elevator on the center trunk.

"Do you need help, sir?" Commander Brendan asked.

"Sure Brendan, I wouldn't mind a veteran's help."

They hopped on the elevator together and shot down to the lower branches. Commander Brendan felt the heat from the fire in the elevator the further down they went. "So how bad do you think it is?" Commander Brendan asked to break the silence on the ride down.

"I hope not too bad. Launch is in three days, and the Big Man is counting on us," Emery Mas jumped out of the elevator. Lower Branch 18 burned as brightly as an orange snake of fire wrapped around its needles. Commander Brendan could barely breathe as the heat forced sweat to bead and drip from his forehead.

The Home Fire Battalion was on scene. They hooked up to the center branch hydrant system and sprayed water on the flames, trying to push the fire out. The Emergency Water and Needle Response

Team was spread over the adjacent branches trying to prevent the spread of the fire. The Sergeant ran up to Klark, the Fire Chief. "Can it be contained to this branch?"

"I hope so. One of the bulbs popped and the wire whipped around, knocking out Timmy, one of Light's guys. We should be able to get this under control," Klark said.

"Good, very good," Emery responded as the flames grew higher. The fire erupted in a flash and knocked everyone down to their knees. As the Home Fire Battalion began to advance on the inferno again, the hook up for the hose blew off the trunk, spraying water everywhere but on the flames. Commander Brendan saw it, dragged himself up from the craggy hot bark and ran to the hose, but the Captain threw him down and ran for it himself.

POP! Another light broke. The shards sprayed, stunning the seasoned Captain. He managed to shake it off but was badly hurt. His initial run turned into a hopping limp as he grabbed the hose. Commander Brendan ran to the trunk hydrant, wiped the sweat from his brow and shut down the water. Then grabbing the hose with his injured Captain, the two hooked it back into the tree trunk hydrant. Emery turned the water back on and the Home Fire Battalion was back to doing what they do best.

"Captain! You okay?" Commander Brendan yelled, struggling to breathe. Captain Mas fell unconscious. The Fire Battalion was getting a handle on the fire and added a second hose line to clean it up. The flames were extinguished and the Medics immediately brought him to the hospital on the upper branches.

Commander Brendan thought about his Captain's sacrifice and the burden of leadership. Sometimes self-sacrifice is the only option. He almost cried. It should have been Brendan who was hit by the bulb, not the Captain.

Chapter 4

CHRISTMAS MYSTERY

The Fire Tailors extinguished the blaze in typical, efficient fashion. Commander Brendan waited for the Home Tree Police Department. He knew staying and helping was what Captain Mas would want. Brendan hoped Mas would be okay. He taught him all he needed to become a Tannenbaum Tailor officer. The events didn't give Brendan much time to worry about his Captain. He stayed to report to his Dad, a lieutenant in the Home Tree Police Department and one of the North Pole's finest.

The blue-and-white gift box car hovered to Branch 18, its bow light spinning on the top. Lt. Holly parked the hovering police vehicle on the end of the branch as to not disrupt a possible crime scene.

"Whoa. Brendan what did you do?" Lt. Holly climbed out of the top of the car.

"Very funny, Dad. We have quite the situation here, something doesn't feel right."

"Son, we can't go on feelings alone." Lt. Holly put a pair of goggles on. He pushed a button and a high pitched, but soft, beep sounded from the right lens of the goggles.

"Are you planning on swimming?" Commander Brendan asked of his father.

"I wish I was but the polar bears won't get out of the pool at the Academy. And these are meant to help. Must you always challenge me like your mother. Jeez." Lt. Holly approached the damaged light wires and bulbs. His head bobbed as he looked through his new goggles.

"But seriously, what are those things?" Commander Brendan asked.

"The boys at Glimmer call them Glimmerlight goggles. They enhance vision and also pick up..."

"Pick up what?"

Lt. Holly examined the socket of the first bulb that exploded and the part of the branch closest to it.

"This can't be... it just can't be." Lt. Holly shook his head.

"Can't be what?" Brendan asked, grimacing.

Commander Brendan's dad searched around and examined the bulb shards strewn across the wet bark of Branch 18.

"Can't be what, Dad?"

"Hey, Brendan, do me a favor. Unscrew what's left of that bulb and give me the serial number?"

"You want me to unscrew it all by myself? It is really wet on this branch. Are you sure it's safe?"

"Yes, my son, it is safe. Lighting shut down power to this strand of lights. Please do it," Lt. Holly said.

Commander Brendan approached the large light socket and pushed the lever to unscrew the bulb. The wheel emerged on the outside of the socket to turn and detach the bulb. He turned the wheel enough so the serial number would show.

"Okay, got it-122247. Now you want to tell me what you are seeing with your Glimmerwhatevers?"

"The lighting department would never leave a bulb that old burning on the Home Tree. We have to move fast. We have to move now."

Commander Brendan shook his head as he ran to catch up to his Dad hopping in the gift box car.

Chapter 5

LIGHTING ENLIGHTENING

Commander Brendan smelled the musk implanted into the seats of his Dad's gift box car. He knew it came from over many years of chasing bad elves and sitting on long stakeouts with fast food as the only dietary option.

"So what is the plan? Where we headed?" Commander Brendan asked.

"Headed to the Lighting warehouse. That bulb was too old to be in that tree," Lt. Holly said. His Glimmerlight goggles sat folded above his brow.

"Don't they reuse old ones and replace the fuses?"

"Yes, kiddo, they do but they always file the serial numbers off of them and give a brand new serial number. The last two numbers indicate the year they were screwed into the Home Tree's wire and socket system. The one that caused the fire was used in 1947. It is 1987. Our elves are awesome at making lasting technology but not that good. Here we are!" Lt. Holly hopped out of the car.

"Hold on Dad!" Commander Brendan was not used to his father moving so fast. Things had always been pretty quiet on the North Pole for the Tree Elf police. His excitement was warranted, though, Brendan supposed, shaking his head.

The Lighting department warehouse resembled a giant C7 light bulb. A C100,000 in other words. A giant Christmas light bulb. Gigantic, in comparison to tree elves, and it stood straight up about 10 feet high but really it was the size of a shed to Santa.

They entered through a door in the bottom screw that spun before opening, granting entry.

All the magnificence of the building's exterior disappeared when entering the interior. Standard brown tone of typical warehouses. No architectural wizardry here. No need for it.

Lt. Holly approached the front shipping and receiving desk. He wore a serious cop look.

"Excuse me!" He shouted, waking the elf behind the desk who'd been caught sleeping on the job.

"Oh elf! Wow! Sorry about that dude." The pimply tree elf responded in slow fashion, wiping the sleep from his eyes.

"Home Tree Police was wondering if I could see the shipping manifest for today and yesterday," Lt Holly said, staring at the clerk.

Commander Brendan laughed. "Seriously?"

"Oh, okay. Hold on, dudes. Let me see..." The desk clerk shuffled his desk full of portable electronic gadgets for the shipping manifest clipboard.

"I think it is hanging on the wall behind you. Actually. Yeah. Pretty...pretty sure that's it." Captain Brendan leaned over the desk.

"Thanks, dude. I got it." The clerk handed the manifest to Lt. Holly.

"Here. while I do this, take these and scan every inch of this place." Lt Holly handed the Glimmerlight goggles over to his son.

"Okay but you still haven't told me what to look for with these things." Commander Brendan fumbled but fastened the goggles to his head. The strap fit tight just above the points of his ears.

"You will see green sparkles around me, yourself, and in our footsteps. Magical imprints. You need to look for blue sparkle prints. Very rare up here..." Lt Holly examined the manifest.

"Uh Dad, there are lots of blue sparkle prints on the desk…and," Commander Brendan's mouth dropped.

Lt. Holly dropped the clipboard and lunged across the desk. The desk clerk tossed the papers on the desk to obscure Lt. Holly's vision.

"Get him, kiddo. He started the fire!"

Chapter 6

MOUNTAIN CLIMBING

Commander Brendan Holly's heart beat quickened. This days' welcome steadily worn by another emergency situation, all but diminished as Brendan ran further in the Lighting warehouse with heavy, but useful, goggles. "What kind of elf is he?"

In the center of the warehouse floor stood a massive pile of the light bulbs ready for processing. The blue sparkle prints led up the mountainous pile. Commander Brendan followed as quickly as possible. The desk clerk traversed the lights pile with effortless grace. He leapt and his hands stuck to the bulbs like a spider's legs to a wall.

"Really, what kind of elf are you? This is ridiculous," Brendan thought. The Tailor Commander scanned the area for a crane or something to catch up. Climbing that pile of lights would slow him down too much. He knew his limitations.

"A glimmerlift would really help right now!" A garland-laden crane stood just to the right of the pile of lights. There were only a few bulbs at the top of the pile. The crane must have recently been used to take some off the pile to processing. Brendan ran to the crane, looking up at the fleeing elf, hoping to reach the crane's controls before the elf reached the top. The tip of the warehouse was only a few inches from the top of the mountain of lights.

"You get him yet, kid?!" Lt. Holly yelled to his son from the front entrance.

"No! Of course not!" Commander Brendan yelled, climbing into the crane's seat.

"Well, why not? He is up there!"

"I know, Dad!" Commander Brendan never operated a crane in his life. All he needed to do was crash the long neck of the crane into the top of the pile to slow his foe down.

The desk clerk, turned fugitive from the law, neared the top of the light mountain, with no sign of slowing down.

"Okay can't be that different from the Icicle's controls," Commander Brendan told himself. He twisted a lever with a light bulb on the end of it. A noise pierced his elven ears and a vibration rattled from under his seat. The crane didn't move but it was on. Brendan pulled another lever and this time it moved.

The top of the crane crashed into the middle of the pile of lights. The part of the pile that stuck out the furthest suffered the greatest damage. Huge shards of glass fell to the warehouse floor and the bulbs at the top began to roll like an avalanche towards the thin veil of glass of the crane's driver seat occupied by Commander Brendan.

Chapter 7

JOVIAL PURSUIT

A green giant C7 light bulb rolled towards the cockpit of the crane. It cracked as it neared the driver's compartment. Commander Brendan jumped out of the driver's seat. The green bulb broke and shards jutted through the glass and through the back rest.

"Phew!"

"Hey, kiddo. You better keep movin'!" Lt. Holly yelled, watching the avalanche of bulbs topple and roll down towards his son and spread over the warehouse floor.

"Right! Thanks Dad!"

Commander Brendan ran in between giant bulbs careening and spinning as they crashed the floor. A blue one entered his field of vision, blocking his path to the front office. Another red bulb smashed into the blue one sending giant shards towards the Commander. He shielded his face and ran parallel to the smashing bulbs, but an orange bulb spun in his altered path.

"Ah! This is not happening! But it is. It totally is!" Commander Brendan slid in between the orange bulb's rotations and hugged the warehouse wall. He kept close to the wall and headed towards the office again. The avalanche stopped. Just the spinning and cracking of a few straggling bulbs filled the echoing walls of the warehouse.

Commander Brendan reached his father back in the office, panting, "Well that was ridiculous. I am used to *taking care* of Christmas light bulbs, not *destroying* them....hahaha. Wow."

"What do you think you are doing?" Lt. Holly asked, his brow furrowed.

Commander Brendan, hands on knees, catching his breath, "What? What do you mean?"

"He is still getting away!" Lt. Holly pointed towards the desk clerk suspected of setting the Home Tree fire. He was hopping up on empty cardboard light bulb boxes towards the domed ceiling of the warehouse.

"Oh, right. I almost died, Dad! You get..."

Lt. Holly's phone rang. "Hold on, Brendan!"

A look of steely resolve washed over his father's face. "Right, right! On my way!" Lt. Holly took off towards the giftbox car.

"What happened?" Commander Brendan yelled.

"Another fire has started on the shopping branch of the Home Tree. They have to be connected. I am headed there now. You can handle him, can't you?"

Commander Brendan's Dad sped away before he could answer. "I am a Tailor Commander! Not a cop! I tailor Christmas trees to a family's needs! I keep their spirits up. Why am I still talking?!"

He turned back towards the boxes and with his Glimmerlight goggles, he saw his assailant's blue sparkle prints and thus his path.

"Sure, I got this. I can do this! Slow down, Q-Bert! I am coming!"

Chapter 8

ASCENT

The desk clerk or bad guy reached the top of the box pile quicker than Brendan could. Again, he moved effortlessly, almost gliding up the boxes, just like he did with bulbs until Brendan smashed through them.

"Almost there Qubes. Wait up!" Commander Brendan yelled, panting only about halfway up the box pile. The sweat glazed his face as he jumped up to the next box, punching holes in the empty boxes for hand holds.

"I thought I was in good shape," Commander Brendan mumbled as he peered towards the summit of the pile. The desk clerk rubbed his hands together and pressed something in his palms.

"What's he doing? Hey, what are you doing? I said to wait!" Commander Brendan yelled, slowing down due to fatigue.

"Oh, that is not fair! Not fair!" The desk clerk jumped from the top of the cardboard box pile to the glass wall of the warehouse closest to him, sticking to the wall and climbing, with actual effort this time. The domed but narrow tip of the light bulb-shaped warehouse was his destination.

"Well, I am definitely not a spider. 'Bout the same size as some but not a spider. Can't climb walls." Commander Brendan shook his head. He looked towards the crane again and began his descent all the way back down the box pile. Going down proved much easier. The wall climb was a riskier and more laboring endeavor for the desk clerk. Commander Brendan had time to raise and ride the neck of the crane to the domed ceiling of the warehouse.

The Tailor Commander sped through the labyrinth of broken bulbs and reached the crane's driver seat. He kicked the green shards out of the driver seat and moved a lever. The seat vibrated again and the crane's neck started to raise and extend towards the ceiling.

"Wish I would have thought of this earlier. That would have been smarter."

Commander Brendan slowly pulled himself to the top of the crane's cockpit. He struggled. Glazed sweat started to bead drop on the cold yellow steel of the crane. He looked up with his goggles beeping. The desk clerk was still a long way from reaching the top of the warehouse.

The neck of the crane thinned out the longer it extended. Commander Brendan began to climb the crane's superstructure.

EEEEEEEK! The crane's neck extending grinded out a deafening pitch, as if the neck never had to work so hard, this worried Commander Brendan. His veins throbbed and heart pounded as he climbed higher up the crane's giraffe-like neck. The X pattern of the crane's steel superstructure made for generous hand and foot holds but they got smaller and smaller the farther up he went.

"How is it going up there, my friend?" Commander Brendan rested his sweaty brow on the crane, then looked towards the clerk now closer to the top. EEEEEK! The crane continued to screech but for one last time as the extension ended. The desk clerk kept shaking his head, wincing in pain and stopped to gather himself.

Commander Brendan continued to climb. "Sensitive to sound? That wasn't that bad!"

The narrowest section of the neck lay above Commander Brendan when the sweat from his previous rest caused his foot to slip. Commander Brendan fell.

Chapter 9

HANGING OUT

Commander Brendan fell towards the sharp, jagged edges of the broken bulbs strewn across the floor. He lifted his head away from the floor.

"The cable! The cable!" Commander Brendan yelled, flailing his arms and clawing at the cable hanging from the crane.

"This is gonna hurt!" Commander Brendan had no choice but to grab the steel cable that hung from the end of the crane's neck. His right hand grasped the cable first. The cable vibrated. His hand burned on the cable from gravity still pulling him down towards the shattered glass of the floor. Brendan's descent slowed and came to a full stop as his left hand gripped the cable as well.

"Ah!" Commander Brendan cried out. His right hand was more injured than his left. The cable still vibrated. He was closer to the ground but not close enough to just fall to the ground without risking more injuries or worse. The elf-adrenaline kept his grip strong.

The Tailor Commander's eyes shut from nerves. Something hard hit him and left debris on his head and burnt hands. He opened his eyes to see bits of coal dropping towards him. The desk clerk was literally playing dirty, flinging bituminous bits to force him to loosen his grip. Brendan could do nothing but wait it out.

"I am sure you have many, many stockings filled with coal! Fling as much as you want. I am not letting go!"

Four more bits hit him.

Some hurt more than others. When the pelting stopped, he looked up towards the domed ceiling. The desk clerk vanished and left nothing but faint blue sparkles leading to the very top of the warehouse.

"Coal." Commander Brendan felt the weight of his failure and his own body as it proved more and more difficult to hold on to the cable. He could think of only one way out. Of course, it would be tricky. He needed to get his elfphone from his pocket.

The very same sweat that caused him to slip kept dripping. Each drop that fell reminded him of how terrible a fall he would suffer should he loose his grip. “Okay Brendan. You can do this.”

His elfphone was in his pants, the right pocket, which was to his advantage since his left hand suffered a lesser burn than his right and could still grasp the cable. The Tailor Commander released his right hand from the cable and flexed the muscles in his left arm. His legs were wrapped around the cable as well but did little to make him feel secure.

With his badly injured right hand Commander Brendan reached for his right side pocket. His elfphone’s larger size made it difficult to pull from his pocket. It required more effort.

He grabbed the phone with his index finger and thumb and pulled. The force of his pull caused the cable to move. His left hand squeezed the cable even tighter. Commander Brendan now held his large elfphone in his right hand and dialed the only friend that could help him in this situation, a friend that could fly.

Chapter 10

JANE

"Jane, um, I need your help," Commander Brendan said.

"What's the matter? You sound serious, which is rare," Jane responded.

"Well, I am just hanging out…"

"You need my help hanging out?"

"Jane, no just shush."

"Wha…ooookay, you called me!"

"Sorry. Sorry. I am literally hanging out on a cable attached to the Bulb warehouse's crane and I might fall into a pit of broken Christmas light bulb glass. There is a bad guy getting away as we speak!" Commander Brendan shouted, with urgency.

"Already on my way!" Jane answered.

But before Commander Brendan could make sure she knew where he was, she ended the call. Brendan reinforced his left-handed grip on the cable and used his right hand to put his phone back in his pocket. He felt better now that he had both hands on the cable. All he had to do was wait. Commander Brendan closed his eyes and grimaced. The Glimmerlight goggles' faint beeps were the only sounds that echoed off the warehouse walls.

Beep.

Beep.

Beep.

Commander Brendan's hands ached. The pain grew more intense with each second that passed. The desk clerk was long gone by now. Brendan's usual confidence weakened to shriveling insecurity as he wondered just how much longer he could hold on. He hoped Jane would get there soon.

He felt a draft. He opened his eyes and there she was. His friend Jane, the Fairy Flyer, flew towards him. Her blond curls stuck out of her brown leather helmet. Her bomber jacket was zipped all the way up from her flight from the Hangar. Her wings gracefully flitted. The sight tugged at his heart.

"Oh, thank Santa, you are here!" Commander Brendan yelled.

Jane hovered towards him. She grabbed him from behind, her forearms around his chest.

"I got you. Now where are we going?" Jane asked.

Commander Brendan let go of the cable. His hand pain lessened but the burns kept him from complete relief.

"We gotta go up. The bad guy went up and out of the warehouse," Brendan said.

"Okay, you got it. Jeez! Putting on a little weight or what?" Jane poked fun as her wings flitted faster on their flight to the domed ceiling of the Bulb warehouse.

"Ha! Very funny! I know I am getting a belly…it is bad," Commander Brendan said.

"I am just kidding! Yikes. Relax. What's with the sporty goggles there?" Jane asked.

"They are pretty cool actually. With these Glimmerlight goggles I can see in the dark and can track magical beings like this bad guy. He's an elf and leaves blue sparkles behind that the goggles can detect."

Jane and Brendan reached the ceiling of the Bulb.

"Now where? You are getting sort of heavy for reals."

"Hold on. Let me see." Commander Brendan scanned the ceiling area. There were blue sparkles at the center of the dome.

"He must have gone right through the tip-top. There must be a roof entrance somewhere."

Jane brought him up to center of the dome.

"There it is," Jane said, flying the Tailor Commander to a small catwalk that led to a ladder that accessed the roof or tip top of the Bulb. She dropped him onto the catwalk rather quickly.

"Whoa! Maybe a little warning!" Commander Brendan said.

Jane shook her head, "Heavy!"

"Okay, what's next? The Fairy Fleet is on high alert due to the fires. Do you need more help? Like catching this bad guy?"

"Lt. Holly and I have reason to believe the guy I was chasing is responsible for the fires." The Commander climbed the ladder, all the while tracking the blue sparkle prints. He reached the tip-top of the bulb. The wintry air soothed his burnt palms. The lights of the North Pole took his breath away. The Home Tree still glistened with the colors of the rainbow. The Wrap and Bag department's gift box architecture and ribbon steps sparkled with blue and gold.

Commander Brendan's sightseeing was cut short.

"Wake up! You think the guy you were chasing is responsible for the fires. Shouldn't we be going after him?!" Jane asked.

"Right. Right," Commander Brendan said, scanning the tip top of the Bulb with his goggles. The blue sparkle prints led to a lights wire adorned with white bulbs.

"So this is how this guy has been getting around?" Commander Brendan said to himself.

"Uh, want to clue me in here, pal?" Jane stood with her mouth agape, eyes wide, palms up.

"He is using the old communication wires to get around."

"You mean the wires that lead to the heart of the city from all of the buildings in downtown."

"Yes and what is in the center of downtown?"

"The North Pole!" Commander Brendan and Jane yelled.

Chapter 11

NORTH POLE

The North Pole stands taller than every other structure in the downtown area. It acts as a both a monument and a communication tower. Wires strung with white light bulbs spring from the top of the North Pole and connect to each building around it, forming an umbrella of lights that illuminate the snowy ground of the city center. The only sight prettier is the Home Tree itself at the entrance to the city.

Jane flew Commander Brendan to the bulb at the top of the Pole at the end of the wire that connected to the Lights warehouse.

"The sparkle prints stop here. This is good. I can take it from here," Commander Brendan said.

"That's fine. I need to get back to the Hangar. There is talk that we might be escorting the Tailor

Icicles to each tree assignment. Lots going on, oh and word is your Captain is in stable condition but won't be able to join your team to your assigned tree, looks like you just got a promotion, *Captain* Brendan," Jane said, resting her wings.

Brendan felt relief that Captain Mas was okay. He took a deep breath. Commander Brendan was now Captain Brendan.

"Oh wow, a Captain now? So sudden? Am I ready for this?"

"You have been a Commander long enough. You are ready Brendan. Start with me, what are my orders?" Jane asked.

"Okay, okay," Brendan, said, breathing heavily.

"Captain, orders, sir?" Jane asked again.

"Could you alert my team to the Hangar? I am going to have get down from here eventually. I would rather have my Icicle pick me up than fall and I know you are busy-" Captain Brendan asked.

"I can definitely get Lily and your team prepped should you need them. Don't hesitate to call me again. I can always help if I can. Oh and Brendan, Captains give orders and don't ask polite questions," Jane said, flitting away.

"Right, you are right, thanks!" Captain Brendan said.

He found himself staring at Jane flying away. His heart raced, yet he felt a powerful calm. "Okay you need to focus. I am a Captain now. I can do this," Captain Brendan thought.

The sparkle prints stopped at the bottom curve of the bulb crowning the Pole. He pushed at the red-and-white-striped Pole. Nothing moved. No maintenance entrance there. He looked around on the other wires for more blue prints. He found a trail curving around the pole from the wire that attached to Santa's house!

Captain Brendan carefully shimmied towards the other wire using the bottom of the Pole's bulb as a safety. There was no cable hanging from a crane to save him should he fall again. The cold metal of the Pole felt good. Captain Brendan reached the wire safely and looked up. A door was open just above him within reach. The blue sparkle prints led to the door. Captain Brendan jumped up. "Ouch!" His hands gripped the side of the doorway and he pulled himself up.

The pain spiked in his hands.

He drove his hands into his armpits for comfort and scanned the inside of the North Pole with his Glimmerlights. The blue sparkle prints were everywhere. The inside of the Pole's top looked like a roughshod apartment, hastily put together, and for temporary use only. It also smelled. "Fruitcake and onions? Gross. What are you up to desk clerk?"

Captain Brendan walked towards a cot with perfectly-smoothed blankets.

"Neat freak but a smelly neat freak," Captain Brendan laughed.

Next to the cot was a pile, an organized pile with an empty GlimmerGuise box, which explains how the mysterious elf blended in with the rest of the tree elves. He used a mask. Not just any mask, but a high tech GlimmerTech mask, the newest model.

"I should get one of these for next year's Halloween party. What do we have here?"

Captain Brendan dug into the pile. He found schematics of every building in the North Pole and a diagram of the Home Tree. Other junk in the pile included a flyer for the graduation ceremony and a wire that led to the bulb illuminating the room. On the bulb's screw, a small pulsing red light cast an eerie glow. "Never seen that before, a light timer or something?"

Upon closer inspection, the pulsing red light came from a small cartridge. The cartridge's red light blinked faster. Thinking about the Home Tree fires, Captain Brendan knew the device's function. He jumped towards the door. The same device that caused both Home Tree fires readied to explode.

Chapter 12

EXPLOSIVE MOTIVE

Captain Brendan felt the heat of the fiery explosion as he leapt from the slipshod apartment. The blue-sparkled wire that led to Santa's house would have to break his fall. The force of the blast pushed him toward the wire. The airborne Captain felt the pull of gravity kick in.

"Here we go again!"

The anticipation of having to use his hands again to break his fall caused the Captain to gulp the frosty air and gnash his teeth. His belly hit the wire first. Then he bear-hugged for a grip. Glass from the bulb rained on top of him. Sparks were carried away by the cold wind.

Captain Brendan stood up. "Well, that wasn't so bad!" The wire was wide enough for tree elves to traverse. Hence how the desk clerk wreaked havoc in North Pole City, using the wires to walk freely between major points of interest. The current point of interest being Santa Claus's home, Brendan continued his pursuit, following the blue sparkle prints.

The white lights dangling from the wire lit his path, causing a blinding glare when using the goggles. He rested the goggles on his forehead and forged ahead carefully so he wouldn't slip.

"What would he want with Santa's house?" Brendan thought. The Big Man's house is a two-story wooden house with no defining feature except that it warms your heart. The snow-frosted rooftop, gutters laced with icicle lights, and the chimney casting out the aroma of wood and delicious cookies defined the image of Christmas and home for many, especially the North Pole elves.

Anger sparked within the Tailor Captain. He hurried his pace towards the roof of Santa's house. He lowered the goggles to quickly check that the prints on the wire were still fresh. Brendan reached the snow of Santa's angled roof and turned off the goggles. The snow showed the way now. The desk clerk wanted to break into Santa's home. The very thought made the Captain angrier.

Chapter 13

SNOWBALL FIGHT

Brendan jumped from the old cable to Santa's roof. The desk clerk's prints led to the attic window. A pane of glass was cracked and broken. At the bottom of the window was a grapple digging its claws into the wooden frame. Captain Brendan looked down with the goggles. Blue prints shown on the rope attached to the grapple all the way down to the attic floor.

The Tailor Captain gingerly pulled his elfphone out from his pocket, hands still paining.

"Lily, you at the Hangar?"

"Yes, sir," Lily's deep, crackly voice responded. "All of us here, prepping the Icicle for launch from the Hangar. We were waiting for your call. Looks like Jane will be escorting us to our tree assignment."

Captain Brendan smiled. Either Jane requested to be with his Tailor Team or it was just a coincidence. Whatever the reason, his heart skipped a beat.

"Okay, great! Lily, look after you launch head over to the roof of Santa's house."

SMACK! A cold fist raked the jaw of Captain Brendan. Lily's voice faded into the distance as his elfphone flew down the slope of Santa's rooftop.

The desk clerk, whose skin was now blue, eyes grey, and nose crooked like an upside down number one, pinned Brendan. The blue elf readied for the knockout blow. Brendan balled up some snow and whitewashed his face.

Brendan pulled the goggles off and punched the gut of the elf still pinning him. The desk clerk rolled off the window sill and slid down the angled rooftop. Captain Brendan, furious, slid down the roof towards him.

The blue elf recovered from the slide, popped up, and threw a snowball at Brendan's face, hitting the Tailor Captain flush to the face.

"Gah!" Brendan rubbed the snow from his eyes and cheek. "I hope you didn't ruin my goggles like you ruined my day!" His slide almost caused a collision when the blue elf jumped like a feline over and above Brendan.

"Seriously, what kind of elf are you?"

The blue elf ran back up the roof towards the attic. Brendan stopped sliding and pulled himself up. Bracing his knees for the slippery trek back towards the attic window. Brendan was so slow compared to his enemy. Brendan thought himself a decent athlete, earning good grades in PE at the Tailor Academy but he couldn't do the things his enemy was doing.

About halfway up, he looked towards the window. The blue elf pulled up a metal sphere attached to a rope. It looked like an ornament. "All this for an ornament?" Brendan thought. Brendan trudged up the rooftop. The blue elf secured the metallic sphere to his back. The ornament-shaped sphere was almost as big as he and Brendan. It made the blue elf look like a caricature of the Hunchback of Notre Dame, especially in the silhouette of the attic lights splashing from the window.

Brendan pushed closer, a few seconds from the window. The blue elf ran back towards the old wire leading back to the North Pole. "More chasing! Don't you get tired?" Brendan yelled, now angling towards the cable. His legs burned. His heart pounded. His breaths were short and labored. Brendan hoped Lily would show up with the Icicle now. The blue elf was getting away again, this time with an object stolen from Santa Claus himself!

Chapter 14

END OF THE LINE

The hunchbacked blue elf hopped onto the cable wire leading back to the North Pole. But Captain Brendan gained on his enemy, due to the metallic sphere slowing his assailant down. A few paces behind, Brendan grabbed for his elfphone. "Oh coal! I really loved that phone!" The phone lay somewhere on Santa's roof, its circuitry freezing in the snow and blustery wind.

As Captain Brendan hopped onto the cable wire, more coal bits were thrown at him, trying to knock him off the wire. The blue elf threw coal with one hand and pulled another instrument from his belt. A yellow light pulsed from it. The blue elf knew he couldn't run away from Brendan with the sphere on his back. New tactics must be applied.

Brendan felt the sting of the coal bits hitting him hard in the torso. He had no choice but to cover up. His pace slowed to not fall off the side of the wire. A yellow light flashed then flickered. The blue elf sawed at the wire with the yellow light, which Brendan now figured was a laser.

Despite a few more coal bits bouncing off of him, Brendan charged towards the yellow laser. "We'll both die!"

"No, my tree elf friend. You will die. I will live."

At this point, the two tiny elves were about a quarter of the way back to the North Pole. A cut cable would certainly cause a death-inducing plummet.

The laser made short work of the thick cable. Brendan tackled the blue elf, but it was too late. The force of gravity pulled both of them down.

Brendan grabbed a hold of the metallic sphere attached to the blue elf's back. They fell towards snowy Santa Claus Lane. The blue elf still held the laser and moved it towards Brendan on his back. The momentum caused them to spin in the cold air.

Brendan's stomach felt like it was protruding from his ears. He held the metallic sphere tight! The blue elf moved the laser to the strap on his left shoulder and cut off the backpack holding the sphere with Captain Brendan attached. Brendan saw his enemy swirl away, then pull out a parachute. "Yep, I guess you will live." Captain Brendan figured he had a few short seconds before he hit the ground.

Chapter 15

NEEDLE NET AND NEED TO KNOW

The impact felt brutal, strong and gloriously painful. Glorious because pain meant he'd survived the fall. Captain Brendan couldn't quite breathe yet but he could still see, in between prolonged blinks, the mesh of his Tailor Team's needle net and Icicle transport above.

"Great catch, Lily," he whispered. The Icicle's hover engines pulsed above as he felt the snow of the ground through the mesh of the needle net. The metallic sphere lay next to him.

Steve and Tonto's banter filled his ears as they approached to help him out of the net.

"Forget calling it a needle net. How about the Commander catcher?" Tonto said.

"Not happenin'," Steve said.

"Why not?" Tonto said.

"It is dumb. Just dumb. And didn't you hear with Captain Mas in the hospital, Brendan is now a Captain. You all right, Cap?" Steve, the Fire Tailor asked.

Brendan felt sore. His hands went from burning to a dull, pounding numbness. He breathed deeper. He felt strange with Steve calling him "Cap". Hearing it from a member of his team made it more real. Brendan hoped to live up to Captain Mas's example.

"Been better. Been better."

Tonto pressed the com in his ear, "Lily, you can detach the net now. Over."

The needle net dropped. Steve and Tonto pulled the net off Brendan and helped him up.

Tonto and Steve carried their Captain towards a hovering Icicle transport.

"So from Tailor Captain to action hero, huh?" Steve asked.

"Yeah, you made some good use of my new needle net. Thanks, friend. We are heading to our assignment now," Tonto said.

"Thanks, guys. I appreciate the catch but he got away."

"Who got…?"

Jane interrupted. She flew out of the Icicle transport's ramp entrance and secured the metallic sphere, still next to the net.

"You boys forget something! Ugh! Captain, I need to see you immediately."

She flew ahead of them and back into the Icicle.

"I see we have another passenger this year." Brendan said.

"Yeah, she is pretty intense. All Tailor Teams have fairies escorting their Icicles to their trees," Steve said as they boarded the Icicle transport.

"Lily, what is the situation report on our tree in Chicago?" Captain Brendan asked, wrapping his hands in bandages.

"Bringing it up now sir," Lily responded. She typed into her computer on the main flight deck of the Icicle.

"Thanks, Lily." Brendan said. He fitted gloves to his bandaged hands.

"Got it, sir. Looks like we have quite the situation on the South-side of Chicago. Apparently our tree's household has suffered a death in the family. The kids lost their grandfather. The tree was just put up, with very little decoration."

"So what you are telling me... is that their spirit levels are low."

"Considerably low, sir. We have our work cut out for us," Lily stated as Jane signaled to come in.

"Sorry. Needed to check in here with my pilot. Be right with you. Lily, keep us in a holding pattern above the Hangar until we get the all clear from the Fleet," Brendan said.

"I need to see you in the cargo hold."

The rest of the team woo-hooed in jest.

"Very funny."

While the Captain and Fairy Flyer made their way down to the rear of the Icicle, a very serious, concerned look adorned the fairy's face. They made it down to the base and she took off her leather helmet with a sigh and let out her beautiful blond hair. She sat the Captain down on a box of equipment.

"You know that metal ball you took from that thief?" She asked.

"What is that?"

"I don't know. I think we should call it in for sure. If that elf was trying to steal it, then it must be pretty important. I think we should call your Dad."

"My elfphone is definitely frozen back on the roof, even with the GlimmerFreeze case on it. Do you have yours?"

Jane unzipped her bomber jacket, reached into a pocket, and gave her phone to Brendan. "Put him on the speaker."

"I was gonna do that anyway." Captain Brendan grabbed the phone and dialed Lt. Holly.

Lt. Holly's voice burst through the tinny speaker of the phone. "Jane, tell me my son didn't screw up?"

Captain Brendan looked confused, then frustrated. "What do you mean? Oh wait, you already talked to him?"

"Well, I gave him an update on the situation after I dropped you off at the North Pole. So, yes, I did, I thought that was what you would want?" Jane said.

"That's fine," Captain Brendan said, sighing. "I don't think I screwed up, Dad. Don't worry. I am fine. Thanks for asking."

"What is the situation? We contained the second bulb explosion in the shopping district, they have to be connected to that clerk," Lt. Holly said.

"You can confirm that, Dad. Get a team up to the bulb on top of the North Pole. You will find all the evidence. The clerk got away but I secured what he stole from Santa's house. It is a big metal ball, but the metal ball might be a case."

"It is a case. You know the ball on the end of the Big Man's hat?"

"Yes. So what?"

"Well, that ball makes Christmas possible."

Chapter 16

PLAN LAUNCH

"What do you mean?" Captain Brendan asked his Dad through the phone.

"This ball slows down time around Santa so he can make it to all the houses he needs on Christmas morning," Lt. Holly said. Jane grabbed Captain Brendan's shoulder in comfort for his impending freak out.

"WHAT?" Brendan yelled. Jane then cupped her hand over the Captain's mouth.

"We have to keep this to ourselves. Ourselves meaning just the three of us for now. The Big Man would want it that way. The less elves that know the better. I understand how you feel about your team but we need to take every precaution. I will order an emergency Icicle launch for Tailor Teams whose families have yet to put up their Christmas trees, to provide cover for you guys. If there was an attempt to steal the Snowball, then the fires were a decoy for the thieves to infiltrate Santa's house and steal it, which you prevented," Lt Holly said.

Jane let Brendan breathe again.

"So wait a minute. Why should we still have the Snowball? Shouldn't we be locking it up?"

"The North Pole is no longer safe. We have to hide the Snowball with your team until Christmas Eve, when the Big Man and I will pick it up. No pressure, though."

Brendan laughed. "Yeah, no pressure indeed."

"I will talk to you later. Expect the airways to be filled with Icicles in a few minutes. That is your cover to leave NP airspace. Got it?" Lt. Holly ordered.

"You got it, Dad. Bye."

"Oh and one more thing. Do NOT under any circumstances use the Snowball. Leave it in the case. You can do this kiddo. Keep me updated," Lt. Holly ended the call.

Captain Brendan shook his head. His responsibilities just increased dramatically.

"Jane, can you have the Fairy Fleet check out the area around the North Pole for the suspect?"

"Already did when Steve and Tonto helped you out of the needle net. Nothing," Jane said.

"He parachuted away from me as I was falling with the metal ball or Snowball. Nothing the Fairy Fleet picked up on their aerial sensors?"

"We did a thorough check. Our suspect has just vanished from the Pole."

"Ugh! I almost had him. How could a blue-skinned elf like him just disappear?" Brendan shook his head.

"Don't worry. Everything will be fine," Jane said while putting on her helmet. She flew out to protect not only the team but Christmas for the whole world as well.

Captain Brendan went back to the cockpit, sat in his chair and looked out the windshield. The roof of the Icicle Hangar opened up. Soon the blue glow of thousands of Icicle's thrusters lit up below.

"Sir, we have the all clear from the Fairy Fleet to leave the Pole," Lily said.

"Join the Icicles launching from the Hangar and then set the course for Chicago," Captain Brendan said.

"Yes sir. Breaking from holding pattern to join launch," Lily said, easing the Icicle into position over the Hangar. In the night sky around them, thousands of blue flames lit up as the Icicles piloted by Tannenbaum Tailors headed towards their assigned trees. Each team was ready to monitor and maintain Christmas spirit through the meticulous care of the Christmas tree- the symbol of togetherness, of family, of love. Captain Brendan felt both joy and fear as this Christmas season could change his life forever.

Chapter 17

SNOW FALL

During the Tailor Team's final approach to their assignment, Captain Brendan worried about the tremendous pressure thrust upon the team. Not only would he have to keep the Snowball safe, but they also were heading to a tree where the Christmas spirit levels remained low due to a loss in the family.

The reason such a low spirit level posed such problems, directly affects how long their tree will stand, and if it will remain up for any amount of time. Many stories over the years tell of families whose spirit levels were so low, they didn't even put up a Christmas tree. If they managed to raise it, they would take it down just as quickly for any number of reasons. Brendan only hoped that this Chicago family's tree would remain standing until Christmas Eve, so the Snowball could be picked up.

Along with all the internal concerns, the team probably questioned the emergency launch, Captain Brendan's rescue, the Blue Alarm, and his meeting with Jane down in the cargo hold. The Captain's attention, however, needed to be turned toward the safe arrival at the assigned tree.

"Prepare for hook up to the tree, Lily," Brendan commanded.

"Initiating vertical-swing procedure," Lily responded as Jane flew in and started yelling.

"Remember this is a furnace entry not a chimney/fireplace entry!"

Brendan nodded. "Yes Jane, I am well aware that this is a furnace entry."

"Well, initiating the vertical swing now might be a little too soon, don't you think?"

Lily interjected, "It is too late. Vertical swing has been initiated!"

Jane then quickly flitted out of the Icicle and surveyed the vents that they would have to somehow enter vertically. Vent covers don't leave much room. The heat decided to kick on. The gush of hot air thrust the Icicle towards the vent. BOOM! Something hit the Icicle and pushed them even faster to a vent crash.

"Something definitely hit us, sir. The heat did kick on but that last hit was from something solid," Lily said.

"Do a quick scan with the sensors and pull us out of this spin!" Brendan yelled.

"Scanned already. Nothing and I can't pull us out of this spin!"

"Come on Lil! We just did this in the simulator! Whoa!" Brendan felt sick.

The Tailor's Icicle didn't have enough time to get back into a horizontal position. The Icicle went into a spin barreling towards the steel vent cover. Brendan saw Jane barely flying, out of control on the outside. The warmed air jostled her wings. She spiraled towards the end of the duct quicker than the Icicle.

"Lily, can you get control?" Brendan yelled as the rest of the Team spun in their swivels.

"Not possible, sir! Brace for impact in 10 seconds!" Lily screamed as she ducked under her console.

Captain Brendan had one option. He quickly climbed down to the cargo hold. His tiny heart nearly pumped out of his chest. He reached the area where they stored the Snowball. He scrambled to open the Snowball's metal case then found a blue button with an ornate snowflake on it. "This has to be it, right?" Captain Brendan pushed the button. Cool air spewed from the case, hitting him right in the face. "Ah, nothing's ever easy!" Brendan said as he pushed down on the fluffy white Snowball nestled in the opened case. He didn't know if it would work but he had no choice. It was their only chance.

Chapter 18

STINGING SNOWBALLS

Suddenly, the tremendous momentum that spun the Icicle lessened considerably. It seemed as though it stopped. Brendan ran up to the cockpit and saw that the rest of the Team was practically frozen in their seats. He paused for a minute to figure out exactly how to grab Jane who was literally inches from slamming into a steel slit of the vent cover. Brendan couldn't believe the Snowball worked!

Jane froze in midair about forty inches away from the Icicle. The Captain grabbed the controls of the Icicle and inched it close to her, threw a candy cane around her waist, and brought her in. He noticed that her body didn't move but her wings moved slowly, steadily. It's amazing how swiftly her wings moved while flying. Even in this slowed down environment, they still gracefully flitted.

Brendan flew the Icicle back about sixty inches and moved it into the horizontal position for a smooth entry into the house. He ran down to the cargo hold and jumped on the Snowball. He felt the tremendous force of time catching up to the Icicle and the team. It jolted the Icicle but everything and everyone remained stable. The possibilities were endless with the Snowball!

"What happened, sir?" Lily asked.

"We had some difficulty with the entry, something hit us for sure, I swear, but I took care of it."

"The last thing I remembered… "

"Lily, don't worry about it. All is well," Brendan said, covering.

She let up due to the apparent exhaustion from the Snowball. Brendan felt the tiredness as well, and he wasn't frozen from it. He looked back at the swivels. The rest of the Tailors continued to sleep totally unaffected by the entire situation. They probably had too much cocoa last night. Jane awoke and stared a hole in his forehead. "How am I still alive and how is the Icicle not decorating the vent cover?"

"Well, can we go to the cargo hold to have this conversation?"

Brendan could feel Jane's raging gaze on the back of his head as they walked to the hold.

"Brendan, we are supposed to protect the Snowball, not use it."

"I had no choice. We were in trouble."

"Yeah, we were in trouble because you screwed up!"

"I know, Jane. I ordered the vertical swing early but something solid hit us. I am sorry. It's not every day a Tailor Team has the mission of protecting Christmas for the whole world from thieves!"

"Do you have any idea what you did?"

"Yes, I made a mistake, went vertical in a furnace entry and put all of us in danger but then I fixed it. I swear something hit..."

"You fixed it by using the Snowball. Didn't you?" Jane asked.

"I had no other choice..."

"Your Dad said to not use it under any circumstances, which means that it probably can be traced or something when you use it."

"We don't know that for sure!" Brendan said.

"Your Dad warned us for a reason Captain," Jane said, as she stormed out of the cargo hold.

Brendan shook his head at putting everyone in danger, and then saving everyone, and by saving everyone possibly putting everyone in danger again. Oh yeah, and by putting the team in danger, he put everything that is wonderful and pure and selfless about the world in grave danger. Brendan reeled from the shift in his responsibilities. Before, he was a capable Commander. Now, a rookie Captain assigned with protecting one of the world's most beloved holidays. He wanted to go home.

Chapter 19

FIRST LIGHT

"Sir, we are safely hooked on to our assigned tree," Lily said.

Captain Brendan congratulated his Pilot, "Well done Lily." He felt comfortable. He could now focus on procedure. The Icicle sat high up in the tree a few branches below the star tree topper. The Tailors were ready to tend to a family's Christmas tree, a family that needed Christmas more this year than any other before.

The Tailors set up the command center behind the star tree topper in a matter of minutes, especially with the extra help from the physically-frustrated Jane, still mad at Brendan for using the Snowball.

"All right, team. Let's have a good tree check. Lily anticipates our First Light in a few minutes.

Billy, Steve, Tonto, and Irene have fun glimmerlifting around. Report any issues with the tree to Lily. We will assess and give you what you need as soon as possible," Captain Brendan commanded.

"Yes, sir. Would you mind tellin' us what exactly is in that metal sphere? We figure it has something to do with Jane being here and the emergency launch. Give it to us straight Captain."

The question was finally asked. Captain Brendan knew his team needed to be briefed at some point no matter how sensitive the Snowball situation was. Jane decided to fly in, at just the right time, to make sure Brendan censored himself. She hadn't been around all day and now she showed up. He wasn't going to tell anyone anyway.

"Well, those issues remain clouded in mystery. We don't know for sure what happened, but we have our orders. Christmas Eve is in just two days. We have our work cut out for us. So, let's not try to concern ourselves with the events back at the Pole."

"Yeah…all right," Steve said and shot Brendan a look. He could tell his Captain was lying. Steve had a gruff look but tremendous smarts.

Brendan glared at Jane. "Let's get to work."

The Tailors split up. The zipping of their Glimmerlifts sounded below the star. Jane just took off. She still wouldn't talk to the Captain.

"Lily, how we doing?"

"Well, sir, the spirit levels are still low. It being the 22nd of December, we really need to boost those levels up or we might not be in business. Oh, getting a message from Steve. Go ahead, over."

"Yeah, everythin' looks good down in the stand. Water levels are steady, the tree seems healthy and in better shape than most trees two days from Christmas Eve. I'm gonna start puttin' in the hydrants and hoses, over."

Lily looked for Brendan's approval.

"Tell him it's a go."

"Roger that Steven. You are a go for hydrants," Lily commanded.

Tonto and Irene called in. The tree's branches checked out healthy. Irene did note that the lights seemed to have not been used recently. First Light might not happen after all, which means they solely relied on the ambient light from lamps in the house, and very small standard issue candy cane lights, which were practically useless anyway.

Billy reported in, said the ornaments were dusty but in good shape overall. All of these reports pointed to only one concrete conclusion that relates to low spirit levels. The tree was healthy and still somewhat fresh, which means that the tree's lights have not been turned on in a while. This leads to the most disturbing fact. The time the family spent around the tree had to be very brief.

Captain Brendan went on the com, "Keep up the routine checks. Hopefully we will have some light in here real soon. This ambient light is too low to really start our work anyway. Out."

Suddenly, the Tailors heard a booming human voice. All human voices are too loud for Tailor's ears. They put on their protective Glimmearphones and listened in.

"I am putting the tree on for a lil' bit, Mom. Is that okay?" an older boy's cracking voice asked.

"Sure, go ahead," an adult female's voice responded.

"After all, it is his birthday and he loved Christmas," the boy said.

Captain Brendan rushed out of the star. He felt a sense of relief that someone, the boy, in the household mustered up some Christmas spirit. Brendan closed his eyes and waited for his favorite part. He felt warmth cover his face and sensed brightness through his closed eyelids.

Brendan opened his eyes to lights of blue, red, orange, white, and purple that blazed and bounced off the ornaments round, sparkly, large, and small. The nine-foot tree was trimmed by several feet of silver garland and tinsel, all beaming Christmas warmth. He sat on a branch, and let his worries and fears of this year's mission momentarily melt away as he took in the view from inside the tree. The warmth of Christmas engulfed him.

The Tailor Captain went back on the com, "Let's do this."

Chapter 20

GLIMMER NIGHT

The Team received a good jolt of energy and worked hard during the First Light. Everything ran smoothly. "How's our spirit levels?"

"They spiked a bit, but not enough to end our worries, sir."

"Well, at least we boosted it a little," Brendan responded, trying to remain optimistic.

The booming voices sounded again. The humans were crying.

"Looks like I spoke too soon."

Lily nodded, looking discouraged.

The com cracked open. Brendan heard the low, grumbling voice of his Fire Tailor.

"Looks like those lights really perked things up, huh?"

"Not funny, Steven," Lily snapped back.

"I don't understand. How can they be sad so close to Christmas?" Billy asked.

"Maybe, they're going through a rough time, Billy. Things don't always go as planned." Brendan almost laughed thinking of their situation.

Not long after the crying, the lights turned off.

"All right everybody. Switch to candy lights for a while then call it a day. Get as much as you can done. Out." Brendan grimaced and shook his head.

"I don't know about this household, sir. The spirit levels show no sign of recovering and maintaining enough strength to make it through Christmas," Lily said.

"We have to keep this tree up, Lily. We never lost a tree with Captain Mas and we sure won't with me in the lead either. We have to make Mas proud. At least, that eleven-year old boy showed some signs of spirit," Captain Brendan said.

"Yes. But does he have enough to help his family get over losing their grandfather."

"He has to. If not, I might have to break the..." Brendan said.

"Brendan we have to talk," Jane said as she flew in.

"Lil', check on everything. If anything happens, call me on the com."

Jane grabbed his hand and his heart pumped faster. She flew him down to the Icicle, a few branches lower than the star, on the backside.

"Your Dad is on his way here."

"What?" Brendan asked.

"Relax," Jane said.

"You told on me! To my Dad? Now he's coming! What are we, five-year-old tattle tales?"

"Oh stop! I had to tell him what happened with our entry, and how you used the Snowball. He's coming up to help in any way he can. He's bringing some extra supplies."

"Oh, so now I can tell everyone that they might be in grave danger."

"Hey, relax."

"Relax! How can I relax? You haven't talked to me in a day since I saved your life. Do I get any thanks? No, I get super-mad Janie, stubborn and grizzled as ever."

"I am sorry. Okay, thank you…but you wouldn't have had to save me… " Her retort was cut short by Lily. "SIR, GET UP HERE NOW."

Their conversations were always cut short.

"Give me a lift?" Brendan asked.

He didn't have to ask. She flew him up to the Star Command Center with amazing speed, much faster than glimmerlifting.

The humans were still crying.

"Brendan, Billy's com went out about three minutes ago and the last thing I heard was a crash."

"What branch was he on?"

"About three levels down on the end of a branch, near a blue icicle ornament, not our Icicle but one that looks a lot like our transport."

Brendan looked at Jane. She didn't waste time. Jane flew down to the Icicle to secure the Snowball. Brendan glimmerlifted down to Billy's last known location: a blue icicle ornament that resembled the Icicle transport.

"Steven!" Brendan yelled into the com.

"Yeah I heard, I'm already on my way. Out."

Irene and Tonto checked in. Brendan told them to head up to the star with Lily.

Steve and Brendan found Billy knocked out. With low candy light visibility, they couldn't see if he was badly hurt. Of course, all of this had to happen in the dark, with human cries in the background.

"Get him to medical now," Brendan told Steve.

"Where you goin'?"

"To find Jane. Now go."

Chapter 21

ICY ICICLE

He lied. Brendan didn't have time to explain that he knew exactly where she went…the Icicle. He zipped around and up slowly approaching the ship's ramp, opened onto one of the upper branches. The darkness crept in around him. A chill ran down his spine. He decided not to yell for Jane, because drawing attention to the Snowball might not be a good idea. If the icicle ornament incident was connected.

Too close to be a coincidence, Brendan continued slowly down the steep staircase to the cargo hold. He felt a hand over his mouth near the first landing.

"Son, be quiet. Don't move at all. Put these on."

It was his Dad, Lt. Holly himself. He handed Brendan another pair of Glimmerlight goggles.

Brendan put them on. Suddenly, he could see a bunch of blue sparkles and footprints. He could practically see in the dark.

"Dad... " Brendan whispered.

"Did I not just tell you to shut up?" He placed his finger against his lips.

Brendan felt the Icicle's staircase shake just a little. Then he heard quick, short footsteps scurrying above. Dad moved slowly to the other side of the staircase directly below the sound of the steps.

He motioned for him to go down to the hold. Brendan stepped down the stairs but, he slipped a little. BONG! The hook of his Glimmerlift bumped the side of the stairs. The patter of the footsteps suddenly stopped. Brendan froze.

"Where did Jane go?" Brendan thought.

He moved his head down to look into the hold. He saw what looked like a pair of flitting wings. Lt. Holly yelled, "Now!" The pair of wings shot up past his face, their momentum knocked him down, as Jane brought the now visible Snowball with her.

Brendan saw his Dad grab the ankle of some sort of creature darkly-dressed that could only be seen as a sparkled outline from the Glimmerlight goggles. This creature must have been the source of all the blue-sparkled footsteps!

Dad pulled the creature down the stairs. The creature kicked him in the face. Brendan quickly jumped on and wrestled the dark figure until his father popped a flare. The creature started screaming.

Brendan screeched too. He went blind for a minute until he ripped the Glimmerlight goggles off. His Dad then punched the creature out and wrapped it up in a stocking.

"Jane, did you get away safely with the package?" Lt. Holly asked into his com.

"Yes, I am already at the safe zone."

"Who the heck is that guy? Is that the desk clerk I chased for twelve hours? Why did you refer to the Snowball as the package? What…is what is going on?" Brendan blurted out, panting after the struggle.

"Kiddo, you really don't want to know, but unfortunately you will have to. Get off your butt and help me with this thing. Oh, and never refer to the Snowball as the Snowball while talking on your communicator."

Chapter 22

ANCIENT DANGERS

The Tailors assembled inside the Star Command Center at the top of the tree.

"How is Billy doing?" Brendan asked Lily.

"He will be fine. Just a bump on the head. More importantly, you owe us an explanation."

Irene chimed in, "Yes, you have been acting strange lately."

"Yeah you have," Steve added, "we definitely don't believe that you don't know anythin' either."

Brendan's Dad entered the room and all conversation stopped. He wasn't big for a tree elf, but he had a presence and reputation that demanded respect. He needed no introduction.

"Relax. It's not his fault that he has been keeping something from you."

Then Lt. Holly dropped the stocking and showed everyone the creature, "What you are seeing is a descendant of the ancient elvish clan, Espiritu. This creature used to be an elf like the ones at the Pole and us, but over the centuries this elf has adapted to its new environment in the dark caves of the South Pole."

"South pole?" Tonto laughed.

"I am serious. The Espiritu were the most brilliant elves in the world. The creative rights to all the world's most enduring toys belong to them. The Espiritu even had a hand in the creation of humankind's technological wonders like the printing press, the light bulb, automotive engines, and even computer technology."

"Wow. This guy looks almost exactly like the one I chased at the North Pole. How could these elves think of Santa and us, for that matter, as enemies?" Brendan asked.

"The Espiritu saw the world very differently than Santa over their long existence. They saw nothing but selfishness and hurt from the human race. They protested Santa's views on mankind and threatened to stop making toys for the world's children. To the Espiritu, all children would grow up to become self-serving, violent creatures, thus losing that which makes man unique: the ability to feel and love selflessly."

"So, what happened after they first protested?" Brendan inquired.

"Well, this might come as a surprise, but Santa didn't always have a Naughty List. One of the compromises he made with the Espiritu was the Naughty and Nice List. Even the list would be mired with controversy. Since Santa picked who was naughty and nice, the Espiritu felt they didn't have enough control. The Naughty List that Santa made was always considerably short. So eventually after years of protests and reconciliations, the Espiritu decided not to listen to Santa anymore. They decided to keep all the toys for themselves, believing human children didn't deserve them anymore.

'Santa tried to get them to stay in the North Pole. He even offered to let one of them judge who should be on the Naughty and Nice list. But it was too late. A large number of the Espiritu left for the South Pole never to make toys again. The Toy-Shortage Crisis of 1095 is true and now you all know the real reason why."

"This creature is one of them, right?" Lily asked.

"Yes, it is."

"Why is it here? Are they here to steal toys or something?"

"If only that were true," Lt. Holly said. He stared at the unconscious dark elf. "No, they are here to destroy Christmas itself. The creature's clan is now known in the North Pole as the Spiritless, entirely bereft of all Christmas spirit. All that is left is a selfish determination to leave the world in darkness."

Chapter 23

T-MINUS 12 TO 12/24

The Tailor Team, including groggy Billy, was fully briefed on the situation. The Team received Glimmerlight goggles and flares. Apparently the South Pole's caves made the Spiritless very sensitive to light. The dark elf they had stopped lay tied up locked in the cargo hold. Brendan felt awful. It was his fault this creature attacked Billy. He used the Snowball and since the Espiritu invented the Snowball their South Pole relatives could trace its magic.

Lily was the most upset, but the other Tailors found it in their hearts to forgive Brendan. Lily had been his number one go-to team member. She had a hard time understanding why he didn't tell her what was going on.

"Lily, I am sorry. Protocol, you know."

"You put us all in danger. I could have called for help, sir."

"I know but we can't draw any attention to ourselves or at least not like I did before."

"Well, can I call for help now?"

"No, we have to stay off all coms to the North Pole for at least twelve more hours until Santa gets here. After that, we will be in the clear. We have to try to stay quiet. We have no idea how many Spiritless are listening in. You would know that better than anyone."

"I suppose you are right. In the meantime, I will beef up security and listen in for any strange interference."

"Also Lily, look through anything and everything that Spiritless elf had with him."

"Yes, um sir. The family's spirit levels have dipped to the lowest point."

"Great... Just great."

The booming voices resounded. The Tailors put their Glimmearphones on. Two female voices continued their conversation…

"It is so hard without him."

"I know, honey. I know."

"Do you really think we should even try to have Christmas?"

"I don't know. It is not helping anyone. Maybe I should take everything down."

The other voice began to weep. Suddenly, Brendan saw Billy zip accidentally into a brittle round ornament, with a piece of blue circular garland inside. He broke it. Shards of the ornament and the spherical blue garland fell at the human's feet.

"What is that?" the younger female asked.

"We must have knocked the ornament down. I will clean it up."

"Oh, Mom! Look at the cute fuzzy thing!"

Another young female walked into the room. "Molly, look at this adorable little thing that broke out of this ornament?"

"Oh, that is so cute."

"We should give it a name and put him in the tree."

"Um... "

"How about Mr. Fuzzy Woo?" The two young females burst into laughter. The Tailors all grinned and clutched their earphones. The tiny elves enjoyed human-caused laughter for the first glorious time in this house since they arrived.

The two young females placed Mr. Fuzzy Woo near the star tree topper.

"Brendan... I mean sir. The spirit levels in the house have risen considerably," Lily said with gusto.

Who would have known that a silly round piece of blue garland could raise the spirits? But it did, and bought them some more time. Brendan's orders from Santa himself, to hide the Snowball in this tree, were more likely to be fulfilled. "Thank you, Mr. Fuzzy Woo," Brendan thought.

Chapter 24

SPIRIT OF PREPARATION

Captain Brendan ordered Billy, Lily, Steven, Tonto, and Irene to go about their usual duties. The lights were actually lit in the tree. The Fuzzy Woo uplift still lingered with only a few hours to go until Santa arrived. In the meantime, Janie, Dad, and Brendan plotted out exactly how to protect the Snowball.

"My last aerial sweep of the tree with the Glimmerlight goggles showed no signs of any other Spiritless," Jane shared.

"Good, I think we were able to contain the Spiritless threat for now. The best place to hide the Snowball would be the tree stand at the bottom, closer to my Boxcar, just in case we have to go mobile. The Icicle has been compromised obviously," Dad added as he pointed at our tree's diagram, one of the many sheets found in our Tailor tree assignment folders.

"Dad, my tree is safe. Believe me. We go mobile and the Snowball is easier to get at, especially in your little square gift Boxcar," Brendan said.

"Well, how are your spirit levels?"

"Right now, they are okay."

"Brendan do we have enough to last until Santa gets here?" Jane asked.

Brendan lowered his head. "Barely"

"Kiddo, get that chin up. Santa didn't just pick your team at random to protect the Snowball."

"Thanks, Dad."

"All right then. We will keep the Snowball behind the star until Santa gets here. Janie, I want you hovering around in a protective pattern as usual. Brendan, keep up the normal protocol. I will stand guard at the Icicle to make sure our uninvited guest stays unconscious."

The Jingle Bells beep of Brendan's com sounded and Lily's voice came in. "Sir, there are some interesting gadgets and gizmos this little guy brought with him. You should really come and check it out…over."

"I will be there in a bit. I am going to check in with everyone again. Out," Brendan said.

They went their separate ways. He saw the team's siblings, Irene and Tonto embracing on a branch surrounded by blue and green lights on his way to check in with them.

Irene's shoulders started shaking. She was crying and obviously scared. Brendan decided that they needed extra help. Exercise emergency powers; an unprecedented decision. After he met with Lily, Brendan wanted off the tree to talk to the eleven-year-old. The more help the better, even if it is from a human and against every rule in the Code.

Chapter 25

GONE BATTY

Brendan met up with Lily back at the Star Command Center. She spread several items out on a table and the captain's chair. She examined a round object with much consternation.

"What is up, Lil?" Brendan asked, as the lights turned off in the tree, marking bedtime for the humans.

"I just have an awful feeling about this item in particular. This seems to be giving off a very low energy signature one that my sensors can barely pick up. I can't seem to figure out its function."

"Well, you figured everything else out, right?"

"Yes, all the other things are really just tools for movement. It's almost as if the Spiritless are practically blind."

"Wait a minute, did you say blind?"

"Yes."

"Didn't Dad say they live in caves?"

"Yes, he did."

"Well, what else lives in caves?"

"Bears, rats...bats."

"Maybe, it is some sort of echolocation instrument...kind of like sonar."

"Sonar! That means it can also be used for movement like the other tools and also could be used to... communicate."

"Lily, destroy it. Get rid of it. The low energy is a broadcast!"

Lily stomped it to shreds, then scanned every piece to make sure no energy was left. Brendan quickly called everyone on the closed com to stay alert and ready.

There were a total of six Tailors, one fairy, and an elf cop. That beacon had been pulsing for hours. The sensitive ears of their visitor's friends were listening. They were investigating their missing comrade. They were bound to show up. The big question: how many ears were listening? Brendan had no idea. It felt like the right time to exercise emergency powers.

Chapter 26

OFF-TREE

On his way to the lower branches, Brendan ran into Tonto on his way to check the water levels in the tree stand. He saw his Captain rappelling faster and faster down to the stand.

"Captain! Where you headed in such a hurry?" Tonto asked.

Tonto was far too bright to buy any lie Brendan would tell. The new Captain was a bad liar anyway. Tonto was talented, came from a long line of quality tree elves, great Tailors. He would be Captain of his own tree one day for sure.

Brendan just came out with it, "I am going off tree to ask the boy for help."

"What? Captain! You aren't serious are you?" Tonto grabbed his arms and looked into his eyes.

Brendan shrugged him off.

"Under purview of the Tailor Code, given certain situations emergency powers are granted to the Captain of the team to, within reason, use whatever means necessary to accomplish the mission and uphold the oath the Tailors take when they graduate from the academy. This is how I see it," Brendan said.

"Going off-tree and breaking the Silence Protocol is a bit much, perhaps too much power, don't you think? Not to mention dangerous! What would Captain Mas do?" Tonto said.

"Tonto, you make a whole lot of sense but, I am the Captain now. Normally I would not think of doing anything like this but if this tree is taken down, if the Snowball is exposed, if we fail...then Christmas is over."

"There has to be another way! The Tailors Code forbids that you do this. The Silence Protocol takes precedence! How do you know if that kid, who looks like he might almost be a teenager and probably doesn't believe in Santa anymore, will not crush you when he sees you? Or worse, capture you and spread the news that we exist?" Tonto said.

"I don't know. But it is worth a shot." He hooked his Glimmerlift to the bottom branch and descended to the tree skirt. "Tonto take care of the tree while I am gone."

Tonto just shook his head and glimmerlifted up the tree. Tonto had a very literal interpretation of the Tailor Code. He is next in line to become Captain and follows the rules to the letter. Ever since his parents died while on a mission, he never takes any chances. Perhaps the burden of leadership will change his mind one day.

Brendan was alone among mountains of wrapped presents. He walked towards the edge of the tree skirt. Nerves rattled. Sweat gleamed from his forehead. He took his hat off for a moment and wiped his brow with his right arm.

"One minuscule step for me, one giant leap for elvenkind."

Brendan stepped down into the fibers of the carpet and headed towards the stairs. He knew the general direction he had to go. If he needed a refresher he would jump.

The fibers were like tall grass, tall enough to obscure his vision. He fastened his Glimmerlight goggles to the back of his head and clicked them on. The family was asleep so he hoped for no interference to the stairs, leading to the bedroom. He leaped to find his way. He saw a big black blob in between him and his destination. The human's poufy dog lay before him...sleeping. At least he hoped.

"I am so tiny and stealthy. No problems just go around the big dog," Brendan thought

He continued through the fibers of the carpet, on a path that would bring him around the dog. A toy with a hole in it lay next to the dog, probably laced with peanut butter or something. "I think they called those congs? Fitting since the dog is as big as King Kong to me."

He moved around the dog successfully. The dog slept. Nothing but breathing could be heard. The dog lay in front of the stairs he needed to ascend. Luckily, Brendan had his trusty Glimmerlift with him! He aimed towards the side railing a couple feet above the dog. His Glimmerlight goggles aided him as he aimed toward the rail's underside.

"GRRRRRR….." a growl sounded to his right.

He thought about taking the shot and zipping away. Instead, he found himself in a staring contest with two black eyes framing a long, snarled snout. The staring was really not a game he entered into voluntarily. "Elves must smell differently?" Brendan tried to figure out a good reason why the dog woke up and how he was going to get away from the giant, poufy, rather angry canine at that.

"Coal," Brendan said, cursing.

Chapter 27

PLAY TIME

The dog's breath hit him like the winds preceding an arctic twister. Except the wind was hot and smelled of something the dog should not be eating nor any living creature for that matter. The growls ceased and then a giant white paw came crashing down! Brendan rolled out of the way, with his Glimmerlift still at the ready in his right hand. He shot towards the dog's cong. The line tightened, the hook fastened inside the dog's toy and he zipped right in.

The inside of the dog's cong smelled like peanuts and it was a bit slimy from leftover peanut butter and probably the...Yep the dog's tongue slithered into the cong. He pressed himself up against the back of the cong. Brendan's head and body shook as the cong turned and tumbled as the dog's paw secured it to the floor. He pressed his body against the wall. He felt the heat of the dog's breath again. The tongue lathered the tip of his shoe and then retreated.

Brendan almost let a breath of relief out when he slid from the back of the inside of the cong to the opening in the front in a flash! Peanut butter stuck to his face. He grabbed the side of the opening tight as the toy shook and jolted up and down. The inside of the cong contracted as the dog's jaw bit down on it. Luckily the dog's jaw muscles weren't that of a larger, more ferocious canine, otherwise, the tiny tree elf would have been smashed. The dog thrashed more. Brendan's grip loosened. The dog's strategy was working. His legs moved closer to the opening where his hands held on! His body was shifting to the side. One more thrash and he would be hanging out of the cong. Too close to the dog's sharp teeth.

"GRRRR!" The dog threw the cong with Brendan now dangling from the opening back towards the tree, well away from the stairs. Brendan let go of the cong. He flew through the air like Jane, except soon he would be falling.

He aimed the Glimmerlift at a wooden table against the wall, across from the tree. He took a shot, the force of the dog's throw depleted. He began to fall. The line from the Glimmerlift seemed to move in slow motion. His little elf body would not take a fall from this height well. “Oh, coal!” He cursed. “Coal! Coal! Coal!”

Chapter 29

COME TO THE STABLE

"Oh, for the love..." The line from the Glimmerlift tightened a few inches from the carpet. Brendan zipped up to the top of the wooden table into some fluffy decorative cotton, used to resemble snow. He rolled around in the fluff, giggled, and yelled, "I love my glimmerlift! I love you! I love you!" He even gave it a kiss as he fastened the hook back to his belt.

The Tailor Captain stood up and surveyed the table top. Statues of Santa, gingerbread houses, snowmen, ice skaters, and miniature pine trees combined for a wonderful Christmas display. He bet it looked even better when the twinkle lights were plugged in.

As he walked on the fluff, he felt underneath the fake snow, lights used to illuminate such a quaint, literally quaint, Christmas village. At the back corner of the table was a dark building. Captain Brendan guessed it had to be the stable with the Baby Jesus on display. His Glimmerlight goggles helped him find a way through the statues and trees to the stable.

The baby lay peacefully in his manger. His mother and father close to him, watching in awe at their newest and greatest gift. The three wise men stood with the finest gifts of the ancient world. Their only compass, the North Star, reminded Brendan of his current objective. He had to make it to the boy's room. Christmas must go on. The moments such as the one on display here, the celebration of a child's birth must endure.

He looked to the top of the stable and realized he might be able to glimmerlift along the twinkle lights hanging from the windows on the wall behind the stable to the stairs. He'd be far away from the carpet and the dog. He aimed his Glimmerlift to the roof of the stable when the lights under the fluff turned on! He quickly ran behind the Baby Jesus. If the lights were turned on, a human must be close!

Chapter 30

JACK

From where Brendan was, behind the Baby Jesus, he could tell that it was the eleven-year-old boy he needed to talk to! What incredible luck! The boy stared at the quaint Christmas village. Brendan kept out of sight but peeked a little. The boy's eyes seemed to glisten with tears, yet also a smile cracked from the side of his mouth. He just looked at the village as if nostalgic about past Christmas memories that danced and played in his memory- memories of happier holiday seasons, when his Grandfather enjoyed the holiday with him.

Brendan didn't know how much time he had until the boy stopped looking at the village. He had to act fast, but he also didn't want to freak him out.

"Ah, whatever," Brendan thought.

He ran out to the snow in front of the nativity scene. The boy's eyes looked towards a porcelain version of Santa's house on the other side of the table. Brendan dug through the cotton snow and grabbed the wire of a light nestled underneath and shook it, hoping to signal him.

"No turning back now!' Brendan said to himself. The boy looked away from Santa's house and turned his gaze towards the nativity scene.

He kept shaking the light and then the boy's eyes rested on Brendan. The boy's mouth opened. He just kept staring, his blue eyes wide. Brendan had to speak up, "Hey kiddo!"

The boy covered his mouth with both hands.

Brendan's voice strained to yell again, "Hello, I am Captain Brendan! What is your name?!"

"Um, my name is Jack! What…what are you?"

"Good, Jack! Nice to meet you? Would you mind holding your palm out? So I can get closer to you so I don't have to yell?"

"Okay." Jack put his palm out and the Tailor climbed onto it and Jack brought Brendan closer to his face.

"Great! Now I can actually talk to you, instead of yell. So you are probably wondering who and… what… I am?"

Chapter 31

TANNENBAUM TAILOR

"Every December, people invite pine trees in their houses for holiday celebrations. People gather around these Christmas trees, or Tannenbaums, and open each other's gifts. The people in the house decide how long the tree will stand, but what they don't realize is just how important the tree is or how much work goes into maintaining the tree's beauty throughout the long holiday."

"Don't you just need to make sure the tree has water?" Jack asked. His talking actually gave his mouth a rest from gaping.

"Well, water isn't the only need for the tree as most people think. The tree's proper care requires something tiny and stealthy…it needs tree elves. I, Captain Brendan Holly, lead a team of Tannenbaum Tailors. Every year a team is assigned a household's tree to take care of. By taking care of this tree, we also take care of the family that depends on that tree to feel the spirit of Christmas."

"So cool! You're a Captain! What do you do?"

"I give orders to each department from my base of operations at the apex or top of the tree. I set up my headquarters in whatever decoration used whether it is a star, an angel, etc. The departments consist of a Visual department, that maintains the sparkle of the ornaments, Lighting, which makes sure every bulb is working and bubble shot, Water and Needle, make sure the tree's waterways are clear and every needle is strong, and finally Emergency Services, otherwise known as Fire. Its function should be self-explanatory."

"Wow!" Jack whispered. "Where do you come from?"

"The Tannenbaum Tailors hail from the North Pole. Every year constant training and simulations of possible scenarios run like clockwork around the Big Man's base of operations until December rolls around and the world stops to appreciate life, even if it's only for a day out of the year."

"The Big Man?"

"Think about it really hard, Jack."

"You mean Santa?" Jack's voice filled with glee.

"Yes, Santa Claus." Brendan confirmed.

"Really? I was starting to doubt he existed! After all, I am almost twelve."

"Well, Jack, you are the only human to *know* that Santa and his elves are real, which makes you very special. But Jack, this knowledge cannot be shared with anyone else. Can you promise me that?" Brendan asked. He stood firm.

"I promise."

"Good, Jack. Now I need your help."

Chapter 32

HONORARY TAILOR

The nearly twelve-year-old boy could hardly believe what he'd just heard. His eyes were wide. He looked more like a younger boy than a tween.

"You want…my help? How can I possibly help?"

"My team knows that your family has suffered a major loss. We get a Spirit Level report and we check the levels every hour on the hour. Your Mother, Vivian, mentioned taking the tree down…"

"Oh, I know. I don't think she will. I guess this Christmas has just been really hard with my Grampa passing away. He loved Christmas and really was the best. We were best buddies. He always took me to baseball games. We watched old movies together…." Jack's brow furrowed and tears welled in his eyelids.

Captain Brendan walked from the middle of Jack's palm to a place closer to his wrist. "Sounds like your grandfather was quite the man."

"He always made me feel better when kids at school would give me a hard time. He always knew what to say. He always told me how good of a guy I was."

"What would he say about skipping Christmas and taking down the tree, Jack?"

"He would understand how sad we all feel but he would never skip Christmas. He would never want us to because of him," Jack answered.

"Well, Jack, this is where you come in. I want to make you an Honorary Tailor. If your Mom comes down here and decides to take the tree down, you have to stop her. It is very important that you stop her. If you don't, Christmas for the whole world will be in jeopardy."

"The whole world? No Christmas? Why?" Jack asked, eyes wide again.

"It is a long story but Santa has chosen my team to protect the Snowball, the device that gives Santa enough time to deliver presents to the world's children in one night."

"Whoa".

"Yeah, pretty serious stuff, if the tree is taken down that will make it easier for the bad guys to steal the Snowball. The best place to hide it and keep it safe is inside the tree until Santa can pick it up in a little over an hour from now."

"Santa…is coming here in about an hour!" Jack said.

"Yes, but you cannot stay down here. Only come down if you hear your Mom. Got it? How tired are you?" Brendan asked.

"I won't be able to sleep now," Jack said.

"Good. Well, my newest Tailor, if you could bring me back to the tree, I would appreciate it."

"Yes, sir. Um, how will I know everything is okay and the Snowball is safe? Should I be concerned about the bad guys you talked about?" Jack gently brought Brendan back in front of the middle branches of the tree.

"Good question. My team will handle them. They are tiny like me. If there are more presents under your tree in a couple hours you will know all is well. Before you go back upstairs, could you turn the lights on in the tree? Remember, Jack. You can't tell anyone about us! It is very important! OH and stay awake. Thanks, Jack!"

Brendan aimed his Glimmerlift towards the middle branches, shot, and zipped into the tree. Even though Brendan just put tons of pressure on the kid, he felt confident that Jack would come through should the need arise. He hoped the need would never arise.

Chapter 33

ZERO HOUR

As time ticked down to 2300 hours and Jack as backup, Brendan walked around the inside branches of the tree feeling a little better. Jack turned the lights back on. What an amazing sight! The beautiful glowing lights, the smell that wonderful smell, the strong needles, all his Tailors, under all this stress, still did a wonderful job of keeping this tree strong. He zipped up the branches to see Jane. He felt he needed to tell her how he felt. For some stupid reason, it felt like the right time.

"Jane, could you stop flitting around for a second, and come here for a minute?"

"Now, you want to talk…really?"

"Oh forget it… " Brendan turned to walk away from her. There was never a right time with her.

"No, I'm sorry. What is it?" Jane said as she landed gracefully. She took her helmet off. Her golden locks lay on her shoulders.

"I just wanted to tell you that I am sorry for putting you in so much danger in the vents and that… that…I... "

"Spit it out. What?"

He took her hand. She didn't brush him off.

"Take a look around you. See how beautiful this tree is?"

The holiday lights danced on her eyes, made them sparkle, as she looked up. "Yes, it is very pretty."

"Well, this tree is nowhere near as beautiful a sight as you."

A tear welled up in her left eye. She hugged him. They held each other tightly. They embraced for a few moments until CRACK! The branch they stood on bent from the Icicle ramming into it. Still hugging, Janie flew them out of the way and the lights went out.

The darkness overwhelmed the Fairy Flyer and Tailor Captain. They could barely see the Icicle, but heard the hum of its thrusters. They thought they were safely away.

"Ah!" Brendan screamed, as the Icicle slammed into the branch they landed on.

Brendan fell, but managed to deploy his Glimmerlift and caught a sturdy branch below the surging Icicle.

Janie swooped down to the Snowball, still behind the tree star, secured it and flew down the tree.

The Icicle powerfully ascended. Brendan had to stop it.

"Something happened to Dad. The Spiritless elf somehow escaped!" Brendan realized.

He zipped up to the hook at the top of the Icicle, which bent considerably as it continued to blast through the top branches. The hook jutted downwards and nearly stabbed him, almost making him an ornament. He rolled out of the way, flipped on to the ramp and jumped in.

He found the crazy elf in the cockpit, with a nose that looked like a flat and crooked upside down number one. The dark elf that eluded him at the North Pole! Number One cackled, as he destroyed the tree top. Brendan leapt towards him. He must have heard Brendan move. The dark elf landed a kick square in Brendan's chest sending him spiraling through the swivel seats and onto the staircase.

"Eeeeee..." Brendan squeaked trying to catch the breath violently forced out of his lungs.

Sprawled on the floor of the Icicle with one hand on his paining chest, he saw his Dad lying unconscious next to the top of the staircase. Brendan shook him, but he didn't budge.

Elf-adrenaline kicked in. The air flowed back into his lungs. His chest no longer ached. Brendan ran towards the cockpit in a fit of rage. The mad, cackling monster used his charge against him. The Captain slammed into the viewport.

More pain this time all over his face.

"We are coming for the Snowball. You can't stop us. This selfish world doesn't deserve Christmas, you idealistic fool!" the Spiritless elf said.

Brendan gathered himself quickly. Being smashed like a bug on the viewport in front of the Spiritless elf, he peeled himself off the glass and kicked him in the face. The controls for the Icicle shifted. They spiraled downwards banging off every branch below like a broken roller coaster, until the Icicle stopped about halfway down the tree, still in the vertical position.

The ugly elf lurched towards the open door and ramp. Brendan used his Glimmerlift and grappled the dark elf's arm. Zipping towards him, Brendan rammed his fist into his face. He shook his hand to rattle the sting off it. The Spiritless elf lay motionless.

Brendan ran to the general area where Lt. Holly lay unconscious. He could barely see with his Glimmerlight goggles busted. He used the candy cane light.

"Stupid useless candy cane!" Brendan hit it to make it work. The weak beam flickered on. He located his Dad, put him over his shoulder, and glimmerlifted to the star.

Chapter 34

THE SPIRITLESS

"Lily, Dad's hurt. I need you to take care of him while I get the Snowball to safety."

"Brendan, I will try, but with our spirit levels incredibly low, we could be taken down very soon."

"Add it to the list of things going wrong. Hey, can you give me your pair of goggles? Mine were busted."

Brendan laid his Dad down on the floor next to him. Thankfully, he was still breathing.

"Take them and be careful."

He zipped down in the dark tree and called Janie.

"Did you make it?"

"Yes, but we have a problem, Your Dad's Boxcar was sabotaged. The Snowball is just sitting here. More Spiritless are here as well. I hear them moving.

I can see them and their footprints with my goggles. What should I do?"

"Stay down there. Don't move or make a sound. Keep your flare handy. The Spiritless have incredible hearing."

"Okay," Jane said.

"Didn't I just tell you to shut up?" Brendan sounded exactly like his father.

He zipped further down the tree and had an idea. He called Steve on the com, smart enough this time to whisper.

"Steve, I want you to set the tree on fire."

"That's a change a' pace. Usually you want me to put those out… "

"I know, but I need you to use the fire to protect the Snowball. Santa arrives in thirty minutes. And I'd prefer it if you don't burn the whole tree down."

"All right, I can set one at the top so it won't spread too fast. Meet me up there. Where are you now?"

"I am heading down to get Jane and the Snowball…oh and call the rest of the team to help you. I want everybody on this. Keep quiet."

The bottom of the tree loomed large and expansive. Brendan steadily zipped towards Jane when he saw the footprints all over the lower branches. The prints looked fresh. From what he could tell there were about five of them. They were scurrying around with strange instruments, used to latch on and off every branch with incredible ease, just like at the Bulb warehouse. He could see his Dad's Boxcar nestled near the trunk right above the stand.

"Jane must be to the left or right of that branch," Brendan realized.

Using his Glimmerlift would make noise and give him away. He would have to climb down the rest of the branches slowly, as to not make a sound. He started down and scanned the branches with the blue-green vision of his goggles.

Brendan saw a blue blob with the goggles! A Spiritless elf scurried to the end of the branch just above him. He rushed back, flipped down to Brendan's branch, and walked in the opposite direction. Another almost grabbed his foot as it used his branch to swing away. That was close.

With the coast seemingly clear, Brendan made his move and climbed down to Dad's Boxcar. Jane, on the right side of it, had the Snowball secured in a net attached to her hip. He knelt close to her and motioned towards her flare, should the Spiritless find them, they could temporarily blind them and escape.

Brendan put up five fingers and counted down with Jane. She nodded her head until three Spiritless elves dropped beneath them to inspect the stand. Brendan glanced down. They scoured the tree stand, letting out a horrendous yelps. "ARK! ARK!"

"Why all the yelling?" Brendan thought.

They were using their echolocation beacons to find Brendan, Jane, and the Snowball. The Spiritless apparently grew tired of using their poor eyesight. Sound would help them find what they need.

Chapter 35

FIRE AND ICE

Jane and Brendan waited just a little while longer until the three nasty elves left the tree stand and sat on a far branch of the tree. Brendan grabbed on to Jane. They decided to fly up and around the tree carefully dodging any impact that might trigger the Snowball's power.

About halfway up, they saw the banged up Icicle. Brendan realized he forgot about the unconscious Number One. Jane dropped him off on the ramp.

He was gone. "How could I be so stupid again? Coal!" Brendan yelled and covered his mouth quickly, but it was too late. Number One, his nemesis Spiritless elf, tackled him out onto the edge of the ramp. This time he had two buddies with him, both kicking Brendan while he was down. The Captain struggled to get to his knees but failed.

Face planted, the Tailor Captain reached for his flare and popped it. They cowered and screamed at the blinding light. Brendan deployed his Glimmerlift. Number One managed to grab hold of his ankle. Together they zipped to the branches just above the Icicle together.

Number One, still blinded by the flare, desperately clawed his way to Brendan's waist. Brendan punched the top of Number One's head. The flare burned bright, still clenched in his fist. Number One slipped trying to block the flare's light from his smallish eyes with one hand. With only one hand around Brendan's ankle, Brendan kicked him off.

The Spiritless elf fell back onto the ramp and not all the way down the tree. Brendan squinted from the pain the punch caused his hand. He hung from the line of his Glimmerlift and waved the flare whose light was sputtering from age.

"Oh, come on! Don't die on me!" Brendan exclaimed.

Jane saw his flare. She swooped in and flew him up to the tip top of the tree where the rest of the team waited.

"Hey, Tonto grab some more needles and put 'em in the pile," Steve whispered. Tonto hurried to the net of dried up needles that were removed for being fire hazards. They stood near the end of the branch and formed a perimeter around the Snowball.

"Wait till Chief Klark hears about this," Steve said as he grabbed his flare and dropped it into the dried-up needles.

"ARK! ARK! ARK!" The Tailor Team and Fairy Flyer heard the yelping of the Spiritless grow nearer as they methodically made their way up the tree.

"ARK! ARK! ARK! ARK!" About midway up, the yelps grew more intense. They, most likely, ran into Number One.

"Ladies and gentlemen, this is where we make our stand," Brendan said to Jane, Steve, Irene, Billy, and Tonto. Lily tended to Lt. Holly, both still inside the Star Command Center.

Steve's fire grew. The needles burned fast and furiously. He remained nearby, with a hose-line in case it got out of control. He felt that by placing the fire on the thinner, upper part of the tree, it would prevent the spread of fire to the other branches. Sound reasoning. Captain Brendan was lucky to have him on his crew, and honored to have him as a friend, despite his grumpy mood.

"I hope this works," Irene said.

"Well, it's our last hope till he gets here. How much longer do we have, Lily?" Brendan asked her in the Star Command Center.

"Sir, Santa should be here in fifteen minutes."

"We can handle fifteen minutes, people," Billy exclaimed as the yelps were right below. They huddled around the fire-guarded Snowball and waited.

The first Spiritless elf shrank away from the fire. Apparently the fire was too bright, but obviously he wasn't, as he tried to take the Tailors head on. He fell down the tree, clutching his face. The next five would not be so dumb, especially Brendan's closest enemy. Two more approached from the interior of the branch, but they stopped about halfway.

"Steve, watch our backs. These guys might be a distraction," Jane said.

Steve turned around and, sure enough, one of them attempted to throw water from the tree stand onto the fire. Steve jumped through the fire and grabbed the dark elf. The Spiritless struggled to free himself from the Fire Tailor's iron grip. Steve gritted his teeth and tossed him off the branch.

Another jumped on his back. With tremendous strength he peeled him off. Through the use of one arm, Steve threw him into the blackness of the lower branches.

"Okay, that leaves at least three more that we know of," Steve mumbled as he breathed heavily.

"Those two have not moved," Brendan said, peering below at the two remaining Spiritless.

"What are they waiting for?" Irene asked.

"I don't know. Stay here and do not move."

Brendan recognized a yellow glow. They were cutting the branch down with the same laser that cut the line from Santa's house to the North Pole.

"Steve! Put the fire out now. Now!"

Steve grabbed for the hose. He was about to open up on the fire, when they all lost balance. The branch broke. They plummeted toward the bottom of the tree.

Chapter 36

TEN MINUTES

When he realized the branch broke, Brendan's heart and stomach felt like they had been left a few feet above where he currently laid. A few feet equals a whole lot for a little elf like him. He checked around for everyone, found Irene and Tonto who were okay. Billy latched onto an angel ornament ironically. Steve was somewhere inside the tree, searching for a hose, because the fire began to spread.

The Fire Tailor hobbled out and sprayed the fire down. Then they heard a strange sound coming from Brendan's com. It sounded like a voice. They listened closely.

The vocal was slow and steady, "ARRRRRRRRRRRRRE..." Brendan looked around and noticed everyone from his Team, except for Steve, was frozen!

"This fire ain't movin' real fast for a pine tree," Steve said.

"That's because we must have hit the Snowball as we fell."

"So, if you hit the Snowball, it slows everything else down?"

"That or everything else stays the same and we speed up. Either way it sounds about right and would make sense considering Santa is the only one who is supposed to use it."

"Well... " Steve stopped, taking a casual look around, "where's the Snowball?"

Both Tailors stared at each other for a few seconds.

"I don't know. You would think it would be right by where we regained consciousness"

"Maybe not...we could've fallen farther after it triggered. It's probably in the upper branches somewhere."

"Well, let's go then, smart guy," Brendan said.

"Alright, alright, the fire is out, big guy," Steve said.

"Are you making fun of me again because you are bigger than me? I can take you down in two seconds." Brendan said.

"You may have to tap that Snowball once or twice," Steve said, laughing. "Two seconds with that guy apparently is a long time."

"We should split up. One of us should yell for the other one if we find it."

Brendan went up and Steve went down. Brendan saw more sparkled footsteps with his goggles. He found the Snowball up against the tree trunk, surrounded by charred needles. The remaining three frozen Spiritless elves were advancing towards it with semi-frozen Jane, outstretched with slow, flitting wings hovering right above the Snowball. Her mouth was open in a growl. Brendan giggled and made faces at her. She couldn't do anything!

After that silliness, he called Steve and informed him of the plan.

Chapter 37

SIX AND A HALF MINUTES

Steve and Brendan stood behind the Spiritless elves as they barreled towards the Snowball. Jane whizzed down, tackled one of them, and flew him into the nearest branch.

"Now, Steve!" Brendan yelled. Steve bear-hugged Jane and fell to a lower branch. The Spiritless elf hopped up to the Snowball that the other two already captured. Brendan let out a "NOOOOO!" and then it worked. He heard Number One say, "Test it."

Sure enough they did. Brendan froze. Didn't move a muscle. The Spiritless saw him freeze and walked over to check. Brendan's adversary scanned him. Brendan's eyes burned. His nostrils so wanted to flare from the stink of fruitcake and onions stemming from Number One's mouth.

Brendan didn't know how much longer he could keep his eyes open. Number One stopped and stared for at least a minute or felt like it anyways. He finally walked away.

"We have it. Let's go." The Spiritless elves started down the tree and disappeared into the ground. They just vanished without a trace, probably some dark elf magic or something. Captain Brendan stayed still examining the area they vanished into when suddenly a large object flickered into sight. A black and blue Icicle transport appeared.

The Tailor Captain maintained his frozen stance while looking at the Spiritless transport that could disappear on demand: a cloaked Icicle, which explains the desk clerk's escape back at the North Pole. Brendan knew something had hit the Icicle, sending them spiraling toward the vent cover earlier. Brendan watched the black and blue Icicle fly away.

Brendan moved again and called Steve, "We are clear. They fell for it. They are gone, at least I hope so."

"Yeah, buddy! Jane is a bit angry…and confused."

"Of course she is…of course she is. Meet up at the star ASAP," Brendan said laughing.

"You got it."

Brendan zipped up to the top of the tree. Lily just pointed at the Spirit Level gauge, at the lowest it could possibly be. This tree was about to be taken down with the Team still in it and a busted Icicle. Their only hope was Jack. The Spiritless could come back in their cloaked Icicle at any time. The suspense was almost too much to bear.

They observed the ornaments being taken off the tree. Brendan couldn't believe it. Santa would be there within minutes. He and the team made it this far. Brendan felt failure's weight push his head down.

Never before had his team failed at their mission to maintain a family's tree, their spirit, their hope-the hope that only Christmas provides. The hope that love endures all hardship and loss.

"Come on, kid!" Brendan yelled.

"Sir, who are you talking about?" Lily asked, surprised.

"I used my emergency powers and told the eleven-year-old kid about everything as an insurance policy should what is about to happen happen!" Brendan shook his head.

"Sir, that the loosest interpretation of emergency powers I have ever heard. You broke the most important rule!" Lily said.

"I know, Lily! Not now! Come on, Jack!"

Jack's Mom started taking ornaments off the tree one by one.

The Spirit Level gauge dropped to zero.

"Mom! Wait, what are you doing? Please don't!" Jack's voiced boomed in Brendan's little elf ears.

"Jack, it is too hard without your Grampa. Go back to bed. I promise we will have Christmas next year," Jack's Mom said.

"Mom, you know Grampa would not want to you to do this. He loved Christmas. Mom, I love Christmas and I love you. Please don't." Jack put his arm around his Mom and started to cry.

She hugged him. "Okay, Jack. It's okay." She held her son as he sobbed. A tear rolled down her cheek. She held him for a few moments longer, "Well, help me put these ornaments back…."

He arrived. A large, stout man dressed in red velvet, quietly walked into the room. He gently put his bag down, and approached the older woman and boy.

The woman jumped. She looked scared and confused. Jack smiled.

"Vivian, your son is right. I remember bringing gifts to your father when he was young. He so loved Christmas and wouldn't want you to take this tree down only a few minutes before Christmas Eve. He loves you and doesn't want you to do this."

She pulled Jack behind her. "You get out of here now! You didn't know my father. Who are you anyway?"

"Mom, that is Santa!" Jack said.

"I am as I appear. I am St. Nick." Then he handed her a small gift. She reluctantly opened it. It was an old Christmas picture of her father and her in front of their tree. "I believe your favorite toy that year was Mousetrap, you wanted it so badly. You were always such a good girl, mainly because of your parents, who really don't want you to do this. After all I would know… I am a saint you know."

She stared at the picture for a few moments, shook her head in disbelief, and wiped the tears from her eyes. She took one more look at Santa then gave him a big hug. Somehow, Vivian trusted and believed him. She knew her parents wouldn't want her to skip Christmas especially because of Jack and his sisters, their grandchildren.

Brendan stood next to his Dad, who remained unconscious.

"What are you doing here?" the older woman asked, still mesmerized by the picture Santa had given her.

"Well, I'm just dropping a few things off," he said with a knowing smile and a sparkle in his eye, "and picking one thing up," he whispered to himself.

His big hand wrapped in a red velvet mitten reached into the tree and took the real Snowball out. He nestled it back into the white ball that hung from his hat. "Now Vivian, I want you to at least try to make merry this Christmas, no matter how difficult it may seem right now. You will understand when you have grandchildren someday. Oh and Jack?"

"Yes San…Santa?"

"Your Grampa told me to tell you to…what was it exactly…" Santa had a lot on his mind especially on Christmas Eve.

"Oh yes, he said, never forget how good of a guy you are. I agree with him. Ho ho ho!"

Then Santa squeezed the Snowball and vanished.

The mother and child both stood for a moment staring at the now empty spot where Santa stood. Still gazing, Vivian slowly sat down on the couch. Holding her new gift from Santa to her heart, she put her head down. Jack now held her as she had just held him moments before. She cried a bit more before looking at the picture and said, "Okay, Dad."

Brendan still hovered over his father, hugged him, and repeated what she said, "Okay, Dad," pleading for him to wake up.

Vivian and Jack then put the ornaments back on. Vivian lit the tree, and woke her daughters and her husband. They sat and held each other around the tree.

Lt. Holly finally awakened and said, "I love you, too, Brendan. I love you, too. Merry Christmas."

The spirit levels spiked to a season high. The Tannenbaum Tailors were not going anywhere until the holidays were officially over.

Chapter 38

HOW? MAGIC.

"How are the Spiritless gone? And why did Steve tackle me?" Jane pressed.

Brendan responded first, "Well, you see. Steven and I were fortunate enough to have touched the Snowball, as it slammed onto one of the lower branches after the Spiritless sawed our branch off."

Steve chimed in, "So with all the time in the world, we borrowed some of Billy's white polish, some fluff from the beard of a plush Santa ornament and..." Brendan continued, "...we painted Mr. Fuzzy Woo white, pasted the fluff on, and switched him and the Snowball. Then I acted as though I were suspended in time, when the Spiritless tested Mr. Fuzzy Woo."

"We made sure we did not just appear in front of them when I hit the Snowball, so we hid on the branch below us. Otherwise, they would have probably figured it out, especially if Steve was standing in front of them. We hung back and Steve jumped you from behind the other Spiritless."

Brendan walked over and removed the restraints and gags from Billy, Irene, and Tonto.

"You three needed restraints and gags to not cause any commotion, due to the possibility they might test it, which they did do, of course." Brendan struggled with Billy's restraints.

"Jeez! Steve, could you have tied Billy up any tighter with this tinsel...man?" Brendan managed to untie him.

"Probably," Steve muttered with a sinister grin.

"That was brilliant!" Jane remarked, surprising all with her show of emotion.

"Brendan and Steve-O saving the day," Billy said.

"No, it wasn't just Steve and I. It was all of us. We are a team!"

Chapter 39

HEAVENLY PEACE

"Lily let's roll out the reports, on this the most joyous day of the year."

"Irene and Tonto, how is it going with my lights, water and needles? Over?"

"Vibrant, plenty, and strong sir, over and out," the cheery siblings answered.

"Steve, how is my favorite Fire Tailor?"

"Great," but he didn't respond on the com, he walked right in, and gave Brendan a big bear hug. While he carried Brendan, he walked over to Lily and picked her up with his other arm and hugged her too. On cue, Jane flew in to join the group hug.

Every Christmas morning Brendan gathered the Tailors to zip through the tree, together, as a team.

"Wow, man this tree has been through a whole lot," Billy shared.

"... A fire, Captain Mas goes down, Brendan gets promoted, invasion of crazy elves, and possible early takedown by the humans," Irene ended.

"Well, it worked out somehow," Tonto said as he zipped up to the next branch.

Brendan followed him, "Not really somehow. We all had a hand in saving this tree and ultimately... Christmas. I still can't believe it!"

"Okay, enough of the sappy stuff, Brend... OH!" Steve exclaimed as he 'lifted right into some old sap sticking to the trunk. They all laughed hysterically.

Lily was the first to his aid. "Are you okay?" as she pulled him up.

"I am fine." Steve looked into her eyes, "Thank you, Lily."

Brendan spoke up, "You are telling me to cut out the sappy stuff!" Tonto and Brendan then began to reenact the whole thing. Tonto mimicked in a girly voice, "Oh, Lily, I am a big Fire Tailor! I have fallen into some sap! Help!"

Brendan rushed to Tonto's side, "I'll save you! Are you okay?" He couldn't hold it much longer. They all burst out laughing again except for Steve, who just grinned and nodded.

"All right, you six goofs! Let's go!" Lt. Holly yelled from the fixed up Icicle. Janie flitted around checking and testing the Icicle, "Hurry it up, elves! Christmas morning awaits!"

Captain Brendan and his Tailors all stood on the branch, right below where the Icicle had crashed. They looked around at the gorgeous tree from the best view, their view, inside. No one felt the need to utter a word or even a sigh.

As a few more moments of dedicated silence passed, they rushed to their given assignments. Billy to a dusty ornament. Steve to fix a hydrant smashed from the sawed branch. Tonto to the tree stand to check water levels. Irene to a light in need of a fuse. Lastly, Lily and Captain Brendan to the top of the tree.

Captain Brendan arrived at the Star Command Center with a sense of accomplishment. He and his team saved Christmas. He smiled as he watched Jack's family gather around the tree to open gifts. The smell of pancakes filled the air. All was well, except, that the good captain knew that things would never be same.

W9-BRE-942

The WINDOW *at the* WHITE CAT

DOVER MYSTERY CLASSICS

The WINDOW *at the* WHITE CAT

Mary Roberts Rinehart

Dover Publications, Inc.
Mineola, New York

Bibliographical Note

This Dover edition, first published in 2017, is an unabridged republication of the work originally published in book form in 1910 by The Bobbs-Merrill Company, Indianapolis, Indiana. It first appeared in *Munsey's Magazine* in 1909 under the title *The Mystery of 1122.*

Library of Congress Cataloging-in-Publication Data

Names: Rinehart, Mary Roberts, 1876–1958 author.
Title: The window at the white cat / Mary Roberts Rinehart.
Description: Dover edition. | Mineola, N.Y. : Dover Publications, Inc., 2017.
| Series: Dover mystery classics
Identifiers: LCCN 2017011497 | ISBN 9780486819235 | ISBN 048681923X
Subjects: | GSAFD: Mystery fiction.
Classification: LCC PS3535.I73 W48 2017 | DDC 813/.54—dc23
LC record available at https://lccn.loc.gov/2017011497

Manufactured in the United States by LSC Communications
81923X02 2018
www.doverpublications.com

Contents

I. Sentiments and Clues. 1
II. Uneasy Apprehensions 10
III. Ninety-eight Pearls 16
IV. A Thief in the Night 24
V. Little Miss Jane 31
VI. A Fountain Pen 39
VII. Concerning Margery 46
VIII. Too Late 52
IX. Only One Eye Closed 58
X. Breaking the News 65
XI. A Night in the Fleming Home 76
XII. My Commission 84
XIII. Sizzling Metal 92
XIV. A Walk in the Park 100
XV. Find the Woman 106
XVI. Eleven Twenty-two Again 112
XVII. His Second Wife 116
XVIII. Edith's Cousin 122
XIX. Back to Bellwood 128
XX. Association of Ideas 136
XXI. A Proscenium Box 145
XXII. In the Room over the Way 151
XXIII. A Box of Crown Derby 155
XXIV. Wardrop's Story 161
XXV. Measure for Measure 166
XXVI. Lovers and a Letter 172

Chapter I

Sentiment and Clues

In my criminal work anything that wears skirts is a lady, until the law proves her otherwise. From the frayed and slovenly petticoats of the woman who owns a poultry stand in the market and who has grown wealthy by selling chickens at twelve ounces to the pound, or the silk sweep of Mamie Tracy, whose diamonds have been stolen down on the avenue, or the staidly respectable black and middle-aged skirt of the client whose husband has found an affinity partial to laces and frip-peries, and has run off with her—all the wearers are ladies, and as such announced by Hawes. In fact, he carries it to excess. He speaks of his wash lady, with a husband who is an ash merchant, and he announced one day in some excitement that the lady who had just gone out had appropriated all the loose change out of the pocket of his overcoat.

So when Hawes announced a lady, I took my feet off my desk, put down the brief I had been reading, and rose perfunctorily. With my first glance at my visitor, however, I threw away my cigar, and I have heard since, settled my tie. That this client was different was borne in on me at once by the way she entered the room. She had poise in spite of embarrassment, and her face when she raised her veil was white, refined, and young.

"I did not send in my name," she said when she saw me glancing down for the card Hawes usually puts on my table. "It was advice I wanted, and I—I did not think the name would matter."

She was more composed, I think, when she found me considerably older than herself. I saw her looking furtively at the graying places over my ears. I am only thirty-five, as far as that goes, but my family, although it keeps its hair, turns gray early—a business asset but a social handicap.

"Won't you sit down?" I asked, pushing out a chair so that she would face the light, while I remained in shadow. Every doctor and every lawyer knows that trick. "As far as the name goes, perhaps you had better tell me the trouble first. Then, if I think it indispensable, you can tell me."

She acquiesced to this and sat for a moment silent, her gaze absently on the windows of the building across. In the morning light my first impression was verified. Only too often the raising of a woman's veil in my office reveals the ravages of tears, or rouge, or dissipation. My new client turned fearlessly to the window an unlined face, with a clear skin, healthily pale. From where I sat, her profile was beautiful, in spite of its drooping suggestion of trouble; her first embarrassment gone, she had forgotten herself and was intent on her errand.

"I hardly know how to begin," she said, "but suppose"—slowly—"suppose that a man, a well-known man, should leave home without warning, not taking any clothes except those he wore, and saying he was coming home to dinner and he—he—"

She stopped as if her voice had failed her.

"And he does not come?" I prompted.

She nodded, fumbling for her handkerchief in her bag.

"How long has he been gone?" I asked. I had heard exactly the same thing before, but to leave a woman like that, hardly more than a girl, and lovely!

"Ten days."

"I should think it ought to be looked into," I said decisively, and got up. Somehow I couldn't sit quietly. A lawyer who is worth anything is always a partisan, I suppose, and I never hear of a man deserting his wife that I am not indignant, the virtuous scorn of the unmarried man, perhaps. "But you will have to tell me more than that. Did this gentleman have any bad habits? That is, did he—er—drink?"

"Not to excess. He had been forbidden anything of that sort by his physician. He played bridge for money; but I believe he was rather lucky." She colored uncomfortably.

"Married, I suppose?" I asked casually.

"He had been. His wife died when I—" She stopped and bit her lips. Then it was not her husband, after all! Oddly enough, the sun came out just at that moment, spilling a pool of sunlight at her feet, on the dusty rug with its tobacco-bitten scars.

"It is my father," she said simply. I was absurdly relieved.

But with the realization that I had not a case of desertion on my hands, I had to view the situation from a new angle.

"You are absolutely at a loss to account for his disappearance?"

"Absolutely."

"You have had no word from him?"

"None."

"He never went away before for any length of time without telling you?"

"No. Never. He was away a great deal, but I always knew where to find him." Her voice broke again and her chin quivered. I thought it wise to reassure her.

"Don't let us worry about this until we are sure it is serious," I said. "Sometimes the things that seem most mysterious have the simplest explanations. He may have written and the letter have miscarried or—even a slight accident would account—" I saw I was blundering; she grew white and wide-eyed. "But, of course, that's unlikely too. He would have papers to identify him."

"His pockets were always full of envelopes and things like that," she assented eagerly.

"Don't you think I ought to know his name?" I asked. "It need not be known outside of the office, and this is a sort of confessional anyhow, or worse. People tell things to their lawyer that they wouldn't think of telling the priest."

Her color was slowly coming back, and she smiled.

"My name is Fleming, Margery Fleming," she said after a second's hesitation, "and my father, Mr. Allan Fleming, is the man. Oh, Mr. Knox, what are we going to do? He has been gone for more than a week!"

No wonder she had wished to conceal the identity of the missing man. So Allan Fleming was lost! A good many highly respectable citizens would hope that he might never be found. Fleming, state treasurer, delightful companion, polished gentleman and successful politician of the criminal type. Outside in the corridor the office boy was singing under his breath. "Oh once there was a miller," he sang, "who lived in a mill." It brought back to my mind instantly the reform meeting at the city hall a year before, where for a few hours we had blown the feeble spark of protest against machine domination to a flame. We had sung a song to that very tune, and with this white-faced girl across from me, its words came back with revolting truth. It had been printed and circulated through the hall.

"Oh, once there was a capitol
That sat on a hill,
As it's too big to steal away
It's probably there still.
The ring's hand in the treasury
And Fleming with a sack.
They take it out in wagon loads
And never bring it back."

I put the song out of my mind with a shudder.

"I am more than sorry," I said. I was, too; whatever he may have been, he was *her* father. "And of course there are a number of reasons why this ought not to be known, for a time at least. After all, as I say, there may be a dozen simple explanations, and— There are exigencies in politics—"

"I hate politics!" she broke in suddenly. "The very name makes me ill. When I read of women wanting to—to vote and all that, I wonder if they know what it means to have to be polite to dreadful people, people who have even been convicts, and all that. Why, our last butler had been a prizefighter!" She sat upright with her hands on the arms of the chair. "That's another thing, too, Mr. Knox. The day after father went away, Carter left. And he has not come back."

"Carter was the butler?"

"Yes."

"A white man?"

"Oh, yes."

"And he left without giving you any warning?"

"Yes. He served luncheon the day after father went away, and the maids say he went away immediately after. He was not there that evening to serve dinner, but he came back late that night, and got into the house using his key to the servants' entrance. He slept there, the maids said, but he was gone before the servants were up and we have not seen him since."

I made a mental note of the butler.

"We'll go back to Carter again," I said. "Your father has not been ill, has he? I mean recently."

She considered.

"I cannot think of anything except that he had a tooth pulled." She was quick to resent my smile. "Oh, I know I'm not helping you," she exclaimed, "but I have thought over everything until I cannot think any more. I always end where I begin."

"You have not noticed any mental symptoms—any lack of memory?"

Her eyes filled.

"He forgot my birthday, two weeks ago," she said. "It was the first one he had ever forgotten, in nineteen of them."

Nineteen! Nineteen from thirty-five leaves sixteen!

"What I meant was this," I explained. "People sometimes have sudden and unaccountable lapses of memory and at those times they are apt to stray away from home. Has your father been worried lately?"

"He has not been himself at all. He has been irritable, even to me, and terrible to the servants. Only to Carter—he was never ugly to Carter. But I do not think it was a lapse of memory. When I remember how he looked that morning, I believe that he meant then to go away. It shows how he had changed, when he could think of going away without a word, and leaving me there alone."

"Then you have no brothers or sisters?"

"None. I came to you—" There she stopped.

"Please tell me how you happened to come to me," I urged. "I think you know that I am both honored and pleased."

"I didn't know where to go," she confessed, "so I took the telephone directory, the classified part under 'Attorneys,' and after I shut my eyes, I put my finger haphazardly on the page. It pointed to your name."

I am afraid I flushed at this, but it was a wholesome douche. In a moment I laughed.

"We will take it as an omen," I said, "and I will do all that I can. But I am not a detective, Miss Fleming. Don't you think we ought to have one?"

"Not the police!" she shuddered. "I thought you could do something without calling a detective."

"Suppose you tell me what happened the day your father left, and how he went away. Tell me the little things too. They may be straws that will point in a certain direction."

"In the first place," she began, "we live on Monmouth Avenue. There are just the two of us, and the servants: a cook, two housemaids, a laundress, a butler and a chauffeur. My father spends much of his time at the capital, and in the last two years, since my old governess went back to Germany, at those times I usually go to mother's sisters' at Bellwood—Miss Letitia and Miss Jane Maitland."

I nodded. I knew the Maitland ladies well. I had drawn four different wills for Miss Letitia in the last year.

"My father went way on the tenth of May. You say to tell you all about his going, but there is nothing to tell. We have a machine, but it was being repaired. Father got up from breakfast, picked up his hat and walked out of the house. He was irritated at a letter he had read at the table—"

"Could you find that letter?" I asked quickly.

"He took it with him. I knew he was disturbed, for he did not even say he was going. He took a car, and I thought he was on his way to his office. He did not come home that night and I went to the office the next morning. The stenographer said he had not been there. He is not at Plattsburg, because they have been trying to call him from there on the long-distance telephone every day."

In spite of her candid face, I was sure she was holding something back.

"Why don't you tell me everything?" I asked. "You may be keeping back the one essential point."

She flushed. Then she opened her pocketbook and gave me a slip of rough paper. On it, in careless figures, was the number "eleven twenty-two." That was all.

"I was afraid you would think it silly," she said. "It was such a meaningless thing. You see, the second night after father left, I was nervous and could not sleep. I expected him home at any time and I kept listening for his step downstairs. About three o'clock I was sure I heard someone in the room below mine—there was a creaking as if the person were walking carefully. I felt relieved, for I thought he had come back. But I did not hear the door into his bedroom close, and I got more and more wakeful. Finally I got up and slipped along the hall to his room. The door was open a few inches and I reached in and switched on the electric lights. I had a queer feeling before I turned on the light that there was someone standing close to me, but the room was empty, and the hall, too."

"And the paper?"

"When I saw the room was empty, I went in. The paper had been pinned to a pillow on the bed. At first I thought it had been dropped or had blown there. When I saw the pin, I was startled. I went back to my room and rang for Annie, the second housemaid, who is also a sort of personal maid of mine. It was half-past three o'clock when Annie came down. I took her into father's room and showed her the paper. She was sure it was not there when she folded back the bedclothes for the night at nine o'clock."

"Eleven twenty-two," I repeated. "Twice eleven is twenty-two. But that isn't very enlightening."

"No," she admitted. "I thought it might be a telephone number, and I called up all the eleven twenty-twos in the city."

In spite of myself, I laughed, and after a moment she smiled in sympathy.

"We are not brilliant, certainly," I said at last. "In the first place, Miss Fleming, if I thought the thing was very serious, I would not laugh—but no doubt a day or two will see everything straight. But, to go back to this eleven twenty-two—did you rouse the servants and have the house searched?"

"Yes. Annie said Carter had come back and she went to waken him, but although his door was locked inside, he did not answer. Annie and I switched on all the lights on the lower floor from the top of the stairs. Then we went down together and looked around. Every window and door was locked, but in father's study, on the first floor, two drawers of his desk were standing open. And in the library, the little compartment in my writing table, where I keep my house money, had been broken open and the money taken."

"Nothing else was gone?"

"Nothing. The silver on the sideboard in the dining room, plenty of valuable things in the cabinet in the drawing room—nothing was disturbed."

"It might have been Carter," I reflected. "Did he know where you kept your house money?"

"It is possible, but I hardly think so. Besides, if he was going to steal, there were so many more valuable things in the house. My mother's jewels as well as my own were in my dressing room, and the door was not locked."

"They were not disturbed?"

She hesitated.

"They had been disturbed," she admitted. "My grandmother left each of her children some unstrung pearls. They were a hobby with her. Aunt Jane and Aunt Letitia never had theirs strung, but my mother's were made into different things, all old-fashioned. I left them locked in a drawer in my sitting room, where I have always kept them. The following morning the drawer was unlocked and partly open, but nothing was missing."

"All your jewelry was there?"

"All but one ring, which I rarely remove from my finger." I followed her eyes. Under her glove was the outline of a ring, a solitaire stone.

"Nineteen from—" I shook myself together and got up.

"It does not sound like an ordinary burglary," I reflected. "But I am afraid I have no imagination. No doubt what you have told me would be meat and drink to a person with an analytical turn of mind. I can't deduct. Nineteen from thirty-five leaves sixteen, according to my mental process, although I know men who could make the difference nothing."

I believe she thought I was a little mad, for her face took on again its despairing look.

"We *must* find him, Mr. Knox," she insisted as she got up. "If you know of a detective that you can trust, please get him. But you can understand that the unexplained absence of the state treasurer must be kept secret. One thing I am sure of: He is being kept away. You don't know what enemies he has! Men like Mr. Schwartz, who have no scruples, no principle."

"Schwartz!" I repeated in surprise. Henry Schwartz was the boss of his party in the state; the man of whom one of his adversaries had said, with the distinct approval of the voting public, that he was so low on the scale of humanity that it would require a special dispensation of Heaven to raise him to the level of total degradation. But he and Fleming were generally supposed to be captain and first mate of the pirate craft that passed with us for the ship of state.

"Mr. Schwartz and my father are allies politically," the girl explained with heightened color, "but they are not friends. My father is a gentleman."

The inference I allowed to pass unnoticed, and as if she feared she had said too much, the girl rose. When she left, a few minutes later, it was with the promise that she would close the Monmouth Avenue house and go to her aunts' at Bellwood, at once. For myself, I pledged a thorough search for her father, and began it by watching the scarlet wing on her hat through the top of the elevator cage until it had descended out of sight.

I am afraid it was a queer hodgepodge of clues and sentiment that I poured out to Hunter, the detective, when he came up late that afternoon.

Hunter was quiet when I finished my story.

"They're rotten clear through," he reflected. "This administration is worse than the last, and *it* was a peach. There have been more suicides than I could count on my two hands, in the last ten years. I warn you—you'd be better out of this mess."

"What do you think about the eleven twenty-two?" I asked as he got up and buttoned his coat.

"Well, it might mean almost anything. It might be that many dollars, or the time a train starts, or it might be the eleventh and the twenty-second letters of the alphabet—k—v."

"K—v!" I repeated. "Why that would be the Latin *cave*—beware."

Hunter smiled cheerfully.

"You'd better stick to the law, Mr. Knox," he said from the door. "We don't use Latin in the detective business."

Chapter II

Uneasy Apprehensions

PLATTSBURG was not the name of the capital, but it will do for this story. The state doesn't matter either. You may take your choice, like the story Mark Twain wrote, with all kinds of weather at the beginning, so the reader could take his pick.

We will say that my home city is Manchester. I live with my married brother, his wife and two boys. Fred is older than I am, and he is an exceptional brother. On the day he came home from his wedding trip, I went down with my traps on a hansom, in accordance with a pre-arranged schedule. Fred and Edith met me inside the door.

"Here's your latchkey, Jack," Fred said as he shook hands. "Only one stipulation—remember we are strangers in the vicinity and try to get home before the neighbors are up. We have our reputations to think of."

"There is no hour for breakfast," Edith said as she kissed me. "You have a bath of your own, and don't smoke in the drawing room."

Fred was always a lucky devil.

I had been there now for six years. I had helped to raise two young Knoxes—bully youngsters, too: the oldest one could use boxing gloves when he was four—and the finest collie pup in our end of the state. I wanted to raise other things—the boys liked pets—but Edith was like all women: she didn't care for animals.

I had a rabbit-hutch built and stocked in the laundry, and a dove-cote on the roof. I used the general bath and gave up my tub to a younger alligator I got in Florida, and every Sunday the youngsters and I had a great time trying to teach it to do tricks. I have always taken it a little hard that Edith took advantage of my getting the measles from Billy, to clear out every animal in the house. She broke the news to me gently, the day the rash began to fade, maintaining that, having lost one cook through the alligator escaping from his tub and being mistaken, in the gloom of the back stairs, for a rubber boot, and picked up under the same misapprehension, she could not risk another cook.

On the day that Margery Fleming came to me about her father, I went home in a state of mixed emotion. Dinner was not a quiet meal: Fred and I talked politics, generally, and as Fred was on one side and I on the other, there was always an argument on.

"What about Fleming?" I asked at last, when Fred had declared that in these days of corruption, no matter what the government was, he was "forninst" it. "Hasn't he been frightened into reform?"

"Bad egg," he said, jabbing his potato as if it had been a politician, "and there's no way to improve a bad egg except to hold your nose. That's what the public is doing; holding its nose."

"Hasn't he a daughter?" I asked casually.

"Yes—a lovely girl, too," Edith assented. "It is his only redeeming quality."

"Fleming is a rascal, daughter or no daughter," Fred persisted. "Ever since he and his gang got poor Butler into trouble and then left him to kill himself as the only way out, I have felt that there was something coming to all of them—Hansen, Schwartz and the rest. I saw Fleming on the street today."

"What!" I exclaimed, almost jumping out of my chair.

Fred surveyed me quizzically over his coffee cup.

" 'Hasn't he a daughter!' " he quoted. "Yes, I saw him, Jack, this very day, in an unromantic four-wheeler, and he was swearing at a policeman."

"Where was it?"

"Chestnut and Union. His cab had been struck by a car, and badly damaged, but the gentleman refused to get out. No doubt you could get the details from the cornerman."

"Look here, Fred," I said earnestly. "Keep that to yourself, will you? And you too, Edith? It's a queer story, and I'll tell you sometime."

As we left the dining room, Edith put her hand on my shoulder.

"Don't get mixed up with those people, Jack," she advised. "Margery's a dear girl, but her father practically killed Henry Butler, and Henry Butler married my cousin."

"You needn't make it a family affair," I protested. "I have only seen the girl once."

But Edith smiled. "I know what I know," she said. "How extravagant of you to send Bobby that enormous hobbyhorse!"

"The boy has to learn to ride sometime. In four years he can have a pony, and I'm going to see that he has it. He'll be eight by that time."

Edith laughed.

"In four years!" she said. "Why, in four years you'll—" Then she stopped.

"I'll what?" I demanded, blocking the door to the library.

"You'll be forty, Jack, and it's a mighty unattractive man who gets past forty without being sought and won by some woman. You'll be buying—"

"I will be thirty-nine," I said with dignity, "and as far as being sought and won goes, I am so overwhelmed by Fred's misery that I don't intend to marry at all. If I do—*if I do*—it will be to some girl who turns and runs the other way every time she sees me."

"The oldest trick in the box," Edith scoffed. "What's that thing Fred's always quoting: 'A woman is like a shadow; follow her, she flies; fly from her, she follows.' "

"Upon my word!" I said indignantly. "And you are a woman!"

"I'm different," she retorted. "I'm only a wife and mother."

In the library Fred got up from his desk and gathered up his papers. "I can't think with you two whispering there," he said. "I'm going to the den."

As he slammed the door into his workroom, Edith picked up her skirts and scuttled after him.

"How dare you run away like that?" she called. "You promised me—" The door closed behind her.

I went over and spoke through the panels.

" 'Follow her, she flies; fly from her, she follows'—oh, wife and mother!" I called.

"For Heaven's sake, Edith," Fred's voice rose irritably. "If you and Jack are going to talk all evening, go and sit on *his* knee and let me alone. The way you two flirt under my nose is a scandal. Do you hear that, Jack?"

"Good night, Edith," I called. "I have left you a kiss on the upper left-hand panel of the door. And I want to ask you one more question: what if I fly from the woman and she doesn't follow?"

"Thank your lucky stars," Fred called in a muffled voice, and I left them to themselves.

I had some work to do at the office, work that the interview with Hunter had interrupted, and half past eight that night found me at my desk. But my mind strayed from the papers before me. After a useless effort to concentrate, I gave it up as useless, and by ten o'clock I was on the street again, my evening wasted, the papers in the libel case of the *Star* against the *Eagle* untouched on my desk, and I the victim of an uneasy apprehension that took me, almost without volition, to the neighborhood of the Fleming house on Monmouth Avenue. For it had occurred to me that Miss Fleming might not have left the house that day as she had promised, might still be there, liable to another intrusion by the mysterious individual who had a key to the house.

It was a relief, consequently, when I reached its corner, to find no lights in the building. The girl had kept her word. Assured of that, I looked at the house curiously. It was one of the largest in the city, not wide, but running far back along the side street; a small yard with a low iron fence and a garage completed the property. The streetlights left the back of the house in shadow, and as I stopped in the shelter of the garage, I was positive that I heard someone working with a rear window of the empty house. A moment later the sounds ceased and muffled footsteps came down the cement walk. The intruder made no attempt to open the iron gate; against the light I saw him put a leg over the low fence, follow it up with the other, and start up the street, still with peculiar noiselessness of stride. He was a short, heavy-shouldered fellow in a cap, and his silhouette showed a prodigious length of arm.

I followed, I don't mind saying in some excitement. I had a vision of grabbing him from behind and leading him—or pushing him, under the circumstances—in triumph to the police station, and another mental picture, not so pleasant, of being found on the pavement by some passerby, with a small punctuation mark ending my sentence of life. But I was not apprehensive. I even remember wondering humorously if I should overtake him and press the cold end of my silver-mounted fountain pen into the nape of his neck, if he would throw up his hands and surrender. I had read somewhere of a burglar held up in a similar way with a shoehorn.

Our pace was easy. Once, the man just ahead stopped and lighted a cigarette, and the odor of a very fair Turkish tobacco came back to me. He glanced back over his shoulder at me and went on without quickening his pace. We met no policemen, and after perhaps five minutes walking, when the strain was growing tense, my gentleman of the rubber-soled shoes swung abruptly to the left and—entered the police station!

I had occasion to see Davidson many times after that, during the strange development of the Fleming case; I had the peculiar experience later of having him follow me as I had trailed him that night, and I had occasion once to test the strength of his long arms when he helped to thrust me through the transom at the White Cat, but I never met him without a recurrence of the sheepish feeling with which I watched him swagger up to the night sergeant and fall into easy conversation with the man behind the desk. Standing in the glare from the open window, I had much the lost pride and self-contempt of a wet cat sitting in the sun.

Two or three roundsmen were sitting against the wall, lazily, helmets off and coats open against the warmth of the early spring night. In a back room others were playing checkers and disputing noisily. Davidson's voice came distinctly through the open windows.

"The house is closed," he reported. "But one of the basement windows isn't shuttered and the lock is bad. I couldn't find Shields. He'd better keep an eye on it." He stopped and fished in his pockets with a grin. "This was tied to the knob of the kitchen door," he said, raising his voice for the benefit of the room, and holding aloft a piece of paper. "For Shields!" he explained, "and signed 'Delia.' "

The men gathered around him. Even the sergeant got up and leaned forward, his elbows on his desk.

"Read it," he said lazily. "Shields has got a wife, and her name ain't Delia."

"Dear Tom," Davidson read in a mincing falsetto. "We are closing up unexpected, so I won't be here tonight. I am going to Mamie Brennan's and if you want to talk to me you can get me by calling up Anderson's drugstore. The clerk is a gentleman friend of mine. Mr. Carter, the butler, told me before he left he would get me a place as parlor maid, so I'll have another situation soon. Delia."

The sergeant scowled. "I'm goin' to talk to Tom," he said, reaching out for the note. "He's got a nice family, and things like that're bad for the force."

I lighted the cigar, which had been my excuse for loitering on the pavement, and went on. It sounded involved for a novice, but if I could find Anderson's drugstore, I could find Mamie Brennan; through Mamie Brennan I would get Delia; and through Delia I might find Carter. I was vague from that point, but what Miss Fleming had said of Carter had made me suspicious of him. Under an arc light I made the first note in my new business of manhunter and it was something like this:

> Anderson's drugstore.
> Ask for Mamie Brennan.
> Find Delia.
> Advise Delia that a policeman with a family is a bad bet.
> Locate Carter.

It was late when I reached the corner of Chestnut and Union Streets, where Fred had said Allan Fleming had come to grief in a cab. But the cornerman had gone, and the night man on the beat knew nothing, of course, of any particular collision.

"There's plinty of 'em every day at this corner," he said cheerfully. "The department sends a wagon here every night to gather up the pieces, automobiles mainly. That trolley pole over there has been sliced off clean three times in the last month. They say a fellow ain't a graduate of the automobile school till he can go around it on the sidewalk without hittin' it!"

I left him looking reminiscently at the pole, and went home to bed. I had made no headway, I had lost conceit with myself and a day and evening at the office, and I had gained the certainty that Margery Fleming was safe in Bellwood and the uncertain address of a servant who *might* know something about Mr. Fleming.

I was still awake at one o'clock and I got up impatiently and consulted the telephone directory. There were twelve Andersons in the city who conducted drugstores.

When I finally went to sleep, I dreamed that I was driving Margery Fleming along a street in a broken taxicab, and that all the buildings were pharmacies and numbered eleven twenty-two.

Chapter III

Ninety-eight Pearls

AFTER such a night I slept late. Edith still kept her honeymoon promise of no breakfast hour and she had gone out with Fred when I came downstairs.

I have a great admiration for Edith, for her tolerance with my uncertain hours, for her cheery breakfast room, and the smiling good nature of the servants she engages. I have a theory that, show me a sullen servant and I will show you a sullen mistress, although Edith herself disclaims all responsibility and lays credit for the smile with which Katie brings in my eggs and coffee to largess on my part. Be that as it may, Katie is a smiling and personable young woman, and I am convinced that had she picked up the alligator on the back stairs and lost part of the end of her thumb, she would have told Edith that she cut it off with the bread knife, and thus have saved to us Bessie the Beloved and her fascinating trick of taking the end of her tail in her mouth and spinning.

On that particular morning, Katie also brought me a letter, and I recognized the cramped and rather uncertain writing of Miss Jane Maitland.

> DEAR MR. KNOX:
>
> Sister Letitia wishes me to ask you if you can dine with us tonight, informally. She has changed her mind in regard to the Colored Orphans' Home, and would like to consult you about it.
>
> Very truly yours,
> Susan Jane Maitland

It was a very commonplace note: I had had one like it after every board meeting of the orphans' home, Miss Maitland being on principle an aggressive minority. Also, having considerable mind, changing it became almost as ponderous an operation as moving a barn, although not nearly so stable.

(Fred accuses me here of a very bad pun, and reminds me, quite undeservedly, that the pun is the lowest form of humor.)

I came across Miss Jane's letter the other day, when I was gathering the material for this narrative, and I sat for a time with it in my hand, thinking over again the chain of events in which it had been the first link, a series of strange happenings that began with my acceptance of the invitation, and that led through ways as dark and tricks as vain as Bret Harte's Heathen Chinese ever dreamed of, to the final scene at the White Cat. With the letter I had filed away a half dozen articles and I arranged them all on the desk in front of me: the letter, the bit of paper with eleven twenty-two on it, that Margery gave me the first time I saw her; a notebook filled with jerky characters that looked like Arabic and were newspaper shorthand; a railroad schedule; a bullet, the latter slightly flattened; a cube-shaped piece of chalk which I put back in its box, labeled poison, with a shudder, and a small gold buckle from a slipper, which I—at which I did not shudder.

I did not need to make the climaxes of my story. They lay before me.

I walked to the office that morning, and on the way I found and interviewed the cornerman at Chestnut and Union. But he was of small assistance. He remembered the incident, but the gentleman in the taxicab had not been hurt and refused to give his name, saying he was merely passing through the city from one railroad station to another, and did not wish any notoriety.

At eleven o'clock Hunter called; he said he was going after the affair himself, but that it was hard to stick a dip net into the political puddle without pulling out a lot more than you went after, or than it was healthy to get. He was inclined to be facetious, and wanted to know if I had come across any more k. v's. Whereupon I put away the notes I had made about Delia and Mamie Brennan and I heard him chuckle as I rang off.

I went to Bellwood that evening. It was a suburban town a dozen miles from the city, with a picturesque station, surrounded by lawns and cement walks. Streetcars had so far failed to spoil its tree-bordered streets, and it was exclusive to the point of stagnation. The Maitland place was at the head of the main street, which had at one time been its drive. Miss Letitia, who was seventy, had had sufficient commercial instinct, some years before, to cut her ancestral acres—*their* ancestral acres, although Miss Jane hardly counted—into building lots, except perhaps an acre which surrounded the house. Thus, the Maitland ladies were reputed to be extremely wealthy. And as they never spent any money, no doubt they were.

The homestead as I knew it was one of impeccable housekeeping and unmitigated gloom. There was a chill that rushed from the old-fashioned center hall to greet the newcomer on the porch, and that seemed to freeze up whatever in him was spontaneous and cheerful.

I had taken dinner at Bellwood before, and the memory was not hilarious. Miss Letitia was deaf, but chose to ignore the fact. With superb indifference she would break into the conversation with some wholly alien remark that necessitated a reassembling of one's ideas, making the meal a series of mental gymnastics. Miss Jane, through long practice, and because she only skimmed the surface of conversation, took her cerebral flights easily, but I am more unwieldy of mind.

Nor was Miss Letitia's dominance wholly conversational. Her sister Jane was her creature, alternately snubbed and bullied. To Miss Letitia, Jane, in spite of her sixty-five years, was still a child, and sometimes a bad one. Indeed many a child of ten is more sophisticated. Miss Letitia gave her expurgated books to read, and forbade her to read divorce court proceedings in the newspapers. Once a recreant housemaid presenting the establishment with a healthy male infant, Jane was sent to the country for a month and was only brought back when the house had been fumigated throughout.

Poor Miss Jane! She met me with fluttering cordiality in the hall that night, safe in being herself for once, with the knowledge that Miss Letitia always received me from a thronelike horsehair sofa in the back parlor. She wore a new lace cap, and was twitteringly excited.

"Our niece is here," she explained as I took off my coat—everything was "ours" with Jane; "mine" with Letitia—"and we are having an ice at dinner. Please say that ices are not injurious, Mr. Knox. My sister is so opposed to them and I had to beg for this."

"On the contrary, the doctors have ordered ices for my young nephews," I said gravely, "and I dote on them myself."

Miss Jane beamed. Indeed, there was something almost unnaturally gay about the little old lady all that evening. Perhaps it was the new lace cap. Later, I tried to analyze her manner, to recall exactly what she had said, to remember anything that could possibly help. But I could find no clue to what followed.

Miss Letitia received me as usual, in the back parlor. Miss Fleming was there also, sewing by a window, and in her straight white dress with her hair drawn back and braided around her head, she looked even younger than before. There was no time for conversation. Miss Letitia launched at once into the extravagance of both molasses and butter on the colored orphans' bread and after a glance at me, and a quick comprehension from my face that I had no news for her, the girl at the window bent over her sewing again.

"Molasses breeds worms," Miss Letitia said decisively. "So does pork. And yet those children think Heaven means ham and molasses three times a day."

"You have had no news at all?" Miss Fleming said cautiously, her head bent over her work.

"None," I returned, under cover of the table linen to which Miss Letitia's mind had veered. "I have a good man working on it." As she glanced at me questioningly, "It needed a detective, Miss Fleming." Evidently another day without news had lessened her distrust of the police, for she nodded acquiescence and went on with her sewing. Miss Letitia's monotonous monologue went on, and I gave it such attention as I might. For the lamps had been lighted, and with every movement of the girl across, I could see the gleaming of a diamond on her engagement finger.

"If I didn't watch her, Jane would ruin them," said Miss Letitia. "She gives 'em apples when they keep their faces clean, and the bills for soap have gone up double. Soap once a day's enough for a colored child. Do you smell anything burning, Knox?"

I sniffed and lied, whereupon Miss Letitia swept her black silk, her colored orphans and her majestic presence out of the room. As the door closed, Miss Fleming put down her sewing and rose. For the first time I saw how weary she looked.

"I do not dare to tell them, Mr. Knox," she said. "They are old, and they hate him anyhow. I couldn't sleep last night. Suppose he should have gone back, and found the house closed!"

"He would telephone here at once, wouldn't he?" I suggested.

"I suppose so, yes." She took up her sewing from the chair with a sigh. "But I'm afraid he won't come—not soon. I have hemmed tea towels for Aunt Letitia today until I am frantic, and all day I have been wondering over something you said yesterday. You said, you remember, that you were not a detective, that some men could take nineteen from thirty-five and leave nothing. What did you mean?"

I was speechless for a moment.

"The fact is—I—you see," I blundered, "it was a—merely a figure of speech, a—speech of figures is more accurate—" And then dinner was announced and I was saved. But although she said little or nothing during the meal, I caught her looking across at me once or twice in a bewildered, puzzled fashion. I could fairly see her revolving my detestable figures in her mind.

Miss Letitia presided over the table in garrulous majesty. The two old ladies picked at their food, and Miss Jane had a spot of pink in each withered cheek. Margery Fleming made a brave pretense, but left her plate almost untouched. As for me, I ate a substantial masculine meal and half apologized for my appetite, but Letitia did not hear. She tore the board of managers to shreds with the roast, and denounced them with the salad. But Jane was all anxious hospitality.

"Please *do* eat your dinner," she whispered. "I made the salad myself. And I know what it takes to keep a big man going. Harry eats more than Letitia and I together. Doesn't he, Margery?"

"Harry?" I asked.

"Mrs. Stevens is an unmitigated fool. I said if they elected her president, I'd not leave a penny to the home. That's why I sent for you, Knox." And to the maid, "Tell Heppie to wash those cups in lukewarm water. They're the best ones. And not to drink her coffee out of them. She let her teeth slip and bit a piece out of one the last time."

Miss Jane leaned forward to me after a smiling glance at her niece across.

"Harry Wardrop, a cousin's son, and—" she patted Margery's hand with its ring—"soon to be something closer."

The girl's face colored, but she returned Miss Jane's gentle pressure.

"They put up an iron fence," Miss Letitia reverted somberly to her grievance, "when a wooden one would have done. It was extravagance, ruinous extravagance."

"Harry stays with us when he is in Manchester," Miss Jane went on, nodding brightly across at Letitia as if she, too, were damning the executive board. "Lately, he has been almost all the time in Plattsburg. He is secretary to Margery's father. It is a position of considerable responsibility, and we are very proud of him."

I had expected something of the sort, but the remainder of the meal had somehow lost its savor. There was a lull in the conversation while dessert was being brought in. Miss Jane sat quivering, watching her sister's face for signs of trouble; the latter had subsided into muttered grumbling, and Miss Fleming sat, one hand on the table, staring absently at her engagement ring.

"You look like a fool in that cap, Jane," volunteered Letitia, while the plates were being brought in. "What's for dessert?"

"Ice cream," called Miss Jane, over the table.

"Well, you needn't," snapped Letitia. "I can hear you well enough. You told me it was junket."

"I said ice cream, and you said it would be all right," poor Jane shrieked. "If you drink a cup of hot water after it, it won't hurt you."

"Fiddle," Letitia snapped unpleasantly. "I'm not going to freeze my stomach and then thaw it out like a drain pipe. Tell Heppie to put my ice cream on the stove."

So we waited until Miss Letitia's had been heated, and was brought in, sicklied over with pale hues, not of thought, but of confectioners' dyes. Miss Letitia ate it resignedly. "Like as not I'll break out, I did the last time," she said gloomily. "I only hope I don't break out in colors."

The meal was over finally, but if I had hoped for another word alone with Margery Fleming that evening, I was foredoomed to disappointment. Letitia sent the girl, not ungently, to bed, and ordered Jane out of the room with a single curt gesture toward the door.

"You'd better wash those cups yourself, Jane," she said. "I don't see any sense anyhow in getting out the best china unless there's real company. Besides, I'm going to talk business."

Poor, meek, spiritless Miss Jane! The situation was absurd in spite of its pathos. She confided to me once that never in her sixty-five years of life had she bought herself a gown, or chosen the dinner. She was snubbed with painstaking perseverance, and sent out of the room when subjects requiring frank handling were under discussion. She was as unsophisticated as a child of ten, as unworldly as a baby, as—well, poor Miss Jane, again.

When the door had closed behind her, Miss Letitia listened for a moment, got up suddenly, and, crossing the room with amazing swiftness for her years, pounced on the knob and threw it open again. But the passage was empty; Miss Jane's slim little figure was disappearing into the kitchen. The older sister watched her out of sight, and then returned to her sofa without deigning explanation.

"I didn't want to see you about the will, Mr. Knox," she began without prelude. "The will can wait. I ain't going to die just yet—not if I know anything. But although I think you'd look a heap better and more responsible if you wore some hair on your face, still in most things I think you're a man of sense. And you're not too young. That's why I didn't send for Harry Wardrop; he's too young."

I winced at that. Miss Letitia leaned forward and put her bony hand on my knee.

"I've been robbed," she announced in a half whisper, and straightened to watch the effect of her words.

"Indeed!" I said, properly thunderstruck. I *was* surprised. I had always believed that only the use of the fourth dimension in space would enable anyone, not desired, to gain access to the Maitland house. "Of money?"

"Not money, although I had a good bit in the house." This also I knew. It was said of Miss Letitia that when money came into her possession, it went out of circulation.

"Not—the pearls?" I asked.

She answered my question with another.

"When you had those pearls appraised for me at the jewelers last year, how many were there?"

"Not quite one hundred. I think—yes, ninety-eight."

"Exactly," she corroborated in triumph. "They belonged to my mother. Margery's mother got some of them. That's a good many years ago, young man. They are worth more than they were then—a great deal more."

"Twenty-two thousand dollars," I repeated. "You remember, Miss Letitia, that I protested vigorously at the time against your keeping them in the house."

Miss Letitia ignored this, but before she went on, she repeated again her catlike pouncing at the door, only to find the hall empty as before. This time when she sat down it was knee to knee with me.

"Yesterday morning," she said gravely, "I got down the box; they have always been kept in the small safe at the top of my closet. When Jane found a picture of my niece, Margery Fleming, in Harry's room, I thought it likely there was some truth in the gossip Jane heard about the two, and—if there was going to be a wedding—why, the pearls were to go to Margery anyhow. But I found the door of the safe unlocked and a little bit open—and ten of the pearls were gone!"

"Gone!" I echoed. "Ten of them! Why, it's ridiculous! If ten, why not the whole ninety-eight?"

"How do I know?" she replied with asperity. "That's what I keep a lawyer for. That's why I sent for you."

For the second time in two days I protested the same thing.

"But you need a detective," I cried. "If you can find the thief, I will be glad to send him where he ought to be, but I couldn't find him."

"I will not have the police," she persisted inflexibly. "They will come around asking impertinent questions, and telling the newspapers that a foolish old woman had got what she deserved."

"Then you are going to send them to a bank?"

"You have less sense than I thought," she snapped. "I am going to leave them where they are, and watch. Whoever took the ten will be back for more, mark my words."

"I don't advise it," I said decidedly. "You have most of them now, and you might easily lose them all; not only that, but it is not safe for you or your sister."

"Stuff and nonsense!" the old lady said, with spirit. "As for Jane, she doesn't even know they are gone. I know who did it. It was the new housemaid, Bella MacKenzie. Nobody else could get in. I lock up the house myself at night, and I'm in the habit of doing a pretty thorough job of it. They went in the last three weeks, for I counted them Saturday three weeks ago myself. The only persons in the house in that time, except ourselves, were Harry, Bella and Hepsibah, who's been here for forty years and wouldn't know a pearl from a pickled onion."

"Then—what do you want me to do?" I asked. "Have Bella arrested and her trunk searched?"

I felt myself shrinking in the old lady's esteem every minute.

"Her trunk!" she said scornfully. "I turned it inside out this morning, pretending I thought she was stealing the laundry soap. Like as not she has them buried in the vegetable garden. What I want you to do is stay here for three or four nights, to be on hand. When I catch the thief, I want my lawyer right by."

It ended by my consenting, of course. Miss Letitia was seldom refused. I telephoned to Fred that I would not be home, listened for voices and decided Margery Fleming had gone to bed. Miss Jane lighted me to the door of the guest room, and saw that everything was comfortable. Her thin gray curls bobbed as she examined the water pitcher, saw to the towels, and felt the bed linen for dampness. At the door she stopped and turned around timidly.

"Has—has anything happened to disturb my sister?" she asked. "She has been almost irritable all day."

Almost!

"She is worried about her colored orphans," I evaded. "She does not approve of fireworks for them on the fourth of July."

Miss Jane was satisfied. I watched her little, old, black-robed figure go lightly down the hall. Then I bolted the door, opened all the windows, and proceeded to a surreptitious smoke.

Chapter IV

A Thief in the Night

THE windows being wide open, it was not long before a great moth came whirring in. He hurled himself at the light and then, dazzled and singed, began to beat with noisy thumps against the barrier of the ceiling. Finding no egress there, he was back at the lamp again, whirling in dizzy circles until at last, worn out, he dropped to the table, where he lay on his back, kicking impotently.

The room began to fill with tiny winged creatures that flung themselves headlong to destruction, so I put out the light and sat down near the window, with my cigar and my thoughts.

Miss Letitia's troubles I dismissed shortly. While it was odd that only ten pearls should have been taken, still—in every other way it bore the marks of an ordinary theft. The thief might have thought that by leaving the majority of the gems he could postpone discovery indefinitely. But the Fleming case was of a different order. Taken by itself, Fleming's disappearance could have been easily accounted for. There must be times in the lives of all unscrupulous individuals when they feel the need of retiring temporarily from the public eye. But the intrusion into the Fleming home, the ransacked desk and the broken money drawer—most of all, the bit of paper with eleven twenty-two on it—here was a hurdle my legal mind refused to take.

I had finished my second cigar, and was growing more and more wakeful, when I heard a footstep on the path around the house. It was black outside; when I looked out, as I did cautiously, I could not see even the gray-white of the cement walk. The steps had ceased, but there was a sound of fumbling at one of the shutters below. The catch clicked twice, as if some thin instrument was being slipped underneath to raise it, and once I caught a muttered exclamation.

I drew in my head and, puffing my cigar until it was glowing, managed by its light to see that it was a quarter to two. When I listened again, the housebreaker had moved to another window, and was shaking it cautiously.

With Miss Letitia's story of the pearls fresh in my mind, I felt at once that the thief, finding his ten a prize, had come back for more. My first impulse was to go to the head of my bed, where I am accustomed to keep a revolver. With the touch of the tall corner post, however, I remembered that I was not at home, and that it was not likely there was a weapon in the house.

Finally, after knocking over an ornament that shattered on the hearth and sounded like the crash of doom, I found on the mantel a heavy brass candlestick, and with it in my hand I stepped into the gloom of the hallway and felt my way to the stairs.

There were no night lights; the darkness was total. I found the stairs before I expected to, and came within an ace of pitching down, headlong. I had kicked off my shoes—a fact which I regretted later. Once down the stairs I was on more familiar territory. I went at once into the library, which was beneath my room, but the sounds at the window had ceased. I thought I heard steps on the walk, going toward the front of the house. I wheeled quickly and started for the door, when something struck me a terrific blow on the nose. I reeled back and sat down, dizzy and shocked. It was only when no second blow followed the first that I realized what had occurred.

With my two hands out before me in the blackness, I had groped, one hand on either side of the open door, which of course I had struck violently with my nose. Afterward I found it had bled considerably, and my collar and tie must have added to my ghastly appearance.

My candlestick had rolled under the table, and after crawling around on my hands and knees, I found it. I had lost, I suppose, three or four minutes, and I was raging at my awkwardness and stupidity. No one, however, seemed to have heard the noise. For all her boasted watchfulness, Miss Letitia must have been asleep. I got back into the hall and from there to the dining room. Someone was fumbling at the shutters there, and as I looked, they swung open. It was so dark outside, with the trees and the distance from the street, that only the creaking of the shutter told it had opened. I stood in the middle of the room, with one hand firmly clutching my candlestick.

But the window refused to move. The burglar seemed to have no proper tools; he got something under the sash, but it snapped, and through the heavy plate glass I could hear him swearing. Then he abruptly left the window and made for the front of the house.

I blundered in the same direction, my unshod feet striking on projecting furniture and causing me agonies, even through my excitement. When I reached the front door, however, I was amazed to find it unlocked, and standing open perhaps an inch. I stopped uncertainly. I was in a peculiar position; not even the most ardent admirers of antique brass candlesticks endorse them as weapons of offense or defense. But, there seeming to be nothing else to do, I opened the door quietly and stepped out into the darkness.

The next instant I was flung heavily to the porch floor. I am not a small man by any means, but under the fury of that onslaught I was a child. It was a porch chair, I think, that knocked me senseless; I know I folded up like a jackknife, and that was all I did know for a few minutes.

When I came to, I was lying where I had fallen, and a candle was burning beside me on the porch floor. It took me a minute to remember, and another minute to realize that I was looking into the barrel of a revolver. It occurred to me that I had never seen a more villainous face than that of the man who held it—which shows my state of mind—and that my position was the reverse of comfortable. Then the man behind the gun spoke.

"What did you do with that bag?" he demanded, and I felt his knee on my chest.

"What bag?" I inquired feebly. My head was jumping, and the candle was a volcanic eruption of sparks and smoke.

"Don't be a fool," the gentleman with the revolver persisted. "If I don't get that bag within five minutes, I'll fill you as full of holes as a cheese."

"I haven't seen any bag," I said stupidly. "What sort of bag?" I heard my own voice, drunk from the shock. "Paper bag, laundry bag—"

"You've hidden it in the house," he said, bringing the revolver a little closer with every word. My senses came back with a jerk and I struggled to free myself.

"Go in and look," I responded. "Let me up from here, and I'll take you in myself."

The man's face was a study in amazement and anger. "You'll take me in! You!" He got up without changing the menacing position of the gun. "You walk in there—here, carry the candle—and take me to that bag. Quick, do you hear?"

I was too bewildered to struggle. I got up dizzily, but when I tried to stoop for the candle, I almost fell on it. My head cleared after a moment, and when I had picked up the candle, I had a good chance to look at my assailant. He was staring at me, too. He was a young fellow, well dressed, and haggard beyond belief.

"I don't know anything about a bag," I persisted, "but if you will give me your word there was nothing in it belonging to this house, I will take you in and let you look for it."

The next moment he had lowered the revolver and clutched my arm.

"Who in the devil's name *are* you?" he asked wildly. I think the thing dawned on us both at the same moment.

"My name is Knox," I said coolly, feeling for my handkerchief—my head was bleeding from a cut over the ear—"John Knox."

"Knox!" Instead of showing relief, his manner showed greater consternation than ever. He snatched the candle from me and, holding it up, searched my face. "Then—good God—where is my traveling bag?"

"I have something in my head where you hit me," I said. "Perhaps that is it."

But my sarcasm was lost on him.

"I am Harry Wardrop," he said, "and I have been robbed, Mr. Knox. I was trying to get in the house without waking the family, and when I came back here to the front door, where I had left my valise, it was gone. I thought you were the thief when you came out, and—we've lost all this time. Somebody has followed me and robbed me!"

"What was in the bag?" I asked, stepping to the edge of the porch and looking around, with the help of the candle.

"Valuable papers," he said shortly. He seemed to be dazed and at a loss what to do next. We had both instinctively kept our voices low.

"You are certain you left it here?" I asked. The thing seemed incredible in the quiet and peace of that neighborhood.

"Where you are standing."

Once more I began a desultory search, going down the steps and looking among the cannas that bordered the porch. Something glistened beside the step, and stooping down I discovered a small brown leather traveling bag, apparently quite new.

"Here it is," I said, not so gracious as I might have been; I had suffered considerably for that traveling bag. The sight of it restored Wardrop's poise at once. His twitching features relaxed.

"By Jove, I'm glad to see it," he said. "I can't explain, but—tremendous things were depending on that bag, Mr. Knox. I don't know how to apologize to you; I must have nearly brained you."

"You did," I said grimly, and gave him the bag. The moment he took it I knew there was something wrong; he hurried into the house and lighted the library lamp. Then he opened the traveling bag with shaking fingers. It was empty!

He stood for a moment, staring incredulously into it. Then he hurled it down on the table and turned on me, as I stood beside him.

"It's a trick!" he said furiously. "You've hidden it somewhere. This is not my bag. You've substituted one just like it."

"Don't be a fool," I retorted. "How could I substitute an empty satchel for yours when up to fifteen minutes ago I had never seen you or your grip either? Use a little common sense. Someplace tonight you have put down that bag, and some clever thief has substituted a similar one. It's an old trick."

He dropped into a chair and buried his face in his hands.

"It's impossible," he said after a pause, while he seemed to be going over, minute by minute, the events of the night. "I was followed, as far as that goes, in Plattsburg. Two men watched me from the minute I got there, on Tuesday; I changed my hotel, and for all of yesterday—Wednesday, that is—I felt secure enough. But on my way to the train I felt that I was under surveillance again, and by turning quickly, I came face to face with one of the men."

"Would you know him?" I asked.

"Yes. I thought he was a detective; you know I've had a lot of that sort of thing lately, with election coming on. He didn't get on the train, however."

"But the other one may have done so."

"Yes, the other one may. The thing I don't understand is this, Mr. Knox. When we drew in at Bellwood Station, I distinctly remember opening the bag and putting my newspaper and railroad schedule inside. It was the right bag then; my clothing was in it, and my brushes."

I had been examining the empty bag as he talked.

"Where did you put your railroad schedule?" I asked.

"In the leather pocket at the side."

"It is here," I said, drawing out the yellow folder. For a moment my companion looked almost haunted. He pressed his hands to his head and began to pace the room like a crazy man.

"The whole thing is impossible. I tell you, that valise was heavy when I walked up from the station. I changed it from one hand to the other because of the weight. When I got here, I set it down on the edge of the porch and tried the door. When I found it locked—"

"But it wasn't locked," I broke in. "When I came downstairs to look for a burglar, I found it open at least an inch."

He stopped in his pacing up and down, and looked at me curiously.

"We're both crazy then," he asserted gravely. "I tell you, I tried every way I knew to unlock that door, and could hear the chain rattling.

Unlocked! You don't know the way this house is fastened up at night."

"Nevertheless, it was unlocked when I came down."

We were so engrossed that neither of us had heard steps on the stairs. The sound of a smothered exclamation from the doorway caused us both to turn suddenly. Standing there, in a loose gown of some sort, very much surprised and startled, was Margery Fleming. Wardrop pulled himself together at once. As for me, I knew what sort of figure I cut, my collar stained with blood, a lump on my forehead that felt as big as a doorknob, and no shoes.

"What is the matter?" she asked uncertainly. "I heard such queer noises, and I thought someone had broken into the house."

"Mr. Wardrop was trying to break in," I explained, "and I heard him and came down. On the way I had a bloody encounter with an open door, in which I came out the loser."

I don't think she quite believed me. She looked from my swollen head to the open bag, and then to Wardrop's pale face. Then I think, womanlike, she remembered the two great braids that hung over her shoulders and the dressing gown she wore, for she backed precipitately into the hall.

"I'm glad that's all it is," she called back cautiously, and we could hear her running up the stairs.

"You'd better go to bed," Wardrop said, picking up his hat. "I'm going down to the station. There's no train out of here between midnight and a flag train at four thirty a.m. It's not likely to be of any use, but I want to see who goes on that train."

"It is only half past two," I said, glancing at my watch. "We might look around outside first."

The necessity for action made him welcome any suggestion. Reticent as he was, his feverish excitement made me think that something vital hung on the recovery of the contents of that Russia leather bag. We found a lantern somewhere in the back of the house, and together we went over the grounds. It did not take long, and we found nothing.

As I look back on that night, the key to what had passed and to much that was coming was so simple, so direct—and yet we missed it entirely. Nor, when bigger things developed, and Hunter's trained senses were brought into play, did he do much better. It was some time before we learned the true inwardness of the events of that night.

At five o'clock in the morning Wardrop came back exhausted and nerveless. No one had taken the four thirty; the contents of the bag were gone, probably beyond recall. I put my dented candlestick back on the mantel, and prepared for a little sleep, blessing the deafness of old age which had enabled the Maitland ladies to sleep through it all. I tried to forget the queer events of the night, but the throbbing of my head kept me awake, and through it all one question obtruded itself—who had unlocked the front door and left it open?

Chapter V

Little Miss Jane

I WAS almost unrecognizable when I looked at myself in the mirror the next morning, preparatory to dressing for breakfast. My nose boasted a new arch, like the back of an angry cat, making my profile Roman and ferocious, and the lump on my forehead from the chair was swollen, glassy and purple. I turned my back to the mirror and dressed in wrathful irritation and my yesterday's linen.

Miss Fleming was in the breakfast room when I got down, standing at a window, her back to me. I have carried with me, during all the months since that time, a mental picture of her as she stood there, in a pink morning frock of some sort. But only the other day, having mentioned this to her, she assured me that the frock was blue, that she didn't have a pink garment at the time this story opens and that if she did, she positively didn't have it on. And having thus flouted my eye for color, she maintains that she did *not* have her back to me, for she distinctly saw my newly raised bridge as I came down the stairs. So I amend this. Miss Fleming in a blue frock was facing the door when I went into the breakfast room. Of one thing I am certain. She came forward and held out her hand.

"Good morning," she said. "What a terrible face!"

"It isn't mine," I replied meekly. "My own face is beneath these excrescences. I tried to cover the bump on my forehead with French chalk, but it only accentuated the thing, like snow on a mountaintop."

" 'The purple peaks of Darien,' " she quoted, pouring me my coffee. "Do you know, I feel so much better since you have taken hold of things. Aunt Letitia thinks you are wonderful."

I thought ruefully of the failure of my first attempt to play the sleuth, and I disclaimed any right to Miss Letitia's high opinion of me. From my dogging the watchman to the police station, to Delia and her note, was a short mental step.

"Before anyone comes down, Miss Fleming," I said, "I want to ask a question or two. What was the name of the maid who helped you search the house that night?"

"Annie."

"What other maids did you say there were?"

"Delia and Rose."

"Do you know anything about them? Where they came from, or where they went?"

She smiled a little.

"What does one know about new servants?" she responded. "They bring you references, but references are the price most women pay to get rid of their servants without a fuss. Rose was fat and old, but Delia was pretty. I thought she rather liked Carter."

Carter as well as Shields, the policeman. I put Miss Delia down as a flirt.

"And you have no idea where Carter went?"

"None."

Wardrop came in then, and we spoke of other things. The two elderly ladies it seemed had tea and toast in their rooms when they wakened, and the three of us breakfasted together. But conversation languished with Wardrop's appearance; he looked haggard and worn, avoided Miss Fleming's eyes, and after ordering eggs instead of his chop, looked at his watch and left without touching anything.

"I want to get the nine thirty, Margie," he said, coming back with his hat in his hand. "I may not be out to dinner. Tell Miss Letitia, will you?" He turned to go, but on second thought came back to me and held out his hand.

"I may not see you again," he began.

"Not if I see you first," I interrupted. He glanced at my mutilated features and smiled.

"I have made you a Maitland," he said. "I didn't think that anything but a prodigal Nature could duplicate Miss Letitia's nose! I'm honestly sorry, Mr. Knox, and if you do not want Miss Jane at that bump with a cold silver knife and some butter, you'd better duck before she comes down. Good-bye, Margie."

I think the girl was as much baffled as I was by the change in his manner when he spoke to her. His smile faded and he hardly met her eyes: I thought that his aloofness puzzled rather than hurt her. When the house door had closed behind him, she dropped her chin in her hand and looked across the table.

"You did not tell me the truth last night, Mr. Knox," she said. "I have never seen Harry look like that. Something has happened to him."

"He was robbed of his traveling bag," I explained, on Fred's theory that half a truth is better than a poor lie. "It's a humiliating experience, I believe. A man will throw away thousands, or gamble them away, with more equanimity than he'll see someone making off with his hair brushes or his clean collars."

"His traveling bag!" she repeated scornfully. "Mr. Knox, something has happened to my father, and you and Harry are hiding it from me."

"On my honor, it is nothing of the sort," I hastened to assure her. "I saw him for only a few minutes, just long enough for him to wreck my appearance."

"He did not speak of Father?"

"No."

She got up and, crossing the wooden mantel, put her arms upon it and leaned her head against them. "I wanted to ask him," she said drearily, "but I am afraid to. Suppose he doesn't know and I should tell him! He would go to Mr. Schwartz at once, and Mr. Schwartz is treacherous. The papers would get it, too."

Her eyes filled with tears, and I felt as awkward as a man always does when a woman begins to cry. If he knows her well enough, he can go over and pat her on the shoulder and assure her it is going to be all right. If he does not know her, and there are two maiden aunts likely to come in at any minute, he sits still, as I did, and waits until the storm clears.

Miss Margery was not long in emerging from her handkerchief.

"I didn't sleep much," she explained, dabbing at her eyes, "and I am nervous, anyhow. Mr. Knox, are you sure it was only Harry trying to get into the house last night?"

"Only Harry," I repeated. "If Mr. Wardrop's attempt to get into the house leaves me in this condition, what would a real burglar have done to me!"

She was too intent to be sympathetic over my disfigured face.

"There was someone moving about upstairs not long before I came down," she said slowly.

"You heard me; I almost fell down the stairs."

"Did you brush past my door, and strike the knob?" she demanded.

"No, I was not near any door."

"Very well." Triumphantly. "Someone did. Not only that, but they were in the storeroom on the floor above. I could hear one person and perhaps two, going from one side of the room to the other and back again."

"You heard a goblin quadrille. First couple forward and back," I said facetiously.

"I heard real footsteps—unmistakable ones. The maids sleep back on the second floor, and— Don't tell me it was rats. There are no rats in my aunt Letitia's house."

I was more impressed than I cared to show. I found I had a half hour before train time, and as we were neither of us eating anything, I suggested that we explore the upper floor of the house. I did it, I explained, not because I expected to find anything, but because I was sure we would not.

We crept past the two closed doors behind which the ladies Maitland were presumably taking out their crimps and taking in their tea. Then up a narrow, obtrusively clean stairway to the upper floor.

It was an old-fashioned, sloping-roofed attic, with narrow windows and a bare floor. At one end a door opened into a large room, and in there were the family trunks of four generations of Maitlands. One on another they were all piled there—little hair trunks, squab-topped trunks, huge Saratogas—of the period when the two maiden ladies were in their late teens—and there were handsome, modem trunks, too. For Miss Fleming's satisfaction I made an examination of the room, but it showed nothing. There was little or no dust to have been disturbed; the windows were closed and locked.

In the main attic were two stepladders, some curtains drying on frames and an old chest of drawers with glass knobs and the veneering broken in places. One of the drawers stood open, and inside could be seen a red and white patchwork quilt, and a grayish thing that looked like flannel and smelled to heaven of camphor. We gave up finally, and started down.

Partway down the attic stairs Margery stopped, her eyes fixed on the white-scrubbed rail. Following her gaze, I stopped, too, and I felt a sort of chill go over me. No spot or blemish, no dirty fingerprint marked the whiteness of that stair rail, except in one place. On it, clear and distinct, every line of the palm showing, was the reddish imprint of a hand!

Margery did not speak; she had turned very white and closed her eyes, but she was not faint. When the first revulsion had passed, I reached over and touched the stain. It was quite dry, of course, but it was still reddish brown; another hour or two would see it black. It was evidently fresh—Hunter said afterward it must have been about six hours old, and as things transpired, he was right. The stain showed a hand somewhat short and broad, with widened fingertips; marked in ink, it would not have struck me so forcibly, perhaps, but there, its ugly red against the white wood, it seemed to me to be the imprint of a brutal, murderous hand.

Margery was essentially feminine.

"What did I tell you?" she asked. "Someone was in this house last night; I heard them distinctly. There must have been two, and they quarreled—" She shuddered.

We went on downstairs into the quiet and peace of the dining room again. I got some hot coffee for Margery, for she looked shaken, and found I had missed my train.

"I am beginning to think I am being pursued by a malicious spirit," she said, trying to smile. "I came away from home because people got into the house at night and left queer signs of their visits, and now, here at Bellwood, where nothing *ever* happens, the moment I arrive things begin to occur. And—just as it was at home—the house was so well locked last night."

I did not tell her of the open hall door, just as I had kept from her the fact that only the contents of Harry Wardrop's bag had been taken.

That it had all been the work of one person, and that that person, having in some way access to the house, had also stolen the pearls, was now my confident belief.

I looked at Bella—the maid—as she moved around the dining room; her stolid face was not even intelligent, certainly not cunning. Heppie, the cook and the only other servant, was partly blind and her horizon was the diameter of her largest kettle. No—it had not been a servant, this mysterious intruder who passed the Maitland silver on the sideboard without an attempt to take it, and who floundered around an attic at night, in search of nothing more valuable than patchwork quilts and winter flannels. It is strange to look back and think how quietly we sat there; that we could see nothing but burglary—or an attempt at it—in what we had found.

It must have been after nine o'clock when Bella came running into the room. Ordinarily a slow and clumsy creature, she almost flew. She had a tray in her hand, and the dishes were rattling and threatening overthrow at every step. She brought up against a chair, and a cup went flying. The breaking of a cup must have been a serious offense in Miss Letitia Maitland's house, but Bella took no notice whatever of it.

"Miss Jane," she gasped, "Miss Jane, she's—she's—"

"Hurt!" Margery exclaimed, rising and clutching at the table for support.

"No. Gone—she's gone! She's been run off with!"

"Nonsense!" I said, seeing Margery's horrified face. "Don't come in here with such a story. If Miss Jane is not in her room, she is somewhere else, that's all."

Bella stooped and gathered up the broken cup, her lips moving. Margery had recovered herself. She made Bella straighten and explain.

"Do you mean—she is not in her room?" she asked incredulously. "Isn't she somewhere around the house?"

"Go up and look at the room," the girl replied, and, with Margery leading, we ran up the stairs.

Miss Jane's room was empty. From somewhere near Miss Letitia could be heard lecturing Hepsibah about putting too much butter on the toast. Her high voice, pitched for Heppie's old ears, rasped me. Margery closed the door, and we surveyed the room together.

The bed had been occupied; its coverings had been thrown back, as if its occupant had risen hurriedly. The room itself was in a state of confusion; a rocker lay on its side, and Miss Jane's clothing, folded as she had taken it off, had slid off on to the floor. Her shoes stood neatly at the foot of the bed, and a bottle of toilet vinegar had been upset, pouring a stream over the marble top of the dresser and down on to the floor. Over the high wooden mantel the Maitland who had been governor of the state years ago hung at a waggish angle, and a clock had been pushed aside and stopped at half-past one.

Margery stared around her in bewilderment. Of course, it was not until later in the day that I saw all the details. My first impression was of confusion and disorder: the room seemed to have been the scene of a struggle. The overturned furniture, the clothes on the floor, the picture, coupled with the print of the hand on the staircase and Miss Jane's disappearance, all seemed to point to one thing.

And as if to prove it conclusively, Margery picked up Miss Jane's new lace cap from the floor. It was crumpled and spotted with blood.

"She has been killed," Margery said in a choking voice. "Killed, and she had not an enemy in the world!"

"But where is she?" I asked stupidly.

Margery had more presence of mind than I had; I suppose it is because woman's courage is mental and man's physical, that in times of great strain women always make the better showing. While I was standing in the middle of the room, staring at the confusion around me, Margery was already on her knees, looking under the high, four-post bed. Finding nothing there she went to the closet. It was undisturbed. Pathetic rows of limp black dresses and on the shelves two black crepe bonnets were mute reminders of the little old lady. But there was nothing else in the room.

"Call Robert, the gardener," Margery said quickly, "and have him help you search the grounds and cellars. I will take Bella and go through the house. Above everything, keep it from Aunt Letitia as long as possible."

I locked the door into the disordered room, and with my head whirling, I went to look for Robert.

It takes a short time to search an acre of lawn and shrubbery. There was no trace of the missing woman anywhere outside the house, and from Bella, as she sat at the foot of the front stairs with her apron over her head, I learned in a monosyllable that nothing had been found in the house. Margery was with Miss Letitia, and from the excited conversation I knew she was telling her—not harrowing details, but that Miss Jane had disappeared during the night.

The old lady was inclined to scoff at first.

"Look in the fruit closet in the storeroom" I heard her say. "She's let the spring lock shut on her twice; she was black in the face the last time we found her."

"I did look; she's not there," Margery screamed at her.

"Then she's out looking for stump water to take that wart off her neck. She said yesterday she was going for some."

"But her clothes are all here," Margery persisted. "We think someone must have got in the house."

"If all her clothes are there, she's been sleepwalking," Miss Letitia said calmly. "We used to have to tie her by a cord around her ankle and fasten it to the bedpost. When she tried to get up, the cord would pull and wake her."

I think after a time, however, some of Margery's uneasiness communicated itself to the older woman. She finished dressing, and fumed when we told her we had locked Miss Jane's door and mislaid the key. Finally, Margery got her settled in the back parlor with some peppermints and her knitting; she had a feeling, she said, that Jane had gone after the stump water and lost her way, and I told Margery to keep her in that state of mind as long as she could.

I sent for Hunter that morning and he came at three o'clock. I took him through the back entrance to avoid Miss Letitia. I think he had been skeptical until I threw open the door and showed him the upset chair, the old lady's clothing, and the bloodstained lace cap. His examination was quick and thorough. He took a crumpled sheet of notepaper out of the wastebasket and looked at it; then he stuffed it in his pocket. He sniffed the toilet water, called Margery, and asked her if any clothing was missing, and on receiving a negative answer asked if any shawls or wraps were gone from the halls or other rooms. Margery reported nothing missing.

Before he left the room, Hunter went back and moved the picture which had been disturbed over the mantel. What he saw made him get a chair and, standing on it, take the picture from its nail. Thus exposed, the wall showed an opening about a foot square, and perhaps eighteen inches deep. A metal door, opening in, was unfastened and ajar, and just inside was a copy of a recent sentimental novel and a bottle of some sort of complexion cream. In spite of myself, I smiled; it was so typical of the dear old lady, with the heart of a girl and a skin that was losing its roses. But there was something else in the receptacle, something that made Margery Fleming draw in her breath sharply, and made Hunter raise his eyebrows a little and glance at me. The something was a scrap of unruled white paper, and on it the figures eleven twenty-two!

Chapter VI

A Fountain Pen

HARRY Wardrop came back from the city at four o'clock, while Hunter was in the midst of his investigation. I met him in the hall and told him what had happened, and with this new apprehension added to the shock of the night before, he looked as though his nerves were ready to snap.

Wardrop was a man of perhaps twenty-seven, as tall as I, although not so heavy, with direct blue eyes and fair hair; altogether a manly and prepossessing sort of fellow. I was not surprised that Margery Fleming had found him attractive—he had the blond hair and offhand manner that women seem to like. I am dark, myself.

He seemed surprised to find Hunter there, and not particularly pleased, but he followed us to the upper floor and watched silently while Hunter went over the two rooms. Beside the large chest of drawers in the main attic, Hunter found perhaps half a dozen drops of blood, and on the edge of the open drawer there were traces of more. In the inner room two trunks had been moved out nearly a foot, as he found by the faint dust that had been under them. With the stain on the stair rail, that was all he discovered, and it was little enough. Then he took out his notebook and there among the trunks we had a little seance of our own, in which Hunter asked questions, and whoever could do so answered them.

"Have you a pencil or pen, Mr. Knox?" he asked me, but I had none. Wardrop felt his pockets, with no better success.

"I have lost my fountain pen somewhere around the house today," he said irritably. "Here's a pencil—not much of one."

Hunter began his interrogations.

"How old was Miss Maitland—Miss Jane, I mean?"

"Sixty-five," from Margery.

"She had always seemed rational? Not eccentric, or childish?"

"Not at all; the sanest woman I ever knew." This from Wardrop.

"Has she ever, to your knowledge, received any threatening letters?"

"Never in all her life," from both of them promptly.

"You heard sounds, you say, Miss Fleming. At what time?"

"About half-past one or perhaps a few minutes later. The clock struck two while I was still awake and nervous."

"This person who was walking through the attics here—would you say it was a heavy person? A man, I mean?"

Margery stopped to think.

"Yes," she said finally. "It was very stealthy, but I think it was a man's step."

"You heard no sound of a struggle? No voices? No screams?"

"None at all," she said positively. And I added my quota.

"There could have been no such sounds," I said. "I sat in my room and smoked until a quarter to two. I heard nothing until then, when I heard Mr. Wardrop trying to get into the house. I went down to admit him, and—I found the front door open about an inch."

Hunter wheeled on Wardrop.

"A quarter to two?" he asked. "You were coming home from—the city?"

"Yes, from the station."

Hunter watched him closely.

"The last train gets in here at twelve thirty," he said slowly. "Does it always take you an hour and a quarter to walk the three squares to the house?"

Wardrop flushed uneasily, and I could see Margery's eyes dilate with amazement. As for me, I could only stare.

"I did not come directly home," he said, almost defiantly.

Hunter's voice was as smooth as silk.

"Then—will you be good enough to tell me where you did go?" he asked. "I have reasons for wanting to know."

"Damn your reasons—I beg your pardon, Margery. Look here, Mr. Hunter, do you think I would hurt a hair of that old lady's head? Do you think I came here last night and killed her, or whatever it is that has happened to her? And then went out and tried to get in again through the window?"

"Not necessarily," Hunter said, unruffled. "It merely occurred to me that we have at least an hour of your time last night, while this thing was going on, to account for. However, we can speak of that later. I am practically certain of one thing: Miss Maitland is not dead, or was not dead when she was taken away from this house."

"Taken away!" Margery repeated. "Then you think she was kidnapped?"

"Well, it is possible. It's a puzzling affair all through. You are certain there are no closets or unused rooms where, if there had been a murder, the body could be concealed."

"I never heard of any," Margery said, but I saw Wardrop's face change on the instant. He said nothing, however, but stood frowning at the floor, with his hands deep in his coat pockets.

Margery was beginning to show the effect of the long day's strain; she began to cry a little, and with an air of proprietorship that I resented, somehow Wardrop went over to her.

"You are going to lie down, Margery," he said, holding out his hand to help her up. "Mrs. Mellon will come over to Aunt Letitia, and you must get some sleep."

"Sleep!" she said with scorn, as he helped her to her feet. "Sleep, when things like this are occurring! Father first, and now dear old Aunt Jane! Harry, do you know where my father is?"

He faced her, as if he had known the question must come and was prepared for it.

"I know that he is all right, Margery. He has been—out of town. If it had not been for something unforeseen that—happened within the last few hours, he would have been home today."

She drew a long breath of relief.

"And Aunt Jane?" she asked Hunter, from the head of the attic stairs, "you do not think she is dead?"

"Not until we have found something more," he answered tactlessly. "It's like where there's smoke there's fire; where there's murder there's a body."

When they had both gone, Hunter sat down on a trunk and drew out a cigar that looked like a bomb.

"What do you think of it?" I asked, when he showed no disposition to talk.

"I'll be damned if I know," he responded, looking around for some place to expectorate and finding none.

"The window," I suggested, and he went over to it. When he came back, he had a rather peculiar expression. He sat down and puffed for a moment.

"In the first place," he began, "we can take it for granted that, unless she was crazy or sleepwalking, she didn't go out in her night-clothes, and there's nothing of hers missing. She wasn't taken in a carriage, providing she was taken at all. There's not a mark of wheels on that drive newer than a week, and besides, you say you heard nothing."

"Nothing," I said positively.

"Then, unless she went away in a balloon, where it wouldn't matter what she had on, she is still around the premises. It depends on how badly she was hurt."

"Are you sure it was she who was hurt?" I asked. "That print of a hand—that is not Miss Jane's."

In reply Hunter led the way down the stairs to the place where the stain on the stair rail stood out, ugly and distinct. He put his own heavy hand on the rail just below it.

"Suppose," he said, "suppose you grip something very hard. What happens to your hand?"

"It spreads," I acknowledged, seeing what he meant.

"Now, look at that stain. Look at the short fingers—why, it's a child's hand beside mine. The breadth is from pressure. It might be figured out this way. The fingers, you notice, point down the stairs. In some way, let us say, the burglar, for want of a better name, gets into the house. He used a ladder resting against that window by the chest of drawers.

"Ladder!" I exclaimed.

"Yes, there is a pruning ladder there. Now then—he comes down these stairs, and he has a definite object. He knows of something valuable in that cubbyhole over the mantel in Miss Jane's room. How does he get in? The door into the upper hall is closed and bolted, but the door into the bathroom is open. From there another door leads into the bedroom, and it has no bolt—only a key. That kind of a lock is only a three-minutes delay, or less. Now then, Miss Maitland was a light sleeper. When she wakened, she was too alarmed to scream; she tried to get to the door and was intercepted. Finally she got out the way the intruder got in, and ran along the hall. Every door was locked. In a frenzy she ran up the attic stairs and was captured up there. Which bears out Miss Margery's story of the footsteps back and forward."

"Good heavens, what an awful thing!" I gasped. "And I was sitting smoking just across the hall."

"He brings her down the stairs again, probably half dragging her. Once, she catches hold of the stair rail, and holds desperately to it, leaving the stain here."

"But why did he bring her down?" I asked, bewildered. "Why wouldn't he take what he was after and get away?"

Hunter smoked and meditated.

"She probably had to get the key of the iron door," he suggested. "It was hidden, and time was valuable. If there was a scapegrace member of the family, for instance, who knew where the old lady kept money, and who needed it badly, who knew all about the house, and who—"

"Fleming!" I exclaimed, aghast.

"Or even our young friend, Wardrop," Hunter said quietly. "He has an hour to account for. The trying to get in may have been a blind, and how do you know that what he says was stolen out of his satchel was not what he had just got from the iron box over the mantel in Miss Maitland's room?"

I was dizzy with trying to follow Hunter's facile imagination. The thing we were trying to do was to find the old lady, and, after all, here we were brought up against the same *impasse*.

"Then where is she now?" I asked. He meditated. He had sat down on the narrow stairs, and was rubbing his chin with a thoughtful forefinger. "One thirty, Miss Margery says, when she heard the noise. One forty-five when you heard Wardrop at the shutters. I tell you, Knox, it is one of two things: either that woman is dead somewhere in this house, or she ran out of the hall door just before you went downstairs, and in that case the Lord only knows where she is. If there is a room anywhere that we have not explored—"

"I am inclined to think there is," I broke in, thinking of Wardrop's face a few minutes before. And just then Wardrop himself joined us. He closed the door at the foot of the boxed-in staircase, and came quietly up.

"You spoke about an unused room or a secret closet, Mr. Hunter," he said, without any resentment in his tone. "We have nothing so sensational as that, but the old house is full of queer nooks and crannies, and perhaps, in one of them, we might find—" he stopped and gulped. Whatever Hunter might think, whatever I might have against Harry Wardrop, I determined then that he had had absolutely nothing to do with little Miss Maitland's strange disappearance.

The first place we explored was a closed and walled-in wine cellar, long unused, and to which access was gained by a small window in the stone foundation of the house. The cobwebs over the window made it practically an impossible place, but we put Robert, the gardener, through it, in spite of his protests.

"There's nothin' there, I tell you," he protested, with one leg over the coping. "God only knows what's down there, after all these years. I've been livin' here with the Miss Maitlands for twenty year, and I ain't never been put to goin' down into cellars on the end of a rope."

He went, because we were three to his one, but he was up again in sixty seconds, with the announcement that the place was as bare as the top of his head.

We moved every trunk in the storeroom, although it would have been a moral impossibility for anyone to have done it the night before without rousing the entire family, and were thus able to get to and open a large closet, which proved to contain neatly tied and labeled packages of religious weeklies, beginning in the sixties.

The grounds had been gone over inch by inch, without affording any clue, and now the three of us faced one another. The day was almost gone, and we were exactly where we started. Hunter had sent men through the town and the adjacent countryside, but no word had come from them. Miss Letitia had at last succumbed to the suspense and had gone to bed, where she lay quietly enough, as is the way with the old, but so mild that she was alarming.

At five o'clock Hawes called me from the office and almost tearfully implored me to come back and attend to my business. When I said it was impossible, I could hear him groan as he hung up the receiver. Hawes is of the opinion that by keeping fresh magazines in my waiting room and by persuading me to the extravagance of Turkish rugs, that he has built my practice to its present flourishing state. When I left the telephone, Hunter was preparing to go back to town and Wardrop was walking up and down the hall. Suddenly Wardrop stopped his uneasy promenade and hailed the detective on his way to the door.

"By George," he exclaimed, "I forgot to show you the closet under the attic stairs!"

We hurried up and Wardrop showed us the panel in the hall, which slid to one side when he pushed a bolt under the carpet. The blackness of the closet was horrible in its suggestion to me. I stepped back while Hunter struck a match and looked in.

The closet was empty.

"Better not go in," Wardrop said. "It hasn't been used for years and it's black with dust. I found it myself and showed it to Miss Jane. I don't believe Miss Letitia knows it is here."

"It hasn't been used for years!" reflected Hunter, looking around him curiously. "I suppose it has been some time since you were in here, Mr. Wardrop?"

"Several years," Wardrop replied carelessly. "I used to keep contraband here in my college days, cigarettes and that sort of thing. I haven't been in it since then."

Hunter took his foot off a small object that lay on the floor, and picking it up, held it out to Wardrop, with a grim smile.

"Here is the fountain pen you lost this morning, Mr. Wardrop," he said quietly.

Chapter VII

Concerning Margery

WHEN Hunter had finally gone at six o'clock, summoned to town on urgent business, we were very nearly where we had been before he came. He could only give us theories, and after all, what we wanted was fact—and Miss Jane. Many things, however, that he had unearthed puzzled me.

Why had Wardrop lied about so small a matter as his fountain pen? The closet was empty: what object could he have had in saying he had not been in it for years? I found that my belief in his sincerity of the night before was going. If he had been lying then, I owed him something for a lump on my head that made it difficult for me to wear my hat.

It would have been easy enough for him to rob himself, and, if he had an eye for the theatrical, to work out just some such plot. It was even possible that he had hidden for a few hours in the secret closet the contents of the Russia leather bag. But, whatever Wardrop might or might not be, he gave me little chance to find out, for he left the house before Hunter did that afternoon, and it was later, and under strange circumstances, that I met him again.

Hunter had not told me what was on the paper he had picked out of the basket in Miss Jane's room, and I knew he was as much puzzled as I at the scrap in the little cupboard, with eleven twenty-two on it. It occurred to me that it might mean the twenty-second day of the eleventh month, perhaps something that had happened on some momentous, long-buried twenty-second of November. But this was May, and the finding of two slips bearing the same number was too unusual.

After Hunter left I went back to the closet under the upper stairs, and with some difficulty got the panel open again. The space inside, perhaps eight feet high at one end and four at the other, was empty. There was a row of hooks, as if at some time clothing had been hung there, and a flat shelf at one end, gray with dust.

I struck another match and examined the shelf. On its surface were numerous scratchings in the dust layer, but at one end, marked out as if drawn on a blackboard, was a rectangular outline, apparently that of a smallish box, and fresh.

My match burned my fingers and I dropped it to the floor, where it expired in a sickly blue flame. At the last, however, it died heroically—like an old man to whom his last hours bring back some of the glory of his prime, burning brightly for a second and then fading into darkness. The last flash showed me, on the floor of the closet and wedged between two boards, a small white globule. I did not need another match to tell me it was a pearl.

I dug it out carefully and took it to my room. In the daylight there I recognized it as an unstrung pearl of fair size and considerable value. There could hardly be a doubt that I had stumbled on one of the stolen gems; but a pearl was only a pearl to me, after all. I didn't feel any of the inspirations which fiction detectives experience when they happen on an important clue.

I lit a cigar and put the pearl on the table in front of me. But no explanation formed itself in the tobacco smoke. If Wardrop took the pearls, I kept repeating over and over, if Wardrop took the pearls, who took Miss Jane?

I tried to forget the pearls, and to fathom the connection between Miss Maitland's disappearance and the absence of her brother-in-law. The scrap of paper, eleven twenty-two, must connect them, but how? A family scandal? Dismissed on the instant. There could be nothing that would touch the virginal remoteness of that little old lady. Insanity? Well, Miss Jane might have had a sudden aberration and wandered away, but that would leave Fleming out, and the paper dragged him in. A common enemy?

I smoked and considered for some time over this. An especially malignant foe might rob, or even murder, but it was almost ludicrous to think of his carrying away by force Miss Jane's ninety pounds of austere flesh. The solution, had it not been for the bloodstains, might have been a peaceful one, leaving out the pearls altogether, but later developments showed that the pearls refused to be omitted. To my mind, however, at that time, the issue seemed a double one. I believed that someone, perhaps Harry Wardrop, had stolen the pearls, hidden them in the secret closet, and disposed of them later. I made a note to try to follow up the missing pearls.

Then—I clung to the theory that Miss Maitland had been abducted and was being held for ransom. If I could have found traces of a vehicle of any sort near the house, I would almost have considered my contention proved. That anyone could have entered the house, intimidated and even slightly injured the old lady, and taken her quietly out the front door, while I sat smoking in my room with the window open, and Wardrop trying the shutters at the side of the house, seemed impossible. Yet there were the stains, the confusion, the open front door to prove it.

But—and I stuck here—the abductor who would steal an old woman, and take her out into the May night without any covering—not even shoes—clad only in her nightclothes, would run an almost certain risk of losing his prize by pneumonia. For a second search had shown not an article of wearing apparel missing from the house. Even the cedar chests were undisturbed; not a blanket was gone.

Just before dinner I made a second round of the grounds, this time looking for traces of wheels. I found none nearby, and it occurred to me that the boldest highwayman would hardly drive up to the door for his booty. When I had extended my search to cover the unpaved lane that separated the back of the Maitland place from its nearest neighbor, I was more fortunate.

The morning delivery wagons had made fresh trails, and at first I despaired. I sauntered up the lane to the right, however, and about a hundred feet beyond the boundary hedge I found circular tracks, broad and deep, where an automobile had backed and turned. The lane was separated by high hedges of osage orange from the properties on either side, and each house in that neighborhood had a drive of its own, which entered from the main street, circled the house and went out as it came.

There was no reason, or, so far as I could see, no legitimate reason, why a car should have stopped there, yet it had stopped and for some time. Deeper tracks in the sand at the side of the lane showed that.

I felt that I had made some progress: I had found where the pearls had been hidden after the theft, and this put Bella out of the question. And I had found—or thought I had—the way in which Miss Jane had been taken away from Bellwood.

I came back past the long rear wing of the house which contained, I presumed, the kitchen and the other mysterious regions which only women and architects comprehend. A long porch ran the length of the wing, and as I passed I heard my name called.

"In here in the old laundry," Margery's voice repeated, and I retraced my steps and went up on the porch. At the very end of the wing, dismantled, piled at the sides with firewood and broken furniture, was an old laundry. Its tubs were rusty, its walls mildewed and streaked, and it exhaled the musty odor of empty houses. On the floor in the middle of the room, undeniably dirty and disheveled, sat Margery Fleming.

"I thought you were never coming," she said petulantly. "I have been here alone for an hour."

"I'm sure I never guessed it," I apologized. "I should have been only too glad to come and sit with you."

She was fumbling with her hair, which threatened to come down any minute, and which hung, loosely knotted, over one small ear.

"I hate to look ridiculous," she said sharply, "and I detest being laughed at. I've been crying, and I haven't any handkerchief."

I proffered mine gravely, and she took it. She wiped the dusty streaks off her cheeks and pinned her hair in a funny knob on top of her head that would have made any other woman look like a caricature. But still she sat on the floor.

"Now," she said, when she had jabbed the last hairpin into place and tucked my handkerchief into her belt, "if you have been sufficiently amused, perhaps you will help me out of here."

"Out of where?"

"Do you suppose I'm sitting here because I like it?"

"You have sprained your ankle," I said, with sudden alarm.

In reply she brushed aside her gown, and for the first time I saw what had occurred. She was sitting half over a trapdoor in the floor, which had closed on her skirts and held her fast.

"The wretched thing!" she wailed. "And I have called until I am hoarse. I could shake Heppie! Then I tried to call you mentally. I fixed my mind on you and said over and over, 'Come, please come.' Didn't you feel anything at all?"

"Good old trapdoor!" I said. "I know I was thinking about you, but I never suspected the reason. And then to have walked past here twenty minutes ago! Why didn't you call me then?" I was tugging at the door, but it was fast, with the skirts to hold it tight.

"I looked such a fright," she explained. "Can't you pry it up with something?"

I tried several things without success, while Margery explained her plight.

"I was sure Robert had not looked carefully in the old wine cellar," she said, "and then I remembered this trapdoor opened into it. It was the only place we hadn't explored thoroughly. I put a ladder down and looked around. Ugh!"

"What did you find?" I asked, as my third broomstick lever snapped.

"Nothing—only I know now where Aunt Letitia's Edwin Booth went to. He was a cat," she explained, "and Aunt Letitia made the railroad pay for killing him."

I gave up finally and stood back.

"Couldn't you—er—get out of your garments, and—I could go out and close the door," I suggested delicately. "You see you are sitting on the trapdoor, and—"

But Margery scouted the suggestion with the proper scorn, and demanded a pair of scissors. She cut herself loose with vicious snips, while I paraphrased the old nursery rhyme, "She cut her petticoats all around about." Then she gathered up her outraged garments and fled precipitately.

She was unusually dignified at dinner. Neither of us cared to eat, and the empty places—Wardrop's and Miss Letitia's—Miss Jane's had not been set—were like skeletons at the board.

It was Margery who, after our pretense of a meal, voiced the suspicion I think we both felt.

"It is a strange time for Harry to go away," she said quietly, from the library window.

"He probably has a reason."

"Why don't you say it?" she said suddenly, turning on me. "I know what you think. You believe he only pretended he was robbed!"

"I should be sorry to think anything of the kind," I began. But she did not allow me to finish.

"I saw what you thought," she burst out bitterly. "The detective almost laughed in his face. Oh, you needn't think I don't know: I saw him last night, and the woman too. He brought her right to the gate. You treat me like a child, all of you!"

In sheer amazement I was silent. So a new character had been introduced into the play—a woman, too!

"You were not the only person, Mr. Knox, who could not sleep last night," she went on. "Oh, I know a great many things. I know about the pearls, and what you think about them, and I know more than that, I—"

She stopped then. She had said more than she intended to, and all at once her bravado left her, and she looked like a frightened child. I went over to her and took one trembling hand.

"I wish you didn't know all those things," I said. "But since you do, won't you let me share the burden? The only reason I am still here is on your account."

I had a sort of crazy desire to take her in my arms and comfort her, Wardrop or no Wardrop. But at that moment, luckily for me, perhaps, Miss Letitia's shrill old voice came from the stairway.

"Get out of my way, Heppie," she was saying tartly. "I'm not on my deathbed yet, not if I know it. Where's Knox?"

Whereupon I obediently went out and helped Miss Letitia into the room.

"I think I know where Jane is," she said, putting down her cane with a jerk. "I don't know why I didn't think about it before. She's gone to get her new teeth; she's been talkin' of it for a month. Not but what her old teeth would have done well enough."

"She would hardly go in the middle of the night," I returned. "She was a very timid woman, wasn't she?"

"She wasn't raised right," Miss Letitia said with a shake of her head. "She's the baby, and the youngest's always spoiled."

"Have you thought that this might be more than it appears to be?" I was feeling my way: she was a very old woman. "It—for instance, it might be abduction, kidnapping—for a ransom.

"Ransom!" Miss Letitia snapped. "Mr. Knox, my father made his money by working hard for it: I haven't wasted it—not that I know of. And if Jane Maitland was fool enough to be abducted, she'll stay a while before I pay anything for her. It looks to me as if this detective business is going to be expensive, anyhow."

My excuse for dwelling with such attention to detail on the preliminary story, the disappearance of Miss Jane Maitland and the peculiar circumstances surrounding it, will have to find its justification in the events that followed it. Miss Jane herself, and the solution of that mystery, solved the even more tragic one in which we were about to be involved. I say *we*, because it was borne in on me at about that time, that the things that concerned Margery Fleming must concern me henceforth, whether I willed it so or otherwise. For the first time in my life a woman's step on the stair was like no other sound in the world.

Chapter VIII

Too Late

At nine o'clock that night things remained about the same. The man Hunter had sent to investigate the neighborhood and the country just outside of the town came to the house about eight, and reported "nothing discovered." Miss Letitia went to bed early, and Margery took her upstairs.

Hunter called me by telephone from town.

"Can you take the nine-thirty up?" he asked. I looked at my watch.

"Yes, I think so. Is there anything new?"

"Not yet; there may be. Take a cab at the station and come to the corner of Mulberry Street and Park Lane. You'd better dismiss your cab there and wait for me."

I sent word upstairs by Bella, who was sitting in the kitchen, her heavy face sodden with grief, and taking my hat and raincoat—it was raining a light spring drizzle—I hurried to the station. In twenty-four minutes I was in the city, and perhaps twelve minutes more saw me at the designated corner, with my cab driving away and the rain dropping off the rim of my hat and splashing on my shoulders.

I found a sort of refuge by standing under the wooden arch of a gate, and it occurred to me that, for all my years in the city, this particular neighborhood was altogether strange to me. Two blocks away, in any direction, I would have been in familiar territory again.

Back of me a warehouse lifted six or seven gloomy stories to the sky. The gate I stood in was evidently the entrance to its yard, and in fact, some uncomfortable movement of mine just then struck the latch, and almost precipitated me backward by its sudden opening. Beyond was a yard full of shadowy wheels and packing cases; the streetlights did not penetrate there, and with an uneasy feeling that almost anything, in this none too savory neighborhood, might be waiting there, I struck a match and looked at my watch. It was twenty minutes after ten. Once a man turned the corner and came toward me, his head down, his long ulster flapping around his legs. Confident that it was Hunter, I stepped out and touched him on the arm. He wheeled instantly, and in the light which shone on his face, I saw my error.

"Excuse me," I mumbled, "I mistook my man."

He went on again without speaking, only pulling his soft hat down lower on his face. I looked after him until he turned the next corner, and I knew I had not been mistaken; it was Wardrop.

The next minute Hunter appeared, from the same direction, and we walked quickly together. I told him who the man just ahead had been, and he nodded without surprise. But before we turned the next corner, he stopped.

"Did you ever hear of the White Cat?" he asked. "Little political club?"

"Never."

"I'm a member of it," he went on rapidly. "It's run by the city ring, or rather it runs itself. Be a good fellow while you're there, and keep your eyes open. It's a queer joint."

The corner we turned found us on a narrow, badly paved street. The broken windows of the warehouse still looked down on us, and across the street was an ice factory, with two deserted wagons standing along the curb. As well as I could see for the darkness, a lumberyard stretched beyond the warehouse, its piles of boards giving off in the rain the aromatic odor of fresh pine.

At a gate in the fence beyond the warehouse Hunter stopped. It was an ordinary wooden gate and it opened with a thumb latch. Beyond stretched a long, narrow, brick-paved alleyway, perhaps three feet wide, and lighted by the merest glimmer of a light ahead. Hunter went on regardless of puddles in the brick paving, and I stumbled after him. As we advanced, I could see that the light was a single electric bulb, hung over a second gate. While Hunter fumbled for a key in his pocket, I had time to see that this gate had a Yale lock, was provided, at the side, with an electric bell button, and had a letter slot cut in it.

Hunter opened the gate and preceded me through it. The gate swung to and clicked behind me. After the gloom of the passageway, the small brick-paved yard seemed brilliant with lights. Two wires were strung its length, dotted with many electric lamps. In a corner a striped tent stood out in grotesque relief; it seemed to be empty, and the weather was an easy explanation. From the two-story house beyond there came suddenly a burst of piano music and a none too steady masculine voice. Hunter turned to me, with his foot on the wooden steps.

"Above everything else," he warned, "keep your temper. Nobody gives a hang in here whether you're the mayor of the town, the champion pool player of the first ward, or the roundsman on the beat."

The door at the top of the steps was also Yale-locked. We stepped at once into the kitchen, from which I imagined that the house faced on another street, and that for obvious reasons only its rear entrance was used. The kitchen was bright and clean; it was littered, however, with half-cut loaves of bread, glasses and empty bottles. Over the range a man in his shirtsleeves was giving his whole attention to a slice of ham, sizzling on a skillet, and at a table nearby a young fellow, with his hair cut in a barber's oval over the back of his neck, was spreading slices of bread and cheese with mustard.

"How are you, Mr. Mayor?" Hunter said, as he shed his raincoat. "This is Mr. Knox, the man who's engineering the *Star-Eagle* fight."

The man over the range wiped one greasy hand and held it out to me.

"The Cat is purring a welcome," he said, indicating the frying ham. "If my cooking turns out right, I'll ask you to have some ham with me. I don't know why in thunder it gets black in the middle and won't cook around the edges."

I recognized the mayor. He was a big fellow, handsome in a heavy way, and "Tommy" to everyone who knew him. It seemed I was about to see my city government at play.

Hunter was thoroughly at home. He took my coat and his own and hung them somewhere to dry. Then he went into a sort of pantry opening off the kitchen and came out with four bottles of beer.

"We take care of ourselves here," he explained, as the newly barbered youth washed some glasses. "If you want a sandwich, there is cooked ham in the refrigerator and cheese—if our friend at the sink has left any."

The boy looked up from his glasses. "It's rat-trap cheese, that stuff," he growled.

"The other man out an hour ago and didn't come back," put in the mayor, grinning. "You can kill that with mustard, if it's too lively."

"Get some cigars, will you?" Hunter asked me. "They're on a shelf in the pantry. I have my hands full."

I went for the cigars, remembering to keep my eyes open. The pantry was a small room: it contained an icebox, stocked with drinkables, ham, eggs and butter. On shelves above were cards, cigars and liquors, and there, too, I saw a box with an endorsement which showed the "honor system" of the Cat Club.

"Sign checks and drop here," it read, and I thought about the old adage of honor among thieves and politicians.

When I came out with the cigars, Hunter was standing with a group of new arrivals; they included one of the city physicians, the director of public charities and a judge of a local court. The latter, McFeely, a little, thin Irishman, knew me and accosted me at once. The mayor was busy over the range, and was almost purple with heat and unwonted anxiety.

When the three newcomers went upstairs, instead of going into the grillroom, I looked at Hunter.

"Is this where the political game is played?" I asked.

"Yes, if the political game is poker," he replied, and led the way into the room which adjoined the kitchen.

No one paid any attention to us. Bare tables, a wooden floor, and almost as many cuspidors as chairs, comprised the furniture of the long room. In one corner was a battered upright piano, and there were two fireplaces with old-fashioned mantels. Perhaps a dozen men were sitting around, talking loudly, with much scraping of chairs on the bare floor. At one table they were throwing poker dice, but the rest were drinking beer and talking in a desultory way. At the piano a man with a red mustache was mimicking the sextette from *Lucia* and a roar of applause met us as we entered the room. Hunter led the way to a corner and put down his bottles.

"It's fairly quiet tonight," he said. "Tomorrow's the big night—Saturday."

"What time do they close up?" I asked. In answer Hunter pointed to a sign over the door. It was a card, neatly printed, and it said, "The White Cat never sleeps."

"There are only two rules here," he explained. "That is one, and the other is, 'If you get too noisy, and the patrol wagon comes, make the driver take you home.' "

The crowd was good-humored; it paid little or no attention to us, and when someone at the piano began to thump a waltz, Hunter, under cover of the noise, leaned over to me.

"We traced Fleming here, through your cornerman and the cabby," he said carefully. "I haven't seen him, but it is a moral certainty he is skulking in one of the upstairs rooms. His precious private secretary is here, too."

I glanced around the room, but no one was paying any attention to us.

"I don't know Fleming by sight," the detective went on, "and the pictures we have of him were taken a good while ago, when he wore a mustache. When he was in local politics, before he went to the legislature, he practically owned this place, paying for favors with membership tickets. A man could hide here for a year safely. The police never come here, and a man's business is his own."

"He is upstairs now?"

"Yes. There are four rooms up there for cards, and a bathroom. It's an old dwelling house. Would Fleming know you?"

"No, but of course Wardrop would."

As if in answer to my objection, Wardrop appeared at that moment. He ran down the painted wooden stairs and hurried through the room without looking to right or left. The piano kept on, and the men at the tables were still engrossed with their glasses and one another. Wardrop was very pale; he bolted into a man at the door, and pushed him aside without ceremony.

"You might go up now," Hunter said, rising. "I will see where the young gentleman is making for. Just open the door of the different rooms upstairs, look around for Fleming, and if anyone notices you, ask if Al Hunter is there. That will let you out."

He left me then, and after waiting perhaps a minute, I went upstairs alone. The second floor was the ordinary upper story of a small dwelling house. The doors were closed, but loud talking, smoke, and the rattle of chips floated out through open transoms. From below, the noise of the piano came up the staircase, unmelodious but rhythmical, and from the street on which the house faced, an automobile was starting its engine, with a series of shot-like explosions.

The noise was confusing, disconcerting. I opened two doors, to find only the usual poker table, with the winners sitting quietly, their cards bunched in the palms of their hands, and the losers, growing more voluble as the night went on, buying chips recklessly, drinking more than they should. The atmosphere was reeking with smoke.

The third door I opened was that of a dingy bathroom, with a zinc tub and a slovenly washstand. The next, however, was different. The light streamed out through the transom as in the other rooms, but there was no noise from within. With my hand on the door, I hesitated—then, with Hunter's injunction ringing in my ears, I opened it and looked in.

A breath of cool night air from an open window met me. There was no noise, no smoke, no sour odor of stale beer. A table had been drawn to the center of the small room, and was littered with papers, pen and ink. At one corner was a tray, containing the remnants of a meal; a pillow and a pair of blankets on a couch at one side showed the room had been serving as a bedchamber.

But none of these things caught my eye at first. At the table, leaning forward, his head on his arms, was a man. I coughed and, receiving no answer, stepped into the room.

"I beg your pardon," I said, "but I am looking for—"

Then the truth burst on me, overwhelmed me. A thin stream was spreading over the papers on the table, moving slowly, sluggishly, as is the way with blood when the heart pump is stopped. I hurried over and raised the heavy, wobbling, gray head. It was Allan Fleming and he had been shot through the forehead.

Chapter IX

Only One Eye Closed

MY FIRST impulse was to rouse the house; my second, to wait for Hunter. To turn loose that mob of half-drunken men in such a place seemed profanation. There was nothing of the majesty or panoply of death here, but the very sordidness of the surroundings made me resolve to guard the new dignity of that figure. I was shocked, of course; it would be absurd to say that I was emotionally unstrung. On the contrary, I was conscious of a distinct feeling of disappointment. Fleming had been our key to the Bellwood affair, and he had put himself beyond helping to solve any mystery. I locked the door and stood wondering what to do next. I should have called a doctor, no doubt, but I had seen enough of death to know that the man was beyond aid of any kind.

It was not until I had bolted the door that I discovered the absence of any weapon. Everything that had gone before had pointed to a position so untenable that suicide seemed its natural and inevitable result. With the discovery that there was no revolver on the table or floor, the thing was more ominous. I decided at once to call the young city physician in the room across the hall, and with something approximating panic, I threw open the door—to face Harry Wardrop, and behind him, Hunter.

I do not remember that anyone spoke. Hunter jumped past me into the room and took in in a single glance what I had labored to acquire in three minutes. As Wardrop came in, Hunter locked the door behind him, and we three stood staring at the prostrate figure over the table.

I watched Wardrop: I have never seen so suddenly abject a picture. He dropped into a chair, and feeling for his handkerchief, wiped his shaking lips; every particle of color left his face, and he was limp, unnerved.

"Did you hear the shot?" Hunter asked me. "It has been a matter of minutes since it happened."

"I don't know," I said, bewildered. "I heard a lot of explosions, but I thought it was an automobile, out in the street."

Hunter was listening while he examined the room, peering under the table, lifting the blankets that had trailed off the couch onto the floor. Someone outside tried the doorknob and, finding the door locked, shook it slightly.

"Fleming!" he called under his breath. "Fleming!"

We were silent, in response to a signal from Hunter, and the steps retreated heavily down the hall. The detective spread the blankets decently over the couch, and the three of us moved the body there. Wardrop was almost collapsing.

"Now," Hunter said quietly, "before I call in Dr. Gray from the room across, what do you know about this thing, Mr. Wardrop?" Wardrop looked dazed.

"He was in a bad way when I left this morning," he said huskily. "There isn't much use now trying to hide anything; God knows I've done all I could. But he has been using cocaine for years, and today he ran out of the stuff. When I got here, about half an hour ago, he was on the verge of killing himself. I got the revolver from him—he was like a crazy man, and as soon as I dared to leave him, I went out to try and find a doctor—"

"To get some cocaine?"

"Yes."

"Not—because he was already wounded, and you were afraid it was fatal?"

Wardrop shuddered; then he pulled himself together, and his tone was more natural.

"What's the use of lying about it?" he said wearily. "You won't believe me if I tell the truth, either, but—he was dead when I got here. I heard something like the bang of a door as I went upstairs, but the noise was terrific down below, and I couldn't tell. When I went in, he was just dropping forward, and—" he hesitated.

"The revolver?" Hunter queried, lynx-eyed.

"Was in his hand. He was dead then."

"Where is the revolver?"

"I will turn it over to the coroner."

"You will give it to me," Hunter replied sharply. And after a little fumbling, Wardrop produced it from his hip pocket. It was an ordinary thirty-eight. The detective opened it and glanced at it. Two chambers were empty.

"And you waited—say ten minutes—before you called for help, and even then you went outside hunting a doctor! What were you doing in those ten minutes?"

Wardrop shut his lips and refused to reply.

"If Mr. Fleming shot himself," the detective pursued relentlessly, "there would be powder marks around the wound. Then, too, he was in the act of writing a letter. It was a strange impulse, this—you see, he had only written a dozen words."

I glanced at the paper on the table. The letter had no superscription; it began abruptly:

> "I shall have to leave here. The numbers have followed me. Tonight—"

That was all.

"This is not suicide," Hunter said gravely. "It is murder, and I warn you, Mr. Wardrop, to be careful what you say. Will you ask Dr. Gray to come in, Mr. Knox?"

I went across the hall to the room where the noise was loudest. Fortunately, Dr. Gray was out of the game. He was opening a can of caviar at a table in the corner and came out in response to a gesture. He did not ask any questions, and I let him go into the death chamber unprepared. The presence of death apparently had no effect on him, but the identity of the dead man almost stupefied him.

"Fleming!" he said, awed, as he looked down at the body. "Fleming, by all that's sacred! And a suicide!"

Hunter watched him grimly.

"How long has he been dead?" he asked.

The doctor glanced at the bullet wound in the forehead, and from there significantly to the group around the couch.

"Not an hour—probably less than half," he said. "It's strange we heard nothing, across the hall there."

Hunter took a clean folded handkerchief from his pocket and, opening it, laid it gently over the dead face. I think it was a relief to all of us. The doctor got up from his kneeling posture beside the couch and looked at Hunter inquiringly.

"What about getting him away from here?" he said. "There is sure to be a lot of noise about it, and—you remember what happened when Butler killed himself here."

"He was reported as being found dead in the lumberyard," Hunter said dryly. "Well, Doctor, this body stays where it is, and I don't give a whoop if the whole city government wants it moved. It won't be. This is murder, not suicide."

The doctor's expression was curious.

"Murder!" he repeated. "Why—who—"

But Hunter had many things to attend to; he broke in ruthlessly on the doctor's amazement.

"See if you can get the house empty, Doctor; just tell them he is dead—the story will get out soon enough."

As the doctor left the room, Hunter went to the open window, through which a fresh burst of rain was coming, and closed it. The window gave me an idea, and I went over and tried to see through the streaming pane. There was no shed or low building outside, but not five yards away the warehouse showed its ugly walls and broken windows.

"Look here, Hunter," I said. "Why could he not have been shot from the warehouse?"

"He could have been—but he wasn't," Hunter affirmed, glancing at Wardrop's drooping figure. "Mr. Wardrop, I am going to send for the coroner, and then I shall ask you to go with me to the office and tell the chief what you know about this. Knox, will you telephone the coroner?"

In an incredibly short time the clubhouse was emptied, and before midnight the coroner himself arrived and went up to the room. As for me, I had breakfasted, lunched and dined on horrors, and I sat in the deserted room downstairs and tried to think how I was to take the news to Margery.

At twelve thirty Wardrop, Hunter and the coroner came downstairs, leaving a detective in charge of the body until morning, when it could be taken home. The coroner had a cab waiting, and he took us at once to Hunter's chief. He had not gone to bed, and we filed into his library sepulchrally.

Wardrop told his story, but it was hardly convincing. The chief, a large man who said very little and leaned back with his eyes partly shut, listened in silence, only occasionally asking a question. The coroner, who was yawning steadily, left in the middle of Wardrop's story, as if in his mind, at least, the guilty man was as good as hanged.

"I am—I was—Mr. Allan Fleming's private secretary," Wardrop

began. "I secured the position through a relationship on his wife's side. I have held the position for three years. Before that I read law. For some time I have known that Mr. Fleming used a drug of some kind. Until a week ago I did not know what it was. On the ninth of May, Mr. Fleming sent for me. I was in Plattsburg at the time, and he was at home. He was in a terrible condition—not sleeping at all, and he said he was being followed by some person who meant to kill him. Finally he asked me to get him some cocaine, and when he had taken it, he was more like himself. I thought the pursuit was only in his own head. He had a man named Carter on guard in his house, and acting as butler.

"There was trouble of some sort in the organization; I do not know just what. Mr. Schwartz came here to meet Mr. Fleming, and it seemed there was money needed. Mr. Fleming had to have it at once. He gave me some securities to take to Plattsburg and turn into money. I went on the tenth—"

"Was that the day Mr. Fleming disappeared?" the chief interrupted.

"Yes. He went to the White Cat, and stayed there. No one but the caretaker and one other man knew he was there. On the night of the twenty-first, I came back, having turned my securities into money. I carried it in a package in a small Russia leather bag that never left my hand for a moment. Mr. Knox here suggested that I had put it down, and it had been exchanged for one just like it, but I did not let it out of my hand on that journey until I put it down on the porch at the Bellwood house, while I tried to get in. I live at Bellwood, with the Misses Maitland, sisters of Mr. Fleming's deceased wife. I don't pretend to know how it happened, but while I was trying to get into the house it was rifled. Mr. Knox will bear me out in that. I found my grip empty."

I affirmed it in a word. The chief was growing interested.

"What was in the bag?" he asked.

Wardrop tried to remember.

"A pair of pajamas," he said, "two military brushes and a clothes brush, two or three soft-bosomed shirts, perhaps a half-dozen collars, and a suit of underwear."

"And all this was taken, as well as the money?"

"The bag was left empty, except for my railroad schedule."

The chief and Hunter exchanged significant glances. Then—

"Go on, if you please," the detective said cheerfully.

I think Wardrop realized the absurdity of trying to make anyone believe that part of the story. He shut his lips and threw up his head as if he intended to say nothing further.

"Go on," I urged. If he could clear himself he must. I could not go back to Margery Fleming and tell her that her father had been murdered and her lover was accused of the crime.

"The bag was empty," he repeated. "I had not been five minutes trying to open the shutters, and yet the bag had been rifled. Mr. Knox here found it among the flowers below the veranda, empty."

The chief eyed me with awakened interest.

"You also live at Bellwood, Mr. Knox?"

"No. I am attorney to Miss Letitia Maitland, and was there one night as her guest. I found the bag as Mr. Wardrop described, empty."

The chief turned back to Wardrop.

"How much money was there in it when you—left it?"

"A hundred thousand dollars. I was afraid to tell Mr. Fleming, but I had to do it. We had a stormy scene, this morning. I think he thought the natural thing—that I had taken it."

"He struck you, I believe, and knocked you down?" asked Hunter smoothly.

Wardrop flushed.

"He was not himself; and, well, it meant a great deal to him. And he was out of cocaine; I left him raging, and when I went home I learned that Miss Jane Maitland had disappeared, been abducted, at the time my satchel had been emptied! It's no wonder I question my sanity."

"And then—tonight?" the chief persisted.

"Tonight, I felt that someone would have to look after Mr. Fleming; I was afraid he would kill himself. It was a bad time to leave while Miss Jane was missing. But—when I got to the White Cat I found him dead. He was sitting with his back to the door, and his head on the table."

"Was the revolver in his hand?"

"Yes."

"You are sure?" from Hunter. "Isn't it a fact, Mr. Wardrop, that you took Mr. Fleming's revolver from him this morning when he threatened you with it?"

Wardrop's face twitched nervously.

"You have been misinformed," he replied, but no one was impressed by his tone. It was wavering, uncertain. From Hunter's face I judged it had been a random shot, and had landed unexpectedly well.

"How many people knew that Mr. Fleming had been hiding at the White Cat?" from the chief.

"Very few—besides myself, only a man who looks after the club-house in the mornings, and Clarkson, the cashier of the Borough Bank, who met him there once by appointment."

The chief made no comment.

"Now, Mr. Knox, what about you?"

"I opened the door into Mr. Fleming's room, perhaps a couple of minutes after Mr. Wardrop went out," I said. "He was dead then, leaning on his outspread arms over the table; he had been shot in the forehead."

"You heard no shot while you were in the hall?"

"There was considerable noise; I heard two or three sharp reports like the explosions of an automobile engine."

"Did they seem close at hand?"

"Not particularly; I thought, if I thought at all, that they were on the street."

"You are right about the automobile," Hunter said dryly. "The mayor sent his car away as I left to follow Mr. Wardrop. The sounds you heard were not shots."

"It is a strange thing," the chief reflected, "that a revolver could be fired in the upper room of an ordinary dwelling house, while that house was filled with people—and nobody hear it. Were there any powder marks on the body?"

"None," Hunter said.

The chief got up stiffly.

"Thank you very much, gentlemen," he spoke quietly. "I think that is all. Hunter, I would like to see you for a few minutes."

I think Wardrop was dazed at finding himself free; he had expected nothing less than an immediate charge of murder. As we walked to the corner for a car or cab, whichever materialized first, he looked back.

"I thought so," he said bitterly. A man was loitering after us along the street. The police were not asleep; they had only closed one eye.

The last train had gone. We took a night electric car to Wynton, and walked the three miles to Bellwood. Neither of us was talkative, and I imagine we were both thinking of Margery, and the news she would have to hear.

It had been raining, and the roads were vile. Once, Wardrop turned around to where we could hear the detective splashing along, well behind.

"I hope he's enjoying it," he said. "I brought you by this road so he'd have to wade in mud up to his neck."

"The devil you did!" I exclaimed. "I'll have to be scraped with a knife before I can get my clothes off."

We both felt better for the laugh; it was a sort of nervous reaction. The detective was well behind, but after a while Wardrop stood still, while I plowed along. They came up together presently, and the three of us trudged on, talking of immaterial things.

At the door Wardrop turned to the detective with a faint smile. "It's raining again," he said, "you'd better come in. You needn't worry about me; I'm not going to run away, and there's a couch in the library."

The detective grinned, and in the light from the hall I recognized the man I had followed to the police station two nights before.

"I guess I will," he said, looking apologetically at his muddy clothes. "This thing is only a matter of form, anyhow."

But he didn't lie down on the couch. He took a chair in the hall near the foot of the stairs, and we left him there, with the evening paper and a lamp. It was a queer situation, to say the least.

Chapter X

Breaking the News

WARDROP looked so wretched that I asked him into my room, and mixed him some whisky and water. When I had given him a cigar, he began to look a little less hopeless.

"You've been a darned sight better to me than I would have been to you, under the circumstances," he said gratefully.

"I thought we had better arrange about Miss Margery before we try to settle down," I replied. "What she has gone through in the last twenty-four hours is nothing to what is coming tomorrow. Will you tell her about her father?"

He took a turn about the room.

"I believe it would come better from you," he said finally. "I am in the peculiar position of having been suspected by her father of robbing him, by you of carrying away her aunt, and now by the police and everybody else of murdering her father."

"I do not suspect you of anything," I justified myself. "I don't think you are entirely open, that is all, Wardrop. I think you are damaging yourself to shield someone else."

His expressive face was on its guard in a moment. He ceased his restless pacing, pausing impressively before me.

"I give you my word as a gentleman—I do not know who killed Mr. Fleming, and that when I first saw him dead, my only thought was that he had killed himself. He had threatened to, that day. Why, if you think I killed him, you would have to think I robbed him, too, in order to find a motive."

I did not tell him that that was precisely what Hunter *did* think. I evaded the issue.

"Mr. Wardrop, did you ever hear of the figures eleven twenty-two?" I inquired.

"Eleven twenty-two?" he repeated. "No, never in any unusual connection."

"You never heard Mr. Fleming use them?" I persisted.

He looked puzzled.

"Probably," he said. "In the very nature of Mr. Fleming's position, we used figures all the time. Eleven twenty-two. That's the time the theater train leaves the city for Bellwood. Not what you want, eh?"

"Not quite," I answered noncommittally, and began to wind my watch. He took the hint and prepared to leave.

"I'll not keep you up any longer," he said, picking up his raincoat. He opened the door and stared ruefully down at the detective in the hall below. "The old place is queer without Miss Jane," he said irrelevantly. "Well, good night, and thanks."

He went heavily along the hall and I closed my door. I heard him pass Margery's room and then go back and rap lightly. She was evidently awake.

"It's Harry," he called. "I thought you wouldn't worry if you knew I was in the house tonight."

She asked him something, for—

"Yes, he is here," he said. He stood there for a moment, hesitating over something, but whatever it was, he decided against it.

"Good night, dear," he said gently and went away. The little familiarity made me wince. Every unattached man has the same pang now and then. I have it sometimes when Edith sits on the arm of Fred's chair, or one of the youngsters leaves me to run to "daddy." And one of the sanest men I ever met went to his office and proposed to his stenographer in sheer craving for domesticity, after watching the wife of one of his friends run her hand over her husband's chin and give him a reproving slap for not having shaved!

I pulled myself up sharply, and after taking off my dripping coat, I went to the window and looked out into the May night. It seemed incredible that almost the same hour the previous night little Miss Jane had disappeared, had been taken away bodily through the peace of the warm spring darkness, and that I, as wide-awake as I was at that moment, acute enough of hearing to detect Wardrop's careful steps on the gravel walk below, had heard no struggle, had permitted this thing to happen without raising a finger in the old lady's defense. And she was gone as completely as if she had stepped over some psychic barrier into the fourth dimension!

I found myself avoiding the more recent occurrence at the White Cat. I was still too close to it to have gained any perspective. On that subject I was able to think clearly of only one thing: that I would have to tell Margery in the morning, and that I would have given anything I possessed for a little of Edith's diplomacy with which to break the bad news. It was Edith who broke the news to me that the moths had gotten into my evening clothes while I was hunting in the Rockies, by telling me that my dress coat made me look narrow across the shoulders and persuading me to buy a new one and give the old one to Fred. Then she broke the news of the moths to Fred!

I was ready for bed when Wardrop came back and rapped at my door. He was still dressed, and he had the leather bag in his hand.

"Look here," he said excitedly, when I had closed the door, "this is not my bag at all. Fool that I was, I never examined it carefully."

He held it out to me, and I carried it to the light. It was an ordinary eighteen-inch Russia leather traveling bag, tan in color, and with gold-plated mountings. It was empty, save for the railroad schedule that still rested in one side pocket. Wardrop pointed to the empty pocket on the other side.

"In my bag," he explained rapidly, "my name was written inside that pocket, in ink. I did it myself—my name and address."

I looked inside the pockets on both sides: nothing had been written in.

"Don't you see?" he asked excitedly. "Whoever stole my bag had this one to substitute for it. If we can succeed in tracing the bag here to the shop it came from, and from there to the purchaser, we have the thief."

"There's no maker's name in it," I said after a casual examination. Wardrop's face fell, and he took the bag from me despondently.

"No matter which way I turn," he said, "I run into a blind alley. If I were worth a damn, I suppose I could find a way out. But I'm not. Well, I'll let you sleep this time."

At the door, however, he turned around and put the bag on the floor, just inside.

"If you don't mind, I'll leave it here," he said.

"They'll be searching my room, I suppose, and I'd like to have the bag for future reference."

He went for good that time, and I put out the light. As an afterthought I opened my door perhaps six inches, and secured it with one of the pink conch shells which flanked either end of the stone hearth. I had failed the night before: I meant to be on hand that night.

I went to sleep immediately, I believe. I have no idea how much later it was that I roused. I wakened suddenly and sat up in bed. There had been a crash of some kind, for the shock was still vibrating along my nerves. Dawn was close; the window showed gray against the darkness inside, and I could make out dimly the larger objects in the room. I listened intently, but the house seemed quiet. Still I was not satisfied. I got up and, lighting the candle, got into my raincoat in lieu of a dressing gown, and prepared to investigate.

With the fatality that seemed to pursue my feet in that house, with my first step I trod squarely on top of the conch shell, and I fell back on to the edge of the bed swearing softly and holding the injured member. Only when the pain began to subside did I realize that I had left the shell on the doorsill, and that it had moved at least eight feet while I slept!

When I could walk, I put it on the mantel, its mate from the other end of the hearth beside it. Then I took my candle and went out into the hall. My door, which I had left open, I found closed; nothing else was disturbed. The leather bag sat just inside, as Wardrop had left it. Through Miss Maitland's transom were coming certain strangled and irregular sounds, now falsetto, now deep bass, that showed that worthy lady to be asleep. A glance down the staircase revealed Davidson, stretching in his chair and looking up at me.

"I'm frozen," he called up cautiously. "Throw me down a blanket or two, will you?"

I got a couple of blankets from my bed and took them down. He was examining his chair ruefully.

"There isn't any grip to this horsehair stuff," he complained. "Every time I doze off I dream I'm coasting down the old hill back on the farm, and when I wake up I'm sitting on the floor, with the end of my backbone bent like a hook."

He wrapped himself in the blankets and sat down again, taking the precaution this time to put his legs on another chair and thus anchor himself. Then he produced a couple of apples and a penknife and proceeded to pare and offer me one.

"Found 'em in the pantry," he said, biting into one. "I belong to the apple society. Eat one apple every day and keep healthy!" He stopped and stared intently at the apple. "I reckon I got a worm that time," he said, with less ardor.

"I'll get something to wash him down," I offered, rising, but he waved me back to my stair.

"Not on your life," he said with dignity. "Let him walk. How are things going upstairs?"

"You didn't happen to be up there a little while ago, did you?" I questioned in turn.

"No. I've been kept busy trying to sit tight where I am. Why?"

"Someone came into my room and wakened me," I explained. "I heard a racket, and when I got up, I found a shell that I had put on the doorsill to keep the door open, in the middle of the room. I stepped on it."

He examined a piece of apple before putting it in his mouth. Then he turned a pair of shrewd eyes on me.

"That's funny," he said. "Anything in the room disturbed?"

"Nothing."

"Where's the shell now?"

"On the mantel. I didn't want to step on it again." He thought for a minute, but his next remark was wholly facetious.

"No. I guess you won't step on it up there. Like the old woman: she says, 'Motorman, if I put my foot on the rail will I be electrocuted?' And he says, 'No, madam, not unless you put your other foot on the trolley wire.' "

I got up impatiently. There was no humor in the situation that night for me.

"Someone had been in the room," I reiterated. "The door was closed, although I had left it open."

He finished his apple and proceeded with great gravity to drop the parings down the immaculate register in the floor beside his chair. Then—

"I've only got one business here, Mr. Knox," he said in an undertone, "and you know what that is. But if it will relieve your mind of the thought that there was anything supernatural about your visitor, I'll tell you that it was Mr. Wardrop, and that to the best of my belief he was in your room, not once, but twice, in the last hour and a half. As far as that shell goes, it was I that kicked it, having gone up without my shoes."

I stared at him blankly.

"What could he have wanted?" I exclaimed. But with his revelation, Davidson's interest ceased; he drew the blanket up around his shoulders and shivered.

"Search me," he said and yawned.

I went back to bed, but not to sleep. I deliberately left the door wide open, but no intrusion occurred. Once, I got up and glanced down the stairs. For all his apparent drowsiness, Davidson heard my cautious movements, and saluted me in a husky whisper.

"Have you got any quinine?" he said. "I'm sneezing my head off."

But I had none. I gave him a box of cigarettes, and after partially dressing, I threw myself across the bed to wait for daylight. I was roused by the sun beating on my face, to hear Miss Letitia's tones from her room across.

"Nonsense," she was saying querulously. "Don't you suppose I can smell? Do you think because I'm a little hard of hearing that I've lost my other senses? Somebody's been smoking."

"It's me," Heppie shouted. "I—"

"You?" Miss Letitia snarled. "What are you smoking for? That ain't my shirt; it's my—"

"I ain't smokin'," yelled Heppie. "You won't let me tell you. I spilled vinegar on the stove; that's what you smell."

Miss Letitia's sardonic chuckle came through the door.

"Vinegar," she said with scorn. "Next thing you'll be telling me it's vinegar that Harry and Mr. Knox carry around in little boxes in their pockets. You've pinned my cap to my scalp."

I hurried downstairs to find Davidson gone. My blankets lay neatly folded, on the lower step, and the horsehair chairs were arranged along the wall as before. I looked around anxiously for telltale ashes, but there were none, save, at the edge of the spotless register, a trace. Evidently they had followed the apple parings. It grew cold a day or so later, and Miss Letitia had the furnace fired, and although it does not belong to my story, she and Heppie searched the house over to account for the odor of baking apples—a mystery that was never explained.

Wardrop did not appear at breakfast. Margery came downstairs as Bella was bringing me my coffee, and dropped languidly into her chair. She looked tired and white.

"Another day!" she said wearily. "Did you ever live through such an eternity as the last thirty-six hours?"

I responded absently; the duty I had assumed hung heavy over me. I had a frantic impulse to shirk the whole thing: to go to Wardrop and tell him it was his responsibility, not mine, to make this sad-eyed girl sadder still. That as I had not his privilege of comforting her, neither should I shoulder his responsibility of telling her. But the issue was forced on me sooner than I had expected, for at that moment I saw the glaring headlines of the morning paper, laid open at Wardrop's plate.

She must have followed my eyes, for we reached for it simultaneously. She was nearer than I, and her quick eye caught the name. Then I put my hand over the heading and she flushed with indignation.

"You are not to read it now," I said, meeting her astonished gaze as best I could. "Please let me have it. I promise you I will give it to you—almost immediately."

"You are very rude," she said without relinquishing the paper. "I saw a part of that; it is about my father!"

"Drink your coffee, please," I pleaded. "I will let you read it then. On my honor."

She looked at me; then she withdrew her hand and sat erect.

"How can you be so childish!" she exclaimed. "If there is anything in that paper that it—will hurt me to learn, is a cup of coffee going to make it any easier?"

I gave up then. I had always thought that people heard bad news better when they had been fortified with something to eat, and I had a very distinct recollection that Fred had made Edith drink something—tea probably—before he told her that Billy had fallen off the back fence and would have to have a stitch taken in his lip. Perhaps I should have offered Margery tea instead of coffee. But as it was, she sat, stonily erect, staring at the paper, and feeling that evasion would be useless, I told her what had happened, breaking the news as gently as I could.

I stood by her helplessly through the tearless agony that followed, and cursed myself for a blundering ass. I had said that he had been accidentally shot, and I said it with the paper behind me, but she put the evasion aside bitterly.

"Accidentally!" she repeated. The first storm of grief over, she lifted her head from where it had rested on her arms and looked at me, scorning my subterfuge. "He was murdered. That's the word I didn't have time to read! Murdered! And you sat back and let it happen. I went to you in time and you didn't do anything. No one did anything!"

I did not try to defend myself. How could I? And afterward when she sat up and pushed back the damp strands of hair from her eyes, she was more reasonable.

"I did not mean what I said about your not having done anything," she said, almost childishly. "No one could have done more. It was to happen, that's all."

But even then I knew she had trouble in store that she did not suspect. What would she do when she heard that Wardrop was under grave suspicion? Between her dead father and her lover, what? It was to be days before I knew, and in all that time I, who would have died, not cheerfully but at least stoically, for her, had to stand back and watch the struggle, not daring to hold out my hand to help, lest by the very gesture she divine my wild longing to hold her for myself.

She recovered bravely that morning from the shock, and refusing to go to her room and lie down—a suggestion, like the coffee, culled from my vicarious domestic life—she went out to the veranda and sat there in the morning sun, gazing across the lawn. I left her there finally, and broke the news of her brother-in-law's death to Miss Letitia. After the first surprise, the old lady took the news with what was nearer complacency than resignation.

"Shot!" she said, sitting up in bed, while Heppie shook her pillows. "It's a queer death for Allan Fleming; I always said he would be hanged."

After that, she apparently dismissed him from her mind, and we talked of her sister. Her mood had changed and it was depressing to find that she spoke of Jane always in the past tense. She could speak of her quite calmly—I suppose the sharpness of our emotions is in inverse ratio to our length of years, and she regretted that, under the circumstances, Jane would not rest in the family lot.

"We are all there," she said, "eleven of us, counting my sister Mary's husband, although he don't properly belong, and I always said we would take him out if we were crowded. It is the best lot in the Hopedale Cemetery; you can see the shaft for two miles in any direction."

We held a family council that morning around Miss Letitia's bed: Wardrop, who took little part in the proceedings and who stood at a window looking out most of the time; Margery on the bed, her arm around Miss Letitia's shriveled neck; and Heppie, who acted as interpreter and shouted into the old lady's ear such parts of the conversation as she considered essential.

"I have talked with Miss Fleming," I said, as clearly as I could, "and she seems to shrink from seeing people. The only friends she cares about are in Europe, and she tells me there are no other relatives."

Heppie condensed this into a vocal capsule, and thrust it into Miss Letitia's ear. The old lady nodded.

"No other relatives," she corroborated. "God be praised for that, anyhow."

"And yet," I went on, "there are things to look after, certain necessary duties that no one else can attend to. I don't want to insist, but she ought, if she is able, to go to the city house, for a few hours, at least."

"City house!" Heppie yelled in her ear.

"It ought to be cleaned," Miss Letitia acquiesced, "and fresh curtains put up. Jane would have been in her element; she was always handy at a funeral. And don't let them get one of those let-down-at-the-side coffins. They're leaky."

Luckily Margery did not notice this.

"I was going to suggest," I put in hurriedly, "that my brother's wife would be only too glad to help, and if Miss Fleming will go into town with me, I am sure Edith would know just what to do. She isn't curious and she's very capable."

Margery threw me a grateful glance—grateful, I think, that I could understand how, under the circumstances, a stranger was more acceptable than curious friends could be.

"Mr. Knox's sister-in-law!" interpreted Heppie.

"When you have to say the letter S, turn your head away," Miss Letitia rebuked her. "Well, I don't object, if Knox's sister-in-law don't." She had an uncanny way of expanding Heppie's tabloid speeches. "You can take my white silk shawl to lay over the body, but be sure to bring it back. We may need it for Jane."

If the old lady's chin quivered a bit, while Margery threw her arms around her, she was mightily ashamed of it. But Heppie was made of weaker stuff. She broke into a sudden storm of sobs and left the room, to stick her head in the door a moment after.

"Kidneys or chops?" she shouted almost belligerently.

"Kidneys," Miss Letitia replied in kind.

Wardrop went with us to the station at noon, but he left us there, with a brief remark that he would be up that night. After I had put Margery in a seat, I went back to have a word with him alone. He was standing beside the train, trying to light a cigarette, but his hands shook almost beyond control, and after the fourth match he gave it up. My minute for speech was gone. As the train moved out, I saw him walking back along the platform, paying no attention to anything around him. Also, I had a fleeting glimpse of a man loafing on a baggage truck, his hat over his eyes. He was paring an apple with a penknife, and dropping the peelings with careful accuracy through a crack in the floor of the platform.

I had arranged over the telephone that Edith should meet the train, and it was a relief to see that she and Margery took to each other at once. We drove to the house immediately, and after a few tears when she saw the familiar things around her, Margery rose to the situation bravely. Miss Letitia had sent Bella to put the house in order, and it was evident that the idea of clean curtains for the funeral had been drilled into her until it had become an obsession. Not until Edith had concealed the stepladder were the hangings safe, and late in the afternoon we heard a crash from the library and found Bella twisted on the floor, the result of putting a teakwood tabouret on a table and from thence attacking the lace curtains of the library windows.

Edith gave her a good scolding and sent her off to soak her sprained ankle. Then she righted the tabouret, sat down on it and began on me.

"Do you know that you have not been to the office for two days?" she said severely. "And do you know that Hawes had hysterics in our front hall last night? You had a case in court yesterday, didn't you?"

"Nothing very much," I said, looking over her head. "Anyhow, I'm tired. I don't know when I'm going back. I need a vacation."

She reached behind her and, pulling the cord, sent the window shade to the top of the window. At the sight of my face thus revealed, she drew a long sigh.

"The biggest case you ever had, Jack! The biggest retainer you ever had—"

"I've spent that," I protested feebly

"A vacation, and you only back from Pinehurst!"

"The girl was in trouble—is in trouble, Edith," I burst out. "Anyone would have done the same thing. Even Fred would hardly have deserted that household. It's stricken, positively stricken."

My remark about Fred did not draw her from cover.

"Of course it's your own affair," she said, not looking at me, "and goodness knows I'm disinterested about it; you ruin the boys, both stomachs and dispositions, and I could use your room *splendidly* as a sewing room—"

"Edith! You abominable little liar!"

She dabbed at her eyes furiously with her handkerchief, and walked with great dignity to the door. Then she came back and put her hand on my arm.

"Oh, Jack, if we could only have saved you this!" she said, and a minute later, when I did not speak: "Who is the man, dear?"

"A distant relative, Harry Wardrop," I replied, with what I think was very nearly my natural tone. "Don't worry, Edith. It's all right. I've known it right along."

"Pooh!" Edith returned sagely. "So do I know I've got to die and be buried someday. Its being inevitable doesn't make it any more cheerful." She went out, but she came back in a moment and stuck her head through the door.

"*That's* the only inevitable thing there is," she said, taking up the conversation—an old habit of hers—where she had left off.

"I don't know what you are talking about," I retorted, turning my back on her. "And anyhow, I regard your suggestion as immoral." But when I turned again, she had gone.

That Saturday afternoon at four o'clock the body of Allan Fleming was brought home, and placed in state, in the music room of the house.

Miss Jane had been missing since Thursday night. I called Hunter by telephone, and he had nothing to report.

Chapter XI

A Night in the Fleming Home

I HAD a tearful message from Hawes late that afternoon, and a little after five I went to the office. I found him offering late editions of the evening paper to a couple of clients, who were edging toward the door. His expression when he saw me was pure relief, the clients', relief strongly mixed with irritation.

I put the best face on the matter that I could, saw my visitors, and left alone, prepared to explain to Hawes what I could hardly explain to myself.

"I've been unavoidably detained, Hawes," I said. "Miss Jane Maitland has disappeared from her home."

"So I understood you over the telephone." He had brought my mail and stood by impassively.

"Also, her brother-in-law is dead."

"The papers are full of it."

"There was no one to do anything, Hawes. I was obliged to stay," I apologized. I was ostentatiously examining my letters and Hawes said nothing. I looked up at him sideways, and he looked down at me. Not a muscle of his face quivered, save one eye, which has a peculiar twitching of the lid when he is excited. It gave him a sardonic appearance of winking. He winked at me then.

"Don't wait, Hawes," I said guiltily, and he took his hat and went out. Every line of his back was accusation. The sag of his shoulders told me I had let my biggest case go by default that day; the forward tilt of his head, that I was probably insane; the very grip with which he seized the doorknob, his "good night" from around the door, that he knew there was a woman at the bottom of it all. As he closed the door behind him, I put down my letters and dropped my face in my hands. Hawes was right. No amount of professional zeal could account for the interest I had taken. Partly through force of circumstances, partly of my own volition, I had placed myself in the position of first friend to a family with which I had had only professional relations; I had even enlisted Edith, when my acquaintance with Margery Fleming was only three days old! And at the thought of the girl, of Wardrop's inefficiency and my own hopelessness, I groaned aloud.

I had not heard the door open.

"I forgot to tell you that a gentleman was here half a dozen times today to see you. He didn't give any name."

I dropped my hands. From around the door Hawes' nervous eye was winking wildly.

"You're not sick, Mr. Knox?"

"Never felt better."

"I thought I heard—"

"I was singing," I lied, looking him straight in the eye.

He backed nervously to the door.

"I have a little sherry in my office, Mr. Knox—twenty-six years in the wood. If you—"

"For God's sake, Hawes, there's nothing the matter with me!" I exclaimed, and he went. But I heard him stand a perceptible time outside the door before he tiptoed away.

Almost immediately after, someone entered the waiting room, and the next moment I was facing, in the doorway, a man I had never seen before.

He was a tall man, with a thin, colorless beard trimmed to a Vandyke point, and pale eyes blinking behind glasses. He had a soft hat crushed in his hand, and his whole manner was one of subdued excitement.

"Mr. Knox?" he asked, from the doorway.

"Yes. Come in."

"I have been here six times since noon," he said, dropping rather than sitting in a chair. "My name is Lightfoot. I am—was—Mr. Fleming's cashier."

"Yes?"

"I was terribly shocked at the news of his death," he stumbled on, getting no help from me. "I was in town and if I had known in time I could have kept some of the details out of the papers. Poor Fleming—to think he would end it that way."

"End it?"

"Shoot himself." He watched me closely.

"But he didn't," I protested. "It was not suicide, Mr. Lightfoot. According to the police, it was murder."

His cold eyes narrowed like a cat's. "Murder is an ugly word, Mr. Knox. Don't let us be sensational. Mr. Fleming had threatened to kill himself more than once; ask young Wardrop. He was sick and despondent; he left his home without a word, which points strongly to emotional insanity. He could have gone to any one of a half-dozen large clubs here, or at the capital. Instead, he goes to a little third-rate political club, where, presumably, he does his own cooking and hides in a dingy room. Is that sane? Murder! It was suicide, and that puppy Wardrop knows it well enough. I—I wish I had him by the throat!"

He had worked himself into quite a respectable rage, but now he calmed himself.

"I have seen the police," he went on. "They agree with me that it was suicide, and the party newspapers will straighten it out tomorrow. It is only unfortunate that the murder theory was given so much publicity. The *Times-Post*, which is Democratic, of course, I cannot handle."

I sat stupefied.

"Suicide!" I said finally. "With no weapon, no powder marks, and with a half-finished letter at his elbow."

He brushed my interruption aside.

"Mr. Fleming had been—careless," he said. "I can tell you in confidence, that some of the state funds had been deposited in the Borough Bank of Manchester, and—the Borough Bank closed its doors at ten o'clock today."

I was hardly surprised at that, but the whole trend of events was amazing.

"I arrived here last night," he said, "and I searched the city for Mr. Fleming. This morning I heard the news. I have just come from the house: his daughter referred me to you. After all, what I want is a small matter. Some papers—state documents—are missing, and no doubt are among Mr. Fleming's private effects. I would like to go through his papers, and leave tonight for the capital."

"I hardly have the authority," I replied doubtfully. "Miss Fleming, I suppose, would have no objection. His private secretary, Wardrop, would be the one to superintend such a search."

"Can you find Wardrop—at once?"

Something in his eagerness put me on my guard.

"I will make an attempt," I said. "Let me have the name of your hotel, and I will telephone you if it can be arranged for tonight."

He had to be satisfied with that, but his eagerness seemed to me to be almost desperation. Oddly enough, I could not locate Wardrop after all. I got the Maitland house by telephone, to learn that he had left there about three o'clock and had not come back.

I went to the Fleming house for dinner. Edith was still there, and we both tried to cheer Margery, a sad little figure in her black clothes. After the meal, I called Lightfoot at his hotel, and told him that I could not find Wardrop, that there were no papers at the house, and that the office safe would have to wait until Wardrop was found to open it. He was disappointed and furious; like a good many men who are physical cowards, he said a great deal over the telephone that he would not have dared to say to my face, and I cut him off by hanging up the receiver. From that minute, in the struggle that was coming, like Fred, I was "forninst" the government.

It was arranged that Edith should take Margery home with her for the night. I thought it a good idea; the very sight of Edith tucking in her babies and sitting down beside the library lamp to embroider me a scarfpin holder for Christmas would bring Margery back to normal again. Except in the matter of Christmas gifts, Edith is the sanest woman I know; I recognized it at the dinner table, where she had the little girl across from her planning her mourning hats before the dinner was half finished.

When we rose at last, Margery looked toward the music room, where the dead man lay in state. But Edith took her by the arm and pushed her toward the stairs.

"Get your hat on right away, while Jack calls a cab," she directed. "I must get home, or Fred will keep the boys up until nine o'clock. He is absolutely without principle."

When Margery came down, there was a little red spot burning in each pale cheek, and she ran down the stairs like a scared child. At the bottom she clutched the newel post and looked behind fearfully.

"What's the matter?" Edith demanded, glancing uneasily over her shoulder.

"Someone has been upstairs," Margery panted. "Somebody has been staying in the house while we were away."

"Nonsense," I said, seeing that her fright was infecting Edith. "What makes you think that?"

"Come and look," she said, gaining courage, I suppose, from a masculine presence. And so we went up the long stairs, the two girls clutching hands, and I leading the way and inclined to scoff.

At the door of a small room next to what had been Allan Fleming's bedroom, we paused and I turned on the light.

"Before we left," Margery said more quietly, "I closed this room myself. It had just been done over, and the pale blue soils so easily I came in the last thing, and saw covers put over everything. Now look at it!"

It was a sort of boudoir, filled with feminine knickknacks and mahogany lounging chairs. Wherever possible, a pale brocade had been used, on the empire couch, in panels in the wall, covering cushions on the window seat. It was evidently Margery's private sitting room.

The linen cover that had been thrown over the divan was folded back, and a pillow from the window seat bore the imprint of a head. The table was still covered, knobby protuberances indicating the pictures and books beneath. On one corner of the table, where the cover had been pushed aside, was a cup, empty and clean-washed, and as if to prove her contention, Margery picked up from the floor a newspaper, dated Friday morning, the twenty-second.

A used towel in the bathroom nearby completed the inventory. Margery had been right; someone had used the room while the house was closed.

"Might it not have been your—father?" Edith asked, when we stood again at the foot of the stairs. "He could have come here to look for something, and lain down to rest."

"I don't think so," Margery said wanly. "I left the door so he could get in with his key, but—he always used his study coach. I don't think he ever spent five minutes in my sitting room in his life."

We had to let it go at that finally. I put them in a cab, and saw them start away; then I went back into the house. I had arranged to sleep there and generally to look after things—as I said before. Whatever scruples I had had about taking charge of Margery Fleming and her affairs had faded with Wardrop's defection and the new mystery of the blue boudoir.

The lower floor of the house was full of people that night, local and state politicians, newspaper men and the usual crowd of the morbidly curious. The undertaker took everything in hand, and late that evening I could hear them carrying in tropical plants and stands for the flowers that were already arriving. Whatever panoply the death scene had lacked, Allan Fleming was lying in state now.

At midnight things grew quiet. I sat in the library, reading, until then, when an undertaker's assistant in a pink shirt and polka-dot cravat came to tell me that everything was done.

"Is it customary for somebody to stay up, on occasions like this?" I asked. "Isn't there an impression that wandering cats may get into the room, or something of that sort?"

"I don't think it will be necessary, sir," he said, trying to conceal a smile. "It's all a matter of taste. Some people like to take their troubles hard. Since they don't put money on their eyes anymore, nobody wants to rob the dead."

He left with that cheerful remark, and I closed and locked the house after him. I found Bella in the basement kitchen with all the lights burning full, and I stood at the foot of the stairs while she scooted to bed like a scared rabbit. She was a strange creature, Bella—not so stupid as she looked, but sullen, morose—"smoldering" about expresses it.

I closed the doors into the dining room and, leaving one light in the hall, went up to bed. A guest room in the third story had been assigned me, and I was tired enough to have slept on the floor. The telephone bell rang just after I got into bed, and grumbling at my luck, I went down to the lower floor.

It was the *Times-Post*, and the man at the telephone was in a hurry.

"This is the *Times-Post*. Is Mr. Wardrop there?"

"No."

"Who is this?"

"This is John Knox."

"The attorney?"

"Yes."

"Mr. Knox, are you willing to put yourself on record that Mr. Fleming committed suicide?"

"I am not going to put myself on record at all."

"Tonight's *Star* says you call it suicide, and that you found him with the revolver in his hand."

"The *Star* lies!" I retorted, and the man at the other end chuckled.

"Many thanks," he said, and rang off.

I went back to bed, irritated that I had betrayed myself. Loss of sleep for two nights, however, had told on me: in a short time I was sound asleep.

I wakened with difficulty. My head felt stupid and heavy, and I was burning with thirst. I sat up and wondered vaguely if I were going to be ill, and I remember that I felt too weary to get a drink. As I roused, however, I found that part of my discomfort came from bad ventilation, and I opened a window and looked out.

The window was a side one, opening on to a space perhaps eight feet wide, which separated it from its neighbor. Across from me was only a blank red wall, but the night air greeted me refreshingly. The wind was blowing hard, and a shutter was banging somewhere below. I leaned out and looked down into the well-like space beneath me. It was one of those apparently chance movements that have vital consequences, and that have always made me believe in the old Calvinistic creed of foreordination.

Below me, on the wall across, was a rectangle of yellow light, reflected from the library window of the Fleming home. There was someone in the house.

As I still stared, the light was slowly blotted out—not as if the light had been switched off, but by a gradual decreasing in size of the lighted area. The library shade had been drawn.

My first thought was burglars: my second—Lightfoot. No matter who it was, there was no one who had business there. Luckily, I had brought my revolver with me from Fred's that day, and it was under my pillow; to get it, put out the light and open the door quietly, took only a minute. I was in pajamas, barefoot, as on another almost similar occasion, but I was better armed than before.

I got to the second floor without hearing or seeing anything suspicious, but from there I could see that the light in the hall had been extinguished. The unfamiliarity of the house, the knowledge of the silent figure in the drawing room at the foot of the stairs, and of whatever might be waiting in the library beyond, made my position uncomfortable, to say the least.

I don't believe in the man who is never afraid: he doesn't deserve the credit he gets. It's the fellow who is scared to death, whose knees knock together, and who totters rather than walks into danger, who is the real hero. Not that I was as bad as that, but I would have liked to know where the electric switch was, and to have seen the trap before I put my head in.

The stairs were solidly built, and did not creak. I felt my way down by the baluster, which required my right hand, and threw my revolver to my left. I got safely to the bottom, and around the newel post; there was still a light in the library, and the door was not entirely closed. Then, with my usual bad luck, I ran into a heap of folding chairs that had been left by the undertaker, and if the crash paralyzed me, I don't know what it did to the intruder in the library.

The light was out in an instant, and with concealment at an end, I broke for the door and threw it open, standing there with my revolver leveled. We—the man in the room and I—were both in absolute darkness. He had the advantage of me. He knew my location, and I could not guess his.

"Who is here?" I demanded.

Only silence, except that I seemed to hear rapid breathing.

"Speak up, or I'll shoot!" I said, not without an ugly feeling that he might be—even probably was—taking careful aim by my voice. The darkness was intolerable: I reached cautiously to the left and found, just beyond the door frame, the electric switch. As I turned it, the light flashed up. The room was empty, but a portière in a doorway at my right was still shaking.

I leaped for the curtain and dragged it aside, to have a door just close in my face. When I had jerked it open, I found myself in a short hall, and there were footsteps to my left. I blundered along in the semi-darkness, into a black void which must have been the dining room, for my outstretched hand skirted the table. The footsteps seemed only beyond my reach, and at the other side of the room the swinging door into the pantry was still swaying when I caught it.

I made a misstep in the pantry, and brought up against a blank wall. It seemed to me I heard the sound of feet running up steps, and when I found a door at last, I threw it open and dashed in.

The next moment the solid earth slipped from under my feet, I threw out my hand, and it met a cold wall, smooth as glass. Then I fell—fell an incalculable distance, and the blackness of the night came over me and smothered me.

Chapter XII

My Commission

When I came to, I was lying in darkness, and the stillness was absolute. When I tried to move, I found I was practically a prisoner: I had fallen into an air shaft, or something of the kind. I could not move my arms, where they were pinioned to my sides, and I was half-lying, half-crouching, in a semi-vertical position. I worked one arm loose and managed to make out that my prison was probably the dumbwaiter shaft to the basement kitchen.

I had landed on top of the slide, and I seemed to be tied in a knot. The revolver was under me, and if it had exploded during the fall it had done no damage. I can hardly imagine a more unpleasant position. If the man I had been following had so chosen, he could have made away with me in any one of a dozen unpleasant ways—he could have filled me as full of holes as a sieve, or scalded me, or done anything, pretty much, that he chose. But nothing happened. The house was impressively quiet.

I had fallen feet first, evidently, and then crumpled up unconscious, for one of my ankles was throbbing. It was some time before I could stand erect, and even by reaching, I could not touch the doorway above me. It must have taken five minutes for my confused senses to remember the wire cable, and to tug at it. I was a heavy load for the slide, accustomed to nothing weightier than political dinners, but with much creaking I got myself at last to the floor above, and stepped out, still into darkness, but free.

I still held the revolver, and I lighted the whole lower floor. But I found nothing in the dining room or the pantry. Everything was locked and in good order. A small alcove off the library came next; it was undisturbed, but a tabouret lay on its side, and a half-dozen books had been taken from a low bookcase, and lay heaped on a chair. In the library, however, everything was confusion. Desk drawers stood open—one of the linen shades had been pulled partly off its roller, a chair had been drawn up to the long mahogany table in the center of the room, with the electric dome overhead, and everywhere, on chairs, over the floor, heaped in stacks on the table, were papers.

After searching the lower floor, and finding everything securely locked, I went upstairs, convinced the intruder was still in the house. I made a systematic search of every room, looking into closets and under beds. Several times I had an impression, as I turned a corner, that someone was just ahead of me, but I was always disappointed. I gave up at last and, going down to the library, made myself as comfortable as I could, and waited for morning.

I heard Bella coming down the stairs, after seven sometime; she came slowly, with flagging footsteps, as if the slightest sound would send her scurrying to the upper regions again. A little later I heard her rattling the range in the basement kitchen, and I went upstairs and dressed.

I was too tired to have a theory about the night visitor; in fact, from that time on, I tried to have no theories of any kind. I was impressed with only one thing—that the enemy or enemies of the late Allan Fleming evidently carried their antagonism beyond the grave. As I put on my collar I wondered how long I could stay in this game, as I now meant to, and avoid lying in state in Edith's little drawing room, with flowers around and a gentleman in black gloves at the door.

I had my ankle strapped with adhesive that morning by my doctor and it gave me no more trouble. But I caught him looking curiously at the blue bruise on my forehead where Wardrop had struck me with the chair, and at my nose, no longer swollen, but mustard-yellow at the bridge.

"Been doing any boxing lately?" he asked, as I laced up my shoe.

"Not for two or three years."

"New machine?"

"No."

He smiled at me quizzically from his desk.

"How does the other fellow look?" he inquired, and to my haltingly invented explanation of my battered appearance, he returned the same enigmatical smile.

That day was uneventful. Margery and Edith came to the house for about an hour and went back to Fred's again.

A cousin of the dead man, an elderly bachelor named Parker, appeared that morning and signified his willingness to take charge of the house during that day. The very hush of his voice and his black tie prompted Edith to remove Margery from him as soon as she could, and as the girl dreaded the curious eyes of the crowd that filled the house, she was glad to go.

It was Sunday, and I went to the office only long enough to look over my mail. I dined in the middle of the day at Fred's, and felt heavy and stupid all afternoon as a result of thus reversing the habits of the week. In the afternoon I had my first conversation with Fred and Edith, while Margery and the boys talked quietly in the nursery. They had taken a great fancy to her, and she was almost cheerful when she was with them.

Fred had the morning papers around him on the floor, and was in his usual Sunday argumentative mood.

"Well," he said, when the nursery door upstairs had closed, "what was it, Jack? Suicide?"

"I don't know," I replied bluntly.

"What do you think?" he insisted.

"How can I tell?" Irritably. "The police say it was suicide, and they ought to know."

"The *Times-Post* says it was murder, and that they will prove it. And they claim the police have been called off."

I said nothing of Mr. Lightfoot, and his visit to the office, but I made a mental note to see the *Times-Post* people and learn, if I could, what they knew.

"I cannot help thinking that he deserved very nearly what he got," Edith broke in, looking much less vindictive than her words. "When one thinks of the ruin he brought to poor Henry Butler, and that Ellen has been practically an invalid ever since, I can't be sorry for him."

"What was the Butler story?" I asked. But Fred did not know, and Edith was as vague as women usually are in politics.

"Henry Butler was treasurer of the state, and Mr. Fleming was his cashier. I don't know just what the trouble was. But you remember that Henry Butler killed himself after he got out of the penitentiary, and Ellen has been in one hospital after another. I would like to have her come here for a few weeks, Fred," she said appealingly. "She is in some sanatorium or other now, and we might cheer her a little."

Fred moaned.

"Have her if you like, petty," he said resignedly, "but I refuse to be cheerful unless I feel like it. What about this young Wardrop, Jack? It looks to me as if the *Times-Post* reporter had a line on him."

"Hush," Edith said softly. "He is Margery's fiancé, and she might hear you."

"How do you know?" Fred demanded. "Did she tell you?"

"Look at her engagement ring," Edith threw back triumphantly. "And it's a perfectly beautiful solitaire, too."

I caught Fred's eye on me, and the very speed with which he shifted his gaze made me uncomfortable. I made my escape as soon as I could, on the plea of going out to Bellwood, and in the hall upstairs I met Margery.

"I saw Bella today," she said. "Mr. Knox, will you tell me why you stayed up last night? What happened in the house?"

"I—thought I heard someone in the library," I stammered, "but I found no one."

"Is that all the truth or only part of it?" she asked. "Why do men always evade issues with a woman?" Luckily, womanlike, she did not wait for a reply. She closed the nursery door and stood with her hand on the knob, looking down.

"I wonder what you believe about all this," she said. "Do you think my father—killed himself? You were there; you know. If someone would only tell me everything!"

It seemed to me it was her right to know. The boys were romping noisily in the nursery. Downstairs Fred and Edith were having their Sunday afternoon discussion of what in the world had become of the money from Fred's latest book. Margery and I sat down on the stairs, and, as well as I could remember the details, I told her what had happened at the White Cat. She heard me through quietly.

"And so the police have given up the case!" she said despairingly. "And if they had not, Harry would have been arrested. Is there nothing I can do? Do I have to sit back with my hands folded?"

"The police have not exactly given up the case," I told her, "but there is such a thing, of course, as stirring up a lot of dust and then running to cover like blazes before it settles. By the time the public has wiped it out of its eyes and sneezed it out of its nose and coughed it out of its larynx, the dust has settled in a heavy layer, clues are obliterated, and the public lifts its skirts and chooses another direction. The NO THOROUGHFARE sign is up."

She sat there for fifteen minutes, interrupted by occasional noisy excursions from the nursery, which resulted in her acquiring by degrees a lapful of broken wheels, three-legged horses and a live water beetle which the boys had found under the kitchen sink and imprisoned in a glass-topped box, where, to its bewilderment, they were assiduously offering it dead and mangled flies. But our last five minutes were undisturbed, and the girl brought out with an effort the request she had tried to make all day.

"Whoever killed my father—and it was murder, Mr. Knox—whoever did it is going free to save a scandal. All my friends"—she smiled bitterly—"are afraid of the same thing. But I cannot sit quiet and think nothing can be done. I *must* know, and you are the only one who seems willing to try to find out."

So it was, that when I left the house a half hour later, I was committed. I had been commissioned by the girl I loved—for it had come to that—to clear her lover of her father's murder, and so give him back to her—not in so many words, but I was to follow up the crime, and the rest followed. And I was morally certain of two things—first, that her lover was not worthy of her, and second, and more to the point, that innocent or guilty, he was indirectly implicated in the crime.

I had promised her also to see Miss Letitia that day if I could, and I turned over the events of the preceding night as I walked toward the station, but I made nothing of them. One thing occurred to me, however. Bella had told Margery that I had been up all night. Could Bella—? But I dismissed the thought as absurd—Bella, who had scuttled to bed in a panic of fright, would never have dared the lower floor alone, and Bella, given all the courage in the world, could never have moved with the swiftness and light certainty of my midnight prowler. It had not been Bella.

But after all, I did not go to Bellwood. I met Hunter on my way to the station, and he turned around and walked with me.

"So you've lain down on the case!" I said, when we had gone a few steps without speaking.

He grumbled something unintelligible and probably unrepeatable.

"Of course," I persisted, "being a simple and uncomplicated case of suicide, there was nothing in it anyhow. If it had been a murder, under peculiar circumstances—"

He stopped and gripped my arm.

"For ten cents," he said gravely, "I would tell the chief and a few others what I think of them. And then I'd go out and get full."

"Not on ten cents!"

"I'm going out of the business," he stormed. "I'm going to drive a garbage wagon: it's cleaner than this job. Suicide! I never saw a cleaner case of—" He stopped suddenly. "Do you know Burton—of the *Times-Post?*"

"No, I've heard of him."

"Well, he's your man. They're dead against the ring, and Burton's been given the case. He's as sharp as a steel trap. You two get together."

He paused at a corner. "Good-bye," he said dejectedly. "I'm off to hunt some boys that have been stealing milk bottles. That's about my size, these days." He turned around, however, before he had gone many steps and came back.

"Wardrop has been missing since yesterday afternoon," he said. "That is, he thinks he's missing. We've got him all right."

I gave up my Bellwood visit for the time, and taking a car downtown, I went to the *Times-Post* office. The Monday morning edition was already under way, as far as the staff was concerned, and from the waiting room I could see three or four men, with their hats on, most of them rattling typewriters. Burton came in in a moment, a red-haired young fellow, with a short thick nose and a muggy skin. He was rather stocky in build, and the pugnacity of his features did not hide the shrewdness of his eyes.

I introduced myself, and at my name his perfunctory manner changed.

"Knox!" he said. "I called you last night over the phone."

"Can't we talk in a more private place?" I asked, trying to raise my voice above the confusion of the next room. In reply he took me into a tiny office, containing a desk and two chairs, and separated by an eight-foot partition from the other room.

"This is the best we have," he explained cheerfully. "Newspapers are agents of publicity, not privacy—if you don't care what you say."

I liked Burton. There was something genuine about him; after Wardrop's kid-glove finish, he was a relief.

"Hunter, of the detective bureau, sent me here," I proceeded, "about the Fleming case."

He took out his notebook. "You are the fourth today," he said. "Hunter himself, Lightfoot from Plattsburg, and McFeely here in town.

Well, Mr. Knox, are you willing now to put yourself on record that Fleming committed suicide?"

"No," I said firmly. "It is my belief that he was murdered."

"And that the secretary fellow, what's his name?—Wardrop?—that he killed him?"

"Possibly."

In reply Burton fumbled in his pocket and brought up a pasteboard box, filled with jeweler's cotton. Underneath was a small object, which he passed to me with care.

"I got it from the coroner's physician, who performed the autopsy," he said casually. "You will notice that it is a thirty-two, and that the revolver they took from Wardrop was a thirty-eight. Question, where's the other gun?"

I gave him back the bullet, and he rolled it around on the palm of his hand.

"Little thing, isn't it?" he said. "We think we're lords of creation, until we see a quarter-inch bichloride tablet, or a bit of lead like this. Look here." He dived into his pocket again and drew out a roll of ordinary brown paper. When he opened it, a bit of white chalk fell on the desk.

"Look at that," he said dramatically. "Kill an army with it, and they'd never know what struck them. Cyanide of potassium—and the druggist that sold it ought to be choked."

"Where did it come from?" I asked curiously. Burton smiled his cheerful smile.

"It's a beautiful case, all around," he said, as he got his hat. "I haven't had any Sunday dinner yet, and it's five o'clock. Oh—the cyanide? Clarkson, the cashier of the bank Fleming ruined, took a bite off that corner right there, this morning."

"Clarkson!" I exclaimed. "How is he?"

"God only knows," said Burton gravely, from which I took it Clarkson was dead.

Chapter XIII
Sizzling Metal

BURTON listened while he ate, and his cheerful comments were welcome enough after the depression of the last few days. I told him, after some hesitation, the whole thing, beginning with the Maitland pearls and ending with my drop down the dumbwaiter. I knew I was absolutely safe in doing so: there is no person to whom I would rather tell a secret than a newspaperman. He will go out of his way to keep it: he will lock it in the depth of his bosom, and keep it until seventy times seven. Also, you may threaten the rack or offer a larger salary; the seal does not come off his lips until the word is given. If then he makes a scare-head of it, and gets in three columns of space and as many photographs, it is his just reward.

So—I told Burton everything, and he ate enough beefsteak for two men, and missed not a word I said.

"The money Wardrop had in the grip—that's easy enough explained," he said. "Fleming used the Borough Bank to deposit state funds in. He must have known it was rotten: he and Clarkson were as thick as thieves. According to a time-honored custom in our land of the brave and home of the free, a state treasurer who is crooked can, in such a case, draw on such a bank without security, on his personal note, which is usually worth its value by the pound as old paper."

"And Fleming did that?"

"He did. Then things got bad at the Borough Bank. Fleming had had to divide with Schwartz and the Lord only knows who all, but it was Fleming who had to put in the money to avert a crash—the word crash being synonymous with scandal in this case. He scrapes together a paltry hundred thousand, which Wardrop gets at the capital, and brings on. Wardrop is robbed, or says he is; the bank collapses and Clarkson, driven to the wall, kills himself, just after Fleming is murdered. What does that sound like?"

"Like Clarkson!" I exclaimed. "And Clarkson knew Fleming was hiding at the White Cat!"

"Now, then, take the other theory," he said, pushing aside his cup. "Wardrop goes in to Fleming with a story that he has been robbed: Fleming gets crazy and attacks him. All that is in the morning—Friday. Now, then—Wardrop goes back there that night. Within twenty minutes after he enters the club he rushes out, and when Hunter follows him, he says he is looking for a doctor, to get cocaine for a gentleman upstairs. He is white and trembling. They go back together, and find you there, and Fleming dead. Wardrop tells two stories: first he says Fleming committed suicide just before he left. Then he changes it and says he was dead when he arrived there. He produces the weapon with which Fleming is supposed to have killed himself, and which, by the way, Miss Fleming identified yesterday as her father's. But there are two discrepancies. Wardrop practically admitted that he had taken that revolver from Fleming—not that night, but the morning before—during the quarrel."

"And the other discrepancy?"

"The bullet. Nobody ever fired a thirty-two bullet out of a thirty-eight caliber revolver—unless he was trying to shoot a double-compound curve. Now, then, who does it look like?"

"Like Wardrop," I confessed. "By Jove, they didn't both do it."

"And he didn't do it himself for two good reasons: he had no revolver that night, and there were no powder marks."

"And the eleven twenty-two, and Miss Maitland's disappearance?"

He looked at me with his quizzical smile.

"I'll have to have another steak, if I'm to settle that," he said. "I can only solve one murder on one steak. But disappearances are my specialty; perhaps, if I have a piece of pie and some cheese—"

But I got him away at last, and we walked together down the street.

"I can't quite see the old lady in it," he confessed. "She hadn't any grudge against Fleming, had she? Wouldn't be likely to forget herself temporarily and kill him?"

"Good Lord!" I said. "Why, she's sixty-five, and as timid and gentle a little old lady as ever lived."

"Curls?" he asked, turning his bright blue eyes on me.

"Yes," I admitted.

"Wouldn't be likely to have eloped with the minister or advertised for a husband, or anything like that?"

"You would have to know her to understand," I said resignedly. "But she didn't do any of those things, and she didn't run off to join a theatrical troupe. Burton, who do you think was in the Fleming house last night?"

"Lightfoot," he said succinctly.

He stopped under a streetlamp and looked at his watch.

"I believe I'll run over to the capital tonight," he said. "While I'm gone—I'll be back tomorrow night or the next morning—I wish you would do two things. Find Rosie O'Grady, or whatever her name is, and locate Carter. That's probably not his name, but it will answer for a while. Then get your friend Hunter to keep him in sight for a while, until I come back anyhow. I'm beginning to enjoy this; it's more fun than a picture puzzle. We're going to make the police department look like a kindergarten playing jackstraws."

"And the second thing I am to do?"

"Go to Bellwood and find out a few things. It's all well enough to say the old lady was a meek and timid person, but if you want to know her peculiarities, go to her neighbors. When people leave the beaten path, the neighbors always know it before the families."

He stopped before a drugstore.

"I'll have to pack for my little jaunt," he said, and purchased a toothbrush, which proved to be the extent of his preparations. We separated at the station, Burton to take his red hair and his toothbrush to Plattsburg, I to take a taxicab, and armed with a page torn from the classified directory to inquire at as many of the twelve Anderson's drugstores as might be necessary to locate Delia's gentleman friend, "the clerk," through him Delia, and through Delia, the mysterious Carter, "who was not really a butler."

It occurred to me somewhat tardily, that I knew nothing of Delia but her given name. A telephone talk with Margery was of little assistance: Delia had been a new maid, and if she had heard her other name, she had forgotten it.

I had checked off eight of the Andersons on my list, without result, and the taximeter showed something over nineteen dollars, when the driver drew up at the curb.

"Gentleman in the other cab is hailing you, sir," he said over his shoulder.

"The other cab?"

"The one that has been following us."

I opened the door and glanced behind. A duplicate of my cab stood perhaps fifty feet behind, and from it a familiar figure was slowly emerging, carrying on a high-pitched argument with the chauffeur. The figure stopped to read the taximeter, shook his fist at the chauffeur, and approached me, muttering audibly. It was Davidson.

"That liar and thief back there has got me rung up for nineteen dollars," he said, ignoring my amazement. "Nineteen dollars and forty cents! He must have the thing counting the revolutions of all four wheels!"

He walked around and surveyed my expense account, at the driver's elbow. Then he hit the meter a smart slap, but the figures did not change.

"Nineteen dollars!" he repeated, dazed. "Nineteen dollars and—look here," he called to his driver, who had brought the cab close, "it's only thirty cents here. Your clock's ten cents fast."

"But how—" I began.

"You back up to nineteen dollars and thirty cents," he persisted, ignoring me. "If you'll back up to twelve dollars, I'll pay it. That's all I've got." Then he turned on me irritably. "Good heavens, man," he exclaimed, "do you mean to tell me you've been to eight drugstores this Sunday evening and spent nineteen dollars and thirty cents, and haven't got a drink yet?"

"Do you think I'm after a drink?" I asked him. "Now look here, Davidson, I rather think you know what I am after. If you don't, it doesn't matter. But since you are coming along anyhow, pay your man off and come with me. I don't like to be followed."

He agreed without hesitation, borrowed eight dollars from me to augment his twelve and crawled in with me.

"The next address on the list is the right one," he said, as the man waited for directions. "I did the same round yesterday, but not being a plutocrat, I used the streetcars and my legs. And because you're a decent fellow and don't have to be chloroformed to have an idea injected, I'm going to tell you something. There were eleven roundsmen as well as the sergeant who heard me read the note I found at the Fleming house that night. You may have counted them through the window. A dozen plainclothesmen read it before morning. When the news of Mr. Fleming's mur— death came out, I thought this fellow Carter might know something, and I trailed Delia through this Mamie Brennan. When I got there I found Tom Brannigan and four other detectives sitting in the parlor, and Miss Delia, in a blue silk waist, making eyes at every mother's son of them."

I laughed in spite of my disappointment. Davidson leaned forward and closed the window at the driver's back. Then he squared around and faced me.

"Understand me, Mr. Knox," he said. "Mr. Fleming killed himself. You and I are agreed on that. Even if you aren't just convinced of it, I'm telling you, and—better let it drop, sir." Under his quiet manner I felt a threat: it served to rouse me.

"I'll let it drop when I'm through with it," I asserted, and got out my list of addresses.

"You'll let it drop because it's too hot to hold," he retorted, with the suspicion of a smile. "If you are determined to know about Carter, I can tell you everything that is necessary."

The chauffeur stopped his engine with an exasperated jerk and settled down in his seat, every line of his back bristling with irritation.

"I prefer learning from Carter himself."

He leaned back in his seat and produced an apple from the pocket of his coat.

"You'll have to travel some to do it, son," he said. "Carter left for parts unknown last night, taking with him enough money to keep him in comfort for some little time."

"Until all this blows over," I said bitterly.

"The trip was for the benefit of his health. He has been suffering—and is still suffering—from a curious lapse of memory." Davidson smiled at me engagingly. "He has entirely forgotten everything that occurred from the time he entered Mr. Fleming's employment, until that gentleman left home. I doubt if he will ever recover."

With Carter gone, his retreat covered by the police, supplied with funds from some problematical source, further search for him was worse than useless. In fact, Davidson strongly intimated that it might be dangerous and would certainly be unpleasant. I yielded ungraciously and ordered the cab to take me home. But on the way, I cursed my folly for not having followed this obvious clue earlier, and I wondered what this thing could be that Carter knew, that was at least surmised by various headquarters men, and yet was so carefully hidden from the world at large.

The party newspapers had come out that day with a signed statement from Mr. Fleming's physician in Plattsburg that he had been in ill health and inclined to melancholia for some time. The air was thick with rumors of differences with his party: the dust cloud covered everything; pretty soon it would settle and hide the tracks of those who had hurried to cover under its protection.

Davidson left me at a corner downtown. He turned to give me a parting admonition.

"There's an old axiom in the mills around here, 'Never sit down on a piece of metal until you spit on it.' If it sizzles, don't sit." He grinned. "Your best position just now, young man, is standing, with your hands over your head. Confidentially, there ain't anything within expectorating distance just now that ain't pretty well het up."

He left me with that, and I did not see him again until the night at the White Cat, when he helped put me through the transom. Recently, however, I have met him several times. He invariably mentions the eight dollars and his intention of repaying it. Unfortunately, the desire and the ability have not yet happened to coincide.

I took the evening train to Bellwood, and got there shortly after eight, in the midst of the Sunday evening calm, and the calm of a place like Bellwood is the peace of death without the hope of resurrection.

I walked slowly up the main street, which was lined with residences; the town relegated its few shops to less desirable neighborhoods. My first intention had been to see the Episcopal minister, but the rectory was dark, and a burst of organ music from the church near reminded me again of the Sunday evening services.

Promiscuous inquiry was not advisable. So far, Miss Jane's disappearance was known to very few, and Hunter had advised caution. I wandered up the street and turned at random to the right; a few doors ahead a newish red brick building proclaimed itself the post office, and gave the only sign of life in the neighborhood. It occurred to me that here inside was the one individual who, theoretically at least, in a small place always knows the idiosyncrasies of its people.

The door was partly open, for the spring night was sultry. The postmaster proved to be a one-armed veteran of the Civil War, and he was sorting rapidly the contents of a mailbag, emptied on the counter.

"No delivery tonight," he said shortly. "Sunday delivery, two to three."

"I suppose, then, I couldn't get a dollar's worth of stamps," I regretted.

He looked up over his glasses.

"We don't sell stamps on Sunday nights," he explained, more politely. "But if you're in a hurry for them—"

"I am," I lied. And after he had gotten them out, counting them with a wrinkled finger, and tearing them off the sheet with the deliberation of age, I opened a general conversation.

"I suppose you do a good bit of business here?" I asked. "It seems like a thriving place."

"Not so bad; big mail here sometimes. First of the quarter, when bills are coming round, we have a rush, and holidays and Easter we've got to hire an express wagon."

It was when I asked him about his empty sleeve, however, and he had told me that he lost his arm at Chancellorsville, that we became really friendly. When he said he had been a corporal in General Maitland's command, my path was one of ease.

"The Maitland ladies! I should say I do," he said warmly. "I've been fighting with Letitia Maitland as long as I can remember. That woman will scrap with the angel Gabriel at the resurrection, if he wakes her up before she's had her sleep out."

"Miss Jane is not that sort, is she?"

"Miss Jane? She's an angel—she is that. She could have been married a dozen times when she was a girl, but Letitia wouldn't have it. I was after her myself, forty-five years ago. This was the Maitland farm in those days, and my father kept a country store down where the railroad station is now."

"I suppose from that the Maitland ladies are wealthy."

"Wealthy! They don't know what they're worth—not that it matters a mite to Jane Maitland. She hasn't called her soul her own for so long that I guess the good Lord won't hold her responsible for it."

All of which was entertaining, but it was much like an old-fashioned seesaw; it kept going, but it didn't make much progress. But now at last we took a step ahead.

"It's a shameful thing," the old man pursued, "that a woman as old as Jane should have to get her letters surreptitiously. For more than a year now she's been coming here twice a week for her mail, and I've been keeping it for her. Rain or shine, Mondays and Thursdays, she's been coming, and a sight of letters she's been getting, too."

"Did she come last Thursday?" I asked overeagerly. The postmaster, all at once, regarded me with suspicion.

"I don't know whether she did or not," he said coldly, and my further attempts to beguile him into conversation failed. I pocketed my stamps, and by that time his resentment at my curiosity was fading. He followed me to the door, and lowered his voice cautiously.

"Any news of the old lady?" he asked. "It ain't generally known around here that she's missing, but Heppie, the cook there, is a relation of my wife's."

"We have no news," I replied, "and don't let it get around, will you?"

He promised gravely.

"I was tellin' the missus the other day," he said, "that there is an old walled-up cellar under the Maitland place. Have you looked there?" He was disappointed when I said we had, and I was about to go when he called me back.

"Miss Jane didn't get her mail on Thursday, but on Friday that niece of hers came for it—two letters, one from the city and one from New York."

"Thanks," I returned, and went out into the quiet street.

I walked past the Maitland place, but the windows were dark and the house closed. Haphazard inquiry being out of the question, I took the ten-o'clock train back to the city. I had learned little enough, and that little I was at a loss to know how to use. For why had Margery gone for Miss Jane's mail *after* the little lady was missing? And why did Miss Jane carry on a clandestine correspondence?

The family had retired when I got home except Fred, who called from his study to ask for a rhyme for mosque. I could not think of one and suggested that he change the word to "temple." At two o'clock he banged on my door in a temper, said he had changed the rhythm to fit, and now he couldn't find a rhyme for "temple!" I suggested "dimple" drowsily, whereat he kicked the panel of the door and went to bed.

Chapter XIV
A Walk in the Park

THE funeral occurred on Monday. It was an ostentatious affair, with a long list of honorary pallbearers, a picked corps of city firemen in uniform ranged around the casket, and enough money wasted in floral pillows and sheaves of wheat tied with purple ribbon, to have given all the hungry children in town a square meal.

Amid all this state Margery moved, stricken and isolated. She went to the cemetery with Edith, Miss Letitia having sent a message that, having never broken her neck to see the man living, she wasn't going to do it to see him dead. The music was very fine, and the eulogy spoke of this patriot who had served his country so long and so well. "Following the flag," Fred commented under his breath, "as long as there was an appropriation attached to it."

And when it was all over, we went back to Fred's until the Fleming house could be put into order again. It was the best place in the world for Margery, for, with the children demanding her attention and applause every minute, she had no time to be blue.

Mrs. Butler arrived that day, which made Fred suspicious that Edith's plan to bring her far antedated his consent. But she was there when we got home from the funeral, and after one glimpse at her thin face and hollow eyes, I begged Edith to keep her away from Margery, for that day at least.

Fortunately, Mrs. Butler was exhausted by her journey, and retired to her room almost immediately. I watched her slender figure go up the stairs, and, with her black trailing gown and colorless face, she was an embodiment of all that is lonely and helpless. Fred closed the door behind her and stood looking at Edith and me.

"I tell you, honey," he declared, "*that* brought into a cheerful home is sufficient cause for divorce. Isn't it, Jack?"

"She is ill," Edith maintained valiantly. "She is my cousin, too, which gives her some claim on me, and my guest, which gives her more."

"Lady-love," Fred said solemnly, "if you do not give me the key to the cellarette, I shall have a chill. And let me beg this of you: if I ever get tired of this life, and shuffle off my mortality in a lumberyard, or a political club, and you go around like that, I shall haunt you. I swear it."

"Shuffle off," I dared him. "I will see that Edith is cheerful and happy."

From somewhere above, there came a sudden crash, followed by the announcement, made by a scared housemaid, that Mrs. Butler had fainted. Fred sniffed as Edith scurried upstairs.

"Hipped," he said shortly. "For two cents I'd go up and give her a good whiff of ammonia—not this aromatic stuff, but the genuine article. That would make her sit up and take notice. Upon my word, I can't think what possessed Edith; these spineless, soft-spoken, timid women are leeches on one's sympathies."

But Mrs. Butler was really ill, and Margery insisted on looking after her. It was an odd coincidence, the widow of one state treasurer and the orphaned daughter of his successor; both men had died violent deaths, in each case when a boiling under the political lid had threatened to blow it off.

The boys were allowed to have their dinner with the family that evening, in honor of Mrs. Butler's arrival, and it was a riotous meal. Margery got back a little of her color. As I sat across from her, and watched her expressions change, from sadness to resignation, and even gradually to amusement at the boys' antics, I wondered just how much she knew, or suspected, that she refused to tell me.

I remembered a woman—a client of mine—who said that whenever she sat near a railroad track and watched an engine thundering toward her, she tortured herself by picturing a child on the track, and wondering whether, under such circumstances, she would risk her life to save the child.

I felt a good bit that way; I was firmly embarked on the case now, and I tortured myself with one idea. Suppose I should find Wardrop guilty, and I should find extenuating circumstances—what would I do? Publish the truth, see him hanged or imprisoned, and break Margery's heart? Or keep back the truth, let her marry him, and try to forget that I had had a hand in the whole wretched business?

After all, I decided to try to stop my imaginary train. Prove Wardrop innocent, I reasoned with myself, get to the bottom of this thing, and then—it would be man and man. A fair field and no favor. I suppose my proper attitude, romantically taken, was to consider Margery's engagement ring an indissoluble barrier. But this was not romance; I was fighting for my life happiness, and as to the ring—well, I am of the opinion that if a man really loves a woman, and thinks he can make her happy, he will tell her so if she is strung with engagement rings to the ends of her fingers. Dangerous doctrine? Well, this is not propaganda.

Tuesday found us all more normal. Mrs. Butler had slept some, and very commendably allowed herself to be tea'd and toasted in bed. The boys were started to kindergarten, after ten minutes of frenzied caphunting. Margery went with me along the hall when I started for the office.

"You have not learned anything?" she asked cautiously, glancing back to Edith, at the telephone calling the grocer frantically for the Monday morning supply of soap and starch.

"Not much," I evaded. "Nothing definite, anyhow. Margery, you are not going back to the Monmouth Avenue house again, are you?"

"Not just yet; I don't think I could. I suppose, later, it will have to be sold, but not at once. I shall go to Aunt Letitia's first."

"Very well," I said. "Then you are going to take a walk with me this afternoon in the park. I won't take no; you need the exercise, and I need—to talk to you," I finished lamely.

When she had agreed, I went to the office. It was not much after nine, but, to my surprise, Burton was already there. He had struck up an acquaintance with Miss Grant, the stenographer, and that usually frigid person had melted under the warmth of his red hair and his smile. She was telling him about her sister's baby having the whooping cough, when I went in.

"I wish I had studied law," he threw at me. " 'What shall it profit a man to become a lawyer and lose his own soul?' as the psalmist says. I like this ten-to-four business."

When we had gone into the inner office, and shut out Miss Grant and the whooping cough, he was serious instantly.

"Well," he said, sitting on the radiator and dangling his foot, "I guess we've got Wardrop for theft, anyhow."

"Theft?" I inquired.

"Well, larceny, if you prefer legal terms. I found where he sold the pearls—in Plattsburg, to a wholesale jeweler named, suggestively, Cashdollar."

"Then," I said conclusively, "if he took the pearls and sold them, as sure as I sit here, he took the money out of that Russia leather bag."

Burton swung his foot rhythmically against the pipes.

"I'm not so darned sure of it," he said calmly.

If he had any reason, he refused to give it. I told him, in my turn, of Carter's escape, aided by the police, and he smiled. "For a suicide it's causing a lot of excitement," he remarked. When I told him the little incident of the post office, he was much interested.

"The old lady's in it, somehow," he maintained. "She may have been lending Fleming money, for one thing. How do you know it wasn't her hundred thousand that was stolen?"

"I don't think she ever had the uncontrolled disposal of a dollar in her life."

"There's only one thing to do," Burton said finally, "and that is, find Miss Jane. If she's alive, she can tell something. I'll stake my fountain pen on that—and it's my dearest possession on earth, next to my mother. If Miss Jane is dead—well, somebody killed her, and it's time it was being found out."

"It's easy enough to say find her."

"It's easy enough to find her," he exploded. "Make a noise about it; send up rockets. Put a half-column ad in every paper in town, or—better still—give the story to the reporters and let them find her for you. I'd do it, if I wasn't tied up with this Fleming case. Describe her, how she walked, what she liked to eat, what she wore—in this case what she didn't wear. Lord, I wish I had that assignment! In forty-eight hours she will have been seen in a hundred different places, and one of them will be right. It will be a question of selection—that is, if she is alive."

In spite of his airy tone, I knew he was serious, and I felt he was right. The publicity part of it I left to him, and I sent a special delivery that morning to Bellwood, asking Miss Letitia to say nothing and to refer reporters to me. I had already been besieged with them, since my connection with the Fleming case, and a few more made no difference.

Burton attended to the matter thoroughly. The one-o'clock edition of an afternoon paper contained a short and vivid scarlet account of Miss Jane's disappearance. The evening editions were full, and while vague as to the manner of her leaving, were minute as regarded her personal appearance and characteristics.

To escape the threatened inundation of the morning paper men, I left the office early, and at four o'clock Margery and I stepped from a hill car into the park. She had been wearing a short, crepe-edged veil, but once away from the gaze of the curious, she took it off. I was glad to see she had lost the air of detachment she had worn for the last three days.

"Hold your shoulders well back," I directed, when we had found an isolated path, "and take long breaths. Try breathing in while I count ten."

She was very tractable—unusually so, I imagined, for her. We swung along together for almost a half hour, hardly talking. I was content merely to be with her, and the sheer joy of the exercise after her enforced confinement kept her silent. When she began to flag a little, I found a bench, and we sat down together. The bench had been lately painted, and although it seemed dry enough, I spread my handkerchief for her to sit on. Whereupon she called me "Sir Walter," and at the familiar jest we laughed like a pair of children.

I had made the stipulation that, for this one time, her father's death and her other troubles should be taboo, and we adhered to it religiously. A robin in the path was industriously digging out a worm; he had tackled a long one, and it was all he could manage. He took the available end in his beak and hopped back with the expression of one who sets his jaws and determines that this which should be, is to be. The worm stretched into a pinkish and attenuated line, but it neither broke nor gave.

"Horrid thing!" Margery said. "That is a disgraceful, heartless exhibition.

"The robin is a parent," I reminded her. "It is precisely the same as Fred, who twists, jerks, distorts and attenuates the English language in his magazine work, in order to have bread and ice cream and jelly cake for his two blooming youngsters."

She had taken off her gloves, and sat with her hands loosely clasped in her lap.

"I wish someone depended on me," she said pensively. "It's a terrible thing to feel that it doesn't matter to anyone—not vitally, anyhow—whether one is around or not. To have all my responsibilities taken away at once, and just to drift around, like this—oh, it's dreadful."

"You were going to be good," I reminded her.

"I didn't promise to be cheerful," she returned. "Besides my father, there was only one person in the world who cared about me, and I don't know where she is. Dear Aunt Jane!"

The sunlight caught the ring on her engagement finger, and she flushed suddenly as she saw me looking at it. We sat there for a while saying nothing; the long May afternoon was coming to a close. The paths began to fill with long lines of hurrying homeseekers, their day in office or factory at an end.

Margery got up at last and buttoned her coat. Then impulsively she held out her hand to me.

"You have been more than kind to me," she said hurriedly. "You have taken me into your home—and helped me through these dreadful days—and I will never forget it; never."

"I am not virtuous," I replied, looking down at her. "I couldn't help it. You walked into my life when you came to my office—was it only last week? The evil days are coming, I suppose, but just now nothing matters at all, save that you are you, and I am me."

She dropped her veil quickly, and we went back to the car. The prosaic world wrapped around us again; there was a heavy odor of restaurant coffee in the air; people bumped and jolted past us. To me they were only shadows; the real world was a girl in black and myself and the girl wore a betrothal ring which was not mine.

Chapter XV
Find the Woman

MRS. Butler came down to dinner that night. She was more cheerful than I had yet seen her, and she had changed her mournful garments to something a trifle less depressing. With her masses of fair hair dressed high, and her face slightly animated, I realized what I had not done before—that she was the wreck of a very beautiful woman. Frail as she was, almost shrinkingly timid in her manner, there were times when she drew up her tall figure in something like its former stateliness. She had beautiful eyebrows, nearly black and perfectly penciled; they were almost incongruous in her colorless face.

She was very weak; she used a cane when she walked, and after dinner, in the library, she was content to sit impassive, detached, propped with cushions, while Margery read to the boys in their night nursery and Edith embroidered.

Fred had been fussing over a play for some time, and he had gone to read it to some manager or other. Edith was already spending the royalties.

"We could go a little ways out of town," she was saying, "and we could have an automobile; Margery says theirs will be sold, and it will certainly be a bargain. Jack, are you laughing at me?"

"Certainly *not*," I replied gravely. "Dream on, Edith. Shall we train the boys as chauffeurs, or shall we buy in the Fleming man, also cheap."

"I am sure," Edith said aggrieved, "that it costs more for horse feed this minute for your gray, Jack, than it would for gasoline."

"But Lady Gray won't eat gasoline," I protested. "She doesn't like it."

Edith turned her back on me and sewed. Near me, Mrs. Butler had languidly taken up the paper; suddenly she dropped it, and when I stooped and picked it up I noticed she was trembling.

"Is it true?" she demanded. "Is Robert Clarkson dead?"

"Yes," I assented. "He has been dead since Sunday morning—a suicide."

Edith had risen and come over to her. But Mrs. Butler was not fainting.

"I'm glad, glad," she said. Then she grew weak and semi-hysterical, laughing and crying in the same breath. When she had been helped upstairs, for in her weakened state it had been more of a shock than we realized, Margery came down and we tried to forget the scene we had just gone through.

"I am glad Fred was not here," Edith confided to me. "Ellen is a lovely woman, and as kind as she is mild; but in one of her—attacks, she is a little bit trying."

It was strange to contrast the way in which the two women took their similar bereavements. Margery represented the best type of normal American womanhood; Ellen Butler the neurasthenic; she demanded everything by her very helplessness and timidity. She was a constant drain on Edith's ready sympathy. That night, while I closed the house—Fred had not come in—I advised her to let Mrs. Butler go back to her sanatorium.

At twelve thirty I was still downstairs; Fred was out, and I waited for him, being curious to know the verdict on the play. The bell rang a few minutes before one, and I went to the door; someone in the vestibule was tapping the floor impatiently with his foot. When I opened the door, I was surprised to find that the late visitor was Wardrop.

He came in quietly, and I had a chance to see him well, under the hall light; the change three days had made was shocking. His eyes were sunk deep in his head, his reddened lids and twitching mouth told of little sleep, of nerves ready to snap. He was untidy, too, and a three days' beard hardly improved him.

"I'm glad it's you," he said, by way of greeting. "I was afraid you'd have gone to bed."

"It's the top of the evening yet," I replied perfunctorily, as I led the way into the library. Once inside, Wardrop closed the door and looked around him like an animal at bay.

"I came here," he said nervously, looking at the windows, "because I had an idea you'd keep your head. Mine's gone; I'm either crazy, or I'm on my way there."

"Sit down, man." I pushed a chair to him. "You don't look as if you have been in bed for a couple of nights."

He went to each of the windows and examined the closed shutters before he answered me.

"I haven't. You wouldn't go to bed either, if you thought you would never wake up."

"Nonsense."

"Well, it's true enough. Knox, there are people following me wherever I go; they eat where I eat; if I doze in my chair they come into my dreams!" He stopped there; then he laughed a little wildly. "That last isn't sane, but it's true. There's a man across the street now, eating an apple under a lamppost."

"Suppose you *are* under surveillance," I said. "It's annoying to have a detective following you around, but it's hardly serious. The police say now that Mr. Fleming killed himself; that was your own contention."

He leaned forward in his chair and, resting his hands on his knees, gazed at me somberly.

"Suppose I say he didn't kill himself?" Slowly. "Suppose I say he was murdered? Suppose—good God—suppose I killed him myself?"

I drew back in stupefaction, but he hurried on.

"For the last two days I've been wondering—if I did it! He hadn't any weapon; I had one, his. I hated him that day; I had tried to save him, and couldn't. My God, Knox, I might have gone off my head and done it—and not remember it. There have been cases like that."

His condition was pitiable. I looked around for some whisky, but the best I could do was a little port on the sideboard. When I came back he was sitting with bent head, his forehead on his palms.

"I've thought it all out," he said painfully. "My mother had spells of emotional insanity. Perhaps I went there, without knowing it, and killed him. I can see him, in the night, when I daren't sleep, toppling over onto that table, with a bullet wound in his head, and I am in the room, and I have his revolver in my pocket!"

"You give me your word you have no conscious recollection of hearing a shot fired."

"My word before Heaven," he said fervently. "But I tell you, Knox, he had no weapon. No one came out of that room as I went in and yet he was only swaying forward, as if I had shot him one moment, and caught him as he fell, the next. I was dazed; I don't remember yet what I told the police."

The expression of fear in his eyes was terrible to see. A gust of wind shook the shutters, and he jumped almost out of his chair.

"You will have to be careful," I said. "There have been cases where men confessed murders they never committed, driven by Heaven knows what method of undermining their mental resistance. You expose your imagination to 'third degree' torture of your own invention, and in two days more you will be able to add full details of the crime."

"I knew you would think me crazy," he put in, a little less somberly, "but just try it once: sit in a room by yourself all day and all night, with detectives watching you; sit there and puzzle over a murder of a man you are suspected of killing; you know you felt like killing him, and you have a revolver, and he is shot. Wouldn't you begin to think as I do?"

"Wardrop," I asked, trying to fix his wavering eyes with mine, "do you own a thirty-two-caliber revolver?"

"Yes."

I was startled beyond any necessity, under the circumstances. Many people have thirty-twos.

"That is, I had," he corrected himself. "It was in the leather bag that was stolen at Bellwood."

"I can relieve your mind of one thing," I said. "If your revolver was stolen with the leather bag, you had nothing to do with the murder. Fleming was shot with a thirty-two." He looked first incredulous, then relieved.

"Now, then," I pursued, "suppose Mr. Fleming had an enemy, a relentless one who would stoop to anything to compass his ruin. In his position he would be likely to have enemies. This person, let us say, knows what you carry in your grip, and steals it, taking away the funds that would have helped to keep the lid on Fleming's mismanagement for a time. In the grip is your revolver; would you know it again?"

He nodded affirmatively.

"This person—this enemy—finds the revolver, pockets it and at the first opportunity, having ruined Fleming, proceeds humanely to put him out of his suffering. Is it far-fetched?"

"There were a dozen—a hundred—people who would have been glad to ruin him." His gaze wavered again suddenly. It was evident that I had renewed an old train of thought.

"For instance?" I suggested, but he was on guard again.

"You forget one thing, Knox," he said, after a moment. "There was nobody else who could have shot him: the room was empty."

"Nonsense," I replied. "Don't forget the warehouse."

"The warehouse!"

"There is no doubt in my mind that he was shot from there. He was facing the open window, sitting directly under the light, writing. A shot fired through a broken pane of one of the warehouse windows would meet every requirement of the case: the empty room, the absence of powder marks—even the fact that no shot was heard. There was a report, of course, but the noise in the clubhouse and the thunderstorm outside covered it."

"By George!" he exclaimed. "The warehouse, of course. I never thought of it." He was relieved, for some reason.

"It's a question now of how many people knew he was at the club, and which of them hated him enough to kill him."

"Clarkson knew it," Wardrop said, "but he didn't do it."

"Why?"

"Because it was he who came to the door of the room while the detectives and you and I were inside, and called Fleming."

I pulled out my pocketbook and took out the scrap of paper which Margery had found pinned to the pillow in her father's bedroom. "Do you know what that means?" I asked, watching Wardrop's face. "That was found in Mr. Fleming's room two days after he left home. A similar scrap was found in Miss Jane Maitland's room when she disappeared. When Fleming was murdered, he was writing a letter; he said: 'The figures have followed me here.' When we know what those figures mean, Wardrop, we know why he was killed and who did it."

He shook his head hopelessly.

"I do not know," he said, and I believed him. He had gotten up and taken his hat, but I stopped him inside the door.

"You can help this thing in two ways," I told him. "I am going to give you something to do: you will have less time to be morbid. Find out, if you can, all about Fleming's private life in the last dozen years, especially the last three. See if there are any women mixed up in it, and try to find out something about this eleven twenty-two."

"Eleven twenty-two," he repeated, but I had not missed his change of expression when I said women.

"Also," I went on, "I want you to tell me who was with you the night you tried to break into the house at Bellwood."

He was taken completely by surprise: when he had gathered himself together his perplexity was overdone.

"With me!" he repeated. "I was alone, of course."

"I mean—the woman at the gate."

He lost his composure altogether then. I put my back against the door and waited for him to get himself in hand.

"There was a woman," I persisted, "and what is more, Wardrop, at this minute you believe she took your Russia leather bag and left a substitute."

He fell into the trap.

"But she couldn't," he quavered. "I've thought until my brain is going, and I don't see how she could have done it."

He became sullen when he saw what he had done, refused any more information, and left almost immediately.

Fred came soon after, and in the meantime I had made some notes like this:

1. Examine warehouse and yard.
2. Attempt to trace Carter.
3. See station agent at Bellwood.
4. Inquire Wardrop's immediate past.
5. Take Wardrop to Dr. Anderson, the specialist.
6. Send Margery violets.

Chapter XVI
Eleven Twenty-two Again

BURTON'S idea of exploiting Miss Jane's disappearance began to bear fruit the next morning. I went to the office early, anxious to get my more pressing business out of the way, to have the afternoon with Burton to inspect the warehouse. At nine o'clock came a call from the morgue.

"Small woman, well dressed, gray hair?" I repeated. "I think I'll go up and see. Where was the body found?"

"In the river at Monica Station," was the reply. "There is a scar diagonally across the cheek to the corner of the mouth."

"A fresh injury?"

"No, an old scar."

With a breath of relief I said it was not the person we were seeking and tried to get down to work again. But Burton's prophecy had been right. Miss Jane had been seen in a hundred different places: one perhaps was right; which one?

A reporter for the *Eagle* had been working on the case all night: he came in for a more detailed description of the missing woman, and he had a theory, to fit which he was quite ready to cut and trim the facts.

"It's Rowe," he said confidently. "You can see his hand in it right through. I was put on the Benson kidnapping case. You remember, the boy who was kept for three months in a deserted lumber camp in the mountains? Well, sir, every person in the Benson house swore that youngster was in bed at midnight, when the house was closed for the night. Every door and window bolted in the morning, and the boy gone. When we found Rowe—after the mother had put on mourning—and found the kid, ten pounds heavier than he had been before he was abducted, and strutting around like a turkey cock, Rowe told us that he and the boy took in the theater that night, and were there for the first act. How did he do it? He offered to take the boy to the show if he would pretend to go to bed, and then slide down a porch pillar and meet him. The boy didn't want to go home when we found him."

"There can't be any mistake about the time in this case," I commented. "I saw her myself after eleven, and said good night."

The *Eagle* man consulted his notebook. "Oh, yes," he asked, "did she have a diagonal cut across her cheek?"

"No," I said for the second time.

My next visitor was a cabman. On the night in question he had taken a small and a very nervous old woman to the Omega ferry. She appeared excited and almost forgot to pay him. She carried a small satchel, and wore a black veil. What did she look like? She had gray hair, and she seemed to have a scar on her face that drew the corner of her mouth.

At ten o'clock I telephoned Burton: "For Heaven's sake," I said, "if anybody has lost a little old lady in a black dress, wearing a black veil, carrying a satchel, and with a scar diagonally across her cheek from her eye to her mouth, I can tell them all about her, and where she is now."

"That's funny," he said. "We're stirring up the pool and bringing up things we didn't expect. The police have been looking for that woman quietly for a week: she's the widow of a coal baron, and her son-in-law's under suspicion of making away with her."

"Well, he didn't," I affirmed. "She committed suicide from an Omega ferry boat and she's at the morgue this morning."

"Bully," he returned. "Keep on; you'll get lots of clues, and remember one will be right."

It was not until noon, however, that anything concrete developed. In the two hours between, I had interviewed seven more people. I had followed the depressing last hours of the coal baron's widow, and jumped with her, mentally, into the black river that night. I had learned of a small fairish-haired girl who had tried to buy cyanide of potassium at three drugstores on the same street, and of a tall, light woman who had taken a room for three days at a hotel and was apparently demented.

At twelve, however, my reward came. Two men walked in, almost at the same time: one was a motorman, in his official clothes, brass buttons and patches around the pockets. The other was a taxicab driver. Both had the uncertain gait of men who by occupation are unused to anything stationary under them, and each eyed the other suspiciously.

The motorman claimed priority by a nose, so I took him first into my private office. His story, shorn of his own opinions at the time and later, was as follows:

On the night in question, Thursday of the week before, he took his car out of the barn for the eleven-o'clock run. Barney was his conductor. They went from the barn, at Hays Street, downtown, and then started out for Wynton. The controller blew out, and two or three things went wrong: all told they lost forty minutes. They got to Wynton at five minutes after two; their time there was one twenty-five.

The car went to the bad again at Wynton, and he and Barney tinkered with it until two forty. They got it in shape to go back to the barn, but that was all. Just as they were ready to start, a passenger got on, a woman, alone—a small woman with a brown veil. She wore a black dress or a suit—he was vague about everything but the color, and he noticed her especially because she was fidgety and excited. Half a block farther a man boarded the car, and sat across from the woman. Barney said afterward that the man tried twice to speak to the woman, but she looked away each time. No, he hadn't heard what he said.

The man got out when the car went into the barn, but the woman stayed on. He and Barney got another car and took it out, and the woman went with them. She made a complete round-trip this time, going out to Wynton and back to the end of the line downtown. It was just daylight when she got off at last, at First and Day Streets.

Asked if he had thought at the time that the veiled woman was young or old, he said he had thought she was probably middle-aged. Very young or very old women would not put in the night riding in a streetcar. Yes, he had had men who rode around a couple of times at night, mostly to sober up before they went home. But he never saw a woman do it before.

I took his name and address and thanked him. The chauffeur came next, and his story was equally pertinent.

On the night of the previous Thursday he had been engaged to take a sick woman from a downtown hotel to a house at Bellwood. The woman's husband was with her, and they went slowly to avoid jolting. It was after twelve when he drove away from the house and started home. At a corner—he did not know the names of the streets—a woman hailed the cab and asked him if he belonged in Bellwood or was going to the city. She had missed the last train. When he told her he was going into town, she promptly engaged him, and showed him where to wait for her, a narrow road off the main street.

"I waited an hour," he finished, "before she came; I dropped to sleep or I would have gone without her. About half-past one she came along, and a gentleman with her. He put her in the cab, and I took her to the city. When I saw in the paper that a lady had disappeared from Bellwood that night, I knew right off that it was my party."

"Would you know the man again?"

"I would know his voice, I expect, sir; I could not see much: he wore a slouch hat and had a traveling bag of some kind."

"What did he say to the woman?" I asked.

"He didn't say much. Before he closed the door, he said, 'You have put me in a terrible position,' or something like that. From the traveling bag and all, I thought perhaps it was an elopement, and the lady had decided to throw him down."

"Was it a young woman or an old one?" I asked again. This time the cabby's tone was assured.

"Young," he asserted, "slim and quick: dressed in black, with a black veil. Soft voice. She got out at Market Square, and I have an idea she took a crosstown car there."

"I hardly think it was Miss Maitland," I said. "She was past sixty, and besides—I don't think she went that way. Still it is worth following up. Is that all?"

He fumbled in his pocket, and after a minute brought up a small black pocketbook and held it out to me. It was the small coin purse out of a leather handbag.

"She dropped this in the cab, sir," he said. "I took it home to the missus—not knowing what else to do with it. It had no money in it—only that bit of paper."

I opened the purse and took out a small white card, without engraving. On it was written in a pencil the figures:

C 1122

Chapter XVII
His Second Wife

WHEN the cabman had gone, I sat down and tried to think things out. As I have said many times in the course of this narrative, I lack imagination: moreover, a long experience of witnesses in court had taught me the unreliability of average observation. The very fact that two men swore to having taken solitary women away from Bellwood that night, made me doubt if either one had really seen the missing woman.

Of the two stories, the taxicab driver's was the more probable, as far as Miss Jane was concerned. Knowing her childlike nature, her timidity, her shrinking and shamefaced fear of the dark, it was almost incredible that she would walk the three miles to Wynton, voluntarily, and from there lose herself in the city. Besides, such an explanation would not fit the bloodstains, or the fact that she had gone, as far as we could find out, in her nightclothes.

Still—she had left the village that night, either by cab or on foot. If the driver had been correct in his time, however, the taxicab was almost eliminated; he said the woman got into the cab at one thirty. It was between one thirty and one forty-five when Margery heard the footsteps in the attic.

I think for the first time it came to me, that day, that there was at least a possibility that Miss Jane had not been attacked, robbed or injured: that she had left home voluntarily, under stress of great excitement. But if she had, why? The mystery was hardly less for being stripped of its gruesome details. Nothing in my knowledge of the missing woman gave me a clue. I had a vague hope that, if she had gone voluntarily, she would see the newspapers and let us know where she was.

To my list of exhibits I added the purse with its enclosure. The secret drawer of my desk now contained, besides the purse, the slip marked eleven twenty-two that had been pinned to Fleming's pillow; the similar scrap found over Miss Jane's mantel; the pearl I had found on the floor of the closet; and the cyanide, which, as well as the bullet, Burton had given me. Add to these the still tender place on my head where Wardrop had almost brained me with a chair, and a blue ankle, now becoming spotted with yellow, where I had fallen down the dumb-waiter, and my list of visible reminders of the double mystery grew to eight.

I was not proud of the part I had played. So far, I had blundered, it seemed to me, at every point where a blunder was possible. I had fallen over folding chairs and down a shaft; I had been a half-hour too late to save Allan Fleming; I had been up and awake, and Miss Jane had got out of the house under my very nose. Last, and by no means least, I had waited thirty-five years to find the right woman, and when I found her, someone else had won her. I was in the depths that day when Burton came in.

He walked into the office jauntily and presented Miss Grant with a club sandwich neatly done up in waxed paper. Then he came into my private room and closed the door behind him.

"Avaunt, dull care!" he exclaimed, taking in my dejected attitude and exhibits on the desk at a glance. "Look up and grin, my friend." He had his hands behind him.

"Don't be a fool," I snapped. "I'll not grin unless I feel like it."

"Grin, darn you," he said, and put something on the desk in front of me. It was a Russia leather bag.

"*The* leather bag!" he pointed proudly.

"Where did you get it?" I exclaimed, incredulous. Burton fumbled with the lock while he explained.

"It was found in Boston," he said. "How do you open the thing, anyhow?"

It was not locked, and I got it open in a minute. As I had expected, it was empty.

"Then—perhaps Wardrop was telling the truth," I exclaimed. "By Jove, Burton, he was robbed by the woman in the cab, and he can't tell about her on account of Miss Fleming! She made a haul, for certain."

I told him then of the two women who had left Bellwood on the night of Miss Jane's disappearance, and showed him the purse and its enclosure. The C puzzled him as it had me. "It might be anything," he said as he gave it back, "from a book, chapter and verse in the Bible to a prescription for rheumatism at a drugstore. As to the lady in the cab, I think perhaps you are right," he said, examining the interior of the bag, where Wardrop's name in ink told its story. "Of course, we have only Wardrop's word that he brought the bag to Bellwood; if we grant that we can grant the rest—that he was robbed, that the thief emptied the bag, and either took it or shipped it to Boston."

"How on earth did you get it?"

"It was a coincidence. There have been a shrewd lot of baggage thieves in two or three eastern cities lately, mostly Boston. The method, the police say, was something like this—one of them, the chief of the gang, would get a wagon, dress like an expressman and go around the depots looking at baggage. He would make a mental note of the numbers, go away and forge a check to match, and secure the pieces he had taken a fancy to. Then he merely drove around to headquarters, and the trunk was rifled. The police got on, raided the place, and found, among others, our Russia leather bag. It was shipped back, empty, to the address inside, at Bellwood."

"At Bellwood? Then how—"

"It came while I was lunching with Miss Letitia," he said easily. "We're very chummy—thick as thieves. What I want to know is"—disregarding my astonishment—"where is the hundred thousand?"

"Find the woman."

"Did you ever hear of Anderson, the nerve specialist?" he asked, without apparent relevancy.

"I have been thinking of him," I answered. "If we could get Wardrop there, on some plausible excuse, it would take Anderson about ten minutes with his instruments and experimental psychology, to know everything Wardrop ever forgot."

"I'll go on one condition," Burton said, preparing to leave. "I'll promise to get Wardrop and have him on the spot at two o'clock tomorrow, if you'll promise me one thing: if Anderson fixes me with his eye, and I begin to look dotty and tell about my past life, I want you to take me by the flap of my ear and lead me gently home."

"I promise," I said, and Burton left.

The recovery of the bag was only one of the many astonishing things that happened that day and the following night. Hawes, who knew little of what it all meant, and disapproved a great deal, ended that afternoon by locking himself, blinking furiously, in his private office. To Hawes any practice that was not lucrative was bad practice. About four o'clock, when I had shut myself away from the crowd in the outer office, and was letting Miss Grant take their depositions as to when and where they had seen a little old lady, probably demented, wandering around the streets, a woman came who refused to be turned away.

"Young woman," I heard her say, speaking to Miss Grant, "he may have important business, but I guess mine's just a little more so."

I interfered then, and let her come in. She was a woman of medium height, quietly dressed, and fairly handsome. My first impression was favorable; she moved with a certain dignity, and she was not laced, crimped or made up. I am more sophisticated now; The Lady Who Tells Me Things says that the respectable women nowadays, out-rouge, out-crimp and out-lace the unrespectable.

However, the illusion was gone the moment she began to speak. Her voice was heavy, throaty, expressionless. She threw it like a weapon: I am perfectly honest in saying that for a moment the surprise of her voice outweighed the remarkable thing she was saying.

"I am Mrs. Allan Fleming," she said, with a certain husky defiance.

"I beg your pardon," I said, after a minute. "You mean—the Allan Fleming who just died?"

She nodded. I could see she was unable, just then, to speak. She had nerved herself to the interview, but it was evident that there was a real grief. She fumbled for a black-bordered handkerchief, and her throat worked convulsively. I saw now that she was in mourning.

"Do you mean," I asked incredulously, "that Mr. Fleming married a second time?"

"He married me three years ago, in Plattsburg. I came from there last night. I—couldn't leave before."

"Does Miss Fleming know about this second marriage?"

"No. Nobody knew about it. I have had to put up with a great deal, Mr. Knox. It's a hard thing for a woman to know that people are talking about her, and all the time she's married as tight as ring and book can do it."

"I suppose," I hazarded, "if that is the case, you have come about the estate."

"Estate!" Her tone was scornful. "I guess I'll take what's coming to me, as far as that goes—and it won't be much. No, I came to ask what they mean by saying Allan Fleming killed himself."

"Don't you think he did?"

"I know he did not," she said tensely. "Not only that: I know who did it. It was Schwartz—Henry Schwartz."

"Schwartz! But what on earth—"

"You don't know Schwartz," she said grimly. "I was married to him for fifteen years. I took him when he had a saloon in the Fifth Ward, at Plattsburg. The next year he was alderman: I didn't expect in those days to see him riding around in an automobile—not but what he was malting money—Henry Schwartz is a moneymaker. That's why he's boss of the state now."

"And you divorced him?"

"He was a brute," she said vindictively. "He wanted me to go back to him, and I told him I would rather die. I took a big house, and kept bachelor suites for gentlemen. Mr. Fleming lived there, and—he married me three years ago. He and Schwartz had to stand together, but they hated each other."

"Schwartz?" I meditated. "Do you happen to know if Senator Schwartz was in Plattsburg at the time of the mur—of Mr. Fleming's death?"

"He was here in Manchester."

"He had threatened Mr. Fleming's life?"

"He had already tried to kill him, the day we were married. He stabbed him twice, but not deep enough."

I looked at her in wonder. For this woman, not extraordinarily handsome, two men had fought and one had died—according to her story.

"I can prove everything I say," she went on rapidly. "I have letters from Mr. Fleming telling me what to do in case he was shot down; I have papers—canceled notes—that would put Schwartz in the penitentiary—that is," she said cunningly, "I did have them. Mr. Fleming took them away."

"Aren't you afraid for yourself?" I asked.

"Yes, I'm afraid—afraid he'll get me back yet. It would please him to see me crawl back on my knees."

"But—he cannot force you to go back to him."

"Yes, he can," she shivered. From which I knew she had told me only a part of her story.

After all she had nothing more to tell. Fleming had been shot; Schwartz had been in the city about the Borough Bank; he had threatened Fleming before, but a political peace had been patched; Schwartz knew the White Cat. That was all.

Before she left she told me something I had not known.

"I know a lot about inside politics," she said, as she got up. "I have seen the state divided up with the roast at my table, and served around with the dessert, and I can tell you something you don't know about your White Cat. A back staircase leads to one of the upstairs rooms, and shuts off with a locked door. It opens below, out a side entrance, not supposed to be used. Only a few know of it. Henry Butler was found dead at the foot of that staircase."

"He shot himself, didn't he?"

"The police said so," she replied, with her grim smile. "There is such a thing as murdering a man by driving him to suicide."

She wrote an address on a card and gave it to me.

"Just a minute," I said, as she was about to go. "Have you ever heard Mr. Fleming speak of the Misses Maitland?"

"They were—his first wife's sisters. No, he never talked of them, but I believe, just before he left Plattsburg, he tried to borrow some money from them."

"And failed?"

"The oldest one telegraphed the refusal, collect," she said, smiling faintly.

"There is something else," I said. "Did you ever hear of the number eleven twenty-two?"

"No—or—why, yes—" she said. "It is the number of my house."

It seemed rather ridiculous, when she had gone, and I sat down to think it over. It was anticlimax, to say the least. If the mysterious number meant only the address of this very ordinary woman, then—it was probable her story of Schwartz was true enough. But I could not reconcile myself to it, nor could I imagine Schwartz, with his great bulk, skulking around pinning scraps of paper to pillows.

It would have been more like the fearlessness and passion of the man to have shot Fleming down in the statehouse corridor, or on the street, and to have trusted to his influence to set him free. For the first time it occurred to me that there was something essentially feminine in the revenge of the figures that had haunted the dead man.

I wondered if Mrs. Fleming had told me all, or only half the truth.

That night, at the most peaceful spot I had ever known, Fred's home, occurred another inexplicable affair, one that left us all with racked nerves and listening, fearful ears.

Chapter XVIII
Edith's Cousin

THAT was to be Margery's last evening at Fred's. Edith had kept her as long as she could, but the girl felt that her place was with Miss Letitia. Edith was desolate.

"I don't know what I am going to do without you, she said that night when we were all together in the library, with a wood fire, for light and coziness more than heat. Margery was sitting before the fire, and while the others talked she sat mostly silent, looking into the blaze.

The May night was cold and rainy, and Fred had been reading us a poem he had just finished, receiving with indifference my comment on it, and basking in Edith's rapture.

"Do you know yourself what it is about?" I inquired caustically.

"If it's about anything, it isn't poetry," he replied. "Poetry appeals to the ear. It is primarily sensuous. If it is more than that it ceases to be poetry and becomes verse."

Edith yawned.

"I'm afraid I'm getting old," she said. "I'm getting the nap habit after dinner. Fred, run up, will you, and see if Katie put blankets over the boys?"

Fred stuffed his poem in his pocket and went resignedly upstairs. Edith yawned again, and prepared to retire to the den for forty winks.

"If Ellen decides to come downstairs," she called back over her shoulder, "please come and wake me. She said she felt better and might come down."

At the door she turned, behind Margery's back, and made me a sweeping and comprehensive signal. She finished it off with a double wink, Edith having never been able to wink one eye alone, and crossing the hall, closed the door of the den with an obtrusive bang.

Margery and I were alone. The girl looked at me, smiled a little, and drew a long breath.

"It's queer about Edith," I said. "I never before knew her to get drowsy after dinner. If she were not beyond suspicion, I would think it a deep-laid scheme, and she and Fred sitting and holding hands in a corner somewhere."

"But why—a scheme?" She had folded her hands in her lap, and the eternal ring sparkled malignantly.

"They might think I wanted to talk to you," I suggested.

"To me?"

"To you. The fact is, I do."

Perhaps I was morbid about the ring: it seemed to me she lifted her hand and looked at it.

"It's drafty in here. Don't you think so?" she asked suddenly, looking back of her. Probably she had not meant it, but I got up and closed the door into the hall. When I came back I took the chair next to her, and for a moment we said nothing. The log threw out tiny red devil sparks, and the clock chimed eight, very slowly.

"Harry Wardrop was here last night," I said, poking down the log with my heel.

"Here?"

"Yes. I suppose I was wrong, but I did not say you were here."

She turned and looked at me closely, out of the most beautiful eyes I ever saw.

"I'm not afraid to see him," she said proudly, "and he ought not to be afraid to see me."

"I want to tell you something before you see him. Last night, before he came, I thought that—well, that at least he knew something of—the things we want to know."

"Yes?"

"In justice to him, and because I want to fight fair, I tell you tonight that I don't believe he knows anything about your father's death, and that I believe he was robbed that night at Bellwood."

"What about the pearls he sold at Plattsburg?" she asked suddenly.

"I think when the proper time comes, he will tell about that too, Margery." I did not notice my use of her name until too late. If she heard, she failed to resent it. "After all, if you love him, hardly anything else matters, does it? How do we know but that he was in trouble, and that Aunt Jane herself gave them to him?"

She looked at me with a little perplexity.

"You plead his case very well," she said. "Did he ask you to speak to me?"

"I won't run a race with a man who is lame," I said quietly. "Ethically, I ought to go away and leave you to your dreams, but I am not going to do it. If you love Wardrop as a woman ought to love the man she marries, then marry him and I hope you will be happy. If you don't—no, let me finish. I have made up my mind to clear him if I can; to bring him to you with a clear slate. Then, I know it is audacious, but I am going to come, too, and—I'm going to plead for myself then, unless you send me away."

She sat with her head bent, her color coming and going nervously. Now she looked up at me with what was the ghost of a smile.

"It sounds like a threat," she said in a low voice. "And you—I wonder if you always get what you want?"

Then, of course, Fred came in, and fell over a hassock looking for matches. Edith opened the door of the den and called him to her irritably, but Fred declined to leave the wood fire, and settled down in his easy chair. After a while Edith came over and joined us, but she snubbed Fred the entire evening, to his bewilderment. And when conversation lagged, during the evening that followed, I tried to remember what I had said, and knew I had done very badly. Only one thing cheered me: she had not been angry, and she had understood. Blessed be the woman that understands!

We broke up for the night about eleven. Mrs. Butler had come down for a while, and had even played a little, something of Tschaikovsky's, a singing, plaintive theme that brought sadness back into Margery's face, and made me think, for no reason, of a wet country road and a plodding, back-burdened peasant.

Fred and I sat in the library for a while after the rest had gone, and I told him a little of what I had learned that afternoon.

"A second wife!" he said, "and a primitive type, eh? Well, did she shoot him, or did Schwartz? The Lady or the Democratic Tiger?"

"The Tiger," I said firmly.

"The Lady," said Fred, with equal assurance.

Fred closed the house with his usual care. It required the combined efforts of the maids followed up by Fred, to lock the windows, it being his confident assertion that in seven years of keeping house, he had never failed to find at least one unlocked window.

On that night, I remember, he went around with his usual scrupulous care. Then we went up to bed, leaving a small light at the telephone in the lower hall—nothing else.

The house was a double one, built around a square hall below, which served the purpose of a general sitting room. From the front door a short, narrow hall led back to this, with a room on either side, and from it doors led into the rest of the lower floor. At one side the stairs took the ascent easily, with two stops for landings, and upstairs the bedrooms opened from a similar, slightly smaller square hall. The staircase to the third floor went up from somewhere back in the nursery wing.

My bedroom was over the library, and Mrs. Butler and Margery Fleming had connecting rooms, across the hall. Fred and Edith slept in the nursery wing, so they would be near the children. In the square upper hall there was a big reading table, a lamp, and some comfortable chairs. Here, when they were alone, Fred read aloud the evening paper, or his latest short story, and Edith's sewing basket showed how she put in what women miscall their leisure.

I did not go to sleep at once. Naturally the rather vital step I had taken in the library insisted on being considered and almost regretted. I tried reading myself to sleep, and when that failed, I tried the soothing combination of a cigarette and a book. That worked like a charm; the last thing I remember is of holding the cigarette in a death grip as I lay with my pillows propped back of me, my head to the light, and a delightful languor creeping over me.

I was wakened by the pungent acrid smell of smoke, and I sat up and blinked my eyes open. The side of the bed was sending up a steady column of gray smoke, and there was a smart crackle of fire under me somewhere. I jumped out of bed and saw the trouble instantly. My cigarette had dropped from my hand, still lighted, and as is the way with cigarettes, determined to burn to the end. In so doing it had fired my bed, the rug under the bed and pretty nearly the man on the bed.

It took some sharp work to get it all out without rousing the house. Then I stood amid the wreckage and looked ruefully at Edith's pretty room. I could see, mentally, the spot of water on the library ceiling the next morning, and I could hear Fred's strictures on the heedlessness and indifference to property of bachelors in general and me in particular.

Three pitchers of water on the bed had made it an impossible couch. I put on a dressing gown, and, with a blanket over my arm, I went out to hunt some sort of place to sleep. I decided on the davenport in the hall just outside, and as quietly as I could, I put a screen around it and settled down for the night.

I was wakened by the touch of a hand on my face. I started, I think, and the hand was jerked away—I am not sure: I was still drowsy. I lay very quiet, listening for footsteps, but none came. With the feeling that there was someone behind the screen, I jumped up. The hall was dark and quiet. When I found no one, I concluded it had been only a vivid dream, and I sat down on the edge of the davenport and yawned.

I heard Edith moving back in the nursery: she has an uncomfortable habit of wandering around in the night, covering the children, closing windows, and sniffing for fire. I was afraid some of the smoke from my conflagration had reached her suspicious nose, but she did not come into the front hall. I was wide-awake by that time, and it was then, I think, that I noticed a heavy, sweetish odor in the air. At first I thought one of the children might be ill, and that Edith was dosing him with one of the choice concoctions that she kept in the bathroom medicine closet. When she closed her door, however, and went back to bed, I knew I had been mistaken.

The sweetish smell was almost nauseating. For some reason or other—association of certain odors with certain events—I found myself recalling the time I had a wisdom tooth taken out, and that when I came around I was being sat on by the dentist and his assistant, and the latter had a black eye. Then, suddenly, I knew. The sickly odor was chloroform!

I had the light on in a moment, and was rapping at Margery's door. It was locked, and I got no answer. A pale light shone over the transom, but everything was ominously quiet, beyond the door. I went to Mrs. Butler's door, next; it was unlocked and partly open. One glance at the empty bed and the confusion of the place, and I rushed without ceremony through the connecting door into Margery's room.

The atmosphere was reeking with chloroform. The girl was in bed, apparently sleeping quietly. One arm was thrown up over her head, and the other lay relaxed on the white cover. A folded towel had been laid across her face, and when I jerked it away I saw she was breathing very slowly, stertorously, with her eyes partly open and fixed.

I threw up all the windows, before I roused the family, and as soon as Edith was in the room I telephoned for the doctor. I hardly remember what I did until he came: I know we tried to rouse Margery and failed, and I know that Fred went downstairs and said the silver was intact and the back kitchen door open. And then the doctor came, and I was put out in the hall, and for an eternity, I walked up and down, eight steps one way, eight steps back, unable to think, unable even to hope.

Not until the doctor came out to me, and said she was better, and would I call a maid to make some strong black coffee, did I come out of my stupor. The chance of doing something, anything, made me determined to make the coffee myself. They still speak of that coffee at Fred's.

It was Edith who brought Mrs. Butler to my mind. Fred had maintained that she had fled before the intruders, and was probably in some closet or corner of the upper floor. I was afraid our solicitude was long in coming. It was almost an hour before we organized a searching party to look for her. Fred went upstairs, and I took the lower floor.

It was I who found her, after all, lying full length on the grass in the little square yard back of the house. She was in a dead faint, and she was a much more difficult patient than Margery.

We could get no story from either of them that night. The two rooms had been ransacked, but apparently nothing had been stolen. Fred vowed he had locked and bolted the kitchen door, and that it had been opened from within.

It was a strange experience, that night intrusion into the house, without robbery as a motive. If Margery knew or suspected the reason for the outrage, she refused to say. As for Mrs. Butler, to mention the occurrence put her into hysteria. It was Fred who put forth the most startling theory of the lot.

"By George," he said the next morning when we had failed to find tracks in the yard, and Edith had reported every silver spoon in its place. "By George, it wouldn't surprise me if the lady in the grave clothes did it herself. There isn't anything an hysterical woman won't do to rouse your interest in her, if it begins to flag. How did anyone get in through that kitchen door, when it was locked inside and bolted? I tell you, she opened it herself."

I did not like to force Margery's confidence, but I believe that the outrage was directly for the purpose of searching her room, perhaps for papers that had been her father's. Mrs. Butler came around enough by morning to tell a semi-connected story in which she claimed that two men had come in from a veranda roof, and tried to chloroform her. That she had pretended to be asleep and had taken the first opportunity, while they were in the other room, to run downstairs and into the yard. Edith thought it likely enough, being a credulous person.

As it turned out, Edith's intuition was more reliable than my skepticism—or Fred's.

Chapter XIX

Back to Bellwood

THE inability of Margery Fleming to tell who had chloroformed her, and Mrs. Butler's white face and brooding eyes made a very respectable mystery out of the affair. Only Fred, Edith and I came down to breakfast that morning. Fred's expression was half amused, half puzzled. Edith fluttered uneasily over the coffee machine, her cheeks as red as the bow of ribbon at her throat. I was preoccupied, and, like Fred, I propped the morning paper in front of me and proceeded to think in its shelter.

"Did you find anything, Fred?" Edith asked. Fred did not reply, so she repeated the question with some emphasis.

"Eh—what?" Fred inquired, peering around the corner of the paper.

"Did—you—find—any—clue?"

"Yes, dear—that is, no. Nothing to amount to anything. Upon my soul, Jack, if I wrote the editorials of this paper, I'd *say* something." He subsided into inarticulate growls behind the paper, and everything was quiet. Then I heard a sniffle, distinctly. I looked up. Edith was crying—pouring cream into a coffee cup, and feeling blindly for the sugar, with her pretty face twisted and her pretty eyes obscured. In a second I was up, had crumpled the newspapers, including Fred's, into a ball, and had lifted him bodily out of his chair.

"When I am married," I said fiercely, jerking him around to Edith and pushing him into a chair beside her, "if I ever read the paper at breakfast when my wife is bursting for conversation, may I have some good and faithful friend who will bring me back to a sense of my duty." I drew a chair to Edith's other side. "Now, let's talk," I said.

She wiped her eyes shamelessly with her table napkin. "There isn't a soul in this house I can talk to," she wailed. "All kinds of awful things happening—and we had to send for coffee this morning, Jack. You must have used four pounds last night—and nobody will tell me a thing. There's no use asking Margery— she's sick at her stomach from the chloroform—and Ellen never talks except about herself, and she's horribly—uninteresting. And Fred and you make a ba-barricade out of newspapers, and fire 'yes' at me when you mean 'no'."

"I put the coffee back where I got it, Edith," I protested stoutly. "I know we're barbarians, but I'll swear to that." And then I stopped, for I had a sudden recollection of going upstairs with something fat and tinny in my arms, of finding it in my way, and of hastily thrusting it into the boys' boot closet under the nursery stair.

Fred had said nothing. He had taken her hand and was patting it gently, the while his eyes sought the headlines on the wad of morning paper.

"You burned that blue rug," she said to me disconsolately, with a threat of fresh tears. "It took me ages to find the right shade of blue."

"I will buy you that Shirvan you wanted," I hastened to assure her.

"Yes, to take away when you get married." There is a hint of the shrew in all good women.

"I will buy the Shirvan and *not* get married."

Here, I regret to say, Edith suddenly laughed. She threw her head back and jeered at me.

"You!" she chortled, and pointed one slim finger at me mockingly. "You, who are so mad about one girl that you love all women for her sake! You, who go white instead of red when she comes into the room! You, who have let your practice go to the dogs to be near her, and then never speak to her when she's around, but sit with your mouth open like a puppy begging for candy, ready to snap up every word she throws you and wiggle with joy!"

I was terrified.

"Honestly, Edith, do I do that?" I gasped. But she did not answer; she only leaned over and kissed Fred.

"Women like men to be awful fools about them," she said. "That's why I'm so crazy about Freddie." He writhed.

"If I tell you something nice, Jack, will you make it a room-size rug?"

"Room size it is.

"Then, Margery's engagement ring was stolen last night and when I commiserated her she said, 'Dear me, the lamp's out and the coffee is cold!' "

"Remarkable speech, under the circumstances," said Fred.

Edith rang the bell and seemed to be thinking. "Perhaps we'd better make it four small rugs instead of one large one," she said.

"Not a rug until you have told me what Margery said." Firmly.

"Oh, that! Why, she said it didn't really matter about the ring. She had never cared much about it anyway."

"But that's only a matter of taste," I protested, somewhat disappointed. But Edith got up and patted me on the top of my head.

"Silly," she said. "If the right man came along and gave her a rubber teething ring, she'd be crazy about it for his sake."

"Edith!" Fred said, shocked. But Edith had gone.

She took me upstairs before I left for the office to measure for the Shirvan, Edith being a person who believes in obtaining a thing while the desire for it is in its first bloom. Across the hall Fred was talking to Margery through the transom.

"Mustard leaves are mighty helpful," he was saying. "I always take 'em on shipboard. And cheer up: land's in sight."

I would have given much for Fred's ease of manner when, a few minutes later, Edith having decided on four Shirvans and a hall runner, she took me to the door of Margery's room.

She was lying very still and pale in the center of the white bed, and she tried bravely to smile at us.

"I hope you are better," I said. "Don't let Edith convince you that my coffee has poisoned you."

She said she was a little better, and that she didn't know she had had any coffee. That was the extent of the conversation. I, who have a local reputation of a sort before a jury, could not think of another word to say. I stood there for a minute uneasily, with Edith poking me with her finger to go inside the door and speak and act like an intelligent human being. But I only muttered something about a busy day before me and fled. It was a singular thing, but as I stood in the doorway, I had a vivid mental picture of Edith's description of me, sitting up puppylike to beg for a kind word, and wiggling with delight when I got it. If I slunk into my office that morning like a dog scourged to his kennel, Edith was responsible.

At the office I found a note from Miss Letitia, and after a glance at it I looked in my railroad schedule for the first train. The note was brief; unlike the similar epistle I had received from Miss Jane the day she disappeared, this one was very formal.

> MR. JOHN KNOX:
>
> Dear Sir—Kindly oblige me by coming to see me as soon as you get this. Some things have happened, not that I think they are worth a row of pins, but Hepsibah is an old fool, and she says she did not put the note in the milk bottle.
>
> Yours very respectfully,
> LETITIA ANN MAITLAND

I had an appointment with Burton for the afternoon, to take Wardrop; if we could get him on some pretext, to Dr. Anderson. That day, also, I had two cases on the trial list. I got Humphreys, across the hall, to take them over, and evading Hawes' resentful blink, I went on my way to Bellwood. It was nine days since Miss Jane had disappeared. On my way out in the train I jotted down the things that had happened in that time: Allan Fleming had died and been buried; the Borough Bank had failed; someone had gotten into the Fleming house and gone through the papers there; Clarkson had killed himself; we had found that Wardrop had sold the pearls; the leather bag had been returned;

Fleming's second wife had appeared, and someone had broken into my own house and, intentionally or not, had almost sent Margery Fleming over the borderland.

It seemed to me everything pointed in one direction, to a malignity against Fleming that extended itself to the daughter. I thought of what the woman who claimed to be the dead man's second wife had said the day before. If the staircase she had spoken of opened into the room where Fleming was shot, and if Schwartz was in town at the time, then, in view of her story that he had already tried once to kill him, the likelihood was that Schwartz was at least implicated.

If Wardrop knew that, why had he not denounced him? Was I to believe that, after all the mystery, the number eleven twenty-two was to resolve itself into the number of a house? Would it be typical of the Schwartz I knew to pin bits of paper to a man's pillow? On the other hand, if he had reason to think that Fleming had papers that would incriminate him, it would be like Schwartz to hire someone to search for them, and he would be equal to having Wardrop robbed of the money he was taking to Fleming.

Granting that Schwartz had killed Fleming—then who was the woman with Wardrop the night he was robbed? Why did he take the pearls and sell them? How did the number eleven twenty-two come into Aunt Jane's possession? How did the leather bag get to Boston? Who had chloroformed Margery? Who had been using the Fleming house while it was closed? Most important of all now—where was Aunt Jane?

The house at Bellwood looked almost cheerful in the May sunshine, as I went up the walk. Nothing ever changed the straight folds of the old-fashioned lace curtains; no dog ever tracked the porch, or buried sacrilegious and odorous bones on the level lawn; the birds were nesting in the trees, well above the reach of Robert's ladder, but they were decorous, well-behaved birds, whose prim courting never partook of the exuberance of their neighbors', bursting their little throats in an elm above the baby perambulator in the next yard.

When Bella had let me in, and I stood once more in the straight hall, with the green rep chairs and the Japanese umbrella stand, involuntarily I listened for the tap of Miss Jane's small feet on the stairs. Instead came Bella's heavy tread, and a request from Miss Letitia that I go upstairs.

The old lady was sitting by a window of her bedroom, in a chintz upholstered chair. She did not appear to be feeble; the only change I noticed was a relaxation in the severe tidiness of her dress. I guessed that Miss Jane's exquisite neatness had been responsible for the white ruchings, the soft caps, and the spotless shoulder shawls which had made lovely their latter years.

"You've taken your own time about coming, haven't you?" Miss Letitia asked sourly. "If it hadn't been for that cousin of yours you sent here, Burton, I'd have been driven to sending for Amelia Miles, and when I send for Amelia Miles for company, I'm in a bad way."

"I have had a great deal to attend to," I said as loud as I could. "I came some days ago to tell you Mr. Fleming was dead; after that we had to bury him, and close the house. It's been a very sad—"

"Did he leave anything?" she interrupted. "It isn't sad at all unless he didn't leave anything."

"He left very little. The house, perhaps, and I regret to have to tell you that a woman came to me yesterday who claims to be a second wife."

She took off her glasses, wiped them and put them on again.

"Then," she said with a snap, "there's one other woman in the world as big a fool as my sister Martha was. I didn't know there were two of 'em. What do you hear about Jane?"

"The last time I was here," I shouted, "you thought she was dead; have you changed your mind?"

"The last time you were here," she said with dignity, "I thought a good many things that were wrong. I thought I had lost some of the pearls, but I hadn't."

"What!" I exclaimed incredulously. She put her hands on the arms of her chair, and leaning forward, shot the words at me viciously.

"I—said—I—had—lost—some—of—the—pearls—well—I—haven't."

She didn't expect me to believe her, any more than she believed it herself. But why on earth she had changed her attitude about the pearls was beyond me. I merely nodded comprehensively.

"Very well," I said, "I'm glad to know it was a mistake. Now, the next thing is to find Miss Jane."

"We have found her," she said tartly. "That's what I sent for you about."

"Found her!" This time I did get out of my chair. "What on earth do you mean, Miss Letitia? Why, we've been scouring the country for her."

She opened a religious monthly on the table beside her, and took out a folded paper. I had to control my impatience while she changed her glasses and read it slowly.

"Heppie found it on the back porch, under a milk bottle," she prefaced. Then she read it to me. I do not remember the wording, and Miss Letitia refused, both then and later, to let it out of her hands. As a result, unlike the other manuscripts in the case, I have not even a copy. The substance, shorn of its bad spelling and grammar, was this:

The writer knew where Miss Jane was; the inference being that he was responsible. She was well and happy, but she had happened to read a newspaper with an account of her disappearance, and it had worried her. The payment of the small sum of five thousand dollars would send her back as well as the day she left. The amount, left in a tin can on the base of the Maitland shaft in the cemetery, would bring the missing lady back within twenty-four hours. On the contrary, if the recipient of the letter notified the police, it would go hard with Miss Jane.

"What do you think of it?" she asked, looking at me over her glasses. "If she was fool enough to be carried away by a man that spells cemetery with one m, she deserves what she's got. And I won't pay five thousand, anyhow, it's entirely too much."

"It doesn't sound quite genuine to me," I said, reading it over. "I should certainly not leave any money until we had tried to find who left this."

"I'm not so sure but what she'd better stay a while anyhow," Miss Letitia pursued. "Now that we know she's living, I ain't so particular when she gets back. She's been notionate lately anyhow."

I had been reading the note again. "There's one thing here that makes me doubt the whole story," I said. "What's this about her reading the papers? I thought her reading glasses were found in the library."

Miss Letitia snatched the paper from me and read it again.

"Reading the paper!" she sniffed. "You've got more sense than I've been giving you credit for, Knox. Her glasses are here this minute; without them she can't see to scratch her nose."

It was a disappointment to me, although the explanation was simple enough. It was surprising that we had not had more attempts to play on our fears. But the really important thing bearing on Miss Jane's departure was when Heppie came into the room, with her apron turned up like a pocket and her dust cap pushed down over her eyes like the slouch hat of a bowery tough.

When she got to the middle of the room she stopped and abruptly dropped the corners of her apron. There rolled out a heterogenous collection of things: a white muslin garment which proved to be a nightgown, with long sleeves and high collar; a half-dozen hair curlers—I knew those—Edith had been seen, in midnight emergencies, with her hair twisted around just such instruments of torture; a shoe buttoner; a railroad map; and one new and unworn black kid glove.

Miss Letitia changed her glasses deliberately, and took a comprehensive survey of the things on the floor.

"Where did you get 'em?" she said, fixing Heppie with an awful eye.

"I found 'em stuffed under the blankets in the chest of drawers in the attic," Heppie shouted at her. "If we'd washed the blankets last week, as I wanted to—"

"Shut up!" Miss Letitia said shortly, and Heppie's thin lips closed with a snap. "Now then, Knox, what do you make of that?"

"If that's the nightgown she was wearing the night she disappeared, I think it shows one thing very clearly, Miss Maitland. She was not abducted, and she knew perfectly well what she was about. None of her clothes were missing, and that threw us off the track; but look at this new glove! She may have had new things to put on and left the old. The map—well, she was going somewhere, with a definite purpose. When we find out what took her away, we will find her."

"Humph!"

"She didn't go unexpectedly—that is, she was prepared for whatever it was."

"I don't believe a word of it," the old lady burst out. "She didn't have a secret; she was the kind that couldn't keep a secret. She wasn't responsible, I tell you; she was extravagant. Look at that glove! And she had three pairs half worn in her bureau."

"Miss Maitland," I asked suddenly, "did you ever hear of eleven twenty-two?"

"Eleven twenty-two what?"

"*Just* the number, eleven twenty-two," I repeated. "Does it mean anything to you? Has it any significance?"

"I should say it has," she retorted. "In the last ten years the Colored Orphans' Home has cared for, fed, clothed, and pampered exactly eleven hundred and twenty-two colored children, of every condition of shape and misshape, brains and no brains."

"It has no other connection?"

"Eleven twenty-two? Twice eleven is twenty-two, if that's any help. No, I can't think of anything. I loaned Allan Fleming a thousand dollars once; I guess my mind was failing. It would be about eleven twenty-two by this time."

Neither of these explanations sufficed for the little scrap found in Miss Jane's room. What connection, if any, had it with her flight? Where was she now? What was eleven twenty-two? And why did Miss Letitia deny that she had lost the pearls, when I already knew that nine of the ten had been sold, who had bought them, and approximately how much he had paid?

Chapter XX

Association of Ideas

I ATE a light lunch at Bellwood, alone, with Bella to look after me in the dining room. She was very solicitous, and when she had brought my tea, I thought she wanted to say something. She stood awkwardly near the door, and watched me.

"You needn't wait, Bella," I said.

"I beg your pardon, sir, but—I wanted to ask you—is Miss Fleming well?"

"She was not very well this morning, but I don't think it is serious, Bella," I replied. She turned to go, but I fancied she hesitated.

"Oh, Bella," I called, as she was going out. "I want to ask you something. The night at the Fleming home, when you and I watched the house, didn't you hear some person running along the hall outside your door? About two o'clock, I think?"

She looked at me stolidly.

"No, sir, I slept all night."

"That's strange. And you didn't hear me when I fell down the dumb-waiter shaft?"

"Holy saints!" she ejaculated. "Was *that* where you fell?"

She stopped herself abruptly.

"You heard that," I asked gently, "and yet you slept all night? Bella, there's a hitch somewhere. You didn't sleep that night, at all; you told Miss Fleming I had been up all night. How did you know that? If I didn't know that you couldn't possibly get around as fast as the—person in the house that night, I would say you had been in Mr. Fleming's desk, looking for—let us say, postage stamps. May I have another cup of coffee?"

She turned a sickly yellow white, and gathered up my cup and saucer with trembling hands. When the coffee finally came back it was brought grumblingly by old Heppie. "She says she's turned her ankle," she sniffed. "Turned it on a lathe, like a table leg, I should say, from the shape of it." Before I left the dining room I put another line in my notebook:

What does Bella know?

I got back to the city somewhat late for my appointment with Burton. I found Wardrop waiting for me at the office, and if I had been astonished at the change in him two nights before, I was shocked now. He seemed to have shrunk in his clothes; his eyeballs were bloodshot from drinking, and his fair hair had dropped, neglected, over his forehead. He was sitting in his familiar attitude, his elbows on his knees, his chin on his palms.

He looked at me with dull eyes when I went in. I did not see Burton at first. He was sitting on my desk, holding a flat can in his hand, and digging out with a wooden toothpick one sardine after another and bolting them whole.

"Your good health," he said, poising one in the air where it threatened oily tears over the carpet. "As an appetite-quencher and thirst-producer, give me the festive sardine. How lovely it would be if we could eat 'em without smelling 'em!"

"Don't you do anything but eat?" Wardrop asked, without enthusiasm.

Burton eyed him reproachfully. "Is that what I get for doing without lunch, in order to prove to you that you are not crazy?" He appealed to me. "He says he's crazy—lost his think works. Now, I ask you, Knox, when I go to the trouble to find out for him that he's got as many convolutions as anybody, and that they've only got a little convolved, is it fair, I ask you, for him to reproach me about my food?"

"I didn't know you knew each other," I put in, while Burton took another sardine.

"He says we do," Wardrop said wearily. "Says he used to knock me around at college."

Burton winked at me solemnly.

"He doesn't remember me, but he will," he said. "It's his nerves that are gone, and we'll have him restrung with new wires, like an old piano, in a week."

Wardrop had that after-debauch suspicion of all men, but I think he grasped at me as a dependability.

"He wants me to go to a doctor," he said. "I'm not sick; it's only—" He was trying to light a cigarette, but the match dropped from his shaking fingers.

"Better see one, Wardrop," I urged—and I felt mean enough about doing it. "You need something to brace you up."

Burton gave him a very small drink, for he could scarcely stand, and we went down in the elevator. My contempt for the victim between us was as great as my contempt for myself. That Wardrop was in a bad position there could be no doubt; there might be more men than Fleming who had known about the money in the leather bag, and who thought he had taken it and probably killed Fleming to hide the theft.

It seemed incredible that an innocent man would collapse as he had done, and yet—at this minute I can name a dozen men who, under the club of public disapproval, have fallen into paresis, insanity and the grave. We are all indifferent to our fellowmen until they are against us.

Burton knew the specialist very well—in fact, there seemed to be few people he did not know. And considering the way he had got hold of Miss Letitia and Wardrop, it was not surprising. He had evidently arranged with the doctor, for the waiting room was empty and we were after hours.

The doctor was a large man, his size emphasized by the clothes he wore, very light in color, and unprofessional in cut. He was sandy-haired, inclined to be bald, and with shrewd, light blue eyes behind his glasses. Not particularly impressive, except as to size, on first acquaintance; a good fellow, with a brisk voice, and an amazingly light tread.

He began by sending Wardrop into a sort of examining room in the rear of the suite somewhere, to take off his coat and collar. When he had gone the doctor looked at a slip of paper in his hand.

"I think I've got it all from Mr. Burton," he said. "Of course, Mr. Knox, this is a little out of my line; a nerve specialist has as much business with psychotherapy as a piano tuner has with musical technique. But the idea is Munsterburg's, and I've had some good results. I'll give him a short physical examination, and when I ring the bell one of you may come in. Are you a newspaperman, Mr. Knox?"

"An attorney," I said briefly.

"Press man, lawyer, or doctor," Burton broke in, "we all fatten on the other fellow's troubles, don't we?"

"We don't fatten very much," I corrected. "We live."

The doctor blinked behind his glasses.

"I never saw a lawyer yet who would admit he was making money," he said. "Look at the way a doctor grinds for a pittance! He's just as capable as the lawyer; he works a damn sight harder, and he makes a tenth the income. A man will pay his lawyer ten thousand dollars for keeping him out of jail for six months, and he'll kick like a steer if his doctor charges him a hundred to keep him out of hell for life! Which of you will come in? I'm afraid two would distract him."

"I guess it is Knox's butt-in," Burton conceded, "but I get it later, Doctor; you promised."

The physical examination was very brief; when I was called in, Wardrop was standing at the window looking down into the street below, and the doctor was writing at his desk. Behind Wardrop's back he gave me the slip he had written.

> Test is for association of ideas. Watch length of time between word I give and his reply. I often get hold of facts forgotten by the patient. A wait before the answering word is given shows an attempt at concealment.

"Now, Mr. Wardrop," he said, "will you sit here, please?"

He drew a chair to the center table for Wardrop, and another, just across, for himself. I sat back and to one side of the patient, where I could see Wardrop's haggard profile and every movement of the specialist.

On the table was an electric instrument like a small clock, and the doctor's first action was to attach it to two wires with small, black rubber mouthpieces.

"Now, Mr. Wardrop," he said, "we will go on with the test. Your other condition is fair, as I told you; I think you can dismiss the idea of insanity without a second thought, but there is something more than brain and body to be considered; in other words, you have been through a storm, and some of your nervous wires are down. Put the mouthpiece between your lips, please; you see, I do the same with mine. And when I give you a word, speak as quickly as possible the association it brings to your mind. For instance, I say 'noise.' Your first association might be 'street,' 'band,' 'drum,' almost anything associated with the word. As quickly as possible, please."

The first few words went simply enough. Wardrop's replies came almost instantly. To "light" he replied "lamp"; "touch" brought the response "hand"; "eat" brought "Burton," and both the doctor and I smiled. Wardrop was intensely serious. Then—

"Taxicab," said the doctor, and, after an almost imperceptible pause, "road" came for the association. All at once I began to see the possibilities.

"Desk." "Pen."

"Pipe." "Smoke."

"Head." After a perceptible pause the answer came uncertainly. "Hair." But the association of ideas would not be denied, for in answer to the next word, which was "ice," he gave "blood," evidently following up the previous word "head."

I found myself gripping the arms of my chair. The dial on the doctor's clocklike instrument was measuring the interval; I could see that now. The doctor took a record of every word and its response. Wardrop's eyes were shifting nervously.

"Hot." "Cold."

"White." "Black."

"Whisky." "Glass," all in less than a second.

"Pearls." A little hesitation, then "box."

"Taxicab" again. "Night."

"Silly." "Wise."

"Shot." After a pause, "revolver."

"Night." "Dark."

"Blood." "Head."

"Water." "Drink."

"Traveling bag." He brought out the word "train" after an evident struggle, but in answer to the next word "lost," instead of the obvious "found," he said "woman." He had not had sufficient mental agility to get away from the association with "bag." The "woman" belonged there.

"Murder" brought "dead," but "shot," following immediately after, brought "staircase."

I think Wardrop was on his guard by that time, but the conscious effort to hide truths that might be damaging made the intervals longer, from that time on. Already I felt sure that Allan Fleming's widow had been right; he had been shot from the locked back staircase. But by whom?

"Blow" brought "chair."

"Gone." "Bag" came like a flash.

In quick succession, without pause, came the words—

"Bank." "Note."

"Door." "Bolt."

"Money." "Letters," without any apparent connection.

Wardrop was going to the bad. When, to the next word, "staircase," again, he said "scar," his demoralization was almost complete. As for me, the scene in Wardrop's mind was already in mine—Schwartz, with the scar across his ugly forehead, and the bolted door to the staircase open!

On again with the test.

"Flour," after perhaps two seconds, from the preceding shock, brought "bread."

"Trees." "Leaves."

"Night." "Dark."

"Gate." He stopped here so long, I thought he was not going to answer at all. Presently, with an effort, he said "wood," but as before, the association idea came out in the next word; for "electric light" he gave "letters."

"Attic" brought "trunks" at once.

"Closet." After perhaps a second and a half came "dust," showing what closet was in his mind, and immediately after, to "match" he gave "pen."

A long list of words followed which told nothing, to my mind, although the doctor's eyes were snapping with excitement. Then "traveling bag" again, and instead of his previous association, "woman," this time he gave "yellow." But, to the next word, "house," he gave "guest." It came to me that in his mental processes I was the guest, the substitute bag was in his mind, as being in my possession. Quick as a flash the doctor followed up—

"Guest." And Wardrop fell. "Letters," he said.

To a great many words, as I said before, I could attach no significance. Here and there I got a ray.

"Elderly" brought "black."

"Warehouse." "Yard," for no apparent reason.

"Eleven twenty-two." "C" was the answer, given without a second's hesitation.

Eleven twenty-two C! He gave no evidence of having noticed any peculiarity in what he said; I doubt if he realized his answer. To me, he gave the impression of repeating something he had apparently forgotten. As if a number and its association had been subconscious, and brought to the surface by the psychologist; as if, for instance, someone prompted a—b, and the corollary "c" came without summoning.

The psychologist took the small mouthpiece from his lips, and motioned Wardrop to do the same. The test was over.

"I don't call that bad condition, Mr.—Wardrop," the doctor said. "You are nervous, and you need a little more care in your habits. You want to exercise, regularly, and you will have to cut out everything in the way of stimulants for a while. Oh, yes, a couple of drinks a day at first, then one a day, and then none. And you are to stop worrying—when trouble comes round, and stares at you, don't ask it to have a drink. Take it out in the air and kill it; oxygen is as fatal to anxiety as it is to tuberculosis."

"How would Bellwood do?" I asked. "Or should it be the country?"

"Bellwood, of course," the doctor responded heartily. "Ten miles a day, four cigarettes, and three meals—which is more than you have been taking, Mr. Wardrop, by two."

I put him on the train for Bellwood myself, and late that afternoon the three of us—the doctor, Burton and myself—met in my office and went over the doctor's record.

"When the answer comes in four-fifths of a second," he said, before we began, "it is hardly worth comment. There is no time in such an interval for any mental reservation. Only those words that showed noticeable hesitation need be considered."

We worked until almost seven. At the end of that time the doctor leaned back in his chair, and thrust his hands deep in his trousers pockets.

"I got the story from Burton," he said, after a deep breath. "I had no conclusion formed, and of course I am not a detective. Things looked black for Mr. Wardrop, in view of the money lost, the quarrel with Fleming that morning at the White Cat, and the circumstance of his leaving the club and hunting a doctor outside, instead of raising the alarm. Still, no two men ever act alike in an emergency. Psychology is as exact a science as mathematics; it gets information from the source, and a man cannot lie in four-fifths of a second. 'Head,' you noticed, brought 'hair' in a second and three quarters, and the next word, 'ice,' brought the 'blood' that he had held back before. That doesn't show anything. He tried to avoid what was horrible to him.

"But I gave him 'traveling bag'; after a pause, he responded with 'train.' The next word, 'lost,' showed what was in his mind; instead of 'found,' he said 'woman.' Now then, I believe he was either robbed by a woman, or he thinks he was. After all, we can only get what he believes himself."

" 'Money—letters'—another slip."

" 'Shot—staircase'—where are the stairs at the White Cat?"

"I learned yesterday of a back staircase that leads into one of the upper rooms," I said. "It opens on a side entrance, and is used in emergency."

The doctor smiled confidently.

"We look there for our criminal," he said. "Nothing hides from the chronoscope. Now then, 'staircase—scar.' Isn't that significant? The association is clear: a scar that is vivid enough, disfiguring enough, to be the first thing that enters his mind."

"Schwartz!" Burton said with awe. "Doctor, what on earth does 'eleven twenty-two C' mean?"

"I think that is up to you, gentlemen. The C belongs there, without doubt. Briefly, looking over these slips, I make it something like this: Wardrop thinks a woman took his traveling bag. Three times he gave the word 'letters,' in response to 'gate,' 'guest' and 'money.' Did he have a guest at the time all this happened at Bellwood?"

"I was a guest in the house at the time."

"Did you offer him money for letters?"

"No."

"Did he give you any letters to keep for him?"

"He gave me the bag that was substituted for his."

"Locked?"

"Yes. By Jove, I wonder if there is anything in it? I have reason to know that he came into my room that night at least once after I went asleep."

"I think it very likely," he said dryly. "One thing we have not touched on, and I believe Mr. Wardrop knows nothing of it. That is, the disappearance of the old lady. There is a psychological study for you! My conclusion? Well, I should say that Mr. Wardrop is not guilty of the murder. He knows, or thinks he knows, who is. He has a theory of his own, about someone with a scar: it may be only a theory. He does not necessarily know, but he hopes. He is in a state of abject fear. Also, he is hiding something concerning letters, and from the word 'money' in that connection, I believe he either sold or bought some damaging papers. He is not a criminal, but he is what is almost worse."

The doctor rose and picked up his hat. "He is a weakling," he said, from the doorway.

Burton looked at his watch. "By George!" he said. "Seven twenty, and I've had nothing since lunch but a box of sardines. I'm off to chase the festive mutton chop. Oh, by the way, Knox, where is that locked bag?"

"In my office safe."

"I'll drop around in the morning and assist you to compound a felony," he said easily. But as it happened, he did not.

Chapter XXI
A Proscenium Box

I WAS very late for dinner. Fred and Edith were getting ready for a concert, and the two semi-invalids were playing pinochle in Fred's den. Neither one looked much the worse for her previous night's experience; Mrs. Butler was always pale, and Margery had been so since her father's death.

The game was over when I went into the den. As usual, Mrs. Butler left the room almost immediately, and went to the piano across the hall. I had grown to accept her avoidance of me without question. Fred said it was because my overwhelming vitality oppressed her. Personally, I think it was because the neurasthenic type of woman is repulsive to me. No doubt Mrs. Butler deserved sympathy, but her open demand for it found me cold and unresponsive.

I told Margery briefly of my visit to Bellwood that morning. She was as puzzled as I was about the things Heppie had found in the chest. She was relieved, too.

"I am just as sure, now, that she is living, as I was a week ago that she was dead," she said, leaning back in her big chair. "But what terrible thing took her away? Unless—"

"Unless what?"

"She had loaned my father a great deal of money," Margery said, with heightened color. "She had not dared to tell Aunt Letitia, and the money was to be returned before she found it out. Then—things went wrong with the Borough Bank, and—the money did not come back. If you know Aunt Jane, and how afraid she is of Aunt Letitia, you will understand how terrible it was for her. I have wondered if she would go—to Plattsburg, and try to find Father there."

"The *Eagle* man is working on that theory now," I replied. "Margery, if there was a letter 'C' added to eleven twenty-two, would you know what it meant?"

She shook her head in the negative.

"Will you answer two more questions?" I asked.

"Yes, if I can."

"Do you know why you were chloroformed last night, and who did it?"

"I think I know who did it, but I don't understand. I have been trying all day to think it out. I'm afraid to go to sleep tonight."

"You need not be," I assured her. "If necessary, we will have the city police in a ring around the house. If you know and don't tell, Margery, you are running a risk, and more than that, you are protecting a person who ought to be in jail."

"I'm not sure," she persisted. "Don't ask me about it, please."

"What does Mrs. Butler say?"

"Just what she said this morning. And she says valuable papers were taken from under her pillow. She was very ill—hysterical, all afternoon."

The gloom and smouldering fire of the *Sonata Apassionata* came to us from across the hall. I leaned over and took Margery's small hand between my two big ones.

"Why don't you tell me?" I urged. "Or—you needn't tell me, I know what you think. But there isn't any motive that I can see, and why would she chloroform you?"

"I don't know," Margery shuddered. "Sometimes—I wonder—do you think she is altogether sane?"

The music ended with the crash of a minor chord. Fred and Edith came down the stairs, and the next moment we were all together, and the chance for a quiet conversation was gone. At the door Fred turned and came back.

"Watch the house," he said. "And by the way, I guess"—he lowered his voice—"the lady's story was probably straight. I looked around again this afternoon, and there are fresh scratches on the porch roof under her window. It looks queer, doesn't it?"

It was a relief to know that, after all, Mrs. Butler was an enemy and a dangerous person to nobody but herself. She retired to her room almost as soon as Fred and Edith had gone. I was wondering whether or not to tell Margery about the experiment that afternoon; debating how to ask her what letters she had got from the postmaster at Bellwood addressed to Miss Jane, and what she knew of Bella. At the same time—bear with me, oh masculine reader, the gentle reader will, for she cares a great deal more for the love story than for all the crime and mystery put together—bear with me, I say, if I hold back the account of the terrible events that came that night, to tell how beautiful Margery looked as the lamplight fell on her brown hair and pure profile, and how the impulse came over me to kiss her as she sat there; and how I didn't, after all—poor gentle reader!—and only stooped over and kissed the pink palm of her hand.

She didn't mind it; speaking as nearly as possible from an impersonal standpoint, I doubt if she was even surprised. You see, the ring was gone and—it had only been an engagement ring anyhow, and everybody knows how binding they are!

And then an angel with a burning sword came and scourged me out of my Eden. And the angel was Burton, and the sword was a dripping umbrella.

"I hate to take you out," he said. "The bottom's dropped out of the sky; but I want you to make a little experiment with me." He caught sight of Margery through the portéires, and the imp of mischief in him prompted his next speech. "She said she must see you," he said, very distinctly, and leered at me.

"Don't be an ass," I said angrily. "I don't know that I care to go out tonight."

He changed his manner then.

"Let's go and take a look at the staircase you fellows have been talking about," he said. "I don't believe there is a staircase there, except the main one. I have hounded every politician in the city into or out of that joint, and I have never heard of it."

I felt some hesitation about leaving the house—and Margery—after the events of the previous night. But Margery had caught enough of the conversation to be anxious to have me to go, and when I went in to consult her she laughed at my fears.

"Lightning never strikes twice in the same place," she said bravely. "I will ask Katie to come down with me if I am nervous, and I shall wait up for the family."

I went without enthusiasm. Margery's departure had been delayed for a day only, and I had counted on the evening with her. In fact, I had sent the concert tickets to Edith with an eye single to that idea. But

Burton's plan was right. It was, in view of what we knew, to go over the ground at the White Cat again, and Saturday night, with the place full of men, would be a good time to look around, unnoticed.

"I don't hang so much to this staircase idea," Burton said, "and I have a good reason for it. I think we will find it is the warehouse, yet."

"You can depend on it, Burton," I maintained, "that the staircase is the place to look. If you had seen Wardrop's face today, and his agony of mind when he knew he had associated 'staircase' with 'shot,' you would think just as I do. A man like Schwartz, who knew the ropes, could go quietly up the stairs, unbolt the door into the room, shoot Fleming and get out. Wardrop suspects Schwartz, and he's afraid of him. If he opened the door just in time to see Schwartz, we will say, backing out the door and going down the stairs, or to see the door closing and suspect who had just gone, we would have the whole situation, as I see it, including the two motives of deadly hate and jealousy."

"Suppose the stairs open into the back of the room? He was sitting facing the window. Do you think Schwartz would go in, walk around the table and shoot him from in front? Pooh! Fudge!"

"He had a neck," I retorted. "I suppose he might have turned his head to look around."

We had been walking through the rain. The White Cat, as far off as the poles socially, was only a half-dozen blocks actually from the best residence portion of the city. At the corner of the warehouse, Burton stopped and looked up at it.

"I always get mad when I look at this building," he said. "My great-grandfather had a truck garden on this exact spot seventy years ago, and the old idiot sold out for three hundred dollars and a pair of mules! How do you get in?"

"What are you going in for?" I asked.

"I was wondering if I had a grudge—I have, for that matter—against the mayor, and I wanted to shoot him, how I would go about it. I think I should find a point of vantage, like an overlooking window in an empty building like this, and I would wait for a muggy night, also like this, when the windows were up and the lights going. I could pot him with a thirty-eight at a dozen yards, with my eyes crossed."

We had stopped near the arched gate where I had stood and waited for Hunter, a week before. Suddenly Burton darted away from me and tried the gate. It opened easily, and I heard him splashing through a puddle in the gloomy yard.

"Come in," he called softly. "The water's fine."

The gate swung to behind me, and I could not see six inches from my nose. Burton caught my elbow and steered me, by touching the fence, toward the building.

"If it isn't locked too tight," he was saying, "we can get in, perhaps through a window, and get upstairs. From there we ought to be able to see down into the club. What the devil's that?"

It was a rat, I think, and it scrambled away among the loose boards in a frenzy of excitement. Burton struck a match; it burned faintly in the dampness, and in a moment went out, having shown us only the approximate location of the heavy, arched double doors. A second match showed us a bar and a rusty padlock; there was no entrance to be gained in that way.

The windows were of the eight-paned variety, and in better repair than the ones on the upper floors. By good luck, we found one unlocked and not entirely closed; it shrieked hideously as we pried it up, but an opportune clap of thunder covered the sound.

By this time I was ready for anything that came; I was wet to my knees, muddy, disreputable. While Burton held the window, I crawled into the warehouse, and turned to perform the same service for him. At first I could not see him, outside. Then I heard his voice, a whisper, from beyond the sill.

"Duck," he said. "Cop!"

I dropped below the window, and above the rain I could hear the squash of the watchman's boots in the mud. He flashed a night lamp in at the window next to ours, but he was not very near, and the open window escaped his notice. I felt all the nervous dread of a real malefactor, and when I heard the gate close behind him, and saw Burton put a leg over the sill, I was almost as relieved as I would have been had somebody's family plate, tied up in a tablecloth, been reposing at my feet.

Burton had an instinct for getting around in the dark. I lighted another match as soon as he had closed the window, and we made out our general direction toward where the stairs ought to be. When the match went out, we felt our way in the dark; I had only one box of wax matches, and Burton had dropped his in a puddle.

We got to the second floor, finally, and without any worse mishap than Burton banging his arm against a wheel of some sort. Unlike the first floor, the second was subdivided into rooms; it took a dozen precious matches to find our way to the side of the building overlooking the club, and another dozen to find the window we wanted. When we were there at last, Burton leaned his elbows on the sill, and looked down and across.

"Could anything be better!" he said. "There's our theater, and we've got a proscenium box. That room over there stands out like a spotlight."

He was right. Not more than fifteen feet away, and perhaps a foot lower than our window, was the window of the room where Fleming had been killed. It was empty, as far as we could see; the table, neat enough now, was where it had been before, directly under the light. Anyone who sat there would be an illuminated target from our window. Not only that, but an arm could be steadied on the sill, allowing for an almost perfect aim.

"Now, where's your staircase?" Burton jeered.

The club was evidently full of men, as he had prophesied. Above the rattle of the rain came the thump-thump of the piano, and a half-dozen male voices. The shutters below were closed; we could see nothing.

I think it was then that Burton had his inspiration.

"I'll bet you a five-dollar bill," he said, "that if I fire off my revolver here, now, not one of those fellows down there would pay the slightest attention."

"I'll take that bet," I returned. "I'll wager that every time anybody drops a poker, since Fleming was shot, the entire club turns out to investigate."

In reply Burton got out his revolver, and examined it by holding it against the light from across the way.

"I'll tell you what I'll do," he said. "Everybody down there knows me; I'll drop in for a bottle of beer, and you fire a shot into the floor here, or into somebody across, if you happen to see anyone you don't care for. I suggest that you stay and fire the shot, because if you went, my friend, and nobody heard it, you would accuse me of shooting from the back of the building somewhere."

He gave me the revolver and left me with a final injunction.

"Wait for ten minutes," he said. "It will take five for me to get out of here, and five more to get into the clubhouse. Perhaps you'd better make it fifteen?"

Chapter XXII

In the Room over the Way

HE WENT away into the darkness, and I sat down on an empty box by the window and waited. Had anyone asked me, at that minute, how near we were to the solution of our double mystery, I would have said we had made no progress—save by eliminating Wardrop. Not for one instant did I dream that I was within less than half an hour of a revelation that changed my whole conception of the crime.

I timed the interval by using one of my precious matches to see my watch when he left. I sat there for what seemed ten minutes, listening to the rush of the rain and the creaking of a door behind me in the darkness somewhere, that swung back and forth rustily in the draft from the broken windows. The gloom was infinitely depressing; away from Burton's enthusiasm, his scheme lacked point; his argument, that the night duplicated the weather conditions of that other night, a week ago, seemed less worthy of consideration.

Besides, I have a horror of making myself ridiculous, and I had an idea that it would be hard to explain my position, alone in the warehouse, firing a revolver into the floor, if my own argument was right, and the club should rouse to a search. I looked again at my watch: only six minutes.

Eight minutes.

Nine minutes.

Everyone who has counted the passing of seconds knows how they drag. With my eyes on the room across, and my finger on the trigger, I waited as best I could. At ten minutes I was conscious there was someone in the room over the way. And then he came into view from the side somewhere, and went to the table. He had his back to me, and I could only see that he was a large man, with massive shoulders and dark hair.

It was difficult to make out what he was doing. After a half-minute, however, he stepped to one side, and I saw that he had lighted a candle, and was systematically reading and then burning certain papers, throwing the charred fragments on the table. With the same glance that told me that, I knew the man. It was Schwartz.

I was so engrossed in watching him that when he turned and came directly to the window, I stood perfectly still, staring at him. With the light at his back, I felt certain I had been discovered, but I was wrong. He shook the newspaper which had held the fragments, out of the window, lighted a cigarette and flung the match out also, and turned back into the room. As a second thought, he went back and jerked at the cord of the window shade, but it refused to move.

He was not alone, for from the window he turned and addressed someone in the room behind.

"You are sure you got them all?" he said.

The other occupant of the room came within range of vision. It was Davidson.

"All there were, Mr. Schwartz," he replied. "We were nearly finished before the woman made a bolt." He was fumbling in his pockets. I think I expected him to produce an apple and a penknife, but he held out a small object on the palm of his hand.

"I would rather have done it alone, Mr. Schwartz," he said. "I found this ring in Brigg's pocket this morning. It belongs to the girl."

Schwartz swore and, picking up the ring, held it to the light. Then he made an angry motion to throw it out of the window, but his German cupidity got the better of him. He slid it into his vest pocket instead.

"You're damned poor stuff, Davidson," he said, with a snarl. "If she hasn't got them, then Wardrop has. You'll bungle this job and there'll be hell to pay. Tell McFeely I want to see him."

Davidson left, for I heard the door close. Schwartz took the ring out and held it to the light. I looked at my watch. The time was almost up.

A fresh burst of noise came from below. I leaned out cautiously and looked down at the lower windows; they were still closed and shuttered. When I raised my eyes again to the level of the room across, I was amazed to see a second figure in the room—a woman, at that.

Schwartz had not seen her. He stood with his back to her, looking at the ring in his hand. The woman had thrown her veil back, but I could see nothing of her face as she stood. She looked small beside Schwartz's towering height, and she wore black.

She must have said something just then, very quietly, for Schwartz suddenly lifted his head and wheeled on her. I had a clear view of him, and if ever guilt, rage, and white-lipped fear showed on a man's face, it showed on his. He replied—a half-dozen words, in a low tone, and made a motion to offer her a chair. But she paid no attention.

I have no idea how long a time they talked. The fresh outburst of noise below made it impossible to hear what they said, and there was always the maddening fact that I could not see her face. I thought of Mrs. Fleming, but this woman seemed younger and more slender. Schwartz was arguing, I imagined, but she stood immobile, scornful, watching him. She seemed to have made a request, and the man's evasions moved her no whit.

It may have been only two or three minutes, but it seemed longer. Schwartz had given up the argument, whatever it was, and by pointing out the window, I supposed he was telling her he had thrown what she wanted out there. Even then she did not turn toward me; I could not see even her profile.

What happened next was so unexpected that it remains little more than a picture in my mind. The man threw out his hands as if to show he could not or would not accede to her request; he was flushed with rage, and even at that distance the ugly scar on his forehead stood out like a welt. The next moment I saw the woman raise her right hand, with something in it.

I yelled to Schwartz to warn him, but he had already seen the revolver. As he struck her hand aside, the explosion came; I saw her stagger, clutch at a chair, and fall backward beyond my range of vision.

Then the light went out, and I was staring at a black, brick wall.

I turned and ran frantically toward the stairs. Luckily, I found them easily. I fell rather than ran down to the floor below. Then I made a wrong turning and lost some time. My last match set me right and I got into the yard somehow, and to the street.

It was raining harder than ever, and the thunder was incessant. I ran around the corner of the street, and found the gate to the White Cat without trouble. The inner gate was unlocked, as Burton had said he would leave it, and from the steps of the club I could hear laughter and the refrain of a popular song. The door opened just as I reached the top step, and I half tumbled inside.

Burton was there in the kitchen, with two other men whom I did not recognize, each one holding a stein of beer. Burton had two, and he held one out to me as I stood trying to get my breath.

"You win," he said. "Although I'm a hardworking journalist and need the money, I won't lie. This is Osborne of the *Star* and McTighe of the *Eagle,* Mr. Knox. They heard the shot in there, and if I hadn't told the story, there would have been a panic. What's the matter with you?"

I shut the door into the grillroom and faced the three men.

"For God's sake, Burton," I panted, "let's get upstairs quietly. I didn't fire any shot. There's a woman dead up there."

With characteristic poise, the three reporters took the situation quietly. We filed through the grillroom as casually as we could; with the door closed, however, we threw caution aside. I led the way up the stairs to the room where I had found Fleming's body, and where I expected to find another.

On the landing at the top of the stairs I came face to face with Davidson, the detective, and behind him Judge McFeely. Davidson was trying to open the door of the room where Fleming had been shot, with a skeleton key. But it was bolted inside. There was only one thing to do: I climbed on the shoulders of one of the men, a tall fellow, whose face to this day I don't remember, and by careful maneuvering and the assistance of Davidson's long arms, I got through the transom and dropped into the room.

I hardly know what I expected. I was in total darkness. I know that when I got the door open at last, when the cheerful light from the hall streamed in, and I had not felt Schwartz's heavy hand at my throat, I drew a long breath of relief. Burton found the electric light switch and turned it on. And then—I could hardly believe my senses. The room was empty.

One of the men laughed a little.

"Stung!" he said lightly. "What sort of a story have you and your friend framed up, Burton?"

But I stopped at that minute and picked up a small nickel-plated revolver from the floor. I held it out, on my palm, and the others eyed it respectfully.

Burton, after all, was the quickest-witted of the lot. He threw open one of the two doors in the room, revealing a shallow closet, with papered walls and a row of hooks. The other door stuck tight. One of the men pointed to the floor; a bit of black cloth had wedged it, from the other side. Our combined efforts got it open at last, and we crowded in the doorway, looking down a flight of stairs.

Huddled just below us, her head at our feet, was the body of the missing woman.

"My God," Burton said hoarsely, "who is it?"

Chapter XXIII

A Box of Crown Derby

We got her into the room and on the couch before I knew her. Her fair hair had fallen loose over her face, and one long, thin hand clutched still at the bosom of her gown. It was Ellen Butler!

She was living, but not much more. We gathered around and stood looking down at her in helpless pity. A current of cold night air came up the staircase from an open door below, and set the hanging light to swaying, throwing our shadows in a sort of ghastly dance over her quiet face.

I was too much shocked to be surprised. Burton had picked up her hat, and put it beside her.

"She's got about an hour, I should say," said one of the newspapermen. "See if Gray is around, will you, Jim? He's mostly here Saturday night."

"Is it—Miss Maitland?" Burton asked, in a strangely subdued voice.

"No; it is Henry Butler's widow," I returned, and the three men were reporters again, at once.

Gray was there and came immediately. Whatever surprise he may have felt at seeing a woman there, and dying, he made no comment. He said she might live six hours, but the end was certain. We got a hospital ambulance, and with the clang of its bell as it turned the corner and hurried away, the White Cat drops out of this story, so far as action is concerned.

Three detectives and as many reporters hunted Schwartz all of that night and the next day, to get his story. But he remained in hiding. He had a start of over an hour, from the time he switched off the light and escaped down the built-in staircase. Even in her agony, Ellen Butler's hate had carried her through the doorway after him, to collapse on the stairs.

I got home just as the cab, with Fred and Edith, stopped at the door. I did not let them get out; a half-dozen words, without comment or explanation, and they were driving madly to the hospital.

Katie let me in, and I gave her some money to stay up and watch the place while we were away. Then, not finding a cab, I took a car and rode to the hospital.

The building was appallingly quiet. The elevator cage, without a light, crept spectrally up and down; my footsteps on the tiled floor echoed and reechoed above my head. A night watchman, in felt shoes, admitted me, and took me upstairs.

There was another long wait while the surgeon finished his examination, and a nurse with a basin of water and some towels came out of the room, and another one with dressings went in. And then the surgeon came out, in a white coat with the sleeves rolled above his elbows, and said I might go in.

The cover was drawn up to the injured woman's chin, where it was folded neatly back. Her face was bloodless, and her fair hair had been gathered up in a shaggy knot. She was breathing slowly, but regularly, and her expression was relaxed—more restful than I had ever seen it. As I stood at the foot of the bed and looked down at her, I knew that as surely as death was coming, it would be welcome.

Edith had been calm, before, but when she saw me she lost her self-control. She put her head on my shoulder, and sobbed out the shock and the horror of the thing. As for Fred, his imaginative temperament made him particularly sensitive to suffering in others. As he sat there beside the bed I knew by his face that he was repeating and repenting every unkind word he had said about Ellen Butler.

She was conscious; we realized that after a time. Once she asked for water, without opening her eyes, and Fred slipped a bit of ice between her white lips. Later in the night she looked up for an instant, at me.

"He—struck my—hand," she said with difficulty, and closed her eyes again.

During the long night hours I told the story, as I knew it, in an undertone, and there was a new kindliness in Fred's face as he looked at her.

She was still living by morning, and was rallying a little from the shock. I got Fred to take Edith home, and I took her place by the bed. Someone brought me coffee about eight, and at nine o'clock I was asked to leave the room, while four surgeons held a consultation there. The decision to operate was made shortly after.

"There is only a chance," a gray-haired surgeon told me in brisk short-dipped words. "The bullet went down, and has penetrated the abdomen. Sometimes, taken early enough, we can repair the damage, to a certain extent, and nature does the rest. The family is willing, I suppose?"

I knew of no family but Edith, and over the telephone she said, with something of her natural tone, to do what the surgeons considered best.

I hoped to get some sort of statement before the injured woman was taken to the operating room, but she lay in a stupor, and I had to give up the idea. It was two days before I got her deposition, and in that time I had learned many things.

On Monday I took Margery to Bellwood. She had received the news about Mrs. Butler more calmly than I had expected.

"I do not think she was quite sane, poor woman," she said with a shudder. "She had had a great deal of trouble. But how strange—a murder and an attempt at murder—at that little club in a week!"

She did not connect the two, and I let the thing rest at that. Once, on the train, she turned to me suddenly, after she had been plunged in thought for several minutes.

"Don't you think," she asked, "that she had a sort of homicidal mania, and that she tried to kill me with chloroform?"

"I hardly think so," I returned evasively. "I am inclined to think someone actually got in over the porch roof."

"I am afraid," she said, pressing her gloved hands tight together. "Wherever I go, something happens that I cannot understand. I never willfully hurt anyone, and yet—these terrible things follow me. I am afraid—to go back to Bellwood, with Aunt Jane still gone, and you—in the city."

"A lot of help I have been to you," I retorted bitterly. "Can you think of a single instance where I have been able to save you trouble or anxiety? Why, I allowed you to be chloroformed within an inch of eternity, before I found you."

"But you did find me," she cheered me. "And just to know that you are doing all you can—"

"My poor best," I supplemented.

"It is very comforting to have a friend one can rely on," she finished, and the little bit of kindness went to my head. If she had not got a cinder in her eye at that psychological moment, I'm afraid I would figuratively have trampled Wardrop underfoot, right there. As it was, I got the cinder, after a great deal of looking into one beautiful eye—which is not as satisfactory by half as looking into two—and then we were at Bellwood.

We found Miss Letitia in the lower hall, and Heppie on her knees with a hatchet. Between them sat a packing box, and they were having a spirited discussion as to how it should be opened.

"Here, give it to me," Miss Letitia demanded, as we stopped in the doorway. "You've got stove lengths there for two days if you don't chop 'em up into splinters."

With the hatchet poised in midair she saw us, but she let it descend with considerable accuracy nevertheless, and our greeting was made between thumps.

"Come in"—thump—"like as not it's a mistake"—bang—"but the expressage was prepaid. If it's mineral water—" crash. Something broke inside.

"If it's mineral water," I said, "you'd better let me open it. Mineral water is meant for internal use, and not for hall carpets." I got the hatchet from her gradually. "I knew a case once where a bottle of hair tonic was spilled on a rag carpet, and in a year they had it dyed with spots over it and called it a tiger skin."

She watched me suspiciously while I straightened the nails she had bent, and lifted the boards. In the matter of curiosity, Miss Letitia was truly feminine; great handfuls of excelsior she dragged out herself, and heaped on Heppie's blue apron, stretched out on the floor.

The article that had smashed under the vigor of Miss Letitia's seventy years lay on the top. It had been a teapot, of some very beautiful ware. I have called just now from my study, to ask what sort of ware it was, and the lady who sets me right says it was Crown Derby. Then there were rows of cups and saucers, and heterogeneous articles in the same material that the women folk seemed to understand. At the last, when the excitement seemed over, they found a toast rack in a lower corner of the box and the "Ohs" and "Ahs" had to be done all over again.

Not until Miss Letitia had arranged it all on the dining-room table, and Margery had taken off her wraps and admired from all four corners, did Miss Letitia begin to ask where they had come from. And by that time Heppie had the crate in the woodbox, and the excelsior was a black and smoking mass at the kitchen end of the grounds.

There was not the slightest clue to the sender, but while Miss Letitia rated Heppie loudly in the kitchen, and Bella swept up the hall, Margery voiced the same idea that had occurred to me.

"If—if Aunt Jane were—all right," she said tremulously, "it would be just the sort of thing she loves to do."

I had intended to go back to the city at once, but Miss Letitia's box had put her in an almost cheerful humor, and she insisted that I go with her to Miss Jane's room, and see how it was prepared for its owner's return.

"I'm not pretending to know what took Jane Maitland away from this house in the middle of the night," she said. "She was a good bit of a fool, Jane was; she never grew up. But if I know Jane Maitland, she will come back and be buried with her people, if it's only to put Mary's husband out of the end of the lot.

"And another thing, Knox," she went on, and I saw her old hands were shaking. "I told you the last time you were here that I hadn't been robbed of any of the pearls, after all. Half of those pearls were Jane's and—she had a perfect right to take forty-nine of them if she wanted. She—she told me she was going to take some, and it—slipped my mind."

I believe it was the first lie she had ever told in her hard, conscientious old life. Was she right? I wondered. Had Miss Jane taken the pearls, and if she had, why?

Wardrop had been taking a long walk; he got back about five, and as Miss Letitia was in the middle of a diatribe against white undergarments for colored children, Margery and he had a half-hour alone together. I had known, of course, that it must come, but under the circumstances, with my whole future existence at stake, I was vague as to whether it was colored undergarments on white orphans or the other way round.

When I got away at last, I found Bella waiting for me in the hall. Her eyes were red with crying, and she had a crumpled newspaper in her hand. She broke down when she tried to speak, but I got the newspaper from her, and she pointed with one work-hardened finger to a column on the first page. It was the announcement of Mrs. Butler's tragic accident, and the mystery that surrounded it. There was no mention of Schwartz.

"Is she—dead?" Bella choked out at last.

"Not yet, but there is very little hope."

Amid fresh tears and shakings of her heavy shoulders, as she sat in her favorite place, on the stairs, Bella told me, briefly, that she had lived with Mrs. Butler since she was sixteen, and had only left when the husband's suicide had broken up the home. I could get nothing else out of her, but gradually Bella's share in the mystery was coming to light.

Slowly, too—it was a new business for me—I was forming a theory of my own. It was a strange one, but it seemed to fit the facts as I knew them. With the story Wardrop told that afternoon came my first glimmer of light.

He was looking better than he had when I saw him before, but the news of Mrs. Butler's approaching death and the manner of her injury affected him strangely. He had seen the paper, like Bella, and he turned on me almost fiercely when I entered the library. Margery was in her old position at the window, looking out, and I knew the despondent droop of her shoulders.

"Is she conscious?" Wardrop asked eagerly, indicating the article in the paper.

"No, not now—at least, it is not likely."

He looked relieved at that, but only for a moment. Then he began to pace the room nervously, evidently debating some move. His next action showed the development of a resolution, for he pushed forward two chairs for Margery and myself.

"Sit down, both of you," he directed. "I've got a lot to say, and I want you both to listen. When Margery has heard the whole story, she will probably despise me for the rest of her life. I can't help it. I've got to tell all I know, and it isn't so much after all. You didn't fool me yesterday, Knox; I knew what that doctor was after. But he couldn't make me tell who killed Mr. Fleming, because, before God, I didn't know."

Chapter XXIV

Wardrop's Story

"I HAVE to go back to the night Miss Jane disappeared—and that's another thing that has driven me desperate. Will you tell me why I should be suspected of having a hand in that, when she had been a mother to me? If she is dead, she can't exonerate me; if she is living, and we find her, she will tell you what I tell you—that I know nothing of the whole terrible business."

"I am quite certain of that, Wardrop," I interposed. "Besides, I think I have gotten to the bottom of that mystery."

Margery looked at me quickly, but I shook my head. It was too early to tell my suspicions.

"The things that looked black against me were bad enough, but they had nothing to do with Miss Jane. I will have to go back to before the night she—went away, back to the time Mr. Butler was the state treasurer, and your father, Margery, was his cashier.

"Butler was not a businessman. He let too much responsibility lie with his subordinates—and then, according to the story, he couldn't do much anyhow, against Schwartz. The cashier was entirely under machine control, and Butler was neglectful. You remember, Knox, the crash, when three banks, rotten to the core, went under, and it was found a large amount of state money had gone too. It was Fleming who did it—I am sorry, Margery, but this is no time to mince words. It was

Fleming who deposited the money in the wrecked banks, knowing what would happen. When the crash came, Butler's sureties, to save themselves, confiscated every dollar he had in the world. Butler went to the penitentiary for six months, on some minor count, and when he got out, after writing to Fleming and Schwartz, protesting his innocence, and asking for enough out of the fortune they had robbed him of to support his wife, he killed himself, at the White Cat."

Margery was very pale, but quiet. She sat with her fingers locked in her lap, and her eyes on Wardrop.

"It was a bad business," Wardrop went on wearily. "Fleming moved into Butler's place as treasurer, and took Lightfoot as his cashier. That kept the lid on. Once or twice, when there was an unexpected call for funds, the treasury was almost empty, and Schwartz carried things over himself. I went to Plattsburg as Mr. Fleming's private secretary when he became treasurer, and from the first I knew things were even worse than the average state government.

"Schwartz and Fleming had to hold together; they hated each other, and the feeling was trebled when Fleming married Schwartz's divorced wife."

Margery looked at me with startled, incredulous eyes. What she must have seen confirmed Wardrop's words, and she leaned back in her chair, limp and unnerved. But she heard and comprehended every word Wardrop was saying.

"The woman was a very ordinary person, but it seems Schwartz cared for her, and he tried to stab Mr. Fleming shortly after her marriage. About a year ago Mr. Fleming said another attempt had been made on his life, with poison; he was very much alarmed, and I noticed a change in him from that time on. Things were not going well at the treasury; Schwartz and his crowd were making demands that were hard to supply, and behind all that, Fleming was afraid to go out alone at night.

"He employed a man to protect him, a man named Carter, who had been a bartender in Plattsburg. When things began to happen here in Manchester, he took Carter to the home as a butler.

"Then the Borough Bank got shaky. If it went down there would be an ugly scandal, and Fleming would go too. His notes for half a million were there, without security, and he dared not show the canceled notes he had, with Schwartz's endorsement.

"I'm not proud of the rest of the story, Margery." He stopped his nervous pacing and stood looking down at her. "I was engaged to marry a girl who was everything on earth to me, and—I was private secretary to the state treasurer, with the princely salary of such a position!

"Mr. Fleming came back here when the Borough Bank threatened failure, and tried to get money enough to tide over the trouble. A half million would have done it, but he couldn't get it. He was in Butler's position exactly, only he was guilty and Butler was innocent. He raised a little money here, and I went to Plattsburg with securities and letters. It isn't necessary to go over the things I suffered there; I brought back one hundred and ten thousand dollars, in a package in my Russia leather bag. And—I had something else."

He wavered for the first time in his recital. He went on more rapidly, and without looking at either of us.

"I carried, not in the valise, a bundle of letters, five in all, which had been written by Henry Butler to Mr. Fleming, letters that showed what a dupe Butler had been, that he had been negligent, but not criminal; accusing Fleming of having ruined him, and demanding certain notes that would have proved it. If Butler could have produced the letters at the time of his trial, things would have been different."

"Were you going to sell the letters?" Margery demanded, with quick scorn.

"I intended to, but—I didn't. It was a little bit too dirty, after all. I met Mrs. Butler for the second time in my life, at the gate down there, as I came up from the train the night I got here from Plattsburg. She had offered to buy the letters, and I had brought them to sell to her. And then, at the last minute, I lied. I said I couldn't get them—that they were locked in the Monmouth Avenue house. I put her in a taxicab that she had waiting, and she went back to town. I felt like a cad; she wanted to clear her husband's memory, and I—well, Mr. Fleming was your father, Margery. I couldn't hurt you like that."

"Do you think Mrs. Butler took your leather bag?" I asked.

"I do not think so. It seems to be the only explanation, but I did not let it out of my hand one moment while we were talking. My hand was cramped from holding it, when she gave up in despair at last, and went back to the city."

"What did you do with the letters she wanted?"

"I kept them with me that night, and the next morning hid them in the secret closet. That was when I dropped my fountain pen!"

"And the pearls?" Margery asked suddenly. "When did you get them, Harry?"

To my surprise his face did not change. He appeared to be thinking.

"Two days before I left," he said. "We were using every method to get money, and your father said to sacrifice them, if necessary."

"My father!"

He wheeled on us both.

"Did you think I stole them?" he demanded. And I confess that I was ashamed to say I had thought precisely that.

"Your father gave me nine unmounted pearls to sell," he reiterated. "I got about a thousand dollars for them—eleven hundred and something, I believe."

Margery looked at me. I think she was fairly stunned. To learn that her father had married again, that he had been the keystone in an arch of villainy that, with him gone, was now about to fall, and to associate him with so small and mean a thing as the theft of a handful of pearls—she was fairly stunned.

"Then," I said, to bring Wardrop back to his story, "you found you had been robbed of the money, and you went in to tell Mr. Fleming. You had some words, didn't you?"

"He thought what you all thought," Wardrop said bitterly. "He accused me of stealing the money. I felt worse than a thief. He was desperate, and I took his revolver from him."

Margery had put her hands over her eyes. It was a terrible strain for her, but when I suggested that she wait for the rest of the story, she refused vehemently.

"I came back here to Bellwood, and the first thing I learned was about Miss Jane. When I saw the bloody print on the stair rail, I thought she was murdered, and I had more than I could stand. I took the letters out of the secret closet, before I could show it to you and Hunter, and later I put them in the leather bag I gave you, and locked it. You have it, haven't you, Knox?"

I nodded.

"As for that night at the club, I told the truth then, but not all the truth. I suppose I am a coward, but I was afraid to. If you knew Schwartz, you would understand."

With the memory of his huge figure and the heavy undershot face that I had seen the night before, I could understand very well, knowing Wardrop.

"I went to that room at the White Cat that night, because I was afraid not to go. Fleming might kill himself or someone else. I went up the stairs, slowly, and I heard no shot. At the door I hesitated, then opened it quietly. The door into the built-in staircase was just closing. It must have taken me only an instant to realize what had happened. Fleming was swaying forward as I caught him. I jumped to the staircase and looked down, but I was too late. The door below had closed. I knew in another minute who had been there, and escaped. It was raining, you remember, and Schwartz had forgotten to take his umbrella with his name on the handle!"

"Schwartz!"

"Now do you understand why I was being followed?" he demanded. "I have been under surveillance every minute since that night. There's probably someone hanging around the gate now. Anyhow, I was frantic. I saw how it looked for me, and if I had brought Schwartz into it, I would have been knifed in forty-eight hours. I hardly remember what I did. I know I ran for a doctor, and I took the umbrella with me and left it in the vestibule of the first house I saw with a doctor's sign. I rang the bell like a crazy man, and then Hunter came along and said to go back; Dr. Gray was at the club.

"That is all I know. I'm not proud of it, Margery, but it might have been worse, and it's the truth. It clears up something, but not all. It doesn't tell where Aunt Jane is, or who has the hundred thousand. But it does show who killed your father. And if you know what is good for you, Knox, you will let it go at that. You can't fight the police and the courts single-handedly. Look how the whole thing was dropped, and the most cold-blooded kind of murder turned into suicide. Suicide without a weapon! Bah!"

"I am not so sure about Schwartz," I said thoughtfully. "We haven't yet learned about eleven twenty-two C."

Chapter XXV

Measure for Measure

MISS Jane Maitland had been missing for ten days. In that time not one word had come from her. The reporter from the *Eagle* had located her in a dozen places, and was growing thin and haggard following little old ladies along the street—and being sent about his business tartly when he tried to make inquiries.

Some things puzzled me more than ever in the light of Wardrop's story. For the third time I asked myself why Miss Letitia denied the loss of the pearls. There was nothing in what he had learned either, to tell why Miss Jane had gone away—to ascribe a motive.

How she had gone, in view of Wardrop's story of the cab, was clear. She had gone by streetcar, walking the three miles to Wynton alone at two o'clock in the morning, although she had never stirred around the house at night without a candle, and was privately known to sleep with a light when Miss Letitia went to bed first, and could not see it through the transom.

The theory I had formed seemed absurd at first, but as I thought it over, its probabilities grew on me. I took dinner at Bellwood and started for town almost immediately after.

Margery had gone to Miss Letitia's room, and Wardrop was pacing up and down the veranda, smoking. He looked dejected and anxious, and he welcomed my suggestion that he walk down to the station with me. As we went, a man emerged from the trees across and came slowly after us.

"You see, I am only nominally a free agent," he said morosely. "They'll poison me yet; I know too much."

We said little on the way to the train. Just before it came thundering along, however, he spoke again.

"I am going away, Knox. There isn't anything in this political game for me, and the law is too long. I have a chum in Mexico, and he wants me to go down there."

"Permanently?"

"Yes. There's nothing to hold me here now," he said.

I turned and faced him in the glare of the station lights.

"What do you mean?" I demanded.

"I mean that there isn't any longer a reason why one part of the earth is better than another. Mexico or Alaska, it's all the same to me."

He turned on his heel and left me. I watched him swing up the path, with his head down; I saw the shadowy figure of the other man fall into line behind him. Then I caught the platform of the last car as it passed, and that short ride into town was a triumphal procession with the wheels beating time and singing: "It's all the same—the same—to me—to me."

I called Burton by telephone, and was lucky enough to find him at the office. He said he had just got in, and as usual, he wanted something to eat. We arranged to meet at a little Chinese restaurant, where at that hour, nine o'clock, we would be almost alone. Later on, after the theater, I knew that the place would be full of people, and conversation impossible.

Burton knew the place well, as he did every restaurant in the city.

"Hello, Mike," he said to the unctuous Chinaman who admitted us. And "Mike" smiled a slant-eyed welcome. The room was empty; it was an unpretentious affair, with lace curtains at the windows and small, very clean tables. At one corner a cable and slide communicated through a hole in the ceiling with the floor above, and through the aperture, Burton's order for chicken and rice, and the inevitable tea, was barked.

Burton listened attentively to Wardrop's story, as I repeated it.

"So Schwartz did it, after all!" he said regretfully, when I finished. "It's a tame ending. It had all the elements of the unusual, and it resolves itself into an ordinary, everyday, man-to-man feud. I'm disappointed; we can't touch Schwartz."

"I thought the *Times-Post* was hot after him."

"Schwartz bought the *Times-Post* at three o'clock this afternoon," Burton said, with repressed rage. "I'm called off. Tomorrow we run a photograph of Schwartzwold, his place at Plattsburg, and the next day we eulogize the administration. I'm going down the river on an excursion boat, and write up the pig-killing contest at the union butchers' picnic."

"How is Mrs. Butler?" I asked, as his rage subsided to mere rumbling in his throat

"Delirious"—shortly. "She's going to croak, Wardrop's going to Mexico, Schwartz will be next governor, and Miss Maitland's body will be found in a cistern. The whole thing has petered out. What's the use of finding the murderer if he's coated with asbestos and lined with money? Mike, I want some more tea to drown my troubles."

We called up the hospital about ten thirty, and learned that Mrs. Butler was sinking. Fred was there, and without much hope of getting anything, we went over. I took Burton in as a nephew of the dying woman, and I was glad I had done it. She was quite conscious, but very weak. She told the story to Fred and myself, and in a corner Burton took it down in shorthand. We got her to sign it about daylight sometime, and she died very quietly shortly after Edith arrived at eight.

To give her story as she gave it would be impossible; the ramblings of a sick mind, the terrible pathos of it all, is impossible to repeat. She lay there, her long, thin body practically dead, fighting the death rattle in her throat. There were pauses when for five minutes she would lie in a stupor, only to rouse and go forward from the very word where she had stopped.

She began with her married life, and to understand the beauty of it is to understand the things that came after. She was perfectly, ideally, illogically happy. Then one day Henry Butler accepted the nomination for state treasurer, and with that things changed. During his term in office he altered greatly; his wife could only guess that things were wrong, for he refused to talk.

The crash came, after all, with terrible suddenness. There had been an all-night conference at the Butler home, and Mr. Butler, in a frenzy at finding himself a dupe, had called the butler from bed and forcibly ejected Fleming and Schwartz from the house. Ellen Butler had been horrified, sickened by what she regarded as the vulgarity of the occurrence. But her loyalty to her husband never wavered.

Butler was one honest man against a complete organization of unscrupulous ones. His disgrace, imprisonment and suicide at the White Cat had followed in rapid succession. With his death, all that was worthwhile in his wife died. Her health was destroyed; she became one of the wretched army of neurasthenics, with only one idea: to retaliate, to pay back in measure full and running over, her wrecked life, her dead husband, her grief and her shame.

She laid her plans with the caution and absolute recklessness of a diseased mentality. Normally a shrinking, nervous woman, she became cold, passionless, deliberate in her revenge. To disgrace Schwartz and Fleming was her original intention. But she could not get the papers.

She resorted to hounding Fleming, meaning to drive him to suicide. And she chose a method that had more nearly driven him to madness. Wherever he turned he found the figures eleven twenty-two C. Sometimes just the number, without the letter. It had been Henry Butler's cell number during his imprisonment, and if they were graven on his wife's soul, they burned themselves in lines of fire on Fleming's brain. For over a year she pursued this course—sometimes through the mail, at other times in the most unexpected places, wherever she could bribe a messenger to carry the paper. Sane? No, hardly sane, but inevitable as fate.

The time came when other things went badly with Fleming, as I had already heard from Wardrop. He fled to the White Cat, and for a week Ellen Butler hunted him vainly. She had decided to kill him, and on the night Margery Fleming had found the paper on the pillow, she had been in the house. She was not the only intruder in the house that night. Someone—presumably Fleming himself—had been there before her. She found a ladies desk broken open and a small drawer empty. Evidently Fleming, unable to draw a check while in hiding, had needed ready money. As to the jewels that had been disturbed in Margery's boudoir, I could only surmise the impulse that, after prompting him to take them, had failed at the sight of his dead wife's jewels. Surprised by the girl's appearance, Mrs. Butler had crept to the upper floor and concealed herself in an empty bedroom. It had been almost dawn before she got out. No doubt this was the room belonging to the butler, Carter, which Margery had reported as locked that night.

She took a key from the door of a side entrance, and locked the door behind her when she left. Within a couple of nights she had learned that Wardrop was coming home from Plattsburg, and she met him at Bellwood. We already knew the nature of that meeting. She drove back to town, half maddened by her failure to secure the letters that would have cleared her husband's memory, but the wiser by one thing; Wardrop had inadvertently told her where Fleming was hiding.

The next night she went to the White Cat and tried to get in. She knew from her husband of the secret staircase, for many a political meeting of the deepest significance had been possible by its use. But the door was locked, and she had no key.

Above her the warehouse raised its empty height, and it was not long before she decided to see what she could learn from its upper windows. She went in at the gate and felt her way, through the rain, to the windows. At that moment the gate opened suddenly, and a man muttered something in the darkness. The shock was terrible.

I had no idea, that night, of what my innocent stumbling into the warehouse yard had meant to a half-crazed woman just beyond my range of vision. After a little she got her courage again, and she pried up an unlocked window.

The rest of her progress must have been much as ours had been, a few nights later. She found a window that commanded the club, and with three possibilities that she would lose, and would see the wrong room, she won the fourth. The room lay directly before her, distinct in every outline, with Fleming seated at the table, facing her and sorting some papers.

She rested her revolver on the sill and took absolutely deliberate aim. Her hands were cold, and she even rubbed them together, to make them steady. Then she fired, and a crash of thunder at the very instant covered the sound.

Fleming sat for a moment before he swayed forward. On that instant she realized that there was someone else in the room—a man who took an uncertain step or two forward into view, threw up his hands and disappeared as silently as he had come. It was Schwartz. Then she saw the door into the hall open, saw Wardrop come slowly in and close it, watched his sickening realization of what had occurred; then a sudden panic seized her. Arms seemed to stretch out from the darkness behind her, to draw her into it. She tried to get away, to run, even to scream—then she fainted. It was gray dawn when she recovered her senses and got back to the hotel room she had taken under an assumed name.

By night she was quieter. She read the news of Fleming's death in the papers, and she gloated over it. But there was more to be done; she was only beginning. She meant to ruin Schwartz, to kill his credit, to fell him with the club of public disfavor. Wardrop had told her that her husband's letters were with other papers at the Monmouth Avenue house, where he could not get them.

Fleming's body was taken home that day, Saturday, but she had gone too far to stop. She wanted the papers before Lightfoot could get at them and destroy the incriminating ones. That night she got into the Fleming house, using the key she had taken. She ransacked the library, finding not the letters that Wardrop had said were there, but others, equally or more incriminating, canceled notes, private accounts that would have ruined Schwartz forever.

It was then that I saw the light and went downstairs. My unlucky stumble gave her warning enough to turn out the light. For the rest, the chase through the back hall, the dining room and the pantry, had culminated in her escape up the back stairs, while I had fallen down the dumbwaiter shaft. She had run into Bella on the upper floor—Bella, who had almost fainted, and who knew her and kept her until morning, petting her and soothing her, and finally getting her into a troubled sleep.

That day she realized that she was being followed. When Edith's invitation came she accepted it at once, for the sake of losing herself and her papers, until she was ready to use them. It had disconcerted her to find Margery there, but she managed to get along. For several days everything had gone well: she was getting stronger again, ready for the second act of the play, prepared to blackmail Schwartz, and then expose him. She would have killed him later, probably; she wanted her measure full and running over, and so she would disgrace him first.

Then—Schwartz must have learned of the loss of the papers from the Fleming house, and guessed the rest. She felt sure he had known from the first who had killed Fleming. However that might be, he had had her room entered, Margery chloroformed in the connecting room, and her papers were taken from under her pillow while she was pretending anesthesia. She had followed the two men through the house and out the kitchen door, where she had fainted on the grass.

The next night, when she had retired early, leaving Margery and me downstairs, it had been an excuse to slip out of the house. How she found that Schwartz was at the White Cat, how she got through the side entrance, we never knew. He had burned the papers before she got there, and when she tried to kill him, he had struck her hand aside.

When we were out in the cheerful light of day again, Burton turned his shrewd, blue eyes on me.

"Awful story, isn't it?" he said. "Those are primitive emotions, if you like. Do you know, Knox, there is only one explanation we haven't worked on for the rest of this mystery—I believe in my soul you carried off the old lady and the Russia leather bag yourself."

Chapter XXVI

Lovers and a Letter

AT NOON that day I telephoned to Margery.

"Come up," I said, "and bring the keys to the Monmouth Avenue house. I have some things to tell you, and—some things to ask you."

I met her at the station with Lady Gray and the trap. My plans for that afternoon were comprehensive; they included what I hoped to be the solution of the Aunt Jane mystery; also, they included a little drive through the park, and a—well, I shall tell about that, all I am going to tell, at the proper time.

To play propriety, Edith met us at the house. It was still closed, and even in the short time that had elapsed it smelled close and musty.

At the door into the drawing room I stopped them. "Now, this is going to be a sort of game," I explained. "It's a sort of button, button, who's got the button, without the button. We are looking for a drawer, receptacle or closet, which shall contain, bunched together, and without regard to whether they should be there or not, a small revolver, two military brushes and a clothes brush, two or three soft bosomed shirts, perhaps a half-dozen collars, and a suit of underwear. Also a small flat package about eight inches long and three wide."

"What in the world are you talking about?" Edith asked.

"I am not talking, I am theorizing," I explained. "I have a theory, and according to it the things should be here. If they are not, it is my misfortune, not my fault."

I think Margery caught my idea at once, and as Edith was ready for anything, we commenced the search. Edith took the top floor, being accustomed, she said, to finding unexpected things in the servants' quarters; Margery took the lower floor, and for certain reasons I took the second.

For ten minutes there was no result. At the end of that time I had finished two rooms, and commenced on the blue boudoir. And here, on the top shelf of a three-corner Empire cupboard, with glass doors and spindle legs, I found what I was looking for. Every article was there. I stuffed a small package into my pocket, and called the two girls.

"The lost is found," I stated calmly, when we were all together in the library.

"When did you lose anything?" Edith demanded. "Do you mean to say, Jack Knox, that you brought us here to help you find a suit of gaudy pajamas and a pair of military brushes?"

"I brought you here to find Aunt Jane," I said soberly, taking a letter and the flat package out of my pocket. "You see, my theory worked out. *Here* is Aunt Jane, and *there* is the money from the Russia leather bag."

I laid the packet in Margery's lap, and without ceremony opened the letter. It began:

My Dearest Niece:

I am writing to you, because I cannot think what to say to Sister Letitia. I am running away! I—am—running—away! My dear, it scares me even to write it, all alone in this empty house. I have had a cup of tea out of one of your lovely cups, and a nap on your pretty couch, and just as soon as it is dark I am going to take the train for Boston. When you get this, I will be on the ocean, the ocean, my dear, that I have read about, and dreamed about, and never seen.

I am going to realize a dream of forty years—more than twice as long as you have lived. Your dear mother saw the continent before she died, but the things I have wanted have always been denied me. I have been of those that have eyes to see and see not. So—I have run away. I am going to London and Paris, and even to Italy, if the money your father gave me for the pearls will hold out. For a year now I have been getting steamship circulars, and I have taken a little French through a correspondence school. That was why I always made you sing French songs, dearie: I wanted to learn the accent. I think I should do very well if I could only sing my French instead of speaking it.

I am afraid that Sister Letitia discovered that I had taken some of the pearls. But—half of them were mine, from our mother, and although I had wanted a pearl ring all my life, I have never had one. I am going to buy me a hat, instead of a bonnet, and clothes, and pretty things underneath, and a switch; Margery, I have wanted a switch for thirty years.

I suppose Letitia will never want me back. Perhaps I shall not want to come. I tried to write to her when I was leaving, but I had cut my hand in the attic, where I had hidden away my clothes, and it bled on the paper. I have been worried since for fear your Aunt Letitia would find the paper in the basket, and be alarmed at the stains. I wanted to leave things in order—please tell Letitia—but I was so nervous, and in such a hurry. I walked three miles to Wynton and took a streetcar. I just made up my mind I was going to do it. I am sixty-five, and it is time I have a chance to do the things I like.

I came in on the car, and came directly here. I got in with the second key on your keyring. Did you miss it? And I did the strangest thing at Bellwood. I got down the stairs very quietly and out onto the porch. I set down my empty traveling bag—I was going to buy everything new in the city—to close the door behind me. Then I was sure I heard someone at the side of the house, and I picked it up and ran down the path in the dark.

You can imagine my surprise when I opened the bag this morning to find I had picked up Harry's. I am emptying it and taking it with me, for he has mine.

If you find this right away, please don't tell Sister Letitia for a day or two. You know how firm your Aunt Letitia is. I shall send her a present from Boston to pacify her, and perhaps when I come back in three or four months, she will be over the worst.

I am not quite comfortable about your father, Margery. He is not like himself. The last time I saw him he gave me a little piece of paper with a number on it and he said they followed him everywhere, and were driving him crazy. Try to have him see a doctor. And I left a bottle of complexion cream in the little closet over my mantel, where I had hidden my hat and shoes that I wore. Please destroy it before your Aunt Letitia sees it.

Good-bye, my dear niece. I suppose I am growing frivolous in my old age, but I am going to have silk linings in my clothes before I die.

YOUR LOVING AUNT JANE

When Margery stopped reading, there was an amazed silence. Then we all three burst into relieved, uncontrolled mirth. The dear, little, old lady with her new independence and her sixty-five-year-old, romantic, starved heart!

Then we opened the packet, which was a sadder business, for it had represented Allan Fleming's last clutch at his waning public credit.

Edith ran to the telephone with the news for Fred, and for the first time that day Margery and I were alone. She was standing with one hand on the library table; in the other she held Aunt Jane's letter, half tremulous, wholly tender. I put my hand over hers, on the table.

"Margery!" I said. She did not stir.

"Margery, I want my answer, dear. I love you—love you; it isn't possible to tell you how much. There isn't enough time in all existence to tell you. You are mine, Margery—mine. You can't get away from that."

She turned, very slowly, and looked at me with her level eyes. "Yours!" she replied softly, and I took her in my arms.

Edith was still at the telephone.

"I don't know," she was saying. "Just wait until I see."

As she came toward the door, Margery squirmed, but I held her tight. In the doorway Edith stopped and stared; then she went swiftly back to the telephone.

"Yes, dear," she said sweetly. "They are, this minute."

A CATALOG OF SELECTED

DOVER BOOKS

IN ALL FIELDS OF INTEREST

A CATALOG OF SELECTED DOVER BOOKS IN ALL FIELDS OF INTEREST

100 BEST-LOVED POEMS, Edited by Philip Smith. "The Passionate Shepherd to His Love," "Shall I compare thee to a summer's day?" "Death, be not proud," "The Raven," "The Road Not Taken," plus works by Blake, Wordsworth, Byron, Shelley, Keats, many others. Includes 13 selections from the Common Core State Standards Initiative. 112pp. 0-486-28553-7

ABC BOOK OF EARLY AMERICANA, Eric Sloane. Artist and historian Eric Sloane presents a wondrous A-to-Z collection of American innovations, including hex signs, ear trumpets, popcorn, and rocking chairs. Illustrated, hand-lettered pages feature brief captions explaining objects' origins and uses. 64pp. 0-486-49808-5

ADVENTURES OF HUCKLEBERRY FINN, Mark Twain. Join Huck and Jim as their boyhood adventures along the Mississippi River lead them into a world of excitement, danger, and self-discovery. Humorous narrative, lyrical descriptions of the Mississippi valley, and memorable characters. 224pp. 0-486-28061-6

ALICE STARMORE'S BOOK OF FAIR ISLE KNITTING, Alice Starmore. A noted designer from the region of Scotland's Fair Isle explores the history and techniques of this distinctive, stranded-color knitting style and provides copious illustrated instructions for 14 original knitwear designs. 208pp. 0-486-47218-3

ALICE'S ADVENTURES IN WONDERLAND, Lewis Carroll. Beloved classic about a little girl lost in a topsy-turvy land and her encounters with the White Rabbit, March Hare, Mad Hatter, Cheshire Cat, and other delightfully improbable characters. 42 illustrations by Sir John Tenniel. A selection of the Common Core State Standards Initiative. 96pp. 0-486-27543-4

THE ARTHUR RACKHAM TREASURY: 86 Full-Color Illustrations, Arthur Rackham. Selected and Edited by Jeff A. Menges. A stunning treasury of 86 full-page plates span the famed English artist's career, from *Rip Van Winkle* (1905) to masterworks such as *Undine, A Midsummer Night's Dream,* and *Wind in the Willows* (1939). 96pp. 0-486-44685-9

THE AWAKENING, Kate Chopin. First published in 1899, this controversial novel of a New Orleans wife's search for love outside a stifling marriage shocked readers. Today, it remains a first-rate narrative with superb characterization. New introductory note. 128pp. 0-486-27786-0

BASEBALL IS . . .: Defining the National Pastime, Edited by Paul Dickson. Wisecracking, philosophical, nostalgic, and entertaining, these hundreds of quips and observations by players, their wives, managers, authors, and others cover every aspect of our national pastime. It's a great any-occasion gift for fans! 256pp. 0-486-48209-X

THE CALL OF THE WILD, Jack London. A classic novel of adventure, drawn from London's own experiences as a Klondike adventurer, relating the story of a heroic dog caught in the brutal life of the Alaska Gold Rush. Note. 64pp. 0-486-26472-6

CANDIDE, Voltaire. Edited by Francois-Marie Arouet. One of the world's great satires since its first publication in 1759. Witty, caustic skewering of romance, science, philosophy, religion, government — nearly all human ideals and institutions. A selection of the Common Core State Standards Initiative. 112pp. 0-486-26689-3

THE CARTOON HISTORY OF TIME, Kate Charlesworth and John Gribbin. Cartoon characters explain cosmology, quantum physics, and other concepts covered by Stephen Hawking's *A Brief History of Time.* Humorous graphic novel–style treatment, perfect for young readers and curious folk of all ages. 64pp. 0-486-49097-1

Browse over 10,000 books at www.doverpublications.com

THE CHERRY ORCHARD, Anton Chekhov. Classic of world drama concerns passing of semifeudal order in turn-of-the-century Russia, symbolized in the sale of the cherry orchard owned by Madame Ranevskaya. Showcases Chekhov's rich sensitivities as an observer of human nature. 64pp. 0-486-26682-6

A CHRISTMAS CAROL, Charles Dickens. This engrossing tale relates Ebenezer Scrooge's ghostly journeys through Christmases past, present, and future and his ultimate transformation from a harsh and grasping old miser to a charitable and compassionate human being. 80pp. 0-486-26865-9

CRIME AND PUNISHMENT, Fyodor Dostoyevsky. Translated by Constance Garnett. Supreme masterpiece tells the story of Raskolnikov, a student tormented by his own thoughts after he murders an old woman. Overwhelmed by guilt and terror, he confesses and goes to prison. A selection of the Common Core State Standards Initiative. 448pp. 0-486-41587-2

CYRANO DE BERGERAC, Edmond Rostand. A quarrelsome, hot-tempered, and unattractive swordsman falls hopelessly in love with a beautiful woman and woos her for a handsome but slow-witted suitor. A witty and eloquent drama. 144pp. 0-486-41119-2

A DOLL'S HOUSE, Henrik Ibsen. Ibsen's best-known play displays his genius for realistic prose drama. An expression of women's rights, the play climaxes when the central character, Nora, rejects a smothering marriage and life in "a doll's house." A selection of the Common Core State Standards Initiative. 80pp. 0-486-27062-9

DOOMED SHIPS: Great Ocean Liner Disasters, William H. Miller, Jr. Nearly 200 photographs, many from private collections, highlight tales of some of the vessels whose pleasure cruises ended in catastrophe: the *Morro Castle, Normandie, Andrea Doria, Europa,* and many others. 128pp. 0-486-45366-9

DUBLINERS, James Joyce. A fine and accessible introduction to the work of one of the 20th century's most influential writers, this collection features 15 tales, including a masterpiece of the short-story genre, "The Dead." 160pp. 0-486-26870-5

THE EARLY SCIENCE FICTION OF PHILIP K. DICK, Philip K. Dick. This anthology presents short stories and novellas that originally appeared in pulp magazines of the early 1950s, including "The Variable Man," "Second Variety," "Beyond the Door," "The Defenders," and more. 272pp. 0-486-49733-X

THE EARLY SHORT STORIES OF F. SCOTT FITZGERALD, F. Scott Fitzgerald. These tales offer insights into many themes, characters, and techniques that emerged in Fitzgerald's later works. Selections include "The Curious Case of Benjamin Button," "Babes in the Woods," and a dozen others. 256pp. 0-486-79465-2

ETHAN FROME, Edith Wharton. Classic story of wasted lives, set against a bleak New England background. Superbly delineated characters in a hauntingly grim tale of thwarted love. Considered by many to be Wharton's masterpiece. 96pp. 0-486-26690-7

FLATLAND: A Romance of Many Dimensions, Edwin A. Abbott. Classic of science (and mathematical) fiction — charmingly illustrated by the author — describes the adventures of A. Square, a resident of Flatland, in Spaceland (three dimensions), Lineland (one dimension), and Pointland (no dimensions). 96pp. 0-486-27263-X

FRANKENSTEIN, Mary Shelley. The story of Victor Frankenstein's monstrous creation and the havoc it caused has enthralled generations of readers and inspired countless writers of horror and suspense. With the author's own 1831 introduction. 176pp. 0-486-28211-2

THE GARGOYLE BOOK: 572 Examples from Gothic Architecture, Lester Burbank Bridaham. Dispelling the conventional wisdom that French Gothic architectural flourishes were born of despair or gloom, Bridaham reveals the whimsical nature of these creations and the ingenious artisans who made them. 572 illustrations. 224pp. 0-486-44754-5

THE GIFT OF THE MAGI AND OTHER SHORT STORIES, O. Henry. Sixteen captivating stories by one of America's most popular storytellers. Included are such classics as "The Gift of the Magi," "The Last Leaf," and "The Ransom of Red Chief." Publisher's Note. A selection of the Common Core State Standards Initiative. 96pp. 0-486-27061-0

THE GOETHE TREASURY: Selected Prose and Poetry, Johann Wolfgang von Goethe. Edited, Selected, and with an Introduction by Thomas Mann. In addition to his lyric poetry, Goethe wrote travel sketches, autobiographical studies, essays, letters, and proverbs in rhyme and prose. This collection presents outstanding examples from each genre. 368pp. 0-486-44780-4

GREAT ILLUSTRATIONS BY N. C. WYETH, N. C. Wyeth. Edited and with an Introduction by Jeff A. Menges. This full-color collection focuses on the artist's early and most popular illustrations, featuring more than 100 images from *The Mysterious Stranger, Robin Hood, Robinson Crusoe, The Boy's King Arthur,* and other classics. 128pp. 0-486-47295-7

HAMLET, William Shakespeare. The quintessential Shakespearean tragedy, whose highly charged confrontations and anguished soliloquies probe depths of human feeling rarely sounded in any art. Reprinted from an authoritative British edition complete with illuminating footnotes. A selection of the Common Core State Standards Initiative. 128pp. 0-486-27278-8

THE HAUNTED HOUSE, Charles Dickens. A Yuletide gathering in an eerie country retreat provides the backdrop for Dickens and his friends — including Elizabeth Gaskell and Wilkie Collins — who take turns spinning supernatural yarns. 144pp. 0-486-46309-5

HEART OF DARKNESS, Joseph Conrad. Dark allegory of a journey up the Congo River and the narrator's encounter with the mysterious Mr. Kurtz. Masterly blend of adventure, character study, psychological penetration. For many, Conrad's finest, most enigmatic story. 80pp. 0-486-26464-5

THE HOUND OF THE BASKERVILLES, Sir Arthur Conan Doyle. A deadly curse in the form of a legendary ferocious beast continues to claim its victims from the Baskerville family until Holmes and Watson intervene. Often called the best detective story ever written. 128pp. 0-486-28214-7

THE HOUSE BEHIND THE CEDARS, Charles W. Chesnutt. Originally published in 1900, this groundbreaking novel by a distinguished African-American author recounts the drama of a brother and sister who "pass for white" during the dangerous days of Reconstruction. 208pp. 0-486-46144-0

HOW TO DRAW NEARLY EVERYTHING, Victor Perard. Beginners of all ages can learn to draw figures, faces, landscapes, trees, flowers, and animals of all kinds. Well-illustrated guide offers suggestions for pencil, pen, and brush techniques plus composition, shading, and perspective. 160pp. 0-486-49848-4

HOW TO MAKE SUPER POP-UPS, Joan Irvine. Illustrated by Linda Hendry. Super pop-ups extend the element of surprise with three-dimensional designs that slide, turn, spring, and snap. More than 30 patterns and 475 illustrations include cards, stage props, and school projects. 96pp. 0-486-46589-6

THE IMITATION OF CHRIST, Thomas à Kempis. Translated by Aloysius Croft and Harold Bolton. This religious classic has brought understanding and comfort to millions for centuries. Written in a candid and conversational style, the topics include liberation from worldly inclinations, preparation and consolations of prayer, and eucharistic communion. 160pp. 0-486-43185-1

THE RED BADGE OF COURAGE, Stephen Crane. Amid the nightmarish chaos of a Civil War battle, a young soldier discovers courage, humility, and, perhaps, wisdom. Uncanny re-creation of actual combat. Enduring landmark of American fiction. 112pp. 0-486-26465-3

RELATIVITY SIMPLY EXPLAINED, Martin Gardner. One of the subject's clearest, most entertaining introductions offers lucid explanations of special and general theories of relativity, gravity, and spacetime, models of the universe, and more. 100 illustrations. 224pp. 0-486-29315-7

THE ROAD NOT TAKEN AND OTHER POEMS, Robert Frost. A treasury of Frost's most expressive verse. In addition to the title poem: "An Old Man's Winter Night," "In the Home Stretch," "Meeting and Passing," "Putting in the Seed," many more. All complete and unabridged. Includes a selection from the Common Core State Standards Initiative. 64pp. 0-486-27550-7

ROMEO AND JULIET, William Shakespeare. Tragic tale of star-crossed lovers, feuding families and timeless passion contains some of Shakespeare's most beautiful and lyrical love poetry. Complete, unabridged text with explanatory footnotes. 96pp. 0-486-27557-4

SANDITON AND THE WATSONS: Austen's Unfinished Novels, Jane Austen. Two tantalizing incomplete stories revisit Austen's customary milieu of courtship and venture into new territory, amid guests at a seaside resort. Both are worth reading for pleasure and study. 112pp. 0-486-45793-1

THE SCARLET LETTER, Nathaniel Hawthorne. With stark power and emotional depth, Hawthorne's masterpiece explores sin, guilt, and redemption in a story of adultery in the early days of the Massachusetts Colony. A selection of the Common Core State Standards Initiative. 192pp. 0-486-28048-9

SELECTED POEMS, Emily Dickinson. Over 100 best-known, best-loved poems by one of America's foremost poets, reprinted from authoritative early editions. No comparable edition at this price. Includes 3 selections from the Common Core State Standards Initiative. 64pp. 0-486-26466-1

SIDDHARTHA, Hermann Hesse. Classic novel that has inspired generations of seekers. Blending Eastern mysticism and psychoanalysis, Hesse presents a strikingly original view of man and culture and the arduous process of self-discovery, reconciliation, harmony, and peace. 112pp. 0-486-40653-9

SKETCHING OUTDOORS, Leonard Richmond. This guide offers beginners step-by-step demonstrations of how to depict clouds, trees, buildings, and other outdoor sights. Explanations of a variety of techniques include shading and constructional drawing. 48pp. 0-486-46922-0

STAR LORE: Myths, Legends, and Facts, William Tyler Olcott. Captivating retellings of the origins and histories of ancient star groups include Pegasus, Ursa Major, Pleiades, signs of the zodiac, and other constellations. "Classic." — *Sky & Telescope.* 58 illustrations. 544pp. 0-486-43581-4

STRIP FOR MURDER, Max Allan Collins. Illustrated by Terry Beatty. Colorful characters with murderous motives populate this illustrated mystery, in which the heated rivalry between a pair of cartoonists ends in homicide and a stripper-turned-detective and her stepson-partner seek the killer. "Great fun." — *Mystery Scene.* 288pp. 0-486-79811-9

SURVIVAL HANDBOOK: The Official U.S. Army Guide, Department of the Army. This special edition of the Army field manual is geared toward civilians. An essential companion for campers and all lovers of the outdoors, it constitutes the most authoritative wilderness guide. 288pp. 0-486-46184-X

SWEENEY TODD THE STRING OF PEARLS: The Original Victorian Classic, James Malcolm Rymer or Thomas Peckett Prest. Foreword by Rohan McWilliam. The inspiration for a long-running Broadway musical, this Victorian novel in the penny dreadful tradition recounts the nefarious doings of a murderous barber and baker who recycle their victims into meat pies. 304pp. 0-486-79739-2

TREASURE ISLAND, Robert Louis Stevenson. Classic adventure story of a perilous sea journey, a mutiny led by the infamous Long John Silver, and a lethal scramble for buried treasure — seen through the eyes of cabin boy Jim Hawkins. 160pp. 0-486-27559-0

TWELVE YEARS A SLAVE, Solomon Northup. The basis for the Academy Award®-winning movie! Kidnapped into slavery in 1841, Northup spent 12 years in captivity. This autobiographical memoir represents an exceptionally detailed and accurate description of slave life and plantation society. 7 illustrations. Index. 352pp. 0-486-78962-4

VARNEY THE VAMPYRE: or, The Feast of Blood, Part 1, James Malcolm Rymer or Thomas Peckett Prest. With an Introduction by E. F. Bleiler. A deathless creature with an insatiable appetite for blood, Varney is the antihero of this epic, which predates *Dracula* and establishes many of the conventions associated with vampirism. Volume 1 of 2. 480pp. 0-486-22844-4

VARNEY THE VAMPYRE: or, The Feast of Blood, Part 2, James Malcolm Rymer or Thomas Peckett Prest. In this gripping Gothic drama of the 1840s, the bloodthirsty title character repeatedly dies but is reborn and forced to renew his relentless search for victims. Volume 2 of 2. 448pp. 0-486-22845-2

VICTORIAN MURDERESSES: A True History of Thirteen Respectable French and English Women Accused of Unspeakable Crimes, Mary S. Hartman. Riveting combination of true crime and social history examines a dozen famous cases, offering illuminating details of the accused women's backgrounds, deeds, and trials. "Vividly written, meticulously researched." — *Choice*. 336pp. 0-486-78047-3

VILLETTE, Charlotte Brontë. Acclaimed by Virginia Woolf as "Brontë's finest novel," this moving psychological study features a remarkably modern heroine who abandons her native England for a new life as a schoolteacher in Belgium. 480pp. 0-486-45557-2

WALDEN; OR, LIFE IN THE WOODS, Henry David Thoreau. Accounts of Thoreau's daily life on the shores of Walden Pond outside Concord, Massachusetts, are interwoven with musings on the virtues of self-reliance and individual freedom, on society, government, and other topics. A selection of the Common Core State Standards Initiative. 224pp. 0-486-28495-6

WHAT EINSTEIN DIDN'T KNOW: Scientific Answers to Everyday Questions, Robert L. Wolke. From simple (How do magnets work?) to complex (Where does uranium get its energy?), this volume offers intriguing insights into scientific facts. Definitive accounts of workings behind everyday phenomena include related do-it-yourself experiments. 240pp. 0-486-49289-3

WORLD WAR II: THE ENCYCLOPEDIA OF THE WAR YEARS, 1941-1945, Norman Polmar and Thomas B. Allen. Authoritative and comprehensive, this reference surveys World War II from an American perspective. Over 2,400 entries cover battles, weapons, and participants as well as aspects of politics, culture, and everyday life. 85 illustrations. 960pp. 0-486-47962-5

WUTHERING HEIGHTS, Emily Brontë. Somber tale of consuming passions and vengeance — played out amid the lonely English moors — recounts the turbulent and tempestuous love story of Cathy and Heathcliff. Poignant and compelling. 256pp. 0-486-29256-8